THE WHISKEY WOMAN OF WILSON'S CREEK

JOHN HUTCHINSON

Green
Heron
Books

Published by Green Heron Books, an imprint of Storied Publishing

Permission requests and other questions may be directed to the Contact page at www.storied.pub.

ISBN: 978-1-951991-20-3

Cover design by Sean Benesh

Edited by Doug Serven

PRAISE FOR WHISKEY WOMAN

Set in the Civil War era, John Hutchison takes an aspiring priest through battlefields, seminary, and a surprising love to that shapes within him a form of charity that no theology classroom could ever fully convey.
Fr. Nathan Carr
Headmaster, The Academy of Classical Christian Studies

Whiskey Woman of Wilson's Creek is a delightful interweaving of history, culture, romance, adventure and the healing traditions of the Ozarks. For those of you who spend too much time with your noses in nonfiction, I highly recommend this delightful escape into the past.
Katrina Bogdon
Doctorate of Naturopathic Medicine

Raised in the region, knowing the caves, rolling hills, plains, and history of Wilson's Creek Battlefield, I was immediately drawn into this story of high adventure, romance, and drama set in the Ozarks. A story with old-fashioned morality anchored in Christian faith, Whiskey Woman of Wilson's Creek is a book that I could not put down until finished.
Lindsey Robison
President, Messiah Project

Hutchinson adeptly sets the stage for the reader to journey back through time and space. The beautiful and feral Ozarks become the backdrop for an intriguing story that takes place during one of the most challenging times in American history. The author's skillful use of nineteenth century regional vernacular is as convincing as the fluid conversations and interplay between the characters. Hutchinson illuminates the spiritual undercurrent throughout the story giving verve to this enjoyable tour-de-force.
Sunni Mercer
Independent Museum Consultant

Author, *TIG*

CONTENTS

ALSO BY JOHN M. HUTCHINSON

Carver's Box

Heart Fire: A Novel of Redemption

Since she has always said this is her
favorite of all of my writings,
the work is dedicated to
my first and best editor:

Jean Ann Hutchinson

PART 1

KRIEGER ANDREWES

ONE

A Battlefield

August 10, 1861

"Kriek! Kriek! Ich sterbe, Ich sterbe. Kriek, pray for me. Kriek...."

"Willi? Willi? Stay with me Willi. Blieb bei mir."

I knew I would receive no response.

Willi died.

And it was not what I might have expected. I had never actually watched anyone die before. To my surprise there was no big sigh or groan, no flopping of the limbs, no perceptible sinking of the body. It all just... ended. I had been watching his eyes when he died. Save for a slight dilation of his pupils and a teensy sinking of those eyes, he looked same a second after his last breath as the second before. Yet, I knew he had died. And I sensed it from looking at his eyes, just the eyes, nothing else. This is how I witnessed his *transitus*.

With the horrors of war all around—the deafening explosions, the shouts, the showers of grape shot and shrapnel, the strange mixture of mud and dust, the screaming of horses and men—despite all of this, Willi's death was for me a sacred moment when the agonies of battle faded to a distant background, an instant when the partition of heaven and earth became so thin that if one listened closely enough choirs of angels could be heard. Through this thin partition, I whispered my prayer for Willi as he had requested, hoping that he would be received into the arms of mercy.

I eased Willi off my lap where I had been cradling his head and rose to my knees. The instant I bent over to close his eyes, a round slammed directly into my right buttock. It knocked me hard to the ground, and, in that split second before the pain registered, I remembered Colonel Sigel's admonition, "Keep hinter dem Horizont, meine Herren, well below the horizon." I groaned and in a reflexive motion, drew my right leg up just in time to take another round. I screamed in agony and in the next heartbeat, a curtain of black fell upon me.

———

"You, nurse! I need a hand here! Y'all come help me out."

"Ain't no nurse."

"Whatever you are, come an' help me out."

"Whatcha fixin' to do?"

"Put a tourniquet on him. Gotta amputate that leg."

Amputate! The word snatched me from nothingness to bursting panic. My eyes snapped open. Four eyes peered down at me.

"He's awake," the one in a bloody apron said.

"Shore 'nough," the other said, one who looked and dressed like a man but sounded like a woman. "Howdy, soldier. You been out like Lottie's eye. Good to have you back."

"Your leg has been shot to smithereens," Bloody Apron said. "Sorry to tell y'all this but we gotta take the leg off."

"Don' know fer shore if'n that's true," Man-Woman said.

The officer looked at Man-Woman, puzzled by her dissension. "Ma'am, all due respect, but I'm the field surgeon here. That leg has been severely wounded. Lord knows how long this man's been lying out here in this field. Amazed he's still breathing. But if that leg doesn't come off in the next few hours, gangrene could set in and then he's a goner. Amputation is the only way to save his life."

"You ain't a-gonna take that leg off hyar in the field is you?"

"No, I'm going to bind it up, give him some opiates, and get him to the field hospital in that farm house to the north. I need your help getting him in the ambulance."

"Gonna die you send him in thar. Why 't'ain't nothin' but an infection farm. Chock full o' animalcules what'll kill 'im sure as a goose goes barefooted."

"Chock full o' what?"

"Animalcules. Li'l critters."

"Look ma'am, all due respect once again, but I don't have time to debate all of this. Now give me a hand... please."

Just then, a groan sounded from one of the nearby bodies lying akimbo on the ground.

Both of my attendants looked around.

Man-Woman pointed to her left. "It's that man o'er thar with his hand on his haid what groaned. Better scoot on o'er thar an' check on 'im. I'll stay with this'un."

She waited until the surgeon knelt to assess the extent of the other man's wounds, then reached down, picked me up as if I were as light as a scarecrow, and carried me briskly into a nearby stand of trees lining a dusty road. There a horse-drawn medicine wagon without insignia awaited us. Gently, she laid me in the back of the wagon and checked my tourniquet, an odd screw device the field surgeon had strapped to my upper leg.

"Gotta get that artery clamped tighter'n a jug ag'in' the bone," she said. "Lookin' perty good fer now. I'll check it a coupla times afore we git home. Now, you gotta have somethin' fer your hurtin'. Sure to be somethin' fierce."

She rolled a blanket and eased it under my head and shoulders to form a pillow. She then opened a side drawer of the medicine wagon, partitioned by a number of cubicles and dividers. After checking through several of them, she retrieved a small bottle filled with little white pills.

"Coupla these orter help," she said.

At her directive, I opened my mouth and received the pills from her hand swallowing them with a slug of water from her canteen. Satisfied with these preparations, she jumped up to the wagon bench and clucked her horse into motion.

"Wait," I said, managing to rise to one elbow. "Where are you taking me?"

"Gonna git that leg fixed up. Now settle back down."

"Who are you?"

"All in good time, soldier. Down you go."

Devoid of energy and in the throes of hot pain, my capacity to protest winked out. I lay back on the makeshift bed as directed. At a steady gait and with no interference from anyone, we drew away from the stench of cordite in the clash that would come to be known as The Battle of Wilson's Creek or Oak Hills if you were a Secessionist. Apparently, everyone was otherwise occupied in the aftermath of the battle and took little notice of us. The Confederate field surgeon, either consumed with the sufferings of the groaning man or indifferent to me, a wounded Federal soldier, gave us no chase whatsoever.

For the next hours, I wandered in and out of awareness, no doubt due to the effects of the little white pills. I could not tell you the route we took nor where on the map we finally arrived. I estimated that I had been wounded somewhere around ten o'clock that morning and lay immobile well into the heat of the day. The sun had sunk low in the Western sky when we came to a halt. Thus, I surmised we had been traveling for at least four hours, given the slow pace of our journey.

When the wagon halted, she carried me again, effortlessly, up a steep slope to the face of a limestone cave. The mouth of the cave had been completely enclosed by a wood-framed wall with a door on the left side and a curtained window on the right. From beneath the center of the wall, there emerged a small burbling creek.

Man-Woman opened the door to the cave, and laid me on a long metal table that rested on a massive mahogany chest with a dozen brass-handled drawers. Beneath us, I could see tightly laid floorboards raised above the small stream that emerged from a shallow spring in the rear of the cave. When I had been deposited on the table, Man-Woman lit half a dozen kerosene lamps and suspended them on hooks attached to a frame above the table. I threw my right arm over my eyes to shield them from the bright glare of the lamps and searched for my voice.

"Who are you and where am I?" I asked again, my voice strained and reedy.

"Now that thar is a perfec'ly reasonable query. Reckon I orter introduce myself proper. Belle Potts is the name. An' who might you be?"

"Krieger, Private Krieger Andrewes," I said.

"Krieger Andrewes? What sorta name is 'at?"

"Long story. Where am I?"

"You're in Belle Potts' surgery. Now, jes' so's you know, I'm a-fixin' to scrub up good an' have a look-see at that limb thar."

"Surgery? Are you a doctor?"

"Naw. I reckon you could say I'se a *healer*."

My alarm bells, already ringing at this strange deportation from the battlefield, now rose to a shuddering clang.

"If you're not a doctor, stay away from me," I said.

"Private Andrewes, no need for you to be skeered. Sure 'nough don' got no sheepskin on the wall with fancy Latin words, but I knowed what I'se about. 'Sides, don' 'pear to me you got much choice. So lay back down an' res' as much as possible while I scrub up."

Belle left my side and moved to a basin affixed to a wall of the cave. There she withdrew a small file and proceeded to clean her fingernails. Laying the file aside, she opened a spigot on a pipe running from some sort of reservoir above the cave down through the rock ceiling to the basin below. Methodically, she scrubbed her hands and forearms with what appeared to be a course, abrasive hunk of soap. The waste water coursed through a pipe extending from the bottom of the basin out through the front wall of the cave and, I presumed, there to be voided into the ground. When she had finished no fewer than ten minutes of washing, she uncorked a bottle of clear fluid and doused her hands.

"That orter do it," she said.

She removed the lid of a plated tin pan and withdrew a set of shears with blunt, curved blades dripping from the solution in which they had been bathed. She brought the shears to my table side along with the bottle. From one of the drawers under the table, she removed a white starched apron and a cotton mask, which she placed over her nose and mouth. Through that mask, she began to clarify what was about to happen. The timbre of her voice changed, and, despite her strange backwoods dialect, she spoke with an unexpectedly gentle and comforting tone, nearly a whisper I would say.

"Private Andrewes, I need to inspect that thar wound, see jes' how much damage was done by 'at Minié ball. Also 'pears you took one in the backside. Gotta look at it too. So's I kin do all that, I gotta cut them britches off'n you."

"But," I said, again with rising alarm. "It's not proper for you to see me without my trousers. I am a seminary student. Such an exposure to a woman would be forbidden."

I tried to sit up. She gently pushed me back down on the table.

"I do unnerstand yer predic'ment Private Andrewes but to be right forthcomin', I don' git a gander at them wounds, yer mighty sure to die. I ain't got no time to waste hyar."

In my diminishment, all resolve ebbed. I gave a reluctant sigh and nodded.

Swiftly she cut my trousers and undergarment away and pitched them into a trash barrel. "Them gots to be burned right away. Now, no use you frettin' 'bout bein' exposed hyar." She turned away, splashed more of the clear liquid on her hands, and extracted a towel from a large armoire near the basin. With her eyes averted, she covered my midsection. Belle then trained her eyes on my wounded leg, studying it from several angles. When she had finished her inspection, she looked directly in my eyes.

"Private Andrewes, I cain't tell precisely what we got hyar. I gotta probe that wound and that's gonna hurt like ole Billy Hades. To make matters worse, I gotta pour a good dose o' this on it." She held up the bottle full of clear liquid. "When that pain reaches the ole noggin, you'll like to scream to high heaven. An' that's okay. Let 'er rip."

"What's in that bottle?"

"Carn whisky."

"Corn whisky?"

"Yup. Made it myself. Pertinear pure alcyhol."

"Why do you have to put that on my leg?"

"Kills the critters."

"What critters?"

"As you is prone to say, *long story*. I'll 'splain it to you when we-un's is all finished hyar. Now, I reckon you best get ready 'cause hyar it comes."

As predicted, I screamed to the roof of the cave and nearly passed completely out when she poured the better part of a pint of corn whiskey on my open wound.

"I'se mighty awful sorrow 'bout that. I truly am but 'twas fer the best b'lieve me."

She closed her eyes to enhance her concentration, inserted a finger into the wound, and probed with an expert touch. With each cry of agony, Belle offered a soothing apology. "Sorrow," she would say. When at last she removed her finger, I took a couple of deep breaths.

"Now, gotta look at yer backside. Kin you roll on over to yer left?"

"That I cannot do."

"Private Andrewes, you got a ball in yer backside. I gots to git it out, clean that thar wound, an' stave off infection what is shore to happen if'n I don'. Come on now. O'er you go."

Against all propriety, I did so, red-faced with embarrassment. Belle seemed quite unfazed at the sight of my bare backside.

"Here comes the carn whiskey," she said and poured a goodly dose on and around the wound.

This time, I managed to stifle my outcry and, to my great relief, I did not experience much discomfort as she prodded this second wound.

"You kin lay back now," she said, removing her cloth mask and putting her hands on her hips. "Time to talk turkey," she said. "Yer a lucky man, Private Andrewes. That Minié ball didn' hit yer knee. Come mighty close, but them knee bones is intact. Now you gots two bones in that lower limb. One's the fibula and t'other's the tibia. Big one's the tibia. Li'l one's the fibula. Yer fibula is shot to pieces. Felt some bone fragments. But, I b'lieve that tibia kin support yer leg all by itself. So, hyar's what I'm a-fixin' to do. I want to put you to sleep an' go in thar, clean that mess out, get shed o' that Minié ball, file down them two stubs of the fibula an' sew you up. Then I'll get that musket ball outta yer behind. That one's no trouble 'tall. Perty simple extraction."

Quite honestly, I didn't know what to say so I just nodded.

"Now here's what you gotta know. I'se perty good at sewin folks up, an' I'll do my best, but I fear you gonna have a bodacious scar on that leg. An' to boot, I'd be plumb hornswaggled if'n you didn't come outta this gimped up a mite. They's a muscle in thar what raises yer foot an' that big ole granddaddy toe. That muscle... it's prob'ly ruined, near as I kin tell. I'm mighty sorrow to have to tell you this."

I lay there trying to absorb what she was saying.

"Gotta be clar here, Private Krieger Andrewes. You'd like to died if'n you'd been treated by that young Reb surgeon. Most o' them field surgeons—both Yankee and Reb—is greener'n goose dung. Oh, I'd allow as to how he means well, but he ain't got no trainin' an' maybe never even done an op'ration afore that nasty battle what you jes' come through. Most o' them doctors don' know nothin' 'bout the critters, an' if'n I'se a bettin' gel, I'd a not give a plugged ring cent fer yer chances in that field hospital. They'd a-hacked off yer limb an' killed you to boot. B'live me you got a fightin' chance with Belle, so whaddya say? Ready fer a nice long nap?"

"I... I don' know. Put me to sleep? Is that with chloroform?"

"Naw, don' use chloroform. that's nasty business. Why you'd likely wake up all staggerin' around like a buck-eyed calf an' fightin' down the nausea. Be plumb miser'ble fer a spell. I use ether. Here, let me show you what I mean."

She walked over to the armoire and retrieved from one of the shelves a box eighteen to twenty inches in length, about a foot wide, and two inches in depth. It had two chambers, with a stationary pipe and a mask running from one of the chambers.

"Now I reckon yer wonderin' why I operate here in a cave. Well, it's a perty constant temperature in hyar—'bout sixty degrees yar round. 'Tain't too hot. 'Tain't too cold. Sixty degrees. That's a good temp fer administerin' ether. This here contraption was figgered out by an English doctor named John Snow. He's daid now, but he was a man away ahaid o' his time. This instrument, called an *inhaler*, allows me to reg'late the flow o' the ether at a constant and proper temp, so's I kin control how much yer suckin' in. Ain't never had a problem with anyone gettin' into anesthesia trouble when I use this. I'll allow as to how ether don' smell too good, but it's fer shore safer'n chloroform."

I closed my eyes and took a deep breath. I had to admit to myself that my strength was once again fading and I had become light-headed.

"Not much choice," I said.

"No sir, an' I believe time is perty critical hyar."

I gave a resigned nod.

Belle patted me on the shoulder and smiled before staging the ether inhaler to my left side. She filled one side with water from a large glass jug, which I later learned had been sterilized by boiling and allowed to cool to cave temperature. She poured liquid ether into the other chamber of the inhaler. Then, moving briskly back to the basin she scrubbed her hands and forearms once again. Of course, when she had completed all of these ablutions, she doused her hands thoroughly with corn whisky. Returning to my side, she scrubbed the inhaler mask with a whiskey-soaked pad.

"'Bout ready hyar?" she asked.

I nodded.

"All right, then. 'Twon't be too bad at first 'cause you a-gonna be suckin' in mostly air. Then I'll add some ether to the mix an' you'll start to fade away. Don' worry none. I'll keep a close eye on yer breathin' an' heart rate. Next time you see me, it'll be all over but the shoutin'. Good luck Private Andrewes, an' I suppose I should add *God's mercy*, you bein' a good Christian an' all."

———

I couldn't open my eyes for the longest time. I'd tug with my eye muscles, but I just couldn't pry the lids open.

I heard Belle's voice in the recesses of my mind. "I see them eyeballs a-rollin' 'round in thar. Kin you hear me Private Andrewes?" I felt a gentle shake on my shoulder. "Come on now, let's be up an' at 'em. You can pop them peepers open."

Another shake.

Finally, I managed to let a bit of light stream in. To my relief, five of the six overhead lanterns had been extinguished so there was only a soft glow in the cave. I took a deep clearing breath and coughed.

"Well, yer back," Belle said, with a wide smile. "An' yer doin' jes' fine. Feel like hearin' 'bout it?"

I nodded... at least I think I nodded.

"'Magine I'll have to go o'er this ag'in later. Yer likely to fergit what I'm about to say. That's perty narmal. You gonna be groggy as an ole bear in walkin' hibernation fer a spell. But, I got right good news fer you. Everthin' went as I hoped. Them Minié balls are a revoltin' form o' ammynition. Plumb shatter ever'thin' they hit. Well, I'm happy to report I got all them bone fragments outta the wound, got the fibula stubs rounded off, and did a real careful sewin'-up job. That round in yer right ham was an ole fashioned musket ball an' it jes' popped out like a pit in a ripe cherry. So, the operation was a fine success. How's yer hurtin'?"

"Hurts."

"I kin 'magine. Well, I'm a-gonna keep you on some opiates fer awhile but not too long. Stay on them too long yer gonna start thinkin' you need 'em more than food, water, an' a perty gel. Cain't have it. So I'll switch you on over to some ginger juice an' I'll put a ginger ooze on yer wounds. Should he'p to ease the pain as yer comin' off them opiates."

"Ginger?"

"Yup. Grow it up in the garden. Gotta have a long, hot summer though. Juice is right tasty and the ooze'll he'p the pain, not so much as them opiates, I'd allow, but you git my drift."

I took a deep breath. "Cold," I said.

"That's perty narmal too. I'll fetch 'nother blanket but afore I do, better take yer tempyture."

Once more she reached into a drawer below me and withdrew a long, slightly bent tube affixed to a graded scale. My face must have registered some concern as to what she planned to do with that tube because she launched into a deep, rollicking belly laugh.

"Now don' you go a-gettin all narvish-like on me. Jes' gonna slide this in yer armpit. I'd allow as to how it'd give a right better readin' if I did put it inside you somewheres, but you've had enough indignity fer one day. Armpit'll do."

"Never had my temperature taken before."

"Naw, don' 'magine you have. 'Tain't a common practice but it'll tell us if'n they's infection."

As she waited for the temperature to register, she carried on with her explanation. "You see, Private Andrewes, most doctors think pus, what they call *laudable pus*, is a good thang 'cause it means pyresis or elevated tempyture ain't a-gonna set in. They's all wrong. Fact o' the matter is, pus means infection, an' infection is bad. Infection means them critters has been livelier'n a tick in a tarpot. If'n you got a temp, infection is afoot. So, we gonna keep an eye on yer temp an' them wounds. How's yer Latin, Private Andrewes?"

"My Latin?"

"Yup, yer Latin."

"I've studied it."

"How 'bout *rubor, dolor, calor,* an' *tumor.* Know what them words mean?"

"Red, pain, heat, and swelling."

"Right. That's what we don' want. Maybe a li'l rubor and dolor'd be okay at first, but after a spell, don' want none o' them thangs 'cause they mean infection too."

She retrieved the thermometer and studied it under one of the lamps. "Good," she said. "Temp's okay. Now, Private Andrewes, I'm a-gonna git you that blanket an' a coupla more o' them opium pills an' skedaddle. Jes' after I finished yer operation, afore you woke up, I got word that Ma Baldridge been called to straw. Baldridges live only a coupla miles from here, so I'll be headin' on over thar, bein' as I'se the only granny-woman in these hyar parts. No big rush. It'll be a *groaner.* All Ma Baldridge's babies is groaners. That's what I call hard labor. Easy labor's a *sneeze out.* Poor ole Ma Baldridge—eight groaners, and one more on the way. Be enough, ask me. Reckon she'd agree. I swear she's the up-an'-comin'est woman in Christian County."

Belle's laughter continued as she covered me with another blanket and administered two more opium pills. She extinguished the last lantern and, save for the early morning light streaming through the window, I reclined in darkness.

I could not help but reflect on my most peculiar circumstances. In less than twenty-four hours, I had watched my friend and neighbor, Willi Swartzendruber's eyes die. I had been mortally wounded, mortal in the sense of near-certain death in a Confederate field hospital. I had been whisked away from the battlefield by a man-woman named Belle who practiced medicine in a cave. And now I lay recuperating from what appeared to have been a most successful surgery.

Peculiar as it all was, I reckoned a prayer would be in order. I gave the Almighty all the thanksgiving and praise I could muster. I sought His continued care, and I included a petition for Ma Baldridge's groaner.

Ozark Glossary

ginger ooze – decoction
narvish-like - worried, uncertain
called to straw - gone into labor
granny-woman – midwife

TWO

Belle's Place

August 11, 1861

When I awakened, I crawled around in my mind for several long seconds trying to remember where I was, when it was, and why I was there. Thankfully, I had a pretty good sense of *who* I was. When I had resolved these several uncertainties, I raised my head to see Belle Potts studying the wound on my calf.

"Howdy, Private Andrewes. Have a good snooze?"

"Seems so," I said.

"Ma Baldridge got herself a new little farm hand," she said. Feisty li'l soul but healthy as a horse, jes' a-squawlin' an' a-bawlin' when I left."

She grazed her fingertips across the sutures. "Happy to report this hyar incision is lookin' fair good. Li'l inflamed hyar an' thar but all total, not bad. Better clench your jaw, cause I'm a-gonna sponge it off with some carn whisky. Won't be as excruciatin' as before, but yer gonna feel it."

She daubed the incision provoking a sharp intake of air and violent squinting of my eyes, but I did not cry out.

"Sorrow 'bout that," she said. "Now I gotta take a look at yer back-side. Can you roll over on yer left?"

I complied, having abandoned all hope of propriety in matters pertaining to my surgery. She tucked the blanket around me so only the wound was visible. I appreciated her attention to my modesty.

"'That's lookin' mighty good too. Now, Private Andrewes, we gotta move you on outta here. The metal table cain't be too comfy. 'Sides, I gotta scrub it up case 'nother poor soul comes on by. So, I'se askin' you to don a loose-fittin' gown, an' then we-uns is gonna hop on o'er to the house."

"House?"

"Shore 'nough. Got a house. 'Parently, you didn' see it when we-uns rode in."

"No, I didn't."

"It's a nice two-story frame house with wood sidin'. I heired it. It'll be a right restful place fer you to 'cuperate in. So sit up here. I'll steady you."

She helped me into a sitting position with reliable hands. I became a bit light headed so she held me until I stabilized.

"Doin' okay now?" she asked, her voice soft and comforting.

"Yes."

"All right then, put on this hyar josie, an' I'll go fetch the crutch I made. Had to guess on the length."

"When did you have time to make a crutch?"

"Oh, don' take long to attach a padded cross piece to a pole. Done it while you was a-snoozin'."

When Belle returned, she eased me down to the floor with directions not to put any weight on my wounded leg.

"Use that crutch on yer right side, an' I'll be your stanchion on t'other side."

She held me tightly around the waist and, with my left arm over her shoulder together, we walked out of the cave door, down the incline, and into a white clapboard house. With each hobble, I wondered how *gimped up* I might ultimately be.

"Don' figger it's a good idee fer you to try them stairs so I'm puttin' you in my own room hyar on the ground floor. Got me a good feather mattress an' jes' changed the tickin' so it's clean as a June rabbit an' sweet smellin' to boot. Don' want you up an about fer 'nother day or so 'til I'm sure them wounds is in good fettle an' you ain't runnin' no fever. I'm a-gonna scrub the surgery an' then take a bath. They's another spring a bit fu'ther down the hill what makes fer a good soak. Speakin' o' baths, not too long from now I'm a-gonna sponge you off. Yer not smellin' too good. Understandable what with the march, battle, surgery, an' all. But no sense in you stinkin' the place up like a riled up civvy cat."

"How long am I going to be here?"

"Don' know fer shore. I'd not be thinkin' too much 'bout that right now. Yer job's to git better. I'll be back in an hour or so. I'll fix you a bait of victuals. You're prob'ly ready to start a-gnawin on that crutch."

When she left the room, and I settled into the bed, images of the recent battle bloomed in my mind, and I began to wonder about Willi's body. By now, I presume it had been found and properly disposed. I hoped someone was taking care of notifying his family.

Willi and I had grown up together. His father, Dolphy, and mother, Greta, had purchased a home next to ours, and Willi had become one of my good friends. He had a younger sister, Gisele, to whom I had developed an early attraction that was not without romantic overtones. Nothing ever came of this affection, however. School and seminary slid in between us.

The Schwartzendrubers were a respectable, God-fearing family, and I knew they would be crushed by the news of Willi's death, despite the pride they carried in his sacrifice for the Union cause. The thought of their mourning, especially Giselle's, depressed my spirits and moved me to prayer. I resolved to visit the Swartzendrubers as soon as my condition permitted a return to St. Louis and to civilian life. My ninety-day period of enlistment would end in four days' time and, from what Belle had implied, I would still be in her recuperative care when my name was struck from the muster roll.

When Belle arrived back at the house some time later, she did not come into the bedroom to check on me. She ascended the stairs instead. Perhaps twenty minutes later, I heard her come back down. Clanking sounds arose from what I presumed was the kitchen.

"I warmed up some bean soup with venison," she said swooping into my room with a tray upon which rested a steaming bowl of soup and a cup of amber liquid—the ginger juice, I surmised. "Prob'ly this soup'll get yer digestive system woke up. Ether's notorious fer shuttin' down the gut. So here, let's try a coupla bites. Take 'er nice an' slow now."

Her picturesque but sometimes rough language chipped at my sensibilities, but gratitude for her ministrations allowed me to ease around these indelicacies. The delicious soup brought to full awareness just how hungry I was. I had not eaten for over twenty-four hours, and my last meal was only a half ration. We had been on half rations for most of the past week, and it certainly took a toll on our stamina in the field. Some of my fellow enlistees passed out along the hot march from Springfield to the battle site.

Belle waited patiently for me to finish the soup. "Feel like settin' fer a spell? Got a cushioned chair in the keepin' room out thar if'n you feel up to it."

"Why not?" I said.

She helped me out to the front room and eased me gingerly into a chair with tufted seat and back. She smelled fresh and berry-scented from her bath, which intensified my discomfort over my own malodors that were intensifying by the hour. Without a single wrinkle of her nose, she put a put a high stool under my right foot to elevate the leg, spread a short blanket over me, and left the room. When she returned, she had a bottle of corn whiskey and two glasses. Holding the glasses in front of her, she snatched the cork out of the bottle with her teeth and poured two fingers in each glass.

"How's 'bout a stopper o' carn whiskey," she said. "Lord only knows you could use it after all you been through."

"I don't drink."

"You don' drink? Well that don' seem quite right. Why not? Li'l stopper o' carn whiskey ever now an' ag'in ain't gonna hurt."

"I took an oath upon entering seminary to abstain from intoxicating liquors except for medicinal purposes and the Holy Sacrament."

"Are you greenin' me? Why'd you go an' do somethin' like 'at?"

"It was a requirement."

"Well, I reckon you could argy that the whiskey hyar is fer *medicinal purposes*, as you say."

"No thank you."

"Suit yerself."

Belle promptly slugged down the contents of both glasses and poured a third before sitting in a cane rocker opposite to me. For the first time since we had met, if you could call it that, I stole a long look at my surgeon-hostess. On that late afternoon, she had shed the man's britches for a long butternut skirt and plain white blouse. Her blonde hair, which had heretofore been hidden either in the crown of a wide-brimmed leather hat or in the confines of a white bonnet, now cascaded down to her shoulders. Except for her raw-boned figure, I had to admit she was attractive; not beautiful but definitely attractive. Was it her chiseled white teeth formed in a slight overbite that I found intriguing? Or could it have been her fresh, bloomy vitality? Perhaps it could have been her gray eyes, soft and inviting, quite feminine, I thought—a noticeable incongruity to her mannish frame. And, as nearly as I could tell, I had but an inch, maybe less, on her. Belle Potts approached six feet in height.

"So, Private Andrewes, here we'uns is. I reckon you figger 'taint proper to be sittin' hyar 'thout a chaperone. 'Bout all I kin say is 'round the hill country all that Eastern propriety's been perty much forsook. Since we'uns is holed up together reckon we make the best of it. You said you had a long story to tell me 'bout yer name. I'd like to hear 'at. Mayhaps you could add a bit more 'bout yerself, where you come from, an' all."

I nodded and stared at Belle for several long seconds. "Very well," I said. "We shall make the best of it. And Miss Potts, I believe you also have a long story to tell about *animalcules*, as you call them. It is *Miss* Potts, is it not?"

She forced a small laugh, "'Fraid so. No chubs in my life. Guess men don' favor this tall, spindlin' body, what my Ma used to say was fish-pole high an' gun-barrel straight. Don' matter, ain't got no time fer a man anyhow."

Her words were carried on a wave of sadness.

"Go on now," she said. "Where'd that name come from an' how'd you git hyar?"

"I got here because *I fights mit Sigel*—Colonel Franz Sigel, leader of my regiment, the Missouri Third. We're mostly Germans from south Saint Louis. Actually, I'm only half German. My mother is a German immigrant from Baden, but my father was born in England. My mother came across the Atlantic in 1836 and settled in New York. That's were she met my father. Ten years ago, they came to Saint Louis, and because my mother's family—all Germans—also made the move, our family settled with relatives in a German neighborhood. Krieger is my mother's maiden name, and she insisted that her German heritage not be lost on me. So, *Krieger* Andrewes. Most call me Krieg. I'd be pleased if you just called me Krieg."

She sipped her corn whiskey. "All right then, Krieg. Yer ma an' pa still alive?"

"My mother is, but my father died two years ago now."

Belle locked her eyes on mine. "Sorrow," she said. "Death of a pa is like a pistol shot on a cold marnin'." After several seconds, she changed course. "So how'd you git in the Fed'ral Army?"

"German settlements in America have formed what they call Turner Societies," I said. "The German word is *turnverein*. These are primarily gymnasiums where we strive for physical health. In addition, though, we have a chess club, a choir, and even a fencing club. Colonel Sigel was my fencing instructor. When the prospect of war came up, we Germans started military drills with wooden rifles. I was only occasionally involved because I was away at school. I had just returned from a break in seminary—this was last May—when Secessionist Governor Jackson began his plot to seize the armory in Saint Louis. Sigel formed up a regiment of Germans and Bohemians that he called *Lyon's Fahnenwacht*. That means Lyon's Color Guard. General Lyon was our leader in this latest battle by Wilson Creek. We got word just before I was hit that General Lyon had been killed, God rest his soul. He was a courageous leader, but I think a bit reckless."

"So you Germans is Union folk, I take it."

"Yes indeed and the Secessionists hate us—call us Black Guards or the—I won't say it—the *Cussed Dutch*, if you will pardon my language."

She smiled. "So how did a pup preacher git hisself inter 'iss regiment?"

"My mother is a pillar of the German Women's Union. She even took the lead in stitching up a regimental flag for Lyon's Fahnenwacht, which she presented to Colonel Sigel before we headed west. You can imagine the pressures on me to join and *fights mit Sigel*. I enlisted for ninety days."

"S'pose you got inter some other battles afore this last-un."

"We left Saint Louis for Rolla by train in June. From there, we marched to Springfield and were supposed to cut off the Secessionists who were retreating back to southwest Missouri from the north. We got into a right serious fight over by Carthage and were nearly routed there. We had to fall back quickly to Sarcoxie. Colonel Sigel is very popular among the Germans and thought to be a great military leader because of his training in Germany. I have to say, however, that I don't hold him in such high regard. His battle tactics seem ill conceived even to my inexpert eye. We seem always to be backing up. One of my non-German comrades says 'I don't fights mit Sigel. I retreats mit Sigel.' I think he has a point."

Belle shook her head. "The whole thing's plumb lunacy. Leaders on both sides is crazier'n bessie bugs, ask me."

"I disagree. We are fighting to preserve this country and to free the Negro."

"Don' you think they's a better way than to jibble healthy young men with grapeshot and Minié balls?"

"Sometime's war is the only alternative."

"Strange comin' from a preacher-to-be. Seems you orter favor peace."

"I do favor peace, but the Church has always held that it is morally acceptable to repel the unjust aggressor."

"Don' say? Well, I reckon the South'd be the first to say you Fed'rals is the unjust aggressor."

"They fired on Fort Sumter first."

"Don'cha suppose they figgered they's aggerpervoked. Way I heerd it, oncet the South pulled away, they wanted the Yankees to vacate the Fort, it now bein' Southern prop'ty an' all."

"But the South had no right to secede."

"Reckon depends on who you talk to on that issue." She paused momentarily as if to collect her thoughts. "Don' know much 'bout Jesus an' all, but from what I heerd, ain't supposed to return evil fer evil. Supposed to love thine enemies."

"But, Belle, the evil of slavery has been resistant to remedy. Jesus demanded sacrificial love and that love compels us to take up arms, to lay down our lives for those who are in bondage."

"Well, they's a-layin' down lives an' then they's a-layin' down lives. If'n you is resistin' force without force yerself, an' git kilt, now that's one thing. But, takin' up a musket an' goin' off to kill folk yerself an' then git kilt, why that's 'nother thing. Don' make no sense to me that y'uns is a-killin' to be a-lovin'. Ever one o' y'uns is misfoolin' yerselves."

I found my ire rising a bit. "This nation has formed a union. A union is a union, not a collection of free-standing states. Perhaps your idealistic notion of human beings loving without force applies to the individual but it certainly doesn't apply to governments."

"Seems to me they's a bigger gum'ment you gotta look to. Way I unnerstand it, God's gum'ment's bigger an' all the gum'ments combined. An' ever who norates 'round 'bout bein' a Christian best foller God in everthin' an' that includes no killin'. Cain't be a-killin' an' a-lovin' at the same time. But I'm jes' squanderin' a 'pinion hyar."

Can't be a-killin' an' a-lovin' at the same time. I couldn't agree. Neither could I muster a response.

Sensing my pause and mounting consternation, she set her glass down on a nearby table. "Seems to me we can keep a-backin' an' forthin' all day long. I recommend we not chase this chigger round the stump no more. T'ain't no sense in argyin' ourselves into a dither. Two different p'ints o' view. You got yers. I got mine. Don' know as how we'll get this reconciled in short order. 'Sides, I got some more curiosities. Like, how'd a German boy—guess mayhaps I orter say German-English boy—wind up studyin' to be a preacher?"

"That's the English side of me. My mother isn't particularly devout, having come out of that German skepticism that swept across the land when she was an impressionable young woman. My father, on the other hand, was a militant member of the Church of England, which we call the Episcopal Church in the States."

"'Piscopal? Strange name. Never heard of it."

"Means *bishop*, governance by bishops."

"Don' know nothin' 'bout that."

I waived the matter off as immaterial. "To continue," I said, warming a bit to my autobiography. "My father insisted that I attend church with him—St. James' Parish in the center of the city. So he and I—did I mention I'm now an only child?—were devout members of the church. From a very early age, I felt myself drawn to the clergy life. I started college studies at Washington University in Saint Louis but finally decided to go to seminary. It's called Cranmer Hall, located out in the woods west of Saint Louis."

"So why do you want to be a preacher, Private Krieger Andrewes? God tap you on the shoulder?"

"Something like that."

She leaned forward in her chair, quite obviously—and surprisingly —interested in what I had to say. Her mouth was slightly open, and she nodded with each thing I said as if confirming it in her own mind.

"Like what?" she said. "Tell me. Hear a voice from heaven?"

"No, it's more of a feeling that this is what I ought to be doing? It's hard to describe."

"So God didn' th'ow a pie in yer face."

"No, it was more of an inner nudge."

"I reckon I unnerstan'. S'pose you could say I had an *inner nudge* what to he'p sick people an' all."

"Tell me about that Miss Belle."

"No *Miss* Belle. Jes' Belle. An' I ain't sayin' nothin' yet since I ain't done hearin' from you. I ain't never chawed the fat with a sem'nary man afore. So what do you do all day in that Cranmeer Hall?"

"We have long days. We're up at five in the morning for early prayers. Then breakfast followed by Morning Prayer. From seven in the morning until noon, we are engaged in recitations and study—Greek, Latin, Hebrew, Dogmatic Theology, Holy Scripture, Practical Theology, Church History, and the like. In the afternoons, we work around the seminary. I'm assigned to the library and have become the de facto seminary librarian. Others are involved in cleaning, repair of the grounds, construction, and so on. Then we have Evening Prayer and dinner. From seven in the evening until ten, we have more recitations and study. Come ten o'clock it's lights out."

"How many yas you got to do this?"

"Three. I have one year to go."

"An' no alkyholic spirits, you say?"

"None. No commerce with the fairer sex either."

"You greenin' me ag'in?"

"No, ma'am. As our dean would say, 'Too much time with a lady spells too little time with the Lord.'"

"'At's plumb ridic'lous. You mean chattin' here with Belle is ag'in the rules."

"I don't suppose it's strictly against the rules, but it would raise eyebrows if it happened frequently."

"That's jes' plain prepost'rous, but I'll tell you this, Krieg Andrewes, if'n that dean gets after you, I'll vouch. You've been a fine gentleman, an' we'uns conducted ourselves in a prim an' proper fashion. Why we's all growed up. Orter be able to cut our own weeds seems to me. To boot, I don' believe settin' a spell with Belle has drawed you too fer away from the Lord."

"No, I...."

Just then, I was stopped in mid-sentence by a sharp rap on the door. Belle jumped to her feet. When she opened the door, I heard a voice crying,

"Belle, we gots a man what's bad injured here. Need yer he'p."

"What happened?"

"Got shot in the haid."

"Shot in the haid? How'd that happen?"

"It's that Irish boy Tommy O'Mally. He runs that saloon on up thar jes' east o' the town square in Springfield. You know the one?"

"I do. Ain't been in it but I knowed 'twas thar."

"Tommy—he's a Union man, an' when them Rebs rolled inter Springfield this marnin', they took o'er his saloon and started a-drinkin' an' whoopin' it up. Didn' pay Tommy nary a cent. Well, you know how them Irish can be. Got his dander up. Mad as a coon in a poke. Grabbed a pistol and started toward the courthouse where Ole Pap—that's Gen'l Price—was settin' up his quarters. Tommy was fixin' to shoot Ole Pap, but one o' them aides-de-camp seed Tommy comin' and shot him instead. Took him to Doc Otis, but the Doc jest shook his haid. Said 'I cain't help Tommy. Only one person in these parts can save Tommy an' that's Belle.' So we loaded him up an' come on down hyar. Can you he'p us Belle? Need you to get that bullet outen him an' cooper him up good."

"Haul him up to the surgery. Put him on that table inside. I'll be up direc'ly."

Belle came back into the house.

"Sorry Krieg, but I gotta get a move on. Best get you back in that bed."

She helped me to my feet, and we virtually double-timed it into her bedroom. She was out of the house in a flash.

I extinguished the lantern by the bed and let darkness settle upon me. The pain in my leg began to intensify. Belle had already reduced the dosage of opiates, and the ginger juice did not compensate. However, I resolved to struggle through the discomfort because I knew my condition and situation were far less critical than the one she faced in the cave.

I recited Evening Prayer from memory. I skipped some portions of the service and had no Bible to read but, all-in-all, it was a refreshing time for me and one that permitted me to pray for Tommy O'Malley who lay *in extremis* in the cave not thirty yards away.

I awoke in the early hours of the morning vaguely aware of a presence in my room. I turned my head to the left and, in the dim light from the front room, I saw Belle sitting statue still in a chair directly next to my bed. She was breathing through parted lips, and tears spilled down her cheeks.

"Belle, what's wrong?" I said, raising myself up on one elbow.

She gave a quick shake of her head.

Instinctively, I placed my hand on her arm. She clasped my hand and held it just as a drowning person might seize a rescue pole. Neither of us said anything. She shuddered and the tears pumped once again. We lingered thus in silence for several long minutes.

"Lost him," she said finally in a strangled voice.

I waited.

"Tommy O'Mally's daid." She spoke her words on a choke. "God knows I tried. Don' rightly know what happened. Had him sedated. Had him trephined. He was doin' good. Gettin' ready to go on in an get that ball out an' clean everthin' up when he slipped away. Somethin' else musta been afoot inside thar I didn' ketch. I knowed how to git a bullet outen a man's haid. Done it afore. 'Twasn't beyond my knowance 'tall."

She squeezed my hand even more tightly. "'At pore man an' his family was a-countin' on me an' I let 'em down."

Despite my wounds, I struggled to a sitting position in my bed and, throwing my seminary prohibitions to the wind, I put my other hand on her shoulder.

"Belle, you can't blame yourself. Most people don't survive gunshots to the head especially when they've been banged around on a ten-mile carriage ride. The other doctor up in Springfield wouldn't even try. At least you tried. It was Tommy's time."

She sniffed and nodded.

"I dare say if anyone could have saved him, it would have been you."

She glanced at me and then quickly turned away. "I thankee fer listenin' to me snubbin' like this. "

"Surely you've lost patients in the past. It's got to be the nature of your work."

"I have, fer shore. It hurts ever'time, too. It hurts to lose one, and I blubber ever time I do. Most times I'se all alone. Kinda nice to have you nearby to take a-holt o' my hand. Yer a mighty kind man, Krieger Andrewes."

She took a deep breath, blotted her tears with a sleeve, and patted my hand. "Well, I orter take a gander at yer wounds, I reckon."

She stood and let my hands slip away. I felt a bit of letdown that this connection had been lost. I experienced a strange emotional mixture of sorrow and gratification. I had come to appreciate that this eccentric hill woman. Despite her mannish dress, her mysterious knowledge of medicine, and her uncommon bravado, she was still very much a woman, a lonely one subject to the sorrows and distresses to which those of an isolated and tender heart are heir.

"Looks like you done waded yer deepest water. Them wounds is a-healing quicker'n a snake goin' through a holler log," she said upon completion of her examination. "I best git to bed an' let you finish yer rest. Come tomorrow, I'm a-gonna git you up on both o' them feet fer a li'l half-hammin' 'round the room. So you sleep good...."

She put her hand on my shoulder. "Thankee again."

"Does a snake really go quickly through a hollow log?" I asked with a grin on my face.

She returned the grin. "I reckon so."

I didn't dare ask what *half-hammin'* meant.

Ozark Glossary

heired - inherited
josie - long undergarment
civvy cat - small spotted skunk
victuals - a meal
stopper - small quantity
greenin' - teasing
chubs - sweethearts, lovers
jibble - cut to pieces
aggerpervoked - to provoke
poke – bag
cooper - treat an open-head injury
snubbin - weep, sob, snivel
half-hammin - skip, hop, and jump
chimney – fireplace

THREE

Belle's Place

August 13, 1861

The low-grade pain in my wounds continued during the course of the night, resulting in restless and limited sleep. When morning dawned, I decided to attempt ambulation on my own.

Arising from the bed, I stood with my foot lifted like a heron in repose on a riverbank. I managed to position my crutch before taking a first tentative step. That seemed easy enough so, emboldened, I took another. In the course of the next few minutes, I managed to transport myself out of the bedroom and into the front room and made for the tufted chair. Just as I leaned toward the arm of the chair, the crutch slipped on the hardwood floor, and I crashed to the floor. The crutch clattered away. By reflexive contortion, I managed to avoid impacting either of my wounds in the fall, but I cracked my head hard on the fireplace hearth.

Seconds later, as I was rubbing a ballooning knot on my head, Belle came thundering down the stairs. She bypassed the last four steps by vaulting over the railing, raced to where I lay jumbled on the floor, and put her arm under my back to support me.

"What in tarnation is you tryin' to do, you cockeyed loon!"

"Sorry," I managed to say.

"You better not have mussed up my stitchin', or I'll whup you 'til you runs rabbits!"

"What does that mean?" I asked as she lifted me into the chair.

"Don' rightly know. Somethin' my Ma used to say. Seems 'propriate in a sitiation where some looby boy goes a-crashin' 'round the house. Now you set still so I can git a gander at that limb."

Belle proceeded to study my wounds. Then, with some obvious disgust, she gently parted my hair and examined the knot on my head.

"'At's a nasty lump on yer noggin. You'll be sore as an unpricked boil fer a spell, but everthin' else done checked out good. So I reckon yer off'n hook fer now. Hope you didn' hurt my chimney none. Now, you keep a-settin' still an' keep a-listin' to the left. Don' want too much weight on them sutures. I'm a-gonna go back upstairs an' make prep'rations fer the day. I'll git some johnnycakes an' ming-mang cookin' afore long."

She looked me straight in the eye, "I'm fixin' to give you a bath today."

With that, she ascended the stairs, and I thought I detected a bit more force in her footfalls. I sat and stewed over what *gettin' a bath* might imply. Thus far, Belle had been very respectful of my desire for modesty and decorum, but a bath is a bath after all and, in my experience, when one is so engaged, one doffs one's clothes. Given my physical limitations and the tone of her language, I worried that she was planning to assume more agency for this enterprise than my comfort level would allow.

———

"Whooee, I done et myself inter the creek," Belle said as she rose from the table and began to gather the breakfast dishes. "How's 'bout you, Krieg, you chambered all you kin chamber?"

I nodded.

"All right, then. I'll clean up these hyar dishes, an' then we-uns'll get on with the day."

I watched her stack the dishes and again raised to myself a question that had periodically surfaced since my rescue from the battlefield.

Why me? Of all the wounded soldiers on that battlefield by Wilson Creek, why had I been selected to benefit from what appeared to be extraordinary good fortune?

Truthfully, I was infused with humility at the thought that I was spared a swift and painful death. Was this in order that I might accomplish some larger and nobler purpose in life? And could Belle have been my healing angel, my feminine Raphael? For a Christian man, it was not difficult to draw such conclusions. I wondered how Belle might answer these questions, and so I engaged her thus.

"Belle, may I ask you a question?" She intuited the seriousness of my intent and stopped her labors to turn and look at me. She placed her hands on the hips of her britches, a stance I realized was common for her.

"I reckon," she said.

"Why me? Why did you pick me? Of all of the soldiers in need of medical help, why did you give me the benefit of your care and devotion?"

She pursed her lips in consideration of my question.

"Reckon that's a good query. Don' rightly know why you, of all them poor souls dyin' on that field. When I ketched it in the breeze that they's a battle goin' on, I j'ined up with some o' the neighbor gels to see whate'er we could do to he'p with thems what was all shot up. When I come down that farm road on my wagon an' took a gander at what had took place by the Wilson, I said to myself, 'Belle, fer you to try to take care 'o all them men is gonna be a hard fight with a short stick.' I pondered the sitiation fer awhile and come to the reckonin' that I best do what I could to save one or two from a shore and certain death. Better to save one or two I figgered than scurry 'round that field like a ragged-bottom buzzard tryin' to fix up a bunch, an' mayhaps save no one. Been wonderin' if'n that was the right choice. Mayhaps givin' comfort to many would be a better thang to do than save jes' one. Don' know. But in yer case, I s'pose you could conclude it was the right choice. As it'd be, you was one o' the first I come upon an' I knowed I could give you a fightin' chance. When the other man groaned an' that sap-green Reb surgeon wandered off, I jes' figured it was one o' them *carpe deim* times. So I grabbed you and shuckled outen thar."

I was astounded to hear the Latin phrase. "*Carpe deim*, as in the writings of Horace?" I asked.

"Don' know 'bout 'at. Jes' 'member Doc J usin' them furrin words, an' I done picked 'em up."

"Who is Doc J?"

"Doctor Joachim Jeremiah Johnson, knowed as Doc J. Well, he's part o' that long yarn I still gotta spin. Mayhaps in candle-light I'll tell you 'bout Doc J. But 'enough o' this gabbin'. I gots to set inter my work an' that includes yer bath."

"But, wait—one more question. How did you know it was a *carpe deim* time? How did you know that at that precise moment, you should pick me up and bring me here?"

She shrugged her shoulders. "Couldn't rightly say. Jes' seemed like the right thang to do."

She stood, leaving me to ponder just how God taps a guardian angel *ad litem* (not to overuse the Latin) and presses her into a saving act.

———

With a large and mysterious leather purchase slung over her shoulder, Belle steadied me into a standing position and supported in our journey down a gentle incline of a hundred yards leading to a small, deep, tree-lined, and spring-fed pool, which I estimated to be a quarter of an acre in size. I noticed along the way that the small creek emerging from the cave emptied into this spring, and from there, the combined waters spilled into a much larger tributary that coursed to a distant river.

"Where does that stream lead to, the one emptying out of the spring?" I asked.

"It's knowed as Johnson Run. It's tributary o' the Finley Fork what empties inter the James River. Case you was wonderin', Wilson Creek, near where you got plugged, also flows inter the James. This hyar spring—perty li'l thang ain't it—it's called Johnson Spring by most folks, but some's now referin' to it as *Belle's Spring*. I ain't ask no one to call it that. They's jes' doin' it. Kinder like the sound... Belle's Spring. Whaddya think, Krieg, you like Belle's Spring?"

"I think it's a perfect name."

"'Course at the moment, you ain't in no position to say otherwise. That's if you don' want me to drop you like a sack 'o pum-grannies."

That did it. I started to laugh uncontrollably, and I could barely catch my breath.

Belle halted our excursion. "What's got yer fancy?"

I continued to laugh, shuddering and weeping without relief. Belle just looked at me as if I had sprouted seven new heads. When pains suddenly erupted in my side, I was able to muster a measure of sobriety, but my grin lingered amid the winces.

"Mind tellin' me why you is so in the gales?" Belle said.

"Nothing really. You just have the funniest way of saying things sometimes."

"I talk jes' like ever'one else in these hyar parts. I reckon you'd like me to talk high falutin' English an' all, but that don' suit me a bit. Fact is, I start talkin' like you, folks 'round hyar'd accuse me o' bein' an odd jenny in a strange stall."

"No. No. I didn't mean that. Quite honestly, I don't tire a bit of hearing you talk. Your language has a quaint, charming, and very colorful character. To my *furrin'* ear, however, some of the pictures you paint are quite amusing."

"All right then, Krieger Andrewes," she effected a graceful curtsy, "Appears I am 'bliged to be in yer service, providin' 'musin' sayin's to tickle yer innards. Now, if'n you can get a-holt o' yerself, let's ease down on this hyar dock."

She helped me onto a small dock that jutted into Belle Spring. When I was seated, she rummaged in her purchase and drew out a hunk of soap, a large irregular sponge, and a folded towel.

"I'm a-gonna leave you fer a few minutes," she said. You get shuck o' that josie and scrub up them parts you'd jes' as soon not have me see. Then kivver up with this hyar towel. I'll be over in the woods yonder. Holler, an' I'll come on back to finish the rest o' you."

I must have expressed a look of concern.

"If'n you ponder on it fer a short time," Belle said. "I imagine you'll come to the real'zation they's not much o' you I h'ain't already seed. An' don' take much noodlin' to realize you can warsh most o' yerself 'thout me around. So hop to. You is ripe an' od'iferous. *Do not* —I say ag'in—DO NOT get them wounds wet."

My fears had been confirmed. Belle fully intended to invade my privacy, but there did not appear to be much I could do to defend myself. She was a woman of strong will, and I had discovered that those eventualities upon which she insisted generally came to pass. I began my sponging, fully resolved to leave only a tiny, unreachable patch in the middle of my back for Belle to wash. I looked around. True to her explanation, Belle had removed herself entirely and was nowhere to be seen

The water was cold and quite refreshing on that hot August morning, and it did feel good to remove the grime of battle, butchery, and travail. Upon closer inspection, it was clear that Belle had already washed me in certain areas, those in close proximity to the wounds. My lower right leg had been shaved and cleansed as, I presumed had my backside.

No doubt these ministrations had been performed while I had been anesthetized. When I had finished washing all I could comfortably reach, I shouted for Belle to return. Not a minute later, she was at my side, which made me wonder if she had been spying upon me from behind a nearby stand of trees, but I dismissed this thought as idle and prurient speculation. I did not want to contemplate further the implications of such an act on her part.

"'At orter improve yer outlook on life a mite," she said. "Need yer back laved?"

I nodded and handed her the sponge.

She knelt behind me and began to hum in a low contralto voice. Instantly, I knew the tune. I picked up her melody and began to sing, "Mutter, o sing mich zur Ruh—Wie noch in schöneren Stunden" Our voices—hers in English and mine in German—blended in this haunting ballad. Slowly, in time with the music, Belle washed my back.

I cannot begin to describe the soothing and salutary effect it had upon me. The washing itself took much longer than necessary, but we both knew that the purpose far exceeded mere cleansing. She was ministering to me, and with each musical caress of the sponge, the miseries of the past several months wafted away, and I savored the bathing of both body and spirit. At a natural point, intuited by both of us, we sang the last note allowing it to drift over the placid surface of the spring.

"'At were right nice, Private Krieger Andrewes. I reckon yer ma taught them German words to 'Mother, oh sing me to rest as in my bright days departed'?"

"When I was sick as a child, and she wanted to sing me to sleep, this was the song."

"You sure sing with a nice coarse voice," she said.

"Coarse?"

"Yup, in 'ese parts we say a feller has a *coarse* voice, if'n he sings deep."

"I must assume, Belle, that you just paid me a compliment, and I thank you. May I return the same—your voice is quite beautiful and, I suppose, coarse for a woman."

She smiled briefly and, in that instant, I detected again that fleeting sadness that lurked just under the surface.

"Now we better get back at it," she said. "Gots to warsh the hair. Hyar, let's slip this clean josie on. Then you orter lie down on yer belly with yer head o'er the water. Don' jostle them stitches."

I complied with her directives and let her soap and rinse my hair several times.

"All right then. One more thang. Yer in need of a shave."

My eyes widened again as she rummaged in the bottom of her seemingly bottomless purchase and retrieved a straight razor. "Put some o' that thar soap on yer face so's I don' knick you. Lather it up some," she said, as if I needed instruction on how to shave.

"I don't need any help shaving."

"I knowed that but ain't no lookin' glass out hyar, an' though I reckon you could peer down inter the spring, it don' seem like a particularly good 'proach when I can see yer face right good an' can shave yer smooth and slick as a peeled onion."

I lathered my face.

With a practiced hand, she scraped away my whiskers. Her labors afforded me a chance to study her countenance in near range. The summer sun had burnished her skin, bringing into relief the very fine white down that directly bordered her hairline. She had a small brown mole on her upper lip that I had not previously noted, but otherwise her complexion was clear and, dare I say—*glowing*? Her lips were slightly parted, and her breath was carried on a fresh minty scent giving further evidence of her uncommon cleanliness and robust good health. On two occasions, she glanced into my eyes and, realizing that I was appraising her, she responded with tiny, tic-like smiles.

"How you get in hyar," she asked, stroking with her forefinger the deep cleft in my chin.

"Like this," I said and tugged the sides of my jaw to open the cleft.

She laughed and carefully applied her blade to this last unshaved area. "You gotta chug in that jaw bone, fer sure. I'd wager it runs in yer family."

"It does. My father has it and so did my brother."

"Did?"

"Yes, died as an infant."

"I'm right sorrow 'bout that, Krieg. Older or younger?"

"Younger."

"So when he died, you come to be an only child, like you said afore."

"Yes. Now I'm the only one. You? You have any brothers or sisters?"

"Naw. Jes' Belle."

She did not elaborate, and I did not pursue the matter.

After drying my face, she leapt to her feet. "Up an' at 'em," she said, lifting me into a standing position. When we arrived back at the house, she led me over to the small creek emerging from the cave and seated me on a flat rock.

"Wait hyar," she said and walked briskly into the house some twenty yards away. A few minutes later, she returned with a small dish and a toothbrush.

"A clean mouth is partic'larly important to a healthy body, Krieg. So it's tooth cleanin' time. Hyar...."

She handed me the toothbrush.

"That's one o' Belle's brushes, but I sloshed it good with carn whiskey an' rinsed it so all my critters is daid." She handed me the dish. "Now take some o' this an' put it on the brush and scrub them choppers good. They's all drossy."

"What is this?" I asked, lifting the small dish.

"Mixture o' blue sage, mint, an' salt. Wet yer brush in the crick an' dip it in the powder."

The mixture puckered my mouth, but it certainly had a cleansing effect, and when I rinsed, a very pleasant and fresh taste lingered in my mouth. I cupped my hand and exhaled into it, smelling my breath. The same minty scent I detected on her breath now pervaded my own. I smiled in satisfaction.

"Got me a whole tin 'o that toothpowder, so you clean them choppers at least oncet a day."

I nodded.

"All right then. We-uns gonna git you back inside, slosh them wounds with some carn whiskey. Then I'm off. Ol' Barty Bramwell's 'bout to have the green quilt put o'er him. Figure poor ol' soul ain't got more'n a day or two, so I'm a-gonna go on o'er to his place'n check up on him, see if he' settin' comfortable havin' made peace with the ground an' all."

"You mean he's dying?"

"That's right."

"Isn't there a clergyman to visit him and see to his comfort during his last hours."

"Oh, I reckon could call on Brother Fryer, but he's dumber'n a mud fence. All that man does is holler, an' what he says don' amount to a sneeze in a whirlwind. He cain't give no comfort to no one. Orter be bored fer the simples."

"Don' seem quite right that you have to do the pastorin'," I said and just then became horrified at the realization that I was beginning to pick up the local diction. I resolved to monitor my speech with a bit more vigilance. Belle didn't skip a beat.

"I figure sometimes you git more healin' with what you say than what you do."

With that, Belle guided me back into the house and, with boring eyes, she admonished me to do nothing to jeopardize the integrity of my rapidly healing sutures. Then she shot out of sight, leaving me to a lonesome afternoon.

———

I rested for a time on the tufted chair and worried that I hadn't gotten word to my mother confirming I was still alive. Since I had been spirited away from the battlefield without notification to anyone, I presumed I had been classified as missing in action. I had no idea what happened after the battle. From what the wagon driver had said the previous evening, it appeared as if the Confederate Army now controlled Springfield and the surrounding countryside, which would effectively place me behind enemy lines. Presumably, my outfit and what remained of Lyon's tattered army had retreated back to the railhead at Rolla. I resolved to write a letter to my mother and then discuss with Belle how I might post it so that it could be delivered back to Saint Louis.

I crutched around the first floor of the house but could find nothing with which to write a note. Ignoring Belle's admonitions for prudence and care, I decided to try the stairs. Staying close to the banister, I managed to haul myself up to the first landing and on to the second floor without incident. As I looked back down the staircase I worried the descent might not be quite so easy. My explorations revealed two bedrooms. One of provided Belle's temporary quarters and the other stood in readiness for a future guest. As I passed by the two rooms, a third beckoned from behind a closed door. I swung through several steps until I was positioned in front of the door. When I turned the knob, the door creaked open to reveal a massive library with floor-to-ceiling bookshelves on all walls. A large oak roll-top desk stood as a silent monitor of what must have been several thousand volumes.

Belle's penchant for cleanliness and order ended at the threshold of the library. It was festooned with cobwebs and layers of dust frosted the shelves and leaves of the books. However, the library was not a mausoleum. It had seen use and recently. The top of the desk was free of dust and several issues of prominent medical journals—*Lancet* and the *New England Journal of Medicine*—lay in scattered disarray around the chair. I gathered several of the journals and noted that they were of recent publication. My observations led me to believe that Belle used the desk for study but did not frequently avail herself of the plethora of surrounding tomes.

I retrieved several volumes at random from various locations in the collection and realized that the range of subject matter was indeed impressive. There were, of course, books on the practice of medicine and midwifery but, in addition, I spotted works of literature, natural history, political economy, philosophy, mathematics, astronomy, and – to my great surprise—religion. I estimated there to be about one hundred books on religion, some of which were required reading in my seminary studies. However, all of these the volumes were arrayed in a completely unsystematic and senseless order. I had known people with large, haphazard libraries who could, upon request instantly locate a particular volume. The collector of this bastion of knowledge —Doctor Joachim Jeremiah Johnson—was no doubt one of those perspicacious pin-pointers of randomly shelved books. To my delight I found a volume of the English *Book of Common Prayer* and the *Holy Bible*, which I set aside for my own personal use. I didn't think Belle would mind if I borrowed these for the duration of my convalescence in order to remain faithful to my daily prayers and study of the Scriptures.

After perhaps thirty minutes of inspection, I decided one service I could provide in return for Belle's medical care would be the cleaning and ordering of this wonderful library. I had, after all, learned a great deal about the cataloguing of monographs and serials in my work at the seminary. Thus, I immersed myself in this work spending the afternoon, hobbling around the room creating separate stacks of books for each subject area on the bare hardwood floor. When I had the shelves completely emptied, I wended my way through the stacks, some of which were as tall as I, and swung my way into Belle's bedroom. There I found two towels, which I moistened in the basin on her nightstand. With these towels, I wiped down the dust on the shelves and swiped away the cobwebs. When these labors drew to a close, I found myself completely exhausted. So, I took a seat in the chair, propped my throbbing leg on a tall pile of books, and said my evening prayers. Having thus finished my devotions, I laid my head on the desk and fell sound asleep.

The door, creaking in the darkness, awakened me.

"Krieg, is you in hyar?"

"Right here," I said.

"What in tarnation is you up to?"

Just then Belle tripped over one of my unseen stacks of books and collapsed on the floor in a jumble of arms, legs, blonde hair, and the collected works of John Milton. I jumped to my foot.

"Belle, are you all right?"

"I reckon," she said. "Didn't hear no snappin' bones."

I reached my hand out and, after some fumbling, found hers.

"Here let me help you up," I said.

"Now that's right kindly o' you, Krieg, but I ain't takin' no chances on pullin' you down hyar with me an' mayhaps bangin' up them sutures. I'll be clumb up thar in a jiffy."

Despite the fact that she raised herself without my assistance, she held on to my hand until she was fully upright.

"I'm a-gonna git some light in hyar. You set yerse'f back down on that chair."

A few minutes later she rejoined me with a lantern and placed in on the desk top while situating herself tentatively one of the stacks of books.

"Now, mind tellin' me what you is doin' up hyar?"

"I was searching for paper, quill, and ink that I might use to write a letter to my mother in Saint Louis when I chanced upon this incredible library."

Her arms were crossed over her chest, eyes crackling like pitch in a hot fire. "Jes' couldn' set still down thar like I told you to, could you? This defyin' o' my directions is aggerpervokin' me somethin' fierce. You tear them sutures loose yer ducks is a-gonna be in a pore puddle. I swear. I cain't leave you fer a minute what yer up cuttin' the weeds somewhar."

"I'm sorry," I said, trying to remember the last time I had been so roundly scolded. If memory serves it was around Christmas when I was thirteen. I had eaten a dozen of my mother's freshly baked spritzgebäck biscuits only to be caught with the last crumbs unswept from my chin.

"So tell me Private Andrewes, jes' what're you fixin' to do hyar?"

"I noticed that the library had become dusty and that the books weren't in a particularly logical order. I thought I might clean the shelves and rearrange the books to permit easier retrieval."

Belle sighed deeply.

"This hyar library's Doc J's. You figgered that out by now I'se shore. I knowed this place was a mess and needed cleanin'. Jes' ain't had the spunk. 'Course since Doc J died, I'se busier'n ants at a picnic."

"Tell me about him."

"Not jes' now. I'm fixin' to warsh up an' git outta these britches. First, I'm gonna he'p you down them stars an' git you settled safe an' sound."

When Belle later joined me in the front room of the house, she presented me with a glass of soft cider and began sipping what I judged to be two fingers of corn whiskey. She had a blue patterned dressing gown over what I presumed was her nightgown. Her dressing gown and unfurled hair gave me a fresh rush of her femininity.

"What're you ganderin' at?" she asked, catching my gaze.

"You."

"What? You ain't favorin' my wrap?"

"Not at all. It looks very nice on you. If I am not too forward, I would wish to compliment you on your appearance this evening."

Even in the dim candlelight I detected a slight flush to her cheeks as she gave her little tic-like smile.

After several long seconds, she changed the subject. "So you want to know 'bout animalcules, Doc J, an' how Belle come by this house."

"I'd be very pleased to hear about all of that," I said.

"All right then. Doc J was nigh unto the best doctor in the whole world. He went to Transylvania Medical School an' studied with a Doctor Quinones. Them Spaniards is way ahead o' us in medical care and treatment. Larnt their medicine from the Moors accordin' to Doc J. After medical school, he did some doctorin' back in Tennessee but he was one o' them restless souls what wants to be on out in the wilds. So, he come hyar many years ago when Springfield was nothing but a tannery an' a tavern. He searched 'round an' found this hyar cave an' spring. Then he brung out some furrin carpenters an' all the wood an' 'pointments you see in this place. Also set up his doctorin' in that cave. Folks from 'round these parts thought he was nuttier'n a fruitcake. But when they seed it or, e'en better, when they got a-cured in it, they come to a different way o' thinkin' 'bout that cave."

She took a sip of her whiskey.

"Now, 'bout them animalcules. Doc J never did cotton to the idee of miasmas – that's poisonous gas – causin' disease. He'd figgered out that they's li'l critters what we cain't see with the nekkid eye. They's what make us sick. Then 'bout ten, twelve yar ago, he read a pamphlet *On the Mode of Communication of Cholera* by that English doctor name o' Snow. 'Member him? He'd be the man what larnt us 'bout ether. Snow also had the idee that li'l critters called animalcules or germs carried disease from one person to the next. So know what Doc J done?"

"He went to England?"

"That's right. Took one o' them big ocean liners all the way to England. He tole me all 'bout it." Belle stared high into the room and sighed deeply. "Someday I'd like to go on one o' them liners. Shore would." She returned her gaze to me. "Whilst in England, Doc J went to hear Doctor Snow at the Westminster Medical Society meetin'. 'Twas in October, 1849. I'd already been livin' hyar a couple of years by then. To hear Doc J tell it, that was quite a meetin'. When Doctor Snow talked about germs there was a-fawnchin' with arguments a-plenty 'bout whether them animalcules is the cause o' disease or not. When the meetin' was o'er, Doc J 'companied fer a spell with Doctor Snow. That's when he larnt 'bout ether an' how to use it edzacktly. Also, Doc J shored up what he heerd at Doctor Quinones's feet — scrubbin' an' sterilizin' is mighty important in preventin' infection an' the spread o' disease. That's why I make carn whiskey kill-devil stout. Mighty fine fer sterilizin'."

She raised her glass in a toast and promptly drained it.

"So, tell me Belle, how did you become acquainted with Doc J?"

"My pa an' me had a mean li'l cabin not so far from hyar. Ma died when I'se six so Pa an' me carried on with them pigs an' chickens we was a-raisin'. Had a garden patch too but 'twas perty scarce fer us. An' then Pa...well he's daid."

A tremble of sadness surfaced.

"I'm sorry," I said.

She waived my condolence away. "Naw. Don' matter none. Doc J took me in. I was jes' a shoot of a gel at the time. His wife had jes' passed an' he said I could he'p him clean an' cook an' take care o' the house. Well that didn' plug up all my time so I asked if'n I could assist him with his doctorin'. For fifteen years we worked side-by-side, me he'pin' him an' larnin' healin'. When he died two yar ago, I jes' kept a-goin'. Not much else to tell."

"You must miss him terribly."

She nodded.

We sat in silence for several minutes, each lost in our own thoughts. I broke the silence with a question that had been on my mind for some time.

"Are you a woman of faith, Belle?"

"You mean do I b'lieve there's a God an' all?"

"Yes."

"Why shore. Don' have to practice medicine fer too long afore you git a perty clar sense that they's a Creator. Jes' take fer example yer eyeball. "At's a gee-wholliker if'n I ever seed one. No human bein' coulda even thunk up setch a thang as the eye. An' that Darwin feller —got his new book up in the liberry. You mighta seed it. He claims our eyeballs is evolved. Don' make no sense to me."

I smiled. "Well, Belle, you aren't alone in your skepticism on that point. It so happens that an English philosopher named William Paley argued the existence of God from the complexity of the human eye."

"Don' know nothin' 'bout William Paley," she said.

"So to continue, if you believe there is a God do you also believe that Jesus Christ is his son and our savior?"

"Don' rightly know, Krieg. Don' rightly know. I knowed I'se supposed to believe all that but cain't say honestly that it's lodged tight in my mind. Only thang I can reckon fer shore is that there's a God an' He's made all that they is in this world. I can also say fer shore that God is the spring from whence all healin' flows. Belle jest he'ps Him out ever now an' then."

I smiled again. "That's a big understanding, a very big understanding."

She smiled in return. "We-uns in these parts would say that's a sockdolager of an understandin'."

My smile erupted in laughter.

Ozark Glossary

looby - clumsy, awkward
ming-mang - mixture of butter and molasses
furrin - as in *foreign* but connotes anyone or anything from outside of the Ozark region
a sack 'o pum-grannies - small gourd-like fruit of uncertain attribution
gales - gleeful, cheerful
chug - dip, fissure
simples - refers to a dull-witted person, one whose skull ought to be bored to vent the dullness
a-fawnchin – disturbance
edzacktly - accurately, precisely
kill-devil stout - strong, high proof
jes' a shoot - nearly mature
gee-wholliker - marvel, wonder

FOUR

Belle's Place

Mid-late August, 1861

B elle mailed my letter home. Somehow, she knew how to get it
into friendly hands in Springfield which, despite the Confederate
occupation, remained predominantly Union in sentiment. She assured
me that these friendly hands would tender the letter to a Union post
office which relieved my mind. Since the war had begun, postal service
in the north remained reliable and punctual.

Therefore, I had confidence that my mother would receive word
that I survived the battle, did not suffer mortal wounds, and was
currently convalescing with superior medical care. This would be an
enormous relief to my mother who, upon the death of my infant
brother, had become doting and over-protective. It seemed my father's
death exacerbated the situation. I also informed them that I had been
present at the moment of Willi's death and would, upon my return to
Saint Louis, make a special effort to visit with his parents and sister
Gisele.

Also, to my great relief, Belle had begun to bandage my leg with sterile cotton wraps which permitted me to wear *butternuts,* a type of brown overalls. I had a strong suspicion the pair I had been given were Belle's, but upon inquiry, she became evasive and never acknowledged ownership. I suspect she was attempting to spare me any embarrassment over wearing her clothes, but when I saw the legs turned up to fit my inseam, I became highly suspicious. Belle's legs were longer than mine, a condition I daresay she preferred not to admit. This fact did not discomfit me. Rather, I found it worth a wry smile.

For the next several days, my life with Belle Potts settled into a routine. During the day, she attended her patients, both in the cave and in their several homes. I worked on the library shelving and cataloguing project.

Satisfied that I could negotiate the stairs safely, Belle granted me permission to ascend and descend at will. In the evening, we spent hours talking on many subjects. Each day, as the sun sank in the western sky, I looked forward to her return and our quiet conversations. I found that Belle needed a few minutes at the beginning of each evening to relieve her mind of the labors of the day by sipping a few fingers of corn whiskey and unburdening herself of the medical crises and sorrows that attended her work. I was comforted by the fact that she was eager to share the triumphs and joys as well. During these confessions, I simply remained silent and tried to provide supportive comments to ease her pains and celebrate her satisfactions.

I was astonished at Belle's remarkable command of basic academic skills, honed no doubt through the tutelage of Doc J. Though her understanding of advanced medicine and midwifery had been well established, I discovered that her knowledge of other great subjects of the mind was woefully lacking. To her credit, she became a veritable sponge as I held forth on such matters as ancient history, Greek mythology, philosophy, language studies, and, of course, religion.

Given her hunger, I took it upon myself to provide some instruction in these matters. To this end, each day as I worked in the library, I would select one particular book to guide our discussions in that span of time that extended—if I were to use Belle's chronology—from *lamp-lightin' time* to *late candle light.*

On one occasion, after a particularly difficult day for Belle, I had opened a volume containing Edmund Spenser's *Faerie Queene,* from which I began to read. After a number of stanzas from the first quarto I glanced up to see her eyelids flutter.

"Belle?" I said.

Her eyes snapped open. "I'se a-listenin'."

"Perhaps it is time to conclude this session," I said in full sympathy of her weariness. "I have come to just the perfect lines to end this night's sojourn into Renaissance poetry. Listen to Spenser's words:

> *The drouping Night thus creepeth on them fast*
> *And the sad humour loading their eye liddes*
> *As messenger of Morpheus on them cast*
> *Sweet slombering deaw, the which to sleepe them biddes.*

Is that not a perfect bedtime sentiment?"

She stretched and smiled languidly. "Who's that Morpheus feller?" she asked over the cloud of a yawn.

"Morpheus was the Greek god of dreams and of sleep. According to ancient mythology, he was the leader of dream spirits and Spenser says he lived in a cave and slept upon an ebony bed surrounded by poppies."

"Now that's right interestin'," she said with another yawn. "Morphine is made from poppies. Don' s'pose morphine was named for Morpheus do you. Seems quite a coincidence that a drug in a high dose what can benight you right quick is made from them flowers found round Morpheus' black bed."

"Couldn't say for certain, but there is a logic to what you say," I said.

"I need to tell you, Krieg, these evenin' sessions is a precious gift fer me. They's swellin' my knowance, an' ever day I cain't wait fer lamplightin' so's we can set a spell an' you can tell me all them things. Real gap fer me, shore is, and it's a miration how much you knowed."

"I'm not quite sure exactly what you said just then, but I think it captures my sentiments as well. I enjoy these evenings."

"That's 'nough fer now," she said. "Let's hit the hay."

We stood, and I leaned forward on my crutches and began to swing toward my room. Belle picked up the lantern and fell in step beside me. I looked at her, puzzled by her proximity. She smiled.

"Jes' carryin' the lamp fer you, Krieg. What did you think, I's crawlin' into the sack with you?"

"No, I merely…."

She started to laugh—a strong, hearty, earthy sound that came out like the tenor bells of the cathedral. I could not help but begin to join in with her. As we made our way across the floor of the house, I could not ever recall having laughed in such perfect resonance with another human being. When we came to my bedside, Belle placed the lantern on my nightstand. She put her hand on my upper arm and leaned her head close to mine.

"Thankee," she said in nothing more than a whisper. "Thankee fer all that you're larnin' me. Now, sleep tight 'cause tomorrow's a big day fer you."

"Why? What's tomorrow going to bring?"

"Been seven days now. Sutures is comin' out. An' we-uns is gonna see how that limb'll hold up when you put a bit o' weight on it. So, Krieger Andrewes—sweet dreams."

For a brief second, a wisp of hair from her forehead grazed my own, and then she slipped out of the door leaving me with suspended breath.

———

I awakened to tiny snips and quick tugs on my leg. When I came fully to my senses, I saw that Belle had peeled back the coverlet beneath which I slept and had begun to remove the sutures.

"Morning Krieg. How's yer tobacky taste today?"

"What?"

"Sleep good?"

"I reckon."

"That's good. Now lie still."

Less than ten minutes later, all of the sutures from my leg and backside had been deposited in a shallow dish.

"All right then. 'Em wounds done healed up edzacktly as I hoped. Now it bein' marnin' an' all, time t' git triggered up. I'll slip on outen hyar. When you is ready, give me a holler."

When she returned she knelt near to where I was standing and directed me—very gently—to lower my foot to the ground. I responded as ordered.

"That hurt?"

"No."

"Show me if'n you can lift yer toes off'n the floor. This is what them medical books call *dorsiflexion.*"

I tried but felt a shooting pain in my calf.

"That hurts when I do that."

"All right then. Don' do that." She put her hand on the back of my right calf. "See if'n that right limb'll take a li'l weight. Not too much, y'hear?"

I discovered I could load the leg a bit, but it began to tremble on me.

"Enough," she said, feeling the tremors in my leg. "Nothin' hyar worries me much. You ain't a-gonna git much use o' that leg for a few more days. Still a-healin' up. But you heavied up that limb pretty good, an' I figger it'll hold all yer pounds afore long. Yer a stout boy fer a preacher, despite yer bein' cooped up with them books an' all, so's I reckon if'n they's anyone who kin lick this thing, yer the one. I figger in a couple of weeks, we-uns'll have you steppin' out like a chicken in high oats. This calls fer black coffee, fatback, an' fried eggs. Let's git on inter the cook-room."

On her way out of the room, she snatched up the musket resting against the wall by my bed and muttered to herself, "Shoulda hung this up afore."

The glorious taste of the breakfast had been intensified by Belle's favorable prognosis. I owed this woman an enormous debt. "Belle, I'm nearly finished with the library. Should wrap it up in a couple of hours. Got anything else I can do around here?" I asked this upon swallowing my last swig of coffee.

"Fancy a ride inter the jillikins?"

"Beg pardon?"

"Jillikins them woods, back country, hide-out country. Ain't you ever heerd o' jillikins?"

"Sorry to say I have not."

"If'n you're a mind, finish up on that liberry. I'm gonna ride on o'er to Dabney Rudolph's. 'Bout three miles as the crow flies. Poor ole Dabney dropped a plow haid on his foot. Pertineer cut 'it off half up from the toes. Got it splunt good an' bandaged, but I need to see how he's farin'. Should be back when marnin's up. Then I gotta go out in the jillikins to get some more plants fer medicine. Figger you kin ride jes' fine."

"That sounds quite nice, Belle. I feel a bit cramped here. It will be a fine day for a ride."

"All right then."

———

Belle returned, pleased with the progress of Dabney Rudoph's foot, and she was in a rather euphoric mood. She danced around the *cook room*, as she called it, humming a medley of tunes. I hadn't seen her express such brightness before. While she could in no way be described as morose or melancholy, to the sensitive observer she harbored her moments of delight. So one can imagine my joy in seeing her in such a state of harmony. I dared not to question her feelings for fear of suddenly quelling them.

We joined labors at the cook room table in packing some dried venison, cheese wrapped in paraffin paper, several fresh peaches, and three canteens of water. Large soft-sided panniers were strapped on an old mule named Rube who would serve as our pack animal for the various plants we would gather. When all of our provisions were packed, Belle steadied me as I swung my injured leg in a careful arc over the saddle.

"Wait fer a short spell," Belle said and rushed back into the house. When she returned, she carried the Bible I had been using for my daily devotions.

"Mind if'n I carry the Bible along?"

"No. Not at all."

"Reckon yer wonderin' why," she said as she mounted her horse.

"I'm a bit curious, yes."

"Well, at night I hear you sayin' your prayers, readin' the Bible, an' all. Ain't never told me nothin' 'bout the Bible in any o' our talkin' in candle light time. I figger we ain't gonna spend the whole time harvestin' plants so mayhaps we can take a short break an' you can edify me some from the Bible."

I could not help but smile, a wide smile. "I'd be very honored to do that," I said.

"Fine. Now let's git to crackin'."

"Lickety-whoop inter the jillikins?" I asked.

Her tenor bell laugh sounded into the wild countryside. "Now don' that take the rag off'n the bush! Krieger Andrewes is now a-talkin like an old citreen."

Belle clucked her horse into motion, and I fell in behind. We traveled to the southeast and were soon beyond any homesteads or other signs of civilization. As we traveled, she explained that Doc J had come to appreciate the medicinal value of many of the herbs and plants native to the Ozark region. He studied with medicine men and healers from several tribes, primarily the Cherokee. After learning the correct techniques and timing for harvesting, he begun to raise his own, which he would dry and store for later compounding. He even learned the Indian prayers before gathering medicinal plants, prayers that offered gratitude to the plants for their sacrifice in the service of his patients. Belle went on to call my attention to a shed on the back of the property that was used for the storage and preparation of these natural medicines. I had noticed this shed but had never ventured in. I expressed a desire to see it when we returned to the house.

After about three miles, she dismounted near a small stream, put her hands on her hips, and looked up at me.

"Reckon you can stay mounted fer now. Jes' gonna gather some bunches o' watercress. When we'uns git to the open woodland yonder, I'll he'p you down so's you kin take a load off whilst I gather some more plants."

As she waded into the water, a blue heron, annoyed by our presence, lifted into the air with several powerful downstrokes of his wings. Belle pointed to him.

"A *fly-up-the-creek*," she said. "Some call 'em *green herons*, but I preference *fly-up-the-creek*."

She leaned over and began to pull large strands of watercress from the upstream side of a small rocky bar jutting into the stream.

"What is watercress for?" I asked.

"Good fer many an ailment. Injuns used it fer liver an' kidney miseries, but I use it to treat skin problems—pimples, blotches, an' setch."

She continued to harvest the watercress for several more minutes and deposited the cuttings on the bank. I glanced into the sky and noticed that dark storm clouds were suddenly beginning to swirl low in the western sky.

"May be in for a storm," I said.

"It's clabberin' up a might fer shore," she said. "We best move on. I knowed a place where we can git in outta the starm. Rock outcrop upstream a poke."

She shook out the watercress and stuffed it into one of the panniers. Just as we reached the outcropping, a torrential rainstorm began to pound the area. Belle helped me off the horse and led me to the dry gravel-strewn floor beneath the outcropping before retrieving our saddles and panniers. She settled in next to me.

"Whoee! 'Iss hyar is a good ole goose drownder if'n I ever seed one."

"Good thing you knew about this place, or we would be drenched by now."

Lightning cracked in the not too distant sky, and the thunder roared, beginning with a low growl and swelling to a magnificent boulder-rolling boom. The wind began to whip driving sheets of rain beneath the rock outcropping. Belle and I huddled closer together and pulled our knees tightly to our chests. Rube and the two horses lowered their heads in misery.

"Gittin' a might crimpy out," Belle said, and it was then I realized she was shivering in her lightweight cotton blouse. Instinctively, I put my arm over her shoulders and rubbed her exposed arm. She smiled in appreciation, and I did not, as no doubt I should have, immediately remove my arm to restore my clerical propriety. Quite frankly, I enjoyed holding her and, if my sensitivities were accurate, she did not mind either. When I finally retrieved my arm we hunkered side-by-side under the outcropping until the cloudburst began to abate.

"'Pears that it's a-gonna fair-up some," Belle said.

She rummaged around in one of the saddlebags and retrieved the Bible.

"Reckon you could larn me somethin' from this hyar Bible while we-uns is waitin' fer the rain to stopper up."

I had been thinking about this opportunity while we were riding, so I paged directly to the eleventh chapter of John and the story of

Jesus raising Lazarus from the dead. Carefully, I read the first forty-five verses ending with the words:

> *And he that was dead came forth, bound hand and foot with grave-clothes: and his face was bound about with a napkin. Jesus saith unto them, Loose him, and let him go. Then many of the Jews, which came to Mary, and had seen the things which Jesus did, believed on him.*

When I had finished, I closed the Bible and looked at Belle whose eyes were fixed on something in the distance.

"Why'd you read that passage?" she asked at last.

"Why do you think I read it?"

"You testin' me, Private Andrewes?"

"Not at all. I'm just curious as to what struck you about this passage."

She thought for the better part of a minute.

"I reckon they's a list o' meanings as long as a well rope in them verses but one or two of 'em stuck tight with me."

"Such as?"

"Such as them sisters callin' fer Jesus to come an' raise they's sick brother. Now I heerd that same callin' many times in my healin' work. I knowed that many folk what need Jesus call on him to he'p 'em. So when you read that story, I said to myself, he's a-readin' a passage what he knowed I'd unnerstand. Seems like them women callin' fer Jesus is somethin' of a prayer, like the prayers of my patients, only them women was prayin' fer Jesus in the flesh an' blood. We can only pray in the spirit. Have I got a bead on 'er?"

"Yes," I smiled to myself. "Your familiarity with healing is certainly one of the reasons I chose that passage. And you are quite insightful to suggest that Mary and Martha gave us an ancient model of what we religious folk call *intercessory* prayer. What else?"

"Remember when I was a-snubbin' o'er Tommy O'Malley?"

"I do."

"'At happens to me a fair amount. The cut o' my jib droops when folks die on me. I jest feel so sorry fer they's families. It comforts me that Jesus wep' when a friend died. I reckon if'n he wasn't ashamed I shouldn't be neither."

"'Jesus wept' is the smallest verse in the Bible and yet one of the most significant."

"And Krieg, I reckon you picked this passage because you're outta sorts 'bout what I said t'other night."

"I don't follow."

"I reservationed some 'bout that feller Jesus bein' the Son o' God an' all. I suspect that consternated you, bein' as savin' souls is your patch to berry in."

I couldn't help but chuckle at what she said. "To be honest, you have once again caught my intent."

"I'll ponder it some, Krieg, I promise you. Now the rain is in tricklin' time, so I'se a-gonna saddle us up. Like to find a black walnut tree fer nuts, bark, an' leaves. Them nuts is good fer ringworm, an' the bark an' leaves can make a good tea fer the cramps. If we-uns is lucky, we can git some hawthorn berries what is good fer heart palpytations an' what not. Motherwort's good fer the heart as well, but I cain't seem to find much of it. Wouldn't mind gettin' some mad-dog weed if'n we'uns kin find it. Got a coupla folks with the nerves what could benefit from it."

While I found her discourse on medicinal plants to be of some interest, it was her response to the reading from John's gospel that intrigued me more. Clearly, Belle possessed a sharp and incisive mind, and her discernment of my purposes in selecting that particular passage amazed me. Her capacity to fathom the emotions and intentions of those around her arose from a rare and invaluable intelligence.

She was clearly no Deist. She did not believe that God made the world and then went off to take tea, having no further concern for His creation. No, not at all. She believed in God's immanence and intervention with her sick patients. It seemed to me that she professed something of an unexamined Unitarianism wherein she did not see Jesus as the Son of God but as just "that feller."

Yet, there appeared to be an openness to further development of her thought in this regard. I resolved not to push it. If the truth be known, Belle was becoming quite dear to me, not just because she had brought me out of the valley of the shadow of death but simply because I was charmed by her mind and spirit. I had no desire to push her or to create in her any discomfort about being in my presence.

———

When we completed our gathering of plants and returned to Belle's house, it was evening, and the sun had just slipped below the horizon. After Rube and the horses had been liveried and the plants hung in the back shed to dry, Belle and I settled once again in our familiar places to finish off the evening in extended conversation and—for Belle—two fingers of corn whiskey. She was the first to speak.

"Been thinkin' 'bout that passage some more."

"Yes."

"What's stuck sideways in my gullet is this business 'bout Jesus bein' the Son of God. Cain't quite swaller it. I heard ole Brother Fryer a few times an' as I done tole you, I can't abide that man. Nothin' but a gammoner. I swear ever' time that man sees me he jumps on me like a duck on a june bug. *Howdee Belle*, he says, *have yer been saved yet? Have yer accepted Jesus as yer Lord an' Savior? You is gwine straight ter hades if'n yer don' get right with the Lord, Belle Potts.* Krieg, evertime I hear that soozified ole fruitjar sucker, I wanna run like a rabbit in a grass fire. Factually, his yammerin' is part o' my problem. I figger anythin' that mussel-haid says ain't worth the powder to blow it to breakfast. So when he goes on 'bout Jesus as Lord and Savior my brain clams up somethin' fierce, and I sets into squeezin' everthin' he says outta my mind."

I couldn't help it. I started to laugh again.

"So what's amusifyin' you now? Evertime I start to chawin', you start gigglin' like an ole fritter-minded woman."

This actually intensified my laughter until that tic-like smile flickered across her face, and I could feel her embarrassment at my laughter. Momentarily sobered, I assured her that I found her descriptions delightful and a pleasure to hear.

"Please forgive me," I said returning to the substance of our exchange. "For indeed the question you raise is an important one. I will admit it is very difficult to accept the idea of a God-man, of a man who is at the same time our God. This difficulty is even greater when we realize that Jesus was both fully God and fully man."

Belle shook her head in perplexity.

"Perhaps the best place to begin is to learn what Jesus said about himself. There are a couple of key points. First, we can assume that only God can forgive sins. Do you accept this?"

"I reckon'"

"Good. N'ow, in the second chapter of Mark's Gospel, Jesus declares his own authority to forgive sins."

"But anyone can go a-claimin'…."

I put my hand out. "Hear me out. In the second chapter of Mark, we have the story of a sick man whose friends bring him to Jesus. The crowd is so thick in and around the house where Jesus is teaching that these friends can't get in to see him. So they climb up on the roof and lower the sick man nearly into Jesus' lap. Seeing their faith, Jesus turns to the sick man and says, 'Son, thy sins be forgiven thee.' Now the pompous religious leaders are incensed and say, as would we, 'who can forgive sins but God only?' To prove that he can forgive sins, Jesus then heals the sick man. So he seals his claim to be God by doing only what God can do and thereby establishes his authority to forgive sins."

Belle pursed her lips and studied me.

I pressed on.

"The second key point is that Jesus claims always to have existed. No mere man existed before all time. Finally, Jesus said he would come again at the end of time and place the entire world under judgment. All of these three claims are outrageous and a person making these claims would either have to be a raging madman, a lunatic, or filled with the greatest evil we humans can possess—namely, the claim to be God ourselves, unless… what he said about himself is really true. This is where faith comes in. If you come to the conclusion that Jesus is a madman, a lunatic, or evil beyond our understanding, then the Christian religion is fakery of the highest order. However, if you come to the conclusion that Jesus was a genuinely good man, who was not insane, and who would not lie, then his claims—not to mention his miracles and the power of his teaching—establish him as none other than the Son of God."

Belle continued to study me, even to the point of uneasiness.

"I'll swiddle this 'round in my haid fer a spell. Candidly, cain't say I'se clarified on the subject, but I thankee for caucusin' with me on it. Still—don' unnerstand what Brother Fryer is windy-spinnin' 'bout, but mayhaps another night you can rectify that fer me. As fer now, I'se plumb tuckered out. Time to git them steps clumb and crawl in.

She didn't even pause when she asked, "You need he'p into yer room?"

"I can make it.

"All right then. We-uns'll work a bit more on heavyin' up that limb tomorry."

"Good night, Belle and thank you for a pleasant day."

"Pleasant for the twain o' us," she said. "Sweet dreams."

She slowly ascended the stairs, but just before she slipped out of sight, she turned back and smiled. That image—a smile in the shadows of the staircase—is forever fixed on the canvas of my mind.

Ozark Glossary

benight - overtake with darkness
gap - opportunity
miration - wonderment, from *admiration*
git triggered up – dressed
cook-room – kitchen
citireen - old-timer, long-time resident
clabberin – cloudy
crimpy – cold
gammoner - one who talks incessantly but is unreliable
soozified - uncouth and conceited

FIVE

Belle's Place

Late August—Early September, 1861

My third and fourth weeks with Belle were marked by steady and notable progress in the rehabilitation of my leg. Day by day, I was able to add more weight and, from all indications, the tibia bone alone would provide the stability I needed for a near-normal gait.

Raising my foot—*what them medical books calls dorsiflexion*—remained a struggle. According to Belle, I had the capacity to raise my foot, which surprised her, but even the short span of inactivity had substantially weakened the affected muscles. Accordingly, she contrived a training program. For example, in one exercise, she positioned me on the porch railing so my foot was several feet off the ground. She hung a canteen on my affected ankle and instructed me to lift it. At first, I failed miserably, but she was a stern and uncompromising taskmaster.

Late on the second day of my exercises, I managed to elevate the canteen by perhaps a half an inch. Belle danced a little jig of joy and promptly added a cup of water to the canteen, which I also had to lift before the exercise could be terminated. I succeeded, but when at last I dropped the canteen from my foot, I was drenched in perspiration and wheezing like a locomotive. Each day, she added more and more water to the canteen so that by the end of the week I could lift a half-full canteen, which I judged to be roughly a quart by volume.

By day, I tried to do things around the house for which Belle lacked the time or inclination. I cleaned the shed she used to dry her medicinal plants and properly labeled the many jars and tins containing powders and emulsifications. I devoted several days to the repair of a split-rail fence that had collapsed, and on another, I hoed weeds from the herb garden. I must say that lifting rails and hoeing a garden on a crutch is no mean accomplishment. Predictably, both of these services occasioned an impassioned rebuke from Belle.

"I swear, Krieger Andrewes, you is the most 'zasperatin' man! Time an' ag'in I charge you not to o'erdo it an' you jes' take the studs, an' they's no argyin' with you. Soon's I'm around the corner, you is up busifyin' yerself an' puttin' your recovery at grave risk. I got half a mind to clew you upside yer noggin. I'd do it too if I thunk it'd do any good."

In the evening we continued our lengthy conversations on a variety of themes. Belle's interests remained quite varied. While she seemed eager to hear more about the contents of the Bible and the genesis of various Christian doctrines, she did not display a disproportionate interest in this subject over others. While I certainly would have preferred a more exclusive focus on theology, I respected her yearning to delve into many areas of study.

On the one month anniversary of my fall in battle, I raised a subject that both of us had avoided for some time—my departure from the Ozarks. "Belle," I said, "I am loathe to raise this matter because I have so appreciated all your care for me and I have relished these evenings together. However, my need to stay here is diminishing each day, and I do feel some urgency to return to my unit for proper discharge and then on to my family. I must return to my studies at the seminary. The fall term begins in about a month, and I need to report to my Bishop and alert the dean that I will be returning for my final year."

Belle's eyes focused on her hands folded atop her lap and emitted a deep sigh. "I knowed this Krieg. You gotta cut your own weeds. I unnerstand. Truly I do. I could curl 'round your boots an' listen to you from sunup to late candle-light. They's jes' so much to larn. Oh, I could read all them books upstairs but I stow things better by hearin' than by seein', so listenin' to you clots things up better in my haid. An' sure as I live an' breathe, yer progressifyin' mighty good. Don' believe you is gonna be bad hipped in the end. Factually, I'se plannin' to try you on a walkin' stick tomorry, see if'n you kin mosey about 'thout them crutches. Doc J used a walkin' stick in his dotin' years, an' I figger he wouldn't mind none if'n you took it. Course, I'd be stretchin' the blanket a bit sayin' I wasn't gonna miss yer he'pin' me 'round the place hyar. I'se still 'bout as tickled with you as if'n I'd a-found a hair in my butter o'er you disobeyin' my d'rections. But I reckon I'll simmer down in time. Don' believe I said thankee for fixin' that fence. Looks right good now."

"My pleasure."

"I suppose you'll be leavin' with a feelin' that the whole field h'ain't been plowed."

"How do you mean?"

"Me not acceptin' the whole kit an' bilin' 'bout Jesus as the Son o' God an' all. Feel like I'se disapp'intin' you, but I jes' ain't thar yet. I'll wag it 'round though, I guarantee you."

"Belle, permit me to offer you every assurance that you are not *disappointing* me. We all grow into our faith in different ways and in different times. For some, it requires the burning of a long, slow fuse. For others it is a sudden explosion. One is not necessarily to be preferred over the other. So, in your case, *wagging* it around is all that the good Lord asks."

"In ponderin' it, seems like I want to believe the way you do I just cain't."

"Be patient with yourself Belle. Be not drawn into the pressures imposed by someone like Brother Fryer."

"Believe me, not havin' no truck with that durgen."

"So," I said, returning to the original topic of discomfort. "How much longer do you figure I need to remain here, assuming I can handle the walking stick?"

"Well, truth be knowed, you kin leave 'bout anytime after demonstratin' proficiency 'thout the crutch. I'se gonna let you take Doc J's harse."

"I couldn't do that without payment," I said. "I'll send money when I get to Saint Louis."

"Naw. Don' want no money. Belle don' need two harses. Besides, ridin' will spare that limb fer a few more days. You keep on mendin' like you is, I cain't see no reason why you won't be fixed up good fer Cranmeer Hall in a few weeks."

This pronouncement cast a somber pall over the room, and both of us lapsed into silence, which remained unbroken until we bade each other good night and repaired to our respective rooms. The next morning, Belle introduced me to Doc J's walking stick, which I mastered quite quickly and, with grim satisfaction, I set my crutch aside. I turned to face Belle.

"This seems easy enough," I said. "If you are in agreement, I'll give it a day and, assuming I've suffered no mishaps, I'll take my leave on the morrow."

Belle shot me the tic-like smile. "All right then," she said. "I reckon I'll be on my way."

She slipped quietly out of my room and disappeared. I did not see her until mid-evening. I had stationed myself in my usual chair prepared to engage in one last lively conversation on whatever subject fancied her. However, she did not reciprocate. Instead, she went up to her room and closed the door. When it became obvious to me that she did not intend to join me for *caucusin'* that evening, I hobbled off to bed permeated with sadness.

I suspected that Belle's seclusion was a form of protection to shield her from the separation that loomed so near. Belle clearly favored my company, and this pleased me greatly. Yet another part of me wondered if her favor didn't arise in the first instance from a profound loneliness. Indeed, in all the time I had been in her home, not a single person came to visit her for reasons other than medical care. She suffered from severe isolation amid the dozens of patients that treasured all she did for them. It was a loneliness that made my heart ache for her. These concerns, along with my pending departure, were on my mind as I finally drifted off to sleep that night.

I could not tell you the precise hour in which this happened, but at some point in the course of the early morning hours, I slowly became aware that I was not the sole occupant of my bed. When this realization bloomed in my consciousness I sat bolt upright. In the moonlight streaming through the window, I beheld Belle Potts clutching the coverlet and looking directly at me.

"Belle, what are you doing!"

"Hold me Krieg. Please hold Belle."

"I cannot hold you Belle, it is not proper."

"Why?"

"You are in my bed. We are not married. It is a complete breach of propriety. Now, please, before this goes any further, I beg of you to leave."

"Don'cha favor holdin' me?"

"It's not...."

"Then put yer arms around me an' pull me close."

"Belle, no."

"Just fer a stitch. Then I'll scuttle outta hyar."

"I can't."

"Why for?"

"We've been over this. I've taken vows. I've made promises. Now, for the love of God—and I mean that—please go back to your own room!"

Suddenly, she threw her arm around my shoulders and pulled me into a smothering embrace. Second by second, my resolve ebbed. Her lips brushed my ear. "Yer gotta a hook inter my heart, Krieg. First time in my life I ever felt such tender affections fer a man. But I knowed you cain't come a-wingin' me, so I'll mosey off now. Let you get some shut-eye. I'se gonna give you a hand gettin' outta hyar tomorry."

With that, she slipped from the room as noiselessly as she entered. I sat upright for several minutes before I eased back under the covers.

———

The banging of a cast-iron skillet awakened me. I grabbed the cane and hobbled out to the cook room to see Belle turning chicken breasts in a skillet atop the quite modern wood stove that Doc J must have imported to these rugged hills.

"Good morning," I said.

"Marnin'." Her voice was subdued.

"Chicken, I see."

"I heard they's still Rebs up Springfield way an' mayhaps Reb Bushwhackers 'long the road up to Rolla. I knowed a nigh cut that'll

allow us to skirt 'round them ruffians. Figgered I'd carry you fer a day
an' then you'd go on from thar. This hyar is food fer the journey."

Belle's mention of the Confederate occupation of Springfield and
the menace of Southern guerrilla sympathizers roaming the countryside blew the war back into my mind. My respite in this Ozark backwater had allowed me to vacate most thoughts of the conflict that
raged across the nation. Long quiet days in the library or garden,
evenings in wide-ranging conversations with Belle, and plant-gathering
excursions had supplanted the horrors of war and allowed me a
breather, not only in body but spirit as well. Now, the eye of the storm
was soon to pass, and I would be leaving the securities of this wayside
hospice to return to my life, not as a soldier of the Union, but as a
soldier of the Lord.

Belle set the chicken on a nearby rack to cool and used the leavings
to cook the giblets as the substance of a delicious gravy with which we
drenched some fresh biscuits for a quiet breakfast. "'Them biscuits'll
stick to our innards fer a spell, I reckon," she said. "Now we-uns best
get to crackin'. Come with me. Got somethin' fer you."

I followed Belle back into the bedroom. She opened the door to a
mahogany armoire and pulled out a black suit of clothes and a white
blouse smelling strongly of starch.

"What is this?" I asked.

"Preacher's clothes."

"For me?"

"Well sure as snakes crawl, 'tain't fer me."

"But why these clothes?"

"Reckon there's safety in bein' a preacher. Don' know that them
Rebs is too keen on pluggin' a man o' the Lord. Oncet you get back on
the main road, this hyar black frock coat an' wide brimmed black hat'll
shew you off as a preacher. 'Sides ain't too fer off'n the mark, since you
is pupilifyin' at Cranmeer Hall anyhow."

"Where did you get these clothes?" I asked in amazement.

"'Bout five yar back, they's a ridin'-round preacher from these parts
what's named Randolph Opdyke. Come down with the cancer and
died. When I'se out on my rounds few days ago, I stopped by the
Widder Opdyke's cabin over in Gully Warshin' Holler. I asked if'n she
had some o' Brother Randolph's suits. She did. He's a tetch shorter'n
you, but they's enough cuff cloth to let 'em out a tad. Widder Opdyke

takes in sewin' an' mendin', so she modified them britches and coat. Best get inter 'em now. We gots to be a-gettin' while the 'gettin's good."

I put on Brother Randolph's clerical suit and caned my way out of the house where Belle was loading our foodstuffs in one of the saddlebags.

"Got one more thing fer you, Krieg," she said. "Mind comin' close hyar?"

I walked over to where she was standing. She turned to face me and looped something over my neck. When I looked down, I beheld a carved oak cross, approximately two inches long, suspended on a thin leather thong. The cross had been shellacked, giving it a shiny veneer and bringing into bold relief the wood grain patterns.

"Where did you get this?" I asked.

"Been carvin' on it ever now an' then. Reckon it'll he'p some if'n anyone doubts yer a preacher."

"It's beautiful. I shall wear it often. Thank you."

"All right then. Git yerself clumb up on that harse. We gotta a lot o' miles to chaunk up afore sunset."

———

Not far behind Belle's house, we picked up a game trail that coursed in an east-by-northeast direction through heavily forested terrain. Rarely did we break into open fields or meadows. The trail was obscure and, at times indistinguishable from the forest floor through which it cut. Despite the difficulty the trail created for us, I was happy for its obscurity because it meant that it had conveyed only woodland creatures. We crossed several small streams en route, which afforded our horses the opportunity to slake their thirst.

We rode steadily with only occasional brief stops. Not another soul appeared on the trail, and there was nary a homestead to be seen. Just before sunset, we came to a small clearing perhaps thirty feet in diameter ringed by pine trees and within a stone's throw of a small stream.

"This hyar'll be a good spot to take a load off fer the night," Belle said over her shoulder.

We set up camp quickly, and Belle gathered some of the plentiful deadfall to make a campfire. She heated up the chicken and made some camp coffee. Predictably, after a satisfying meal, she quaffed a shot of corn whiskey.

"How far do you think we've come?" I asked.

"Cain't say fer shore. Rode perty hard but trail's slow. I figger eighteen, twenty mile."

I nodded.

"Gots to stay on the trail fer another twenty mile or so tomorry. I figger then you'll be outta the clutches o' them Rebs. From what I heerd, oncet you is past the Niangua River, you'll be in Fed'ral territory an' you can travel the main road to Rolla."

Belle stirred the fire with a stick and then leaned over to withdraw a sheet of paper from her saddlebag.

"Stick 'iss note in yer bag. Jes' when the trail peters out an you is 'proximatin' the main road, they's a farm run by an ole coot name o' Owen MacDougall. I knowed him fer many a yar. Give' Owen that note, an' he'll bed you down fer the night an' his woman'll cook you a bite o' supper."

"Belle, you've thought of everything. I'll never be able to thank you for all you've done for me."

The little tic-smile flitted across her face, but she said nothing.

As the fire ebbed from red to orange and darkness enveloped the clearing, Belle and I crawled under blankets separated by a good ten yards. Before we drifted into sleep, Belle raised up on one elbow.

"You shore you got to go, Krieg?"

"I'm afraid so."

"You could hole up with Belle. We could be a-pullin' in the same direction. I'd do my healin', an' you could keep the place from dilapidatin'."

"Belle, there's nothing for me in these hills. I would grow weary of maintenance, and I cannot ignore the call of God."

She lowered herself and said nothing more.

The next morning, we ate leftover chicken and saddled the horses in silence. Then, without warning, Belle gave me a little shove as if to usher me out of her existence. She mounted her horse and rode away. I watched as she slipped out of sight into the thick forest. She never looked back.

Ozark Glossary

take the studs – grow stubborn
durgen - uncouth, unsophisticated hill person
come a-wingin' - to court or woo
a nigh cut - a back road, generally private
chaunk – to chew

SIX

Cranmer Hall

October, 1861

Agatha tolled five times at five o'clock in the morning. I could hear Mr. Peterslie, the sexton, sound out his tell-tale cough as he walked away from the seminary bell, named after Saint Agatha, the patron saint of bell makers. I raised myself and glanced around the dormitory room to see my fellow seminarians, depleted in number by the War, groaning and rubbing the sleep from their eyes. Only nine of us had arrived for the fall term, and I presumed that most of the absentees had elected to enlist in one or the other of two armies. To be sure, most of us were pro-Union and had strong abolitionist views, but we had a few students from Confederate states who certainly maintained their geographic allegiances. Those who enrolled at the seminary that fall did so for a variety of reasons, including pacifist convictions, a higher sense of purpose, and health limitations. I was the only one who had seen any military action and was one of three remaining seniors.

"And so it begins," Marty Muldown said as he hauled his corpulent frame to a standing position and fumbled around the wall hooks for his blouse, trousers, and cassock.

"Up and at 'em, gentlemen," I said directing my voice to the far beds where the two new freshmen leaned on their arms blinking in bewilderment. "Matins at five-fifteen and tardiness is punishable by death." I had been chosen as Preceptor of the Freshmen, which meant that I bore multiple responsibilities, including helping first-year students understand the rule of life at the seminary, serving as counselor and confidante, assisting with certain of the first-year classes, and recommending necessary discipline to the Dean.

It was a singular honor to be chosen as Preceptor, and I had little doubt it had been conferred upon me because of the supposed maturity I had gained during my brief time as a member of the Missouri Third Regiment. The fact that I was a wounded veteran of the Battle of Wilson's Creek and something of a local hero no doubt factored into the faculty's decision to appoint me.

"He means what he says, too," Marty enjoined. "Death is the prescribed sentence for tardiness—either death or a meeting with the Dean—and I assure you, reverend sirs, death is to be preferred."

The other senior, Smithson Hamilton, who stood apart affixing his cincture in silence, was a taciturn man, flinty, arrogant, and aloof. He rarely said anything, and when he did, good-natured banter was not part of his repertoire. None of us cared much for Smithson. His rigorous and inflexible personality seemed incompatible with the compassion of Christ. Marty and I predicted that his prickly standoffishness made him eminently qualified to be crowned with the mitre of a bishop. (The cynicism with which Marty and I salved the strictness and severity of our life at Cranmer Hall kept us *a-wadin' through the deep waters*, as Belle might have said.)

Belle.

It seemed not a waking moment passed without her surfacing from the depths of my mind. I had hoped that returning to Saint Louis, mustering out with an honorable discharge, submitting to my mother's lavish affections, and resuming my studies at the seminary would crowd Belle out of my thoughts, but thus far this had not been the case. No amount of physical industry or mental activity could rid me of her image. And, when my momentarily un-tethered attentions did have the freedom to wander, the events at Belle's place blossomed brightly in the garden of my mind.

I must confess that my memories of the night when Belle slipped into my bed had progressed to more concupiscent fantasies. Indeed, Belle fluttered about my mind even as we walked in silence from the dormitory to the chapel like a line of black ants to a drop of syrup on a cookhouse floor.

As soon as we were all seated in the choir—seminarians and faculty —Marty, who was the appointed reader for the day, began the service.

"In the Name of the Father, and the Son, and the Holy Ghost" he said.

To which we all responded, "Amen."

"Let us make with a pure heart and humble voice, our confession to Almighty God, devoutly saying…"

In unison we declaimed:

> Most Gracious God, the fountain of all mercy, who desirest not the death of a sinner, nor despisest the tears of the penitent, we miserable sinners humbly prostrate our souls and bodies before Thy most adorable Majesty, and with a true and hearty sorrow, accuse and condemn ourselves. We confess, O Lord God, that we have grievously sinned against Thee in thought…, word…, and deed…, through our fault, through our great fault, through our exceeding great fault. But have thou mercy on us, O most Merciful Father, for Thy Son's sake, Jesus Christ our Lord and only Advocate. Amen."

At the words *thought*, *word*, and *deed*, as was our custom at Cranmer House, we inserted silent pauses for reflection. And I most certainly reflected. Given my lustful thoughts, I had begun to wonder if I could truly be deemed a follower of Christ and worthy of the calling to ministry. These doubts seemed particularly intense on that first morning back in the chapel among my brethren and professors who also surrendered themselves to confession for whatever sins they may have committed—and if there be a gradation of sins, theirs were much paler than my own I was sure.

When the service had ended, I felt a measure of restoration as we walked across the grounds to the Refectory. Though it bore a strange name of Latin origin, it stood before us as little more than a log cabin.

Our breakfast consisted of a simple bowl of oatmeal with unrefined sugar and raisins, which we washed down with several cups of strong coffee. During breakfast, the seminarians were to remain silent while faculty members read from the works of one of the great spiritual lights of the faith: Origen, Augustine of Hippo, John Chrysostom, Peter Abelard, Anselm, and the like. To be perfectly honest, much of this went in one ear and out the other, but I'm sure the faculty felt some satisfaction in bathing us in the spiritual classics.

This is perhaps an appropriate point for me to explain a bit more about my seminary and how it came into being. In the decade of the 1830s and a few years beyond, scholars at the University of Oxford published a series of tracts in which they argued that the Church of England, the Anglican Church, and its daughter church, the American Episcopal Church, constituted one of three great branches of the larger Catholic Church along with the Roman and Orthodox divisions. These same tracts called for a recovery of certain elements of Roman Catholic doctrine and greater ceremony in the services of the Church.

In the United States, General Theological Seminary in New York and Nashotah House in Wisconsin embraced the Oxford or Tractarian Movement, as it was sometimes known. While the Protestant Theological Seminary in Virginia remained true to the opposite doctrinal pole —Protestant, evangelical, and liturgically reserved—it drew students largely from the Middle Atlantic and Southern States. The Philadelphia Divinity School was only a few years old at the time and had developed a churchmanship somewhere between the Anglo-Catholic and Evangelical extremes, the *broad church*, as it was called. Cranmer Hall was formed to educate Episcopal clergymen in the low-church, strictly Protestant tradition with an eye toward developing missionaries for the west.

In 1850, the Bishop of Saint Louis raised sufficient money to buy an abandoned farmhouse and several acres of surrounding land. Following the remodeling of the farmhouse to create classrooms, the other buildings were constructed in what might be described as austere and rustic architecture. The one exception was our chapel—a structure elegant in its simplicity with none of the adornments, statuary, crucifixes, or other appointments now common in many parishes. A parish church in New York that had installed a newer, better instrument, donated a fine organ. The unadorned altar was simply referred to as the

Lord's Table. The *Lord's Supper*—never referred to as the *Eucharist* and only occasionally *Holy Communion*—was celebrated but once a month and on the highest of holy days. Preaching of the Word far overshadowed the sacramental services of the seminary.

Following our breakfast on that opening morning, we had a half hour of personal time before the first recitation. For the seniors, the first recitation was Practical Theology, taught by The Most Reverend Thaddeus Worthingham, dean of the seminary. This yearlong course had been designed to take the two years of the theological erudition to which we had been exposed and translate it into practical skills for preaching, pastoral care, Christian education, and the conversion of souls.

Smithson, Marty, and I took our seats at one of the tables in a classroom on the ground floor the old farmhouse. Peering out from his perch in the front of the room sat *Mister* Worthingham. As a militant low churchman, he forbade anyone to call him *Father* or to refer to him as a *Priest* of the Church, though that was technically his office.

"Gentlemen," Dean Worthingham said looking over the top of his old-fashioned pince nez glasses, "as you know, this is Practical Theology. We shall begin with prayer." He launched into a long, extemporaneous prayer ranging over many petitions, the central theme of which was an invitation for the Holy Ghost to join us in our studies.

I always found these supplications to be a bit odd. Inasmuch as God is all-powerful, all-good, all-knowing, and *all-present*, why would we have to invite Him to join us? It seemed to me that in gathering together in His name, He was inviting us to join Him. However, I was a lowly seminarian and not in a position to question or challenge the prayers of our venerable Dean.

The other aspect of Dean Worthingham's prayers that never ceased to amaze me was his capacity to murmur with only the barest of lip movements. Marty and I opined—privately, of course—that should the Dean's religious calling lapse, he could easily join the great ventriloquist Jonathan Harrington and tour the country to great acclaim.

After outlining the nature of the course and presenting a tortuous recitation on Stephen's sermon in the Book of Acts, he gave us our assignment for the following day.

"Now, gentlemen, for tomorrow, I shall ask each of you to prepare a ten-minute testimonial…." Here he paused, removed his glasses, and stared directly at each of us for several long seconds. "Testimonials," he resumed, "are commonplace in our sister churches of the Great Reformation but have become diminished if not outright eschewed and disdained among the Papists and Puseyites who have infiltrated our denominational ranks." (He exploded the Ps in *Papists and Puseyites* with spittle-laced disdain.)

"However," he continued. "A testimony is a powerful way to witness to the workings of our heavenly Father in our daily lives. Testimonies can be instruments of conversion of the lost and ratification of the faith for those not so far along in the Christian journey. Therefore, you shall esteem and practice the art of Christian testimony. To this end, I wish to hear a brief summary of how the Lord has worked directly in your life. You are to undergird your reflections with appropriate Scripture. Ten minutes... no more."

Aware of Dean Worthingham's hearing difficulties, Marty whispered—without visible lip movement—"Ten minutes... no more."

Marty's mimicry forced me to stifle a laugh, which the dean noticed.

"Mr. Andrewes, are you experiencing an uncontrollable twitch of your lips?"

"No, reverend sir. Sorry for any distraction."

"Then, since you are of sound mind and body, perhaps you could conclude our recitation with prayer, Mr. Andrewes."

I complied.

We had an hour before our second recitation, so Marty and I returned to the Refectory to see if there were any dregs of coffee left. Smithson, of course, went his own way despite our invitation to join us. I'm certain Smithson found Marty and me to be such depraved and irreverent souls that we were not only unworthy of the cloth, but his pious attentions as well. Perhaps he was correct in this assumption, but Marty and I agreed he didn't have to be so sanctimonious about it.

———

"So what was it like at Wilson's Creek?" Marty asked grimacing over the residue of coffee grounds that laced his first swig from a cracked and stained crockery cup.

"Tough fight, Marty. We had camped near Springfield and in the early morning hours, the Third and Fifth Missouri Regiments split away from General Lyon's main army. This came at the instigation of our commander, Colonel Sigel. We traveled south to a position behind the Confederate forces. When we opened fire with our cannons, the Secessionists were completely surprised and fell into disarray. Sigel pressed forward, and we overtook the field in which they had been camping and progressed all the way to a main road called the Old Wire Road. We held this position and spotted soldiers advancing down the road from the northeast. We thought they were Union. They fired on us, but Colonel Sigel deemed their firing to be a mistake and held us back. When we finally realized enemy forces had engaged us, we were nearly overrun. We scattered. Most of my regiment retreated south, back to our original position while others, including myself, raced across the field to the west. Just as we were arriving at one of the farm roads the Secessionists who were hiding in the trees to our right ambushed us. Before we were able to return fire, several of us were shot, including myself. I may have been the only one of the wounded who survived. I don't know. I wound up in a hospital separated from my comrades."

I decided not to go into the details of my rescue and to carefully choose my words when they touched on my relationship with Belle Potts.

"So where did you get hit?"

"Took a round in the lower leg." I lifted my trouser cuff to display the scar, which had healed to a thin white line with shell-pink margins. My dark leg hair had nearly grown out, so the scar was less visible.

"I took one in the hip too." I smiled. "However, I'll wager you would prefer not to inspect that wound."

Marty laughed. "I'll pass. I'm surprised they didn't amputate your leg. Isn't that what those field surgeons usually do with a shot-up leg?"

"I reckon it depends upon the doctor you draw. The one who attended me felt the leg could be saved. Not much more to say."

Fortunately, Marty accepted this explanation and probed no more deeply into the circumstances surrounding my unconventional surgery and subsequent recovery under the tender care of Belle Potts. Just then, Agatha sounded for our second recitation of the day. I stood and grabbed my cane. It occurred to me that within the next couple of weeks my need for the walking stick would be unnecessary. I would still have a slight limp and no doubt would not be engaged in any foot races in the near term. Save for a barely noticeable hitch in my gait and morning stiffness in the leg, I had nearly a full recovery.

My condition contrasted dramatically with that of so many of the wounded soldiers on both sides. Upon my return to St. Louis I was appalled to discover that some of the soldiers wounded at Wilson's Creek had just recently been treated – nearly a month after the battle. Here I was, nearly fully recovered, and some of my comrades-in-arms remained in the very clothes in which they had been felled.

———

"Gentlemen, welcome to your third and decidedly unnecessary year of Hebrew," the Reverend Professor Doctor Lucretius Livermore began. "I have argued that it is senseless to have but two years of study in New Testament Greek and three years in Hebrew. You all possess more than sufficient knowledge of the ancient languages to provide pastoral care. After all, who among your parishioners-to-be will be sufficiently practiced in Greek and Hebrew to challenge you on the fine points of ancient linguistics? However, my entreaties to the dean and trustees have fallen on deaf ears. So, gentlemen, I begin with a profound apology."

Here, Doctor Livermore fell to his knees and prostrated himself on the floor, his cassock clinging to his girth, wailing in penitence. Marty and I were instantly convulsed in laughter because this was vintage Livermore. His antics in class were legendary. Smithson Hamilton stared straight ahead in stoic silence. Not unexpectedly, Professor Livermore was quite incapable of rising to his feet on his own. Marty and I rushed to assist him while Smithson remained stiff as a statue in his seat.

"Thank you for your succor and aid," Marty whispered to Smithson as we passed back to our seats. Predictably, Smithson made no response, but the quick smile on Doctor Livermore's face indicated that he appreciated the sarcasm.

The ninety minutes allotted for our third-year Hebrew class raced by, and I was pleased that we had this *unnecessary* additional year of study if, for no other reason, than it gave us one more opportunity to study with the jocund and irreverent Doctor Livermore. Though I recognized a third year of Hebrew might be superfluous, it did satisfy my appetite for the study of languages. I had a good command of five languages—German, English, Greek, Latin, and now Hebrew—and enjoyed the challenges afforded by ancient texts. Doctor Livermore opined on one occasion that I should consider taking a doctorate in classics. However, I had no desire for education beyond the Bachelor of Divinity degree.

When class ended, I reported to the library, opening it for the first time in three months. A dozen new books had been deposited on the counter, giving rise to my first duty, the cataloguing and shelving of these new volumes. As I opened the door, the familiar scents assailed me—the smells of must and dust, old furniture wax and vellum, aged wood and leather, binding paste and kerosene lamps. I closed my eyes, inhaled deeply, and smiled at the peace this place brought to my soul.

In the twitch of an instant, I was transported back to another library on the second floor of Belle's home. A swirl of sadness overcame me. Would that I could retrieve one of the many volumes that spread before me in that upstairs library and sit with Belle for an evening of conversation.

I had nearly completed my cataloguing when Marty and two of the middlers came into the library. Since the term was but a half-day old, I knew they were not entering the library for scholarly purposes. They were there to exchange the events of their lives, reminisce, and *squander a 'pinion*, as Belle might say. I joined them around one of the tables.

"Doesn't even feel like a war out here does it?" said Minard Kinsey, a feeblish middler who, in his freshman year, had martialed the highest marks in the history of the institution. Despite his chronic health problems and frail physique, Minard never ceased to amaze us with his capacity to endure the rigors and severities of seminary life. Whenever questions arose regarding his future ability to withstand the stresses of ministry, we were quick to caution, "Don't be too sure. He seems to prosper in adversity."

Marty joined the conversation. "With this martial law, I had to get a pass just to travel through St. Louis from my home to the Seminary."

"We all did," I added. "But I will tell you this, gentlemen. Even though the martial law imposes certain strictures upon us, we certainly have a less riotous city. It was open warfare last spring. There were skirmishes and protests, name-calling, rock-throwing, and even occasional gunfire erupting hotbeds of rebel activity. The Secessionists hate the Germans, and we *Black Dutch*, as they call us, have been singled out for harassment and insult. Now, however, particularly down in my neighborhood—Wards Three, Four, and Five in south Saint Louis—it's pretty peaceful. The place is crawling with Federals. In fact, Lafayette Park is a military camp, if you can believe that. The Germans are all Unionists in a Union enclave surrounded by Union troops. So, my family and neighbors are as safe as they can be under the circumstances."

"Wish I could say the same," Minard said. "It's dangerous out west. Our abolitionist family in Booneville is vulnerable. Don't know if you are aware, but there was a hard-fought battle in Booneville back in June. Then some of the Secessionists attacked again just two weeks ago not long before I left to come back here. Our home guard troops repulsed them, but the whole area is ripe for further conflict. I pray almost hourly for my family."

These thoughts stimulated two long and violent consumptive coughs from Minard. We all looked on in empathic silence as he struggled to regain control. I shot a glance toward Marty. He shook his head. Minard was everybody's frail little brother, and we worried about him.

Our conversations broke up thirty minutes later after everyone had completed a brief recapitulation of his activities over the summer months. I spent the balance of the afternoon dusting the shelves and refilling all of the lamps with kerosene. My labors brought the library into a state of readiness for the term and within the next few days it would become a center of study and hushed discussion. A few of the volumes would become hot commodities among students as assignments were issued, and I would have to provide for fair and reasonable access to all in need. The seminary was not yet sufficiently funded to procure multiple copies of those books in heaviest use.

Later that evening, after hearing a fine lecture on the letters of Saint John, I returned to the dormitory and sat at the simple two-drawer desk next to my bed. All of my necessary possessions were arranged in those drawers except for my few clothes and cassock, which I hung on wall hooks above my bed.

In the dim light, I began to prepare my testimonial for the

following day in Dean Worthingham's class, but my mind drifted to Belle. I tried to shake these images from my mind but they clung like an electrostatic charge. They were with me two hours later when I settled under my coverlet and drifted off to sleep, quite exhausted by the intensity of the first day of classes.

———

"For our third and final testimony on this day, we turn to you, Mr. Andrewes," Dean Worthingham said in his high nasal twang. "Please proceed as have the others. Offer us your testimony and include your Scriptural reference. I yield the floor to you."

I stood before our tiny class, smoothed the front of my cassock, placed my script upon the lectern, propped my cane against the wall, opened my Bible to the pre-selected page, and cleared my throat. Marty rolled his eyes, but I did not permit this to unsettle me.

"Most reverend sir and fellow classmates.... As you all know, I was wounded in the right leg during a battle against the Confederate Army in the southwest corner of our state. This battle has come to be known as the Battle of Wilson's Creek, an engagement in which the Free-State forces were repulsed by Rebels. The round I took shattered my fibula and rendered me a candidate for amputation. A Confederate field surgeon found me and set about preparing me for surgery. As an aside, I must say that, despite the hostilities of this war, the surgeons on both sides treat all of the wounded regardless of uniform. It is one of the great examples of charity and magnanimity in the midst of the brutalities and atrocities of battle. I offer this as a sign that Christian compassion and sacrifice can be found in even the most horrendous moments. But I digress.

"At the very moment this field surgeon began his preparations for amputation, another *doctor* arrived on the scene and agreed to take my case. This second doctor determined that my leg could be saved, operated to remove the shattered bone fragments, and oversaw my recuperation. The ministrations of this doctor prevented infection and my recovery time was miraculously short. In due time, perhaps within the fortnight, I shall be secure enough on my feet to jettison this cane. I may still favor the wounded leg and amble along with a bit of a limp, but considering the fact that field amputations are more often fatal than not, I feel as if the Almighty has spared me."

My classmates and Dean Worthingham listened with rapt attention as I proceeded with my testimony.

"I say all of this in the form of prefatory remarks because another miracle happened on my journey home. As you may know, throughout the southern area of Missouri, in the Ozark region, there are bands of Secessionist partisans, ruffians who demolish bridges and railroad tracks, sever telegraph lines, and raid the homes and settlements of Union sympathizers. Just as I was approaching Rolla on my return to Saint Louis, I was waylaid by just such a group, under the leadership of one Jubal Jagger. It seems that several months earlier, Federal troops had attacked Jubal's farm setting his house afire as retribution for his Southern sympathies. You will be horrified to learn that Jubal's wife and young son were trapped in the house and killed. Jubal escaped and chose to exact his own revenge. His brothers Isaac and Walter, along with several others, joined Jubal to form a raiding party that ambushes Federal patrols and couriers.

"I was ambushed by Jubal Jagger. Discovering I was a Union man, they had every intention of murdering me. Nothing I could say in my own defense could dissuade them from their homicidal intentions. Despite the fact that I wore a black coat and trousers common among preachers, they tore me from my horse, tied me to a tree, and prepared to fire upon me. I had around my neck this item...."

I reached under my cassock and retrieved the polished wooden cross that Belle had given me. I placed it around my neck. My audience watched with undivided attention.

"This cross had been given to me by a close friend. I grasped it in my hand just as Jubal Jagger took aim. I prayed aloud to our Heavenly Father to spare me but, if that were not His will, I desired His forgiveness and a swift entry into His nearer presence.

"The rifle misfired.

"Jubal and his men looked at one another. They drew no other conclusion than God had heard my prayer and caused the rifle to jam. Jubal stared at his musket in disbelief and then announced, 'We bes' not trifle with the Almighty.' They let me go on my way under God's protection."

I grasped my well-worn Bible from under the lectern.

"Here, I turn to the *Book of Ezra*. You will recall that following the Decree of Cyrus the Great, the Israelites were permitted to return from the Exile to Jerusalem and rebuild the Temple. Ezra himself gathered a large number of returnees and they set up camp on the banks of a canal in Babylon. Listen now to these words from the eighth chapter of Ezra:

> *Then we departed from the river of Ahava on the twelfth day of the first month, to go unto Jerusalem: and the hand of our God was upon us, and he delivered us from the hand of the enemy, and of such as lay in wait by the way.*

Gentlemen, I offer this passage from the sacred text to demonstrate that even today, God protects us in our journeys. He protected the ancient Israelites from their enemies along the way and He protected me. Though I had not fasted, as did the Israelites, I demonstrated my faith in prayer and by clutching this holy amulet. I stand before you today as a witness to the assurance that *the hand of our God is upon all them for good that seek him; but his power and his wrath is against all them that forsake him.*"

The room rested in silence as I sat down. Even Smithson seemed moved by what I said.

———

The second class of the day, the *unnecessary* Hebrew class, had just gotten underway with Professor Livermore's usual larking about. On this particular occasion, he hauled himself up to stand atop the desk in front of the class, tore off his clerical collar, and placed it precariously on his baldpate. He digressed from his lecture on the development of the Hebrew language and proceeded to rant about the lamentable state of Christian education in Episcopal parishes throughout the country. Such digressions were common and led us to opine in private that Professor Livermore would prefer to teach practical theology than classical languages.

"The faithful couldn't differentiate the Book of Deuteronomy from a goat horn!" he shouted. "We don't teach the faith! And that's a requirement of the Great Commission! Mr. Andrewes, recite the Great Commission."

Such commands were common in Doctor Livermore's classes, but he did catch me a bit flatfooted.

"I'm waiting...." he said, trying to glare fiercely at me but unable to suppress the twinkle in his eye.

I managed to collect my thoughts. "And... and... *Jesus came and spake unto them, saying, all power is given unto me in heaven and in earth. Go ye therefore, and teach all nations, baptizing them in the name of the Father, and of the Son, and of the Holy Ghost...*"

"Teach what? Teach what, Mr. Andrewes?"

I stared blankly at him, not certain what he wished me to say.

"How does the rest of it go, Mr. Andrews?"

Fortunately, I did recall the next verse, "*Teaching them to observe all things whatsoever I have commanded you...*"

At this point, he stomped upon the desk, first one shoe, then the other. "Yes! Finally! Your job, gentlemen, is to *teach* the faith. It must be at the center of everything you do in your ministry. Teach! Teach! Teach! Jesus himself commands you to do this! Is this abundantly clear, gentlemen?"

We all nodded in unison. Satisfied that he had made his point, Professor Livermore prepared to lower his substantial body from the desk when Dean Worthingham came rushing through the door of the classroom and ordered Professor Livermore to come down from his perch and follow him with all due haste. When they had left, the three of us looked at one another.

"What is this all about?" Marty asked.

Smithson and I shrugged. Marty then walked to the window and looked onto the central oval.

"Soldiers," Marty said. "Looks to be about five of them and they are escorting the faculty into the chapel."

"Let's find out what is happening," I said, and we all rushed out of the classroom toward to the chapel.

Ozark Glossary

Papists – Catholics
Puseyites - followers of Edward Pusey, a leader in the Oxford
movement
middlers - second-year seminarians

SEVEN

Cranmer Hall

Fall, 1861—Spring, 1862

All nine of us streamed onto the seminary grounds and sprinted to the chapel. When we arrived, the Dean, Professor Livermore, and the other two faculty members, Professors Crane and Hildebrand, were seated in the front pew. The five soldiers were arrayed before them and one, a lieutenant by insignia, was explaining this unscheduled roundup.

"As you know," the lieutenant said. "We are under a state of martial law imposed upon not only the City of Saint Louis, but all of Missouri. A requirement of martial law is that all officials and clergymen are to sign a loyalty oath on pain of banishment. We are here to secure those signatures."

The young lieutenant then swept his eyes across the four men seated before him.

"Who among you is the Reverend Lucretius Livermore?"

"I am he," Doctor Livermore said, his eyes hooded with suspicion.

"Sir," the lieutenant continued, "we are particularly concerned to receive your signed oath of loyalty. You are a native of Columbia,

South Carolina. Your brother is a high-ranking Confederate officer, is he not? These ties of home and family have placed you on a list of suspected Southern sympathizers, and thus we desire your public declaration of loyalty to the United States of America."

Doctor Livermore rose and walked to a position directly in front of the lieutenant. Two of the other soldiers reached for their pistols.

"At ease, gentlemen," Professor Livermore said. "I mean no one any harm. However, I do wish to make it quite clear that you shall not get from me a signed declaration of loyalty to the United States of America nor, I would add, will you get a signed declaration of loyalty to the Confederate States of America."

Dean Worthingham reached forward to put his hand on Doctor Livermore's arm.

"Please, Lucretius, remain calm. The loyalty oath is something we must all sign. As Christians we are bound to the civil government. *Render to Caesar....*"

Shaking off the Dean's hand, Doctor Livermore thundered. "As a minister in Christ's Church I am bound to only one kingdom—the Kingdom of God—and I am bound to only one constitution—the Holy Bible!"

The lieutenant put his hand on Doctor Livermore's shoulder in an attempt to restrain his outburst. Doctor Livermore thrust the offending hand aside.

"Let him speak!" came a shout from the rear of the chapel.

We all turned to see Minard Kinsey walking briskly to the front of the chapel, his face red, his eyes shooting sparks of anger.

"Professor Livermore is quite right," Minard said. "There are two kingdoms—the spiritual kingdom of God and the civil kingdom of this world. He, all of us...," Minard swept his arm in a wide circle. "All of us are bound by duty of the soul to swear our allegiance to only one kingdom—that of God. Both sides in this unfortunate conflagration are guilty of colossal sin. We seminarians and our faculty have the obligation to denounce sin, including the sins of this nation. By refusing to take an oath of loyalty, our good Professor Livermore here is standing apart from the sinful intentions of those who wage war!"

At this point, Minard was overcome with a paroxysm of coughing. I could not help it. I rose to my feet.

"Sirs," I said. "I am a wounded veteran of this war." I walked down the aisle to stand by Minard. I made certain my limp was pronounced and my cane tapping with amplified strokes. "As such, I believe I may speak with a certain authority, a certain credibility. I was once a devotee of the just-war theory and joined the home guard of Colonel Sigel with patriotic enthusiasm. However, a friend—a friend who is not even a Christian—pointed out to me that *a-killin'* and *a-lovin'* are not compatible. I did not accept what my friend said at first, but in the months of my recovery, I have come to appreciate the truth of this. As Christians, we are bound to love even our enemies, even those who might torture us. History is drenched with the blood of Christian martyrs who have gone to their deaths without resistance and with hearts of love. As Christ loves us, we are to love the world. That is what it means to be a citizen of the Kingdom of God."

I put my arm around Minard's tiny shoulders. "My brave friend here has spoken the truth. He and I stand with Professor Livermore."

The lieutenant put his hand up. "I have no time for your religious debate. I have my orders. You must understand that failure to sign the oath will brand you as disloyal, and you will be imprisoned. The students who are not yet ordained and in office, your sexton, and your cook are not under this requirement of martial law. However, the four of you—Worthingham, Livermore, Crane, and Hildebrand—are under this obligation. I will leave these oaths with you. We shall return tomorrow to retrieve them. If you have not signed them, prepare to be arrested."

With that, the five soldiers left the chapel.

When the soldiers stomped from the chapel, a fearful silence descended upon us until Dean Worthingham pointed to the floor and thirteen cassock-clad men, nine seminarians, and four ordained faculty members dropped to their knees in prayer. The dean invoked the Lord's aid in protecting the seminary from the strictures of martial law. Special prayers were offered for the popular Professor Livermore who, as the day wore on, continued his refusal to sign the loyalty oath. The faculty members urged him to do so but, in time, backed away respecting Professor Livermore's *action of conscience*, as he described it.

Early the following morning, the soldiers returned to the seminary and gathered three signed oaths of allegiance. Seeing none from Professor Livermore, they proceeded to arrest him and march him off campus. Dean Worthingham immediately saddled his horse to follow the soldiers, leaving us to wonder what fate awaited our favorite instructor. Recitations were canceled for the remainder of the day as we milled about waiting for Dean Worthingham to return.

A pall of anxiety shrouded Cranmer Hall. All study had been abandoned and we wandered the grounds in muted conversation. The midday weather added to our disquiet as a roiling thunderstorm spilled torrents of rain, corralling us in the Refectory to await for what we feared would be the worst of news.

A drenched and long-faced Dean Worthingham finally returned at three o'clock that afternoon. As he doffed his saturated hat and coat, we gathered to hear his report. He blew his nose on a soggy handkerchief and began. "Gentlemen, Professor Livermore has been detained in the Myrtle Street Prison, the former slave pen known sardonically as *Hotel de Lynch*. It took me some time to find out what the authorities plan to do with him. Finally, I tracked down the Provost Marshal, who informed me that Professor Livermore would be held in temporary custody before being brought before a military commission to be examined."

The faculty and seminarians exchanged worried glances.

"I protested," Dean Worthingham continued. "I assured the Provost Marshal that Lucretius Livermore did not have a seditionist bone in his body. A godly soul devoted to teaching the faith, I said. The Provost Marshal, a man of some sympathy, assured me that if this were in fact true and if no evidence of treason could be mustered against Professor Livermore, he would simply be banished from the city for failing to sign the oath."

"Then he won't be back?" I asked.

"Unlikely," Dean Worthingham said.

"What happens to his language courses?"

"That is undecided at this point. We shall resume classes tomorrow. I would like to meet with the faculty at this time, so I would ask the students to leave us. We will let you know how we plan to deal with this unfortunate course of events when we have developed a response. Gentlemen, please keep us and Cranmer Hall in devout prayer."

We seminarians removed ourselves from the Refectory. Marty returned to the dormitory and adopted his usual response to stressful news by crawling in for a long nap. I asked the freshmen and middlers to join me in the library where I tried to assure them that while this was a blow to the seminary, it was not a lethal blow. I shared my every confidence that Dean Worthingham and the faculty would draw up an appropriate plan of action that would not compromise our seminary education. Comforted by my remarks, several remained in the library in an attempt to study while others wandered off to *cut their own weeds*, as Belle would have put it.

Despite the tensions of the day—or perhaps because of them—my thoughts turned to Belle. I replayed in my mind our lovely time together under the rock outcropping while gathering medicinal plants. Lost in my dreamy musings, I did not see Dean Worthingham until he stood directly before me at my library table. When I finally awakened to his presence, I jumped to my feet.

"Sorry, reverend sir," I said. "I did not see you enter."

"Quite all right Mister Andrewes. I wonder if I might have a private word with you in my office."

"Of course," I said.

He turned and led me in silence to the office building, a ramshackle structure that had been a former tenant house. When we entered his tiny office overflowing with books in shelves and stacks upon the floor, Dean Worthingham bade me sit in the single guest chair. He retreated behind his desk and removed a stack of pamphlets and papers, thus permitting him to see me clearly as he spoke.

"Mister Andrewes," he said, rubbing his tongue across his incisors. "We have been discussing how to accommodate the loss of a faculty member—perhaps our most prized faculty member—if the seminarians were to be polled."

I nodded, wondering where this conversation would lead.

"We have developed a proposal—the other faculty members and I. As you, know, Professor Livermore himself decried the necessity for a third year of Hebrew."

"Yes, sir."

"I don't know that I agree but, under the circumstances, we have no choice but to cancel it."

I nodded again.

"However," the dean continued, "we cannot abandon the languages, especially Greek for the underclassmen."

"No, sir."

"It has not been lost upon us that you have an uncommon mastery of the classical languages. It surpasses that of the remaining faculty members. Therefore, we would summon you to assume teaching responsibilities for the first two years of Greek and Latin, as well as elementary Hebrew. We believe you can handle these responsibilities while continuing to complete your own education. All tuition and fees for the remainder of your senior year will be cut in half. What do you say?"

Suffice it to say, I could say nothing. The offer floored me and I felt a surge of anxiety.

"Mister Andrewes...."

"Sir, I am rendered speechless."

"Please know you have the full confidence of the faculty. We would ask you to begin tomorrow."

Recovering my senses, I sought to borrow some time. "May I have some time to consider this and pray about it?"

"Of course. You have the next two hours. I would like to announce your acceptance at supper."

Two hours? Announce acceptance? Apparently, Dean Worthingham had already received a direct revelation from God and had made my decision for me. Whatever considerations and prayers I might have were, in his mind, merely for my own edification. I stood, mumbled some words of thanks, and scrambled out of his office. At some level, I had to admit, I was flattered by the offer but could not imagine how I would balance my own studies with the responsibility of bringing the underclassmen to a point of competence in the classical languages.

Back in the dormitory, I awakened Marty and shared the substance of my meeting with the Dean. As he blinked to full awareness, Marty offered congratulations and his assurance that I was the right man for the job. "I reckoned the faculty might go in this direction," he said. "You are the only one of us who has sufficient command of Greek, Latin, and Hebrew to do this work. Who else would they get? It's not as if Saint Louis overflows with linguists."

I nodded, accepting the truth of what he said. "Will you pray with me about this?" I asked.

"Of course. What are friends in Christ for?"

Sitting on our respective beds, we bowed our heads and voiced prayers for the Lord's guidance and support. In the end, I had to conclude that if God had called me to this difficult service, He would provide the wherewithal to succeed. The prayers afforded me some comfort, but a niggling unease remained in the back of my mind, no doubt the Lord's way of prompting me to future prayer.

———

As the next several weeks unfolded, I settled into my new routine. I worked late into the evenings and rose before Agatha tolled in the morning. While I could not keep this schedule indefinitely, I reasoned I would survive for the remaining eight months of my time at seminary. To my relief, these extra efforts seemed to be working. I managed to keep up with my own studies, and the students under my tutelage made progress in their command of the ancient languages.

Again, and again, in those few moments when my thoughts were my own, memories of Belle percolated into my conscious awareness. On one level, I savored these memories, reviewing them with the faintest of smiles. On another level, they were an unhealthy distraction. When such pangs of conscience struck me, I shook my head and tried to focus my attention once again upon the immediate tasks at hand.

I told myself repeatedly that my mooning was no doubt unrequited. I knew Belle had developed a particular affection for me, but surely she would have come to her senses and realized that I was but one more patient in the long string of those who had come under her care. Certainly many others had come to occupy her attentions in the weeks since we parted.

I confess, however, try as I might, I was unsuccessful in banishing her image from my mind. Of course, in flashes of brutal self-examination, I asked myself if I loved Belle Potts, but I never permitted myself to answer this question.

Aside from Professor Livermore's arrest, Cranmer Hall remained an island of seclusion from the war. Only sporadic reports of the hostilities seeped into our rustic campus. We considered this a blessing because it kept us from the distractions that would otherwise consume our much needed mental energies. To be sure, we were generally aware that the declaration of martial law, suspension of the writ of *habeas corpus*, and the various military trials worked systematically to suppress secessionist activity. Saint Louis became a Union stronghold, a haven for loyal refugees, a prison camp for rebels, and a medical center for the wounded. Wagons and trainloads of wounded soldiers streamed into the city swamping the hospitals. Confederate captives swelled the prisons far beyond capacity.

While most of us remained oblivious to these conditions, Dean Worthingham did not. As an off-campus resident of Saint Louis, he witnessed these horrible circumstances and could no longer stand aside while the community had such pressing needs.

Consequently, as the fall term neared its conclusion, he gathered the faculty and seminarians to announce that we were to do our collective part in serving those in need. Two days each week, we were to be dispatched into the city to attend the sick and dying as well as prisoners of war. Our class schedule was reduced and several courses dropped from the curriculum, including Practical Theology, which Dean Worthingham pronounced *superfluous* in light of the practical theologies we would inevitably learn in pastoral service to the city.

Dean Worthingham assigned the seminarians and faculty members to hospitals, prisons, and other refuges. "Mister Andrewes, Laclede Hospital for you. Do you know it?"

"Yes, sir."

"It's operated by the Roman Catholic Sisters of Holy Compassion. They are a medical order but are so consumed with caring for the wounded, they suffer for time to provide spiritual solace. Your role, Mister Andrewes, is to report their Mother Superior and lend her your aid in tending to the spiritual state of the wounded and dying."

I nodded in acceptance and so began my service among the wounded soldiers of the United States of America, a ministry I found simultaneously exhausting and enlivening. No other activity inside or out of the classroom confirmed so decidedly my vocation to the ordained ministry. I prayed fervently for all of the patients, offered comfortable words, shared my own wartime experiences, and aided not a few to faith in Jesus Christ. Sadly, medical care in Saint Louis proved far more primitive than the unconventional practice of medicine in Belle Potts' surgery. Many soldiers died.

I remember vividly one young man—Roger Partridge was his name—from Sheboygan, Wisconsin. He had suffered a wound almost identical to my own. Unfortunately, he received no immediate medical attention until his arrival in Saint Louis, where his leg was immediately amputated at the knee.

The animalcules attacked with a vengeance, and infection set in. By the time I reached him, he was at the point of death. I stayed with him praying, sponging his forehead with a cold cloth, and murmuring words of assurance. Being a Roman Catholic, he asked to make his confession. I had never heard a confession before but assured him that I would receive it.

Possessing neither the office nor appropriate words to pronounce absolution, I whispered an impromptu prayer, made the sign of the cross on his forehead, and assured him that his sins had been forgiven. He slipped away in peace. I had a strong sense of *déjà vu* and found my mind back on the battlefield in southwest Missouri when Willi died in my arms. Just as on that occasion, Roger's eyes mysteriously revealed the moment of death, apprehended more by sensation or intuition than the subtle physical signs. With one hand, I closed his lifeless eyes and sat lost in my own thoughts.

Of course, Roger's death by systemic infection, along with all of the other deaths I witnessed each week, prompted me to ask again that inevitable question, *why me?* Why had I, out of all of the thousands of wounded soldiers, been selected by Belle Potts to receive the benefit of her advanced and irregular medicine? As a man of faith, I recognized this to be divine intervention and no mere coincidence. However, God's intentions remained unclear. I presumed that He had some larger purpose in store for me, but seated beside Roger Partridge's deathbed, I could not fathom what it might be.

———

Our term closed a few days before Christmas. We were given a break until January 6, 1862, the Epiphany. On that day, we were to be back on campus for an evening service of the Lord's Supper to celebrate Epiphany where, in one service, we would commemorate both the coming of the Magi and the baptism of Jesus. During the break, those of us who were residents of Saint Louis and those who could not afford the journey home, continued to provide our community service in support of the war effort.

Unlike some, I did not stay at the seminary during the two weeks between terms. I returned home because Laclede Hospital was closer to our ward than to the seminary campus. On Christmas Day, I invited the five remaining seminarians to our house for one of my mother's splendid feasts. Only Smithson declined. He offered no reason. "Too much fun," Marty opined with his usual wry tone. "Can't celebrate after all. Jesus wouldn't approve. Poor sod needs to re-read the miracle at Cana. Seems it was a great party. Still talking about it nineteen hundred years later."

We had a rollicking good time that Christmas Day and for a brief moment were able to forget about the war and the severity of those conditions in which we ministered. My sainted mother prepared both ham and turkey arrayed on large platters with baked beans, pickles, and German bread pudding with raisins. She served her spice cake for dessert, which nearly brought tears to the eyes of my fellow students who had lived for over three months on the meager and unsatisfying meals of the Refectory. We all repaired to the parlor after dinner to sing favorite Christmas carols—*O Come All Ye Faithful, Deck the Halls, Hark the Herald Angels Sing,* and a delightful new tune called *Jingle Bells.*

Unbeknownst to me, my mother had prepared a stocking for all of the seminarians in which she had placed a new starched and ironed handkerchief, a fresh apple and orange, and a lovingly knitted pair of black woolen socks. Needless to say, such unexpected generosity moved all of my brothers, who responded with long hugs and profuse expressions of gratitude. As the seminarians left, she pressed into Marty's ample hand a full stocking for Smithson.

On Epiphany I concluded my work at Laclede Hospital early and returned to Cranmer Hall to prepare for the evening service. I had been chosen to preach the sermon, so I entered a side door of the chapel, directly into the sacristy where I donned the appropriate vestments and joined in the preparatory prayers led by our celebrant, Dean Worthingham. Since it was common for local residents to attend our services at the seminary, we expected a full church on Epiphany, which heightened my apprehension. Sensing my anxiety, Dean Worthingham put a hand on my shoulder. "Think of it this way," he said. "A winning racehorse is always keyed up prior to the race. It is natural and a good thing for you to be tense in preparation for the delivery of a sermon. It signals the presence of the Holy Spirit. Beware the day you no longer find yourself edgy." I've never forgotten that important bit of counsel.

Just as we were concluding our preparations, the small pipe organ in our chapel erupted with astonishing flourishes, trills, and other ornamentations of that great Epiphany hymn *Brightest and Best of the Sons of the Morning.* This surely could not be Professor Hildebrand, who normally played the organ for our services. He was barely competent to produce the melody and surely could not have produced such a lively musical fanfare. Our collective jaws dropped, and all eyes fixed on Dean Worthingham, who bore a very smug smile.

"Who is that?" I asked.

"You'll see," Dean Worthingham said. "Now, remember gentlemen. Service always starts on time."

We lined up for the procession. Since the back of the organ faced the congregation, I could not see who was playing the instrument. The prelude concluded, and we began the stately march down the central aisle as the organist led us in *O Come Thou Great Jehovah.* It was not until I had taken my place in the sanctuary of the chapel that I discovered who had been playing the organ.

A raven-haired woman in a burgundy gown with white tatted collar poured herself into the keyboard of the organ with a virtuosity it had never known. She wore no head covering, an unusual omission for a woman in an Episcopal church. However, I delighted in its absence because it freed the curls and ringlets to bounce and spring with abandon as her body jumped and rocked with every chord.

When she finished the last notes of the processional, she pivoted on the organ stool and presented those of us in the sanctuary a broad smile that exposed a perfect array of ultra-white teeth. This black-eyed marvel had ambushed our masculine sensibilities, and it took all of my powers of concentration to focus on the opening segments of the service. Apparently, I had not been fully successful in harboring my thoughts because the first lines of my sermon were delivered with a stumbling and inarticulate tongue.

Somehow, perhaps through divine mercy, I managed to assemble myself sufficiently to preach a more than passable sermon, one that garnered the praise of many present. It even received a smile and nod from Dean Worthingham. But the most prized compliment of all came from the young woman at the organ.

"I must say I was moved by your sermon, Mister Andrewes," she said as she walked down the aisle to where I was standing.

Her words clove tongue to palate, and it took several seconds before I could release it and mumble my thanks. Then, to my great surprise, I managed to ask how she knew my name.

"Let me introduce myself," she said. "I am Annie Worthingham, Uncle Thad's niece. I know your name because Uncle has spoken highly of you and noted that you would be offering the sermon tonight."

Just then, having shed his vestments, Dean Worthingham approached us with uncommon speed. Clearly, he intended to maintain all manner of decorum within the seminary grounds.

"Annie will be staying with Mrs. Worthingham and me indefinitely," he said. "She is my brother Thomas's daughter. He is a widower, his wife having died several years ago. Thomas and Annie are staunch Union loyalists from Cooper County to the west. As you may know, that county is in what we call *Little Dixie*, where Southern sympathies run high. Though the Confederate troops have been routed in that area, guerrilla warfare remains a scourge. Bushwhackers continue to terrorize Unionists—burning homes and farms, looting, and murdering those faithful to the United States. Thomas simply felt it was no longer safe for his daughter. And..." he continued, his eyes twinkling like creek water on a bright morning, "she can play the organ in a fashion to which we are quite unaccustomed."

"It is a nice instrument," she said, lowering her eyes. "Though I fear it needs tuning."

"And that shall have to wait," Dean Worthingham said. "Finances being what they are."

"Uncle tells me you fought and were wounded some months ago," Annie said.

"Yes. Wilson's Creek. I was shot in the leg." I did not disclose the site of my other wound.

"You are fortunate, Mister Andrews. I can barely detect a limp."

"Fortunate indeed. I had a fine surgeon. I cast aside my cane several weeks ago and though progress is slow at this point, I continue to enjoy improvements in my gait. If I walk or stand too long, a grinding ache sets in, but I cannot complain."

Our conversation slipped into silence for several long seconds.

"So, tell me Miss Worthingham, how did you come to be so proficient on the organ?"

Annie glanced back to her uncle as if to inquire if lengthier conversation would be permitted. He nodded, and she fixed her dark eyes upon mine.

"Several strokes of good fortune, I would say. My father is a banker and we did not suffer financially. Before I was born, he bought my mother a piano, which she played with natural talent. I appear to have inherited her musical ability and she taught me to play as a very young child. Before Uncle Thad became dean of the seminary—perhaps you already know this—he was rector of our Episcopal parish. He had an organ installed in the church, and I began to play as a child. Before my mother died, she taught me to play, for she had become an excellent organist."

"I see the strokes of good fortune in what you say," I said.

"But it doesn't end there. I became very skilled at playing, but no one could take me to the next level of expertise. My father located a great organ performer, a cathedral organist in Kansas City, and for several years, I lived with him and his wife. We played daily on a great organ and he taught me church hymnody. So there you have it. The nurturing of my love for music and the organ."

I nodded with a smile.

"I hear you have your own proficiencies, Mister Andrewes."

"Oh? How so?"

"You are a gifted linguist, I'm told."

"*Gifted* is perhaps too strong a word. I do enjoy the study of ancient languages and, until Professor Livermore's untimely departure, learned from one who could deepen my understanding. I enjoy, therefore I study diligently these classical languages, but I hardly admit to being gifted."

"You are too modest."

"Nay, accurate."

"Whatever you say, Mister Andrewes."

Just then, Dean Worthingham interrupted our conversation. "Annie, we should be on our way."

"Of course, Uncle."

She offered me a brief curtsy. "I've enjoyed our conversation, Mister Andrewes. Goodbye."

I reciprocated with a brief bow but said nothing more.

She joined her uncle at the entrance to the chapel and slipped into the night.

In mid-April 1862, at the beginning of Holy Week, I received a most unexpected invitation. Dean Worthingham detained me briefly after chapel. "Mister Andrewes," he said with a whisper and a furtive glance. "Mrs. Worthingham and I would like to invite you to Easter dinner at our home, if you would find that acceptable."

"Easter dinner?"

"Yes, unless you have other plans."

"Well, my mother always prepares a sumptuous feast for Easter. She would want her only son home, I fear."

"Why don't you invite her come with you to our home?"

"That would be delightful. I shall ask her."

"Excellent!" Dean Worthingham said, poking his fist in the air.

"Sir," I said. "May I ask, why me?"

"Mrs. Worthingham and I always invite individual faculty members to our home for dinner once each academic semester. The others have already attended one of these dinners, and it occurred to me that you are—well—something of a faculty member and there is no reason for you to be passed over."

"That is very kind of you, but what of the other seminarians? They still think of me as one of them."

Dean Worthingham interrupted me with a wave of his hand. "You needn't worry about your brothers in the faith. Mrs. Worthingham and I will include them in a later invitation. If they ask you about it, simply tell them that you are first on the list. Their turn is coming."

Following the Easter service at Cranmer Hall, one of muted glory given the war, I joined the Dean, his wife, and Annie on the wagon ride to the Worthingham home. My mother graciously declined the invitation since she had invited others for Easter dinner. She assured me that while I would be missed, it was a singular honor to have been invited to the Dean's home, and I should attend without reservation.

On this occasion, Marty's mother invited those seminarians detained by lack of funds or long journeys home to the Muldown's house. This relieved any guilt I might have harbored over my prize invitation. Naturally, Smithson declined Mrs. Muldown's offer, causing Dean Worthingham to wonder aloud if the man were truly suited for the ministry. Recognizing these qualms about Smithson's admissibility to the priesthood to be a rare breach of confidentiality, the two women and I refrained from comment. A part of me, hardly the better part, flowered at the thought that the dean would say such a thing about one seminarian in front of another. Clearly, he thought of me as more than just a student.

The Easter dinner, prepared by the Worthinghams' long-serving cook, Lizzie May, could not have been more delicious. Ham, studded with cloves and baked with precious slices of pineapple, was served on a platter ringed with buttered red potatoes. Acorn squash slathered in maple syrup and freshly baked bread adorned the table.

Dean Worthingham opened a bottle of sherry and poured three glasses. I remained true to my vow of abstinence despite the Dean's assurance that on a feast day—*the* feast day in the Christian calendar— I could be granted temporary release from my vow. Thanking him for his grace, I politely declined the small glass of ruby-red wine and accepted a cup of chilled lemonade instead. We savored each bite and sip. A feast such as this was rare during the war, and we were all thankful for the provision.

Our dinner spanned nearly two hours before concluding with Lizzie May's splendid bread pudding topped with a frothy whipped cream. Cups of tea in hand, we strolled into the parlor to continue our conversation, which inevitably turned to the war. Since we seminarians had limited news, I looked forward to Dean Worthingham's report.

"Our state is solidly in Union hands," he said, sipping the last of his tea. "Earlier this year, troops of the rebellious State Guard were run out of Missouri into northern Arkansas. Union General Curtis was bound and determined to follow up by driving all remaining Confederate troops out of the state. A month ago, he encountered General Price and his Army of the West at Pea Ridge in northern Arkansas. Price outnumbered Curtis but the Union forces were victorious."

I interrupted. "Sir, do you know if my old unit, the Missouri Third under Franz Sigel, participated in the battle?"

"Oh yes. Sigel is now a general, as you may know, and he has been credited with the victory. Word reaching us here in Saint Louis confirms that the German troops under Sigel fought with uncommon valor. I am told that Sigel's strategic mind governed the Union offensive."

I sat back, proud of my former comrades-in-arms but worried for their wellbeing. Old Pap Price was a formidable opponent and surely there would have been casualties among my friends and fellow soldiers. Annie intuited my mixed emotions and shot me a glance of sympathy.

"Now, we have to mop up the Bushwhackers that continue to terrorize the countryside," Dean Worthingham continued, tapping his knee lightly with a fist. "Particularly in the Kansas border counties, Little Dixie, and to a lesser extent in the southwest."

Mention of southwest Missouri instantly filled my mind with images of Belle. The fears I held for my Army brethren merged with worry for her and how she might be faring in such menacing times. As I thus pondered my own connections to the hostilities along the Missouri-Arkansas line, Mrs. Worthingham excused herself, leaving Annie and me with the Dean. There was little chance that we would be left alone. The societal strictures that had been absent during my time in the Ozarks had been reimposed. I spent hours alone with Belle Potts, but there was absolutely no chance that I could be left alone with Annie.

"A penny for your thoughts," Annie said, ignoring her uncle's presence.

I glanced at the Dean, who retrieved a newspaper and puffed upon his pipe.

"Doubtless, I know a lot of the boys who were in that fight in Arkansas," I said returning my gaze to my knees. "Neighbors, friends, fellow soldiers who re-enlisted. Worried is all."

She nodded. "Do you miss soldiering?"

"I don't miss the long marches, poor food, terror of battle, and miserable conditions. But I do miss the serving my country. I miss my brothers in arms. The camaraderie, I suppose. I feel guilty about the luxury of study, a soft bed, and reasonable food while other young men are fighting and dying for a noble cause."

"You have done your part."

"I suppose you are right. I really can't re-enlist. I have only half of the bones in my lower right leg. I could not keep up in a long march, and my leg could not stand the pounding and twisting required in battle. And my conscience, I confess, is trending to pacifism."

"I do admire you, Mister Andrewes. I once thought of lending my services to the war effort, perhaps as a nurse. But I discovered that I could not stand the sight of blood, so I simply backed away from any idyllic notion of supporting the Union cause, even though I fervently believe it." She raised a wondering eyebrow. "I suppose I should be ashamed of myself."

Her admission, while unbecoming, touched me by its honesty. I quickly rationalized that not all were emotionally equipped for the carnage of war. She at least had this modicum of self-awareness. "I understand," I said with less than full candor.

After a long moment, she raised her face to mine. "On this Easter Day, mightn't we talk of more pleasant things?"

"Of course," I said.

"Please excuse me for a moment," Dean Worthingham said, rising from his chair and fanning a cloud of pipe smoke with his hands. "I shall return momentarily."

Annie and I glanced at one another, surprised to have lost our chaperone, if only for a *moment*. She wasted no time in seizing the opportunity. In hushed tones, she asked, "What will you do when you finish your studies this spring?"

In similarly subdued tones, I said "Seek ordination, I suppose, and then on to a curacy somewhere. Wherever the Bishop wishes me to go."

"You will be very good. No doubt you will have your own church in short order, if that's what you wish to do."

Her remark struck me as curious. "Why do you say *if*? It's what I've labored to do these past years."

"I sense some reservation."

"Really? What have I said or done that causes this impression?"

"I can't say for certain. You seem… well… somewhere else."

"You're mistaken, I fear. I have been very focused on my studies, my teaching, my preceptorship, my work at Laclede Hospital. I don't feel as if I'm *somewhere else*."

"Call it woman's intuition."

"It would seem woman's intuition is not foolproof."

She offered a wan smile. "I'm sure you are right, Mister Andrewes."

"Please… I should think by now you could call me Krieger, or Krieg as my friends do."

"Are we friends now."

"I can think of no other term… Annie"

She smiled again, more brightly this time. "I like that."

"And what of you, Annie. What will you do in the months to come?"

"I suppose I will remain in Saint Louis indefinitely. I love playing for the seminarians, but I long for a larger venue, a church with a more versatile organ—more stops, more pipes, more manuals."

"Marriage and family, I presume?"

"Marriage, perhaps. No children. It's a terrible thing to admit, I'm sure, but I don't particularly care for children and wouldn't, even if they were my own."

I was once again taken aback by her self-disclosure and found nothing to say in response.

"Marriage will have to be under certain conditions," she continued. "I loathe the domestic arts. I have no skill with them and they draw me away from my music. So I will have to have certain accommodations—a cook, a housekeeper. Do I shock you, Krieg?"

"It's not what I'm used to."

"I know. Do you find me a dreadful person?"

"Not at all. I admire your honesty."

Dean Worthingham returned to the parlor.

EIGHT

All Souls Parish—Saint Louis

Late Spring—Summer, 1862

Key events of my life unfolded rapidly following that Easter conversation in the Worthingham parlor. I finished my senior year, passed final examinations, and received the faculty's recommendation that I be awarded a Bachelor of Divinity degree. Marty also received a positive recommendation.

Unfortunately, Smithson had been asked to leave the seminary, confirming the faculty's conclusion that he was not suited to the ordained ministry. While we students agreed with this assessment, we found it sad and wished Smithson well as he departed. In a rare moment of humility, he thanked us for our sentiments, which only added to our cheerless gazes as we watched him walk off the campus, valise in hand.

Commencement at Cranmer Hall was a modest affair tucked into the Sunday morning worship service. Marty and I received oversized sheepskin diplomas with grand flourishes on the Latin letters. In his commencement sermon, Dean Worthingham commented on these emblems of our graduation.

"Gentlemen," he said, peering over the top of his pince nez glasses. "These fine diplomas may seem out of character for such a countrified place of learning, but I assure you they couldn't be more fitting. You see, it is not the campus—the buildings and trappings—that define a seminary. It is the quality of the faculty, the rigor of the curriculum, the dedication of its students, and most of all a focus on Christ our Lord that make a seminary truly great. We have all of those elements on full display here at Cranmer Hall. Thus, the symbol of your successful time here—your diploma—should be elegant, even ostentatious."

Here, the dean paused to let his remarks take effect. "There is a further lesson in all of this, gentlemen. A church does not consist of the facilities or its trappings—a stately building, beautiful appointments, impressive music, expensive vessels, elegant vestments. We Episcopalians are particularly vulnerable to this vision of a church. No, a church consists of people united in the love, worship, and service of the Lord our God. And that devotion to God should be unbounded, overflowing, ostentatious. Never, ever forget that. The day you do, you will fail in your sacred work."

That Sunday of commencement was clear and unseasonably warm. Flowering dogwoods and redbuds, native to the area, adorned the forested areas surrounding our campus. Following the service, a reception table had been set up with a large bowl of cranberry punch, flanked by a variety of cookies and sweetmeats.

Congratulations and good cheer abounded. For over an hour, the war disappeared from our conversation as we enjoyed our refreshments and basked in the splendor of the day. As the reception drew to a close and I walked arm-in-arm with my mother, Annie sidled up to me.

I introduced Annie to my mother who gave me a short wink and a kiss before excusing herself to begin her ride to the south. Annie wasted no time in offering her own form of congratulations by inviting me to a picnic on the following day, chaperoned by the Worthinghams, of course. I nodded my acceptance.

Since the park at Lafayette Square had been commandeered as a military camp, we were forced to select another venue for our picnic, and there weren't many options. When we piled into the carriage, Dean Worthingham announced we would travel west along Olive Plank Road to Creve Coeur Lake. He expressed confidence we could find a grassy spot to recline and enjoy Lizzie May's fried chicken and whatever other delights she might have packed in the basket.

Niggles of guilt squirmed in the back of my mind. With the war in full tilt, I felt I should be at the bedside of wounded and dying soldiers. However, assured by Dean Worthingham's counsel that a day or two out of my labors would not be ungodly, I repressed my personal reservations.

After a delicious repast of fried chicken, potato salad, and crisp apples, Mrs. Worthingham wandered down to admire the lake. Dean Worthingham lay on the picnic blanket and, mindless of his oversight responsibilities, fell sound asleep.

When her uncle's snores assured us of a measure of privacy, Annie lowered her voice to a whisper.

"And so, here we are,"

"Indeed," I said.

With butterflies of excitement fluttering within, I found myself at a loss for words. Fortunately, Annie had the presence of mind to move us out of the awkward silence.

"It is another beautiful spring day," she said.

I nodded.

"It is nice to be with you, Krieg."

"As it is with you, Annie."

"You know, my aunt and uncle urged me to invite you on this picnic."

"You don't say."

She offered a brief snicker. "Why do you suppose that is?"

"I couldn't say."

"Don't be daft. He wants us to court."

"That's a very forward suggestion Miss Worthingham."

She snickered again. "Are you averse to such an arrangement?"

"I don't think so."

"That doesn't sound very certain."

I took a deep breath and held it. "No, I suppose not. It's just that I've never courted anyone before."

"And I've never been courted. So we'll have to figure this out together won't we?"

"It would seem so."

"Since my father is not here, I presume you will present my uncle with a card requesting the opportunity to court me."

I tried to hide my reservation with a feigned cough. "Yes," I said. "I'll look into that."

She eyed me with a half-smile of puzzlement. Little did Annie know that in those brief seconds, the only image in my mind was that of Belle with her sun-burnished skin, fine white down along her hairline, and a mole gracing her upper lip. In those seconds, an irrational sense of betrayal pricked me. There was no reason why I should have felt this way. No promises had been made to Belle.

I had just emerged from the strictures imposed upon seminarians. And I was in the presence of a beautiful, accomplished, and very eligible young woman whom I had just promised to court. I desperately needed to reorient my mind and quickly. Again I vowed to wrest Belle from my thoughts.

————

Two weeks following graduation, Marty and I knelt before the bishop in our cathedral church and were ordained to the Sacred Order of Deacons. This conferral of Holy Orders put us in a transitional position. Six months to a year hence, we would be ordained as priests in the church. Immediately, I was assigned to serve as the Curate of All Souls Episcopal Church, an affluent parish on the western boundary of Saint Louis.

The rector, my new boss, would be the irascible Reverend Doctor Gridley Fitzsimmons, whose legendary temperament branded him as Saint Gridley the Grump. When the bishop saw my apprehension at this assignment, he cryptically said, "To the strongest donkey goes the heaviest load." I judged this to be a backhanded compliment, but it did little to ease my trepidation.

All Souls stood in majesty on a slight rise in the terrain and, in addition to the church itself, the grounds sported several additional buildings. Doctor and Mrs. Fitzsimmons resided in the palatial rectory, along with their obnoxious little pug named Jerome (named after the contentious Saint Jerome, I presume). Jerome had lost most of his lower jaw due to the removal of a cancerous growth. As a result, his tongue lapped over the remnant of his jaw in a fountain of perpetual drool.

One of the other buildings, a drafty two-room hut, would serve as my All Soul's home. To label it as spartan would be an understatement. The hut consisted of a bed, a table, two rickety chairs, a pot-bellied stove, and a rough-hewn cross on the wall.

Upon entering for the first time, I wondered aloud, "Dear me, am I a hermit?" After wallowing a few moments in self-pity, I snapped to and unpacked my few belongings, including the pillow and blanket I had been advised to bring. The drooping bed reminded me of a hammock and my efforts to tighten the bed ropes were only partially successful. However, I reminded myself that a saggy bed in a breezy hut certainly beat an Army bedroll on rocky ground in a rainstorm.

The morning after my arrival at All Souls, Doctor Fitzsimmons summoned me to his office, a large book-lined room in the labyrinthine recesses of the church. Behind the closed door of his office I heard the slamming of books, the kicking of furniture, and the hurling of epithets worthy of a barroom brawl.

I knocked.

"Enter!"

I slipped into the office to see a tiny black-cassocked man with a face pinched into a permanent scowl.

"Yes?" he said. "What can I do for you?"

"I'm Deacon Andrewes," I said, and after a several second pause, "reporting for duty as you requested."

He studied me for several long and awkward seconds.

"Sit," he said and returned to his desk chair stepping over the books and papers he had just scattered in some unexplained fit of pique. He leaned back in his chair, bisected his lips with a forefinger, and continued to study me. "So, you've just graduated from that hunting lodge they call a seminary—all freshly scrubbed and on the high road to saving humanity."

"I'm not sure I'd put it quite that way," I said.

"No, I'm sure you wouldn't. I hear you were wounded on the battlefield."

"Yes sir."

"*Hmph.* You crippled?"

"Not badly."

"*Hmph.* Stamina good?"

"I believe so."

"Good. You will do everything around here I don't want to do, which is almost everything. I conduct services, preach sermons, and write my memoirs—that's about it. You do everything else. Sometimes you will conduct services and preach sermons while I write my memoirs. You follow?"

"Yes, I think so but what is *everything else*?"

"I just told you. Everything but conducting services, preaching sermons, and writing memoirs. Now help me find my favorite quill—a white one with a gray tip. Then get out. I have work to do."

I surmised that the tantrum I heard related to the misplacement of his pen, so I began searching in earnest hoping to prevent another outburst. After several minutes, I spotted the missing quill under the desk, retrieved it, and handed it to Doctor Fitzsimmons. Without acknowledging my effort, he snatched the pen and returned to his work.

Carefully, I backed away and eased through the door, closing it with a soft snick. Just then, a chuckle from behind punctuated my trepidation. I turned to see a portly man with a baldpate and jovial air. A wide grin split his gray beard and mustache.

"I see you have met Saint Gridley," he said.

"Yes, sir, I guess you could call that a meeting."

He huffed twice with merriment and put his arm over my shoulder. "Come," he said. "There is fresh lemonade in the Carlyle House. Have you been there yet?"

"No, sir."

"It's an old home. Used to be the rectory, but when we built Saint Gridley's new house, we turned it into a fellowship hall for meetings, lectures, and so on. Mrs. Ballou, our housekeeper, maintains the kitchen. She made lemonade."

"If I'm not too forward, sir," I said. "I don't believe I know who you are."

"Ah, of course. How rude of me. I'm J. Robert Applegate, the Senior Warden. I go by *Bobble*, my mother's nickname for me, which has had an annoying persistence. I'm an attorney by profession but now retired and serving the Lord. I spend time each day here at the church. Gridley needs a supporting hand every now and then, but I'm quite delighted you are here to take some of the load from my shoulders."

For the next hour, as we sipped lemonade, Bobble laid out the things I would be expected to do. The list was lengthy, including all pastoral visitation, management of the parish records, catechesis, and the formation of a new Christian education program for children. Further, I was to evangelize the neighborhood door-to-door. The neighborhood, Mister Applegate informed me, was unbounded since no parish lines had been drawn. Therefore, effectively, all of Saint Louis and its surroundings were considered my field of evangelization.

Sadly, the press of these and many other duties would likely prevent me from continuing my care of the sick and wounded at Laclede Hospital. As I sat on my bed that second evening at All Souls, I grieved the loss of my time at the hospital, for I had developed a keenness for this work as the core of my service to the Lord. I vowed to do what I could to manage my portfolio of responsibilities in such a way that, in time, I might carve out at least a half-day now and then to travel to the center of the city and assist the Sisters of Holy Compassion, all of whom had become my dear friends.

In a brusque and uncompromising voice, Saint Gridley informed me that I was to have no role in the upcoming Sunday service. I was to sit with Mrs. Fitzsimmons and *watch how things get done around here.* I had expected Saint Gridley's wife to be a cringing and obsequious woman, given her husband's snappish character. To my surprise, she presented a sunny disposition full of smiles and eye twinkles. When I was introduced to her, in a decidedly forward move, she threw her arms around me and cooed her pleasure at my arrival. "Doctor Fitzsimmons *so* needs you Deacon Andrewes. You have no idea how much."

As we prepared for the service, I escorted Mrs. Fitzsimmons to the front pew on the left, the one traditionally reserved for a recotr's family. The organist began a prelude, softly and simply at first, then rolling into a magnificent array of embellishments and ornamentations. When the prelude concluded, the characteristically reserved Episcopal congregation murmured its appreciation.

The service adhered strictly to the language, ritual, and ceremony of the *Book of Common Prayer.* I found nothing to surprise me, but I did harbor some trepidation about assuming my place in the rotation for officiating and preaching. Doctor Fitzsimmon's sermon exemplified the dry, uninspiring, and academic rhetoric against which Dean Worthingham had railed during our seminary days.

"Jesus told stories," the dean would say. "You have no better model. Tell stories. It's what people will remember." I can still hear him say *personalize, picture, portray.* Dean Worthingham drummed into our skulls the difference between a sermon for the laity and a theological treatise for the learned. Apparently, Doctor Fitzsimmons had not mastered this distinction. More likely, the contrast had never crossed his mind.

When the service drew to a close, Doctor Fitzsimmons almost grudgingly introduced me as the new Curate. Of course, well-wishers besieged me with greetings and immediate invitations for suppers in the days to come. As the crowd dissipated by foot, carriage, or horse-back, I began my trek to the Hermitage.

Just then a voice called from behind. "Good morning, Krieg." I turned to see Annie Worthingham walking toward me.

"Annie! What are you doing here?"

"Did you not hear me?"

"That was you on the organ?"

She nodded. "Guilty as charged."

"Why didn't you tell me? I couldn't see you in the organ loft."

"I wanted to surprise you. Doctor Fitzsimmons has hired me. We'll be at All Souls together. Isn't that wonderful."

"I'm sure it is."

"I'm pleased my uncle agreed to let you court me. However, why have you not yet called?"

"I'm not certain of propriety in our case. I don't know if it is considered acceptable for us to court in the open."

She laughed. "Honestly, Krieg. You are too straight-laced. What if we are seen as *courting in the open*? I rather think most people will find it delightful... so long as we have a chaperone, of course."

For reasons I cannot explain, I balked at her breezy assurances. The idea of a public display of our courtship among members of my new cure disquieted me. A restrained, sub-rosa, and appropriately chaste relationship would be acceptable, but anything more visible would create within me an unacceptable level of concern. When I disclosed my sentiments on this matter, Annie crossed her arms and with irri-table sighs accepted my conditions for the time being.

Thus, I settled into a routine that consisted of officiating services and preaching on alternate Sundays, performing my other assigned duties, and arranging to meet Annie on the weekends. As might be expected, our relationship deepened, but our trysts were uncorrupted by all but the barest and briefest physical contact—a brushing of the hands, a compression of shoulders, her *accidental* touch of my knee beneath the tablecloth. Though I thought of myself as red-blooded, I found considerable relief in maintaining our current level of affection and no more. I cannot explain why I held myself in check, not pressing my ardor to the brink. I have little doubt that Annie would have given me a good deal more rope had the opportunity presented itself. Inexplicably, it would have been more rope than I was willing to take.

————

As the dog days of summer were rinsed away by unseasonable late August rains, Annie informed me that her father, Thomas Worthingham, would be visiting in early September. As she did so, she lowered her face and simultaneously raised her eyes to mine. In a soft voice she said, "Father will be here for most of a week, just in case you have anything you want to ask him."

I immediately grasped her meaning and it threw me into a whirlpool of consternation. *Fond, entranced by, appreciative...* these would be adjectives that described my feelings for Annie. I enjoyed our times together, our courtship. Yet I could not, in good conscience and with absolute certainty, say I *loved* her. Questions swirled in my mind. Could I grow to love her? Would I ever have the opportunity again to find a romantic companion of such beauty and accomplishment? Did I stand ready to make that pivotal decision and seek her father's permission to wed? If I did not seize this opportunity, would it forever pass me by? Would she wait if I sought to delay?

"Krieg?" she said, jerking me out of my maelstrom of questions. "Are you quite all right?"

"Yes, quite all right," I said, trying to draw myself together.

"Of course, you may have no questions for Father," she said, her gaze sliding to the ground.

Reckoning that my best defense at the moment would be a coy

response I simply said, "Oh, I'm sure I'll have a question or two for him."

This seemed to satisfy her for the moment. She smiled and returned her eyes to mine.

———

For the next ten days, I wrestled with my pillow in the night hours trying to find answers to the questions that lodged in my mind. I prayed about the decisions facing me, but it seemed as if my prayers evaporated by the time they reached the ceiling of my Hermitage. I received no word from the Lord. Lacking clear direction, I resolved to *stew along in my own juice,* to use Belle's turn of phrase, hoping that in the fitting moment, the right decision and attendant words would arise like a phoenix from the ashes of my charred mind. Though her quaint sayings occasionally popped into my brain, I thought less about Belle. Perhaps the passage of time, my relationship with Annie, and the future spread before me had begun to attenuate my thoughts of Belle. Perhaps, at last, she was fading into the pages of my distant memory, a bittersweet but liberating thought. Prolonged and vivid images of her would have further wracked my already tormented mind.

Thomas Worthingham arrived on a sultry Sunday afternoon in early September. I had been invited to Dean Worthingtham's home for a late lunch to await with Annie her father's arrival. Taut as a fiddle string, I picked at my food and struggled to make small talk. All at the table intuited the reasons for my jitters. They knew that meeting Annie's father could be a propitious event. No doubt, hope sprang in their hearts. After all, Annie and I were a *perfect* match. A vigorous young clergyman, well educated, and seasoned by battle, married to a talented and beautiful sacred musician—what could be more ideal? What better couple to help usher in the Kingdom of God?

To be honest, I still had not resolved the uncertainty in my mind. I had made no decision. After days of internal turmoil, I concluded that I would simply have to live in the moment and follow the Lord's leading. However, since He had been frustratingly silent to this point, I wondered if He would provide any guidance whatsoever. I munched quietly on a bite of red potato and inwardly screamed to God for help. I couldn't look at Annie, who sat across from me at the table. In fact, I couldn't look at much of anything but my red potatoes. When I did steal a glance around, I thought I detected bemused expressions on the Worthinghams' faces. Annie simply regarded me with obvious expectation.

When the knock sounded, Annie jumped to her feet. "Daddy!" she shouted and ran from the table. The Worthinghams rose slowly to follow her, and I sat there with my innards *squirmin' like a worm in hot ashes.* I shook my head to rid my mind of this unbidden reminder of Belle and stepped slowly into the parlor where Thomas Worthingham received hearty handshakes and hugs. Annie's father was a tall, portly man with a tight, impeccably trimmed beard and mustache.

As she hugged him, he looked over her shoulder and spotted me standing on the periphery of the room. He raised his eyebrows. "And you must be Deacon Andrewes."

"Yes sir," I said and strode three steps to shake his hand, outstretched behind his clinging daughter. As Annie pivoted away, he said, "Annie has written a great deal about you in recent weeks. I am pleased finally to make your acquaintance."

I took an instant liking to the man. He was one of those rare souls to whom people are magnetically drawn. I have not yet determined why some people have this nearly universal effect. There is an air about them, a demeanor, an indefinable attraction that is almost always accidental and unintended. Thomas Worthingham exuded a warmth and openhandedness that drew me to him.

Was this the message from God? Had the Almighty finally answered my prayers of indecision by placing this charismatic man in my path? Would not my immediate attraction to him ease me toward resolution of my unrest? Could he tip the balance in favor of his daughter who now hung on his arm with a smile of unremitting joy? I could not help but wonder.

Thomas Worthingham accepted a plate of food, and we joined him around the dining table. He reported on the recent victories of the Union forces in Little Dixie. At Compton's Ferry on the Grand River and the later battle of Yellow Creek, Union Colonel Odon Guitar defeated Colonel John Poindexter of the Confederate States. Thomas Worthingham expressed the hope of all Unionists in Little Dixie that the Secessionist menace would once and for all be eliminated. The articulate fashion with which he related the battle scenes and his honey-laced baritone voice added to the man's charm. As I pondered his potential role as my father-in-law, he ended his report and fixed an eye on me.

"So, Deacon Andrewes," he said.

"Krieg, please."

"All right, Krieg, I understand you served the Union cause at Wilson's Creek and came away missing one of the bones allotted to you by the Almighty."

"Yes, sir. I was struck in the leg and a Confederate ball shattered the fibula in my right leg. A very fine surgeon removed the bone and treated me in the days to follow."

"Curious," he said with raised eyebrows. "I've not heard of a field surgeon providing post-operative care. Usually that is left to nurses and others."

"Yes, sir. I was fortunate."

"Well, he must have been a very compassionate surgeon."

"Indeed."

"Well, enough of that. Let us pray that Mister Lincoln will bring this dreadful conflict to a speedy end before every family in America loses a loved one." He paused to place a last bite of brisket in his mouth. He continued to engage my eyes. "So, you are now in the Lord's army. I trust you find your work satisfactory and in accord with your calling."

"I believe so, sir."

"Good. It is a noble work—not one that will bring you great wealth—but surely great gratification."

"I hope so."

"As do I, Krieg. As do I. Gratification in one's work brings stability, something very much needed in these turbulent times." He turned to Mrs. Worthingham. "Superb fare. I thank you for your hospitality. Now, if you will excuse me, I'll take my grip to my room. It's been a tiring journey, and I would like to rest for a time."

As he stood, we all rose in unison. Out of courtesy, I raced to grab his carpetbag and lead him to the upstairs room where he would lodge for the days to come. I placed the bag on a chair in the room. He clapped me on the shoulder and whispered his thanks with a nod and smile. In that moment, I knew he expected me to ask the as-yet unasked question, and soon.

NINE

All Souls Parish—Saint Louis

September, 1862

When I returned to the first floor, I noted that Annie and Mrs. Worthingham had gone for a brief walk while Lizzie Mae cleared the dishes and cleaned the dining area. Dean Worthingham sat in the parlor packing tobacco into his pipe. I stood in the entrance to the parlor.

"There's a trick to packing a pipe," he said in that restricted murmur of his. "If you do it right, you only have to light it once. If you don't, you are forever striking locofocos to keep the thing lit." He tamped the plug into the bowl with his thumb. "There. Perfect. You don't smoke, do you Krieg?"

"No sir. Never did take to it. Makes me cough."

"Pity. It calms the nerves and settles a meal."

He struck a locofoco and puffed his tobacco into flame. As the flame died and the ember appeared, he shook out the match. "Sit. Sit," he said.

As I settled into a wingback chair, he stared at me through the aromatic smoke. "I'm curious," he said. "You are under no obligation to tell me, but do you intend to ask my brother for Annie's hand?"

His forthright question took me aback. Yet, I knew he meant no offense. After all, Dean Worthingham had been my loyal mentor and employer. He could only have good intentions in asking. He would want only the best for his niece and me, so I accepted his question as something far deeper than mere curiosity.

In that moment, I felt the Worthingham family pressures mounting upon me: Thomas's "timely" arrival, Annie's demur question, and now the Dean's direct inquiry. As seconds uncoiled, I felt my resistances crumbling. I took a deep breath. "I believe so, sir. At a suitable time, I will speak with your brother, Mister Worthingham."

"Do you love her, Krieg?"

"Yes, sir, I believe I do."

"Believe, but aren't sure?"

His question stoppered the breath in my throat. I nodded slowly. "Yes, I do... love her that is." There. I had said it. In a hushed voice to be sure, but I had said it. *And now, niggling mind-worm, away with you!*

He smiled. "Good. Though it is not my place, I offer my blessing, and I have no doubt that you are in store for two *ayes*—one from my brother and one from Annie. I shall keep you in my prayers."

"Thank you, sir."

————

The occasion presented itself the following Sunday. Of course, Thomas Worthingham attended All Souls to hear his daughter play on the organ and, secondarily, to hear me preach. When the service ended, Thomas found me alone in the sacristy removing my surplice and stole.

With a brief wave of his hand, he caught my attention. "Just wanted to pop in to say that your sermon this morning was meaty and well-rendered. I appreciated how you wove stories and tales into the text. Would that more preachers would do so. Well done."

"Thank you, sir," I said.

He turned to leave.

"Mister Worthingham," I said. "May I have a word with you?"

He looked at me over his shoulder. "But of course."

"I would like to speak with you privately. Perhaps you wouldn't mind closing the door behind you."

He came into the room and pulled the heavy door shut with a soft snick of the latch.

I smoothed the front of my cassock.

He waited on the tiptoe of expectation.

"Sir, this may not be the most appropriate place," I said, my voice cracking a trifle, "but I wager I won't have many private moments with you. So I thought I should seize the moment, *carpe diem* and all that."

He said nothing, but I detected a bemused smile beneath his mustache. Encouraged, I continued. "As you know, Annie and I have grown close these last months. She is a lovely young woman and I'm… I'm… well, I would be honored if you would bestow upon me permission to ask her hand in marriage."

He said nothing, filling the pause with an unnerving silence. His smile had not widened. Indeed, his expression remained unchanged.

Suddenly, he barked a short laugh, strode toward me, and engulfed me in a suffocating bear hug. While still clinching me, he bellowed, "At long last! At long last! Indeed, you may ask my darling Annie to marry you. Yes. Yes. Yes. She has been waiting with bated breath for many days, hoping you would take this momentous step." He pulled away but continued to hold my upper arms.

He locked eyes with me. "She is the apple of my eye, Krieg, a precious soul. You are to take care of her in every way. If you ever cause her harm or treat her ill, you best light out for a distant and unknown land. For if I ever find you, your future from that moment on will be severely compromised. Am I clear?"

I nodded, vigorously and without breathing.

"Good!" he said. "Now, get on with it. She is waiting."

And she was. As Thomas Worthingham guided me out of the church with his paternal arm over my shoulder, we saw Annie standing alone under a great oak tree cooling herself with an Oriental folding fan.

"I shall leave you two," Worthingham said and spun away with a wink to his daughter.

As if on cue, Annie curled her arm in mine. "You've never shown me where you live. May I see the Hermitage, as I believe you call it?"

I looked around, unnerved by the thought of stealing away to my rooms. Though Annie, it now seemed clear, would soon be my wife, it still would be a breach of propriety for her to be found alone with me in my private space, especially on the campus of All Souls Parish. However, with no one in sight, I threw caution to the wind and led her quickly to my Hermitage.

Once inside, she did a slow scan, taking in the sparse furnishings. "Oh my," she said as she tiptoed to the door of the bedroom. Leaning on the doorframe she peered into the bedroom but did not enter. "Oh my," she said again. "I can see why you call it a hermitage."

"I don't spend much time here," I said. "I don't need much."

Having finished her inspection, she turned and walked slowly toward me. A diffident smile crossed her face. "What did you and Daddy talk about?" Her shoulders swiveled in anticipation."

"This and that," I said, warming to her expectant game.

"This and that? Not terribly forthcoming today are we Deacon Andrewes."

"It may be none of your business, Miss Worthingham."

"Is that so?"

"Could be?"

She drew closer. I could feel the full length of her body against mine. "Are you certain it's none of my business?"

"Let me think. If memory serves…."

"Yes."

"Your name did come up."

"Do tell."

I could smell her breath, feel it on my lips. "Ah yes, now I remember."

"Mmm hmm."

"I had a question for your father."

"I thought you might."

"I asked him if he thought it might rain."

She closed her fist and popped me lightly on the chest before renewing the swivel, more intense this time. "You did *not* ask him about the weather."

"I might have."

"But I know you didn't. What did you ask him?"

I pursed my lips.

She gave me a small shove. "Out with it!"

"If you insist." Slowly, I lowered myself on one knee, took her hand in mine. "Annie Worthingham, with your father's blessing, I would be forever grateful if you would be my wife."

She squealed. And hopped twice.

Then she dropped to her knees, threw her arms around my neck, and kissed me long, deeply, and with unrestrained force. I yielded and felt the last strand of reserve snap and recede.

Ozark Glossary

locofocos - early term for matches

.

PART 2

BELLE POTTS

TEN

Belle's Place

Late October, 1862

I sat in my desk chair an' give a gander 'round the liberry. All tidied an' corded up, thanks to Krieger Andrewes. Been cogitatin' on him off an' on fer o'er a month o' Sundays now. Cain't rightly say how come he stays a-clumped up in my haid. If'n I'se right honest with myself, have to 'fess that I come doe-eyed 'round him.

Fine man, I'd have to say. Keen as a briar whip an' as sweet to ole Belle as any man what's ever been by. I miss him somethin' fierce even after all 'ese days. He done set my heart to a-quiverin' and it's a-quiverin' some still. H'ain't had many opportunities to cozy up to a man, truth be told. As I 'splained afore, Belle ain't plump and curvy what mos' men like. I'se all lanky an' little with it. Oh, I knowed I'se highly sought when it comes to healin,' but when it comes to wingin', them boys look at ole Belle like she's dirt on a stick. Not Krieg, though. That man keered fer me, I knowed he did. He jes' couldn't stay hyar in 'ese hills, what with sem'nary an' all. Even if'n he'd no sem'nary to go back to, he'd be too high-toned fer jakey ole Belle livin' out hyar in the jillikins. Now there I go, getting' all clabbery an' down in the dumps.

I had me a good snub. H'ain't had one in awhile. Reckon I needed it but I gots to get over that Fed'ral private what stuck a hook in my heart. Ever time life slows a mite, he comes a-ridin' into my haid an' canters about. I'se manifold times a-wonderin' what he's doin' at a partic'lar moment, an' so 'twas as I'se settin' in the liberry on that blustery October day. Is he in book time? Is he a-prayin'? What's he eatin'? Where's he livin'? How's that gimpy leg? Is he thinkin' about ole Belle an' the times what we had together? An' o' course, my little brain starts a-thinkin' 'bout whether he's a-courtin' some lively lass or no. Hard to 'magine he's not, handsome man an' all. Yup, I gotta rid my mind o' him, or I'll go plumb tetched.

I reckoned I could snap outen it if'n I'd got back to work. So, I picked up the medical journal I'se readin' and checked oncet again fer the symptoms. Ole Buster Morton had been laid up with a bait o' miseries an' sure 'nough, they matched thems o' white blood—bein' tared all the time, losin' weight, bone pain, an' all bruised up like a dropped love apple. I hove a big sigh an' stood up. Time to lock down the diagnosis.

I left the liberry and hurried on o'er to the surgery. I'd collected a vial o' Buster's blood the afternoon afore an' set it to coolin' in the crick. I smeared a tetch o' that blood on a clean slide, added a drop o' acetic acid, an' slipped it under the new Zeiss micryscope what Doc J bought jes' afore he died. After a spell o' careful eyein', I come to the conclusion that Buster's blood was all swole up with them puffy white cells. Yup, white blood fer certain sure. T'ain't much one kin do fer white blood, an' it'd git Buster afore long I'se sure. I'd give him some Fowler's Solution, what's got arsenic in it, an' hope fer the best.

I opened my pharmacy, hauled out a big bottle of Fowler's, and poured some in a smaller bottle what I could give to Buster. I checked the clock hangin' thar on the surgery wall. Showed a few minutes afore noon. I reckoned I could mosey on out to the Morton place and dose that poor ole boy up with some Fowler's and then let 'em down gentle on the diagnosis. Cain't ne'er tell. White blood is daidly, sure as a wagon wheel's round. Howsome'er, I'd seen a few linger on fer a time, afore crossin' the Jordan. Maybe ole Buster'd be one o' them.

I'd layer some hope on that possibility. Course if'n Krieg was here, he'd be a-prayin up a storm. H'ain't ne'er been much fer prayin', though I'll allow as to how it sure he'ps from time to time, maybe ever'time, come to think on it.

I fetched my hat, tucked my hair up under the band, an' headed out. Some o' them brown oak and yeller maple leaves was a-blowin' in the bluster. Felt the first inklin's o' winter waftin' in on them li'l wind gusts. I hitched my new bay harse —name o' Blancey—to the medicine wagon and clumb aboard.

I named my harse Blancey—short for Amb'lance—cause that's what she pulls mostly. I pulled my collar 'round my neck and we-uns —Blancey 'n' me—ambled eastward on the road what led to the Morton's place. It's a might fer and snaky, but I reckoned I could spend the time cogitatin' on how to break the white blood news to Buster and the missus. Her name would be Lena. Goin' to hit 'em hard. They's been most of they's life all peert and gaily so's to find out that the green carpet ain't so far off fer Buster's a tough chaw to swaller. Hard enough to drop that kind o' load on strangers, but to do so with friends who is such mannersome folk makes it double-hard. Why I'd a-knowed them Mortons since afore any remembrance.

I come upon a turn in the road and unioned up with Swan Creek. I'd foller it pertineer to the Mortons. So I let Blancey carry me along lost in my own meanderin's. High in the trees a blue canary—some call 'em indigo buntin's, but I larned 'em as blue canaries—was singin' up a storm. Afore he passed on, my pa tole me the blue canaries say, *see it... see it... where... where.* It ain't spot on, but if'n you listen close, you can come near to hearin' 'em say them words. Perty li'l song fer a perty li'l bird. It'd a-been a right cheerful drive out along Swan Creek if'n it hadn't been jimmed up by the duty what I had to perform. I druther shinny up a thorn tree with an armload o' eels than give the bad news to Buster and Lena Morton.

I arrived to the Mortons 'long 'bout mid-afternoon. Buster was settin' on the porch o' they's double-pen cabin puffin' away on his corncob pipe whilst Lena done some knittin'. I didn't cotton much to Buster smoking a pipe. Folks what smoke all the time don't seem to feel in the high pink most o' the time. Figgered Buster needed all the strength he could muster to keep the white blood from draggin' him down too soon. O'er time, smokin' tobacky and spittin' ambeer takes the starch outer a person. I suspicioned too that tobacky might cause some kinds o' cancer. Seed a lot of cancer in thems what smoke fer a long spell. Cain't be sure, but I got my hunches.

As soon as the Mortons spotted me, they commenced to wavin'. As I drawed near, Lena stood and hollered inter the house. "Cordell! Cordy Morton! Come on out hyar, see what the cat drug in."

Seconds later, the Mortons' growed boy, Cordell, plugged up the doorway. I misremembered jes' how big that lad was. H'ain't seed him fer a coon's age. Last I heered, he was a steamboat captain on the Miss'sippi. Wondered why he come back home. Jes' in time to hear my bad news too.

Have to allow as to the fact that Cordy was a right handsome lad —seemed handsomer'n the last time I seed him. Wheat shock o' golden hair and a full set o' pure white chompers linin' that big grin o' his. He'd a-chucked his one-suspender butternuts fer them blue seaman's britches what's buttoned on both sides. Ne'er did figger out why a man would want side buttons, but there they was.

A nice white lace-up shirt hung on his wide shoulders. Them laces was partial undone an' his shirt was akimbo givin' me a peek at his chest all fluffed up with yaller curls. I 'verted my eyes. No sense in gittin' my mind cluttered with them kind o' thoughts, 'specially given what I'd druv out to do.

"Well, if'n it ain't Belle Potts, the Ozark croaker" Cordy hollered. "You come all the way out hyar to welcome me home?"

"Don' go puffin' yerself up Cordy. Better question is how come you meandered back hyar to the hills?"

"Why to see you, o' course."

"Don'cha be pourin' water on my wheel, Cordy Morton. Don'cha be actin' like the cock o' the walk jes' cause you is now a high an' mighty captain. I'se knowed you since you was knee high to a mole cricket, an' I don' care how much water you done plowed, you still got a tick in yer naval."

Cordy th'owed up his hands in defeat an' spread his grin a bit wider. Ever since we-uns was youngsters, Cordy an' me have jawed at one 'nother—all good-natured an' seemly, 'o course. Cordy's got all his jackstraws but h'ain't no match fer Belle when it come to word-sparrin'.

We more or less drifted apart after I went to work for Doc J an' soon's he turned eighteen, he 'bandoned the hills fer the river. From the time he was a wee tyke, Cordy Morton had a hankerin' fer water. He's allus fishin', giggin', noodlin', paddlin', wadin', an' swimmin'. I swear, that boy growed gills.

One day, he commenced to floatin' on the Gasconade River in a canoe an' paddled plumb to the Miss'sippi. Never looked back, 'til now o' course. One thang led to 'nother, and perty soon he's workin' the steamboats an' clawin' his way to the top rung o' the wheelhouse ladder.

I'd allow as to how it was good to see him ag'in. Be that as it may, I had a sad duty to perform, so I put him aside in my mind. I clumb down from the medicine wagon and walked slow-like o'er to where Buster an' Lena was a-settin' on the porch. I knelt down an' settled back on my feet so's not to tower o'er 'em while I pitched the sorrow news.

No call to be high an' mighty at a time like this. Cordy 'peared to have reckoned somethin' was afoot. He stayed in the doorway all clammed up, a bit o' worry etched on his brow.

"Buster," I said. "Know how you been feelin' o' late? Tard. Tard as a kitty cat in sunshine time. Sleepin' all the time. 'T'ain't common with you."

He nodded in knowance. I kep' a-goin'. "Buster, you 'member when I leeched that blood outen you yestiday?"

"Yup. Didn't much care for it, have to say."

"Don' blame you. Gettin' stuck with a big holler needle ain't no joyful thang. Important though. I took a long look at yer blood under my micryscope."

"Yeah?"

"Mmhmm. Seems you got a overabundance of what we call white corpuscles."

"White corpuscles?"

"Yes, sir."

"'At good or bad?"

"Sorrow to say, 'tain't real good."

"Howzzat?"

"Means you got a disease what we call *white blood*."

Buster th'owed me a long, sad look. "Is white blood, what you call it, gonna git me?"

"'Fraid so. Maybe not right soon, but got no cure fer it."

Fer quite a few seconds, no smoke puffed outen Buster's pipe. Lena stopped knittin'. She didn' look up. Jes' stared down at them knittin' needles with her forearms on her knees. Wind riffled her skirt. Cordy'd disappeared from the doorframe. I set there a-waitin'. T'weren't much to say. Busted my heart inter li'l pieces watchin' them good folk strugglin' inside to git a grip on all what I tole 'em.

"Gonna be a painful end, Belle?" Buster asked, his voice soft as bellows wind.

"Pain could pile up at times, fer sure," I said. "I got a couple of thangs what might he'p. I'll fetch 'em"

I stood, relieved to be doin' somethin'. Settin' through them long silent moments pains my soul. Gotta be done but 'tain't no picnic.

I moseyed o'er to the wagon. Found the Fowler's Solution, a wee bottle o' laudanum in rhubarb tincture, and a poke o' boneset. Handed 'em to Lena.

"What we'uns got hyar is Fowler's Solution. Shown to be o' some use with the white blood. Take a couple o' spoonfuls ever day. I got more, an' I'll bring it when I come back in a few days. Got here some dried boneset. Make a poultice and lay it on them parts o' Buster what are hurtin' partic'lar' bad. In the little bottle, I mixed up some rhubarb tincture and laudanum fer when the pain gets really bad. Foller?"

Lena nodded and took the medicines inter the cabin.

Poor ole Buster jes' stared off at the trees. I hunkered down to my knees, put my arms 'round him, an' held him fer a spell tryin' to draw some o' that pain an' gloom inter my own self. He allowed me to holt him, an' I knowed it he'ped a mite to have 'nother soul to comfort with.

After a time, he patted me on my back. "I thankee," he said. "I knowed you wasn't wantin' to make this trip all the way out to deliver yer findin's. But I'se not wantin' to hear it from anyone else. You go on now. We'll be all right, leas' fer a spell. Mind checkin' on Cordy? Seems he vamoosed at hearin' the news. You know Cordy. He's a big ole boy but don' do well when bad news comes a-callin'. He'll be a-holed up in the barn. Reckon he could use a pat on the back."

Now ain't that jes' like Buster. All caught up in his own miseries but thinkin' more o' his boy than hisself. I done as Buster asked an' spotted Cordy settin' on a stump in the barn whittlin' away with his jackknife. Didn' look up when I come near. Jes' kep' on a-whittlin'. I laid a hand on his shoulder.

"Awful sorrow, Cordy. Turrible thang to walk inter. I reckon yer pa an' ma is mighty glad to have you back hyar in the hills. Ole Buster's farmin' days is drawin' to a close. He's a-gonna need he'p 'round the place."

Cordy nodded. Still stoppered up. Suggin' inside, I reckon. I let some time reel out afore changin' the subject.

"Why did you come back Cordy? I thunk after you lit out fer the big river, we'd ne'er lay eyes on you ag'in."

Cordy nodded oncet more, pitched the whittle twig, and closed his knife.

"Couldn' cotton to it no more," he said. "Fed'ral army commandeered the steamboats fer transportin' troops an' supplies. Treated us steamboat boys like buck privates. Some o' them officers figgered they knowed more 'bout navigatin' the river than thems o' us what's been doin' it fer yars now. Put us in danger an', ever now an' ag'in, causin' more'n one boat to founder.

I jes' listened as Cordy warmed to the subject.

"Fortnight ago," Cordy continued, "One o' them jackleg Fed'ral officers, name o' Clancy, ordered me to steam through a nasty patch o' river all lodged up with trees, branches, an' root wads—remnants o' a recent storm. Said the boat would plow it all aside. I argyed with him to no avail. I refused to take the order an' Clancy come plumb unhinged an' pitched a fit. Whacked his ridin' crop on the railin' so hard it busted. Quite a sight to behold. I jes' shrugged. Ever now an' ag'in, bad idees gotta have their day in the sun, so I done what he ordered. Shore 'nough, we crashed inter them trees an' branches lurkin' in the river, breached the hull, and that ole boat commenced to take on water somethin' fierce. We was close 'nough to shore to git the men to safety. Lost two harses though, not to mention the valuable ord'-nance. That did it. I tole Clancy, 'twere his boat, his mess, an' his problem. Caught a ride back to Saint Louis and made my way home."

"Seems like 'twas meant to be."

"Seems so."

We lingered quiet fer a time.

"Getting' on toward candle time," Cordy said. "Ma'll fix some supper, you got a mind to stay."

"I best be headin' off," I said. "Try to git home afore dark."

Cordy nodded.

I clapped him on the shoulder. "Be back in a few days, Cordy. Good to see you."

"Same," he said.

I said my goodbyes to Buster an' Lena, clumb back on the wagon, and clucked Blancey inter a trot. We made good time an' arrived back to the house afore th' half-light winked out.

Whilst curryin' Blancey, I'se overcome with melancholy. I reckon the sad sitiation with the Mortons clouded me up good. Seems I shoulda been able to do somethin' more fer Buster, but I'se reached the limit o' medical knowance. Had to allow as to how Buster's in the hands o' the Almighty now.

Be nice if'n Krieg was hyar to put in a word with Him.

I shook my haid. Thar I go ag'in. Ruminatin' on Krieg like some ole nanny goat a-chewin' her cud. But O my! It'd sure be right wonderful if'n he coulda come through that door an' set with me fer a spell, talk about a book from Doc J's liberry. Be mighty nice.

Course I knowed he'd be a-fixin' to preach, or fixin' to pray o'er some poor soul, or settin' with some high-falutin' folk. Or mayhaps a-sparkin' some perty li'l thang what caught his eye. I knowed it. Gots to figger out some way to pitch that man outta my li'l brain when I'se all alone an' feelin' low as a snake belly. Jes' gots to figger it out.

———

Coupla days passed with nothin' much to fret 'bout save fer a young shaver, Georgie Kingston, what got a copperhead bite on his fanger. His ma come to me, I reckon, since I'd he'ped her with other medical needs o'er the yars. She had the good sense to ligate Georgie's fanger 'tweenst the bite and first knuckle. No doubt it slowed the spread o' the venom.

I plopped him on the table in the surgery and bathed his hand in b'iled water what had cooled whilst I preparated a poultice of tobacky leaves. I'se not 'tall certain tobacky he'ps a snake bite but no harm in givin' it a shot. Main treatment'd be a mixture o' clay an' coneflower oil what seemed to leech the venom outen the wound an' cancel out what's left. After a spell, I replaced the tobacky poultice with the clay an' coneflower mash.

Poor li'l feller was skeered as a gnat in a spider web. I sung him a few songs an' stroked his forehead. Seemed to conciliate him some and his ma calmed a mite as well. I knowed Georgie was a right fortunate lad. Seems as if'n them copperhead bites is a fur piece less deadly than a rattlebiter or a mocc'sin. Kinder hard to tell, but didn't figger that copperhead went an' spilt his whole load inter the boy. So, I'se perty sure he'd come through it okay.

Howsome'er he'd be turrible sick. Sure as meat'll fry, he'd be sick. I kep' him in the surgery under some warm blankets fer a good long spell 'til he dozed off. Then I give his ma some d'rections fer the next few days an' sent him home. I'd ride out an' check on him ever few days 'til I'se certain the whole thang had blowed o'er.

One afternoon, coupla days later, I'se out in the garden cuttin' the last herbs o' the season afore the frost come to these ole stony hills. I heerd a harse nickerin' an' blowin' down aside the house. I meandered oe'er and saw Cordy on what looked like a new-broke harse. Critter was swingin' and roundin' somethin' fierce. Tail's high and ears was pricked. Cordy was like to wrasslin' a wild pig. Have to admit, caused me to commence a belly laugh. Come to think on it, hadn't laughed like that in a coon's age.

"Whatcha got there Cordy?" I hollered out. "Seems you jes' broke him a coupla minutes ago."

Cordy ripped out a few cuss words afore simmerin' down to *miserable, hay-burnin' hunk o' crowbait.*

"Peers you been a-ridin' a boat wheel too long, Cordy. Cain't remember how to ride a harse."

"'T'ain't me. 'Orn'ry plug orter be rendered fer glue!'"

Cordy finally got hisse'f dismounted an' his frisky horse hitched to the porch railin'. I sobered a might, suddenly worried Cordy'd come with bad news 'bout Buster.

"Everthang all right to home, Cordy?" I asked.

He nodded an' brushed the dust off his breeches. "Fine. Pa's weatherin' the storm in good fettle fer now. That's why I come by today. Seems Pa don' wanna slither o'er to a warm rock, curl up, an' die like an ole corn snake. He tole Ma he hankered to kill a coupla meat goats, roast 'em on the spit, an' have the neighbors o'er fer a feast. We-uns reckoned that was a fine idee, so plans was laid fer Satu'day a week. Be mighty pleased if'n you'd come, Belle. We-uns is gonna whoop it up good with harseshoes, a hayride, tug-o-war, apple bobbin', an' who knows what else. I'se hopin' to git Merle Clayburn to bring his fiddle so's we-uns kin dance some. Yup, you'd be as welcome as cold water on a hot day."

I give my lips a li'l purse to cover my ponderin' o' the invytation. Had to 'fess sounded perty good. Might be a right ideal antidote fer what's causin' me to be all discomfited an' feelin' like I got drug through the soap kettle. Been busier'n a git-flipper's thumb to boot. Hain't had much rest o' late. Yup, goin' to the Morton's be a fine idee. Not too sure 'bout the dancin' part. I h'ain't cut too much rug in my day. Truth be told, I h'ain't cut no rug ever. I'se bettin' Cordy kin dance up a storm. Fer a big boy, he's foot-light an' agile, even though he don' seem to be too good at settlin' his harse.

"I'd be plumb tickled to come," I said. "I thankee fer askin'. Kin you set a bit. Got some cold sugar coffee in the crick."

"Naw, best be off. Got to track down Merle an' git him to bring his fiddle. Much obliged though."

Cordy pinched the brim o' his hat an' clumb back up on that cantank'rous harse what done three full circles afore Cordy could swing his leg o'er the saddle. Couldn't he'p it. Started gigglin' ag'in like a freckled schoolgirl as Cordy rid outta sight a-quirtin' his harse and cussin' up a storm.

———

Far as the war went, thangs had been fair calm round our parts fer six months or so. Oh, they's a skirmish hyar an' a tussle thar but all-in-all, our Ozark area become somethin' of a conflictual backwater, leastways as fer as the armies went. After that battle o'er by the Wilson, what the Secessionists more or less won, them Fed'rals roared back in an' re-took Springfield. Made it inter a major s'ply depot an' was buildin' some forts to provide some added security.

Only real action—and 'tain't nothin' to trifle at—is them cussed Bushwhackers. Rovin' bands o' Secesh sympathizers ridin' 'round terrorizin' the countryside. They's preferred tactic was to burn plumb to the ground the houses of them what's s'pected o' bein' Fed'ral sympathizers.

Half the time, they got 'er wrong. Burnt down houses o' innocent folk. Plunder, murder, an' ravishin' was all part an' parcel o' them raids. So despite the abeyance o' battles an' setch, thangs kep' on perty tense in them days. Ever'body all edgy an' trepidatious, fearin' them thugs would come a-runnin' on they's prop'ty and cut loose all manner o' mayhem.

Worstest Bushwhacker o' the bunch was Jubal Jagger. 'long with his brothers Isaac an' Walter. Now they's a trio if'n ever they was one. Jubal was a bitter ole man, all twisted an' blinkied by the sad course o' his life and, oh mercy, he harbored a fierce hate o' the Fed'rals and all who put in with 'em.

On the one hand, I felt sorter sorry fer him on account o' his mighty sufferin'. On t'other hand, jes' b'cause he hit a turrible rough patch, don' give him no cause fer terrorizin' the countryside. He p'isoned his brothers' minds with his bittersome outlook and hornswoggled a passel o' young roustabouts fawnchin' and fumin' fer some wild action. He done give the Fed'rals fits with his raids on supply trains, cuttin' telegraph lines, an' robbin' Union depots.

Fact o' the matter—I knowed Jubal a bit. Six or seven yar prior, his sister Lucinda swallered a watermelon seed and come to Jubal's to take to straw. Jubal come git me to be Lucinda's granny-woman.

Sad story. Baby was born daid. Baby girl. Jes' nothin' I coulda done to save the li'l thang. Reckon she died a week or two afore Lucinda started a-strawin'. Cord strangled fer shore. I prob'ly shouldn't say setch a thang but it might a-been jes' as well. Lucinda was perty feisty an' o'er-rim. I harbored consid'rable doubt what she could be a good ma. Turns out, soon's she was outta the straw, she up an' left Jubal's place.

'At's the only contac' I had with Jubal, and I kin vouch that he was a diff'rent man in them former days. To be sure, he was distressed with Lucinda's franzyin' ways, but all-in-all he seemed to be happy an' brimmin' with good will. Sad how a turrible blow like as he suffered can cause a feller's corn to sour right on the cob. But that's what happened to Jubal. Took to the bush an' commenced to settin' fire to hades.

———

Satu'day a week come. Time fer the doin's at the Morton place. I wandered about in my room chawin' what to wear. Didn' have none o' them fancy dresses with petticoats and crinolines, all puffy an' flouncy like I seed in the magazines. Why I didn' e'en wear chemises on the underside, jes' drawers, more like men folk wore. No corset neither but bein' shaped like a sapling, don' reckon I needed one.

Only consolatin' I could muster was that most o' the other ladies was a bit short on fancy clothes too. I finally settled on a simple white blouse an' long navy blue skirt—what I'd argy was my best clothes. Didn' own a link o' jewelry, so I settled fer plaitin' some perty flowers in my hair. Managed some crimpin' and wavin' in my hair to boot. Nothin' too high-wrought, mind you'uns, but a notch above jes' the straight combin' what I usually done.

Might mention too that o'er the yars I'd been 'sper'mentin' with a tincture o' honeysuckle to sweeten a gel's redolence. Didn' have it quite right yet bein's as it didn' last. Smelled perty when first applicated but 'vaporated too soon. Nevertheless, I grabbed the little blue bottle o' tincture on my way outen the door an' figgered I'd splash it on jes' as I's moseyin' up the Morton's lane. I'll admit I planned to sidle up to Cordy right early an' let him have a sniff. Not quite sure what I'd hoped would happen thereafter, but I'se feeling a bit feisty that day an' felt like steppin' out some. Not my usual deportment and it give me a niggle o' self-puffery, feelin' all womanly an' ever'thang.

I set out in the medicine wagon jes' past noon, hopin' to arrive a tetch early to check on Buster. I shore hoped Cordy's pronouncement was true, that his pa was weatherin' the storm fair good so far. Had to admire ole Buster's gumption havin' a hoedown at his place. I reckon he'd decided to celebrate his life afore kickin' the bucket. As Blancey an' I clopped along, I jes' hoped Buster felt right 'nough to enjoy the festivities what was sure to come. If need be, I could prop him up with a bit more laudanum. I watched the laudanum perty careful like with most patients, it bein' addictive an' all. But I figgered *what the heigh*! Worryin' 'bout addiction don' much enter inter it when a feller's dyin'.

'Bout halfway to the Mortons I stopped to give Blancey a handful o' oats. Found a little pack o' cheese wrapped in paraffin paper and had one o' them sensations what makes you think you been someplace afore.

I'se suddenly mindful o' my last day with Krieger Andrewes. Jes' afore we parted ways we had some cheese what was wrapped in paraffin paper. A li'l quiver o' dolefulness run through me as I took a bite. Thinkin' o' him put me in a whipsaw. My unripe plans fer meetin' up with Cordy didn' quite tally with my lingerin' feelin's fer Krieger.

As I'se been sayin', been a-tryin' extry hard o' late to rid my mind o' that man. No matter what trick I conjured, thoughts o' him slipped in an' outen my mind all the live-long day. Cain't honestly say all o' them thoughts was innocent or pure. Mostly they was but not ever'-time. I had seed him mother-naked to be sure an' that dastardly part o' me would hold sway oncet an' a while leadin' me to think thoughts I oughtn't.

Preposterous, I knowed, to be all jimmed up in my mind 'bout a feller I wouldn't ne'er see ag'in. More'n preposterous really, seein's how I'se now whipsawed by the whole thang.

Don' make no sense to get all contrite 'bout wantin' to do whate'er I'se wantin' to do with Cordy 'cause Krieg's a-bungin' up my brain. No sense 'tall.

I'se so exasp'rated standin' there by the wagon, I th'owed the last scrap o' cheese inter the woods an' shook my head so hard some o' them flowers come a-flyin' out. Got 'em back in after a fashion and clucked Blancey inter a trot, tryin' to fix my mind on Buster an' his deterioratin' condition, preparations fer the comin' winter, the promise o' homeopathy, rememb'rances o' John Milton's poems, ways to stretch out the sniffin' time on my honeysuckle tincture.... anythin' to get off'n the whipsaw.

Ozark Glossary

all lanky an' little with it – slender
wingin - courting, dating
jakey – countrified
jillikins – backwoods
puffy white cells – leukemia
snaky - long and winding
gaily - in good health, lively spirits
mannersome – polite, kind
ambeer - tobacco juice
croaker - physician, doctor
got a tick in yer naval - native of the Ozark hill country
noodlin' - catching fish, particularly catfish, with bare hands
git-flipper - guitar player
blinkied – soured
swallered a watermelon seed - became pregnant
o'er-rim – promiscuous
franzyin' – immoral

ELEVEN

Belle's Place

Late October, 1862

'Bout a quarter mile from the Morton farm, the road crests on a high hill givin' one a panoramic view o' them beautiful Ozark hills risin' inter the sky like fresh leavened loaves.

On this partic'lar day, I stopped on that crest to take in the autumn colors—the orange-browns, yaller-browns, an' brown-browns o' the oaks; the 'casional sweet gum red; the bright gold o' the maples. Story goes that one time them hills was all kivvered with pines. Kin still see some plotches o' pine hyar an' thar, 'long with some junipers and cedars, but mostly now them hills is kivvered with hardwoods.

Sittin' thar surveyin' that beautiful land give me a sense o' peace what calmed me a good bit after the consternatin' whipsaw I'd jes' gone through. I'se in no hurry to move along that marnin'. Jes' let the land-peace warsh o'er me. Had a deep within me a sense o' bein' home. Sometimes they's no better sense than to feel you is home. Course, come to think on it, that's likely a feelin' Krieger Andrewes wouldn't ne'er experience if'n he were sittin' by me, bein' a city boy an' all.

Wouldn't have a flicker o' the feelin'. Might allow as to how it was beautiful but 'twouldn't be home to him. I reckon that's 'nother reason fer me to continue elbow-greasin' to scrub him outta my ever'day thinkin'.

Quite a number o' folks had already come by when I driv' the wagon through the Morton's gate. A quick gander 'bout told me they was mostly neighbors from the nearby farms. I could hear strains o' Merle Claiborne's fiddle music comin' from the barn. Kids was a-runnin' around wild. I spotted a clump o' youth—boys an' gels—off to one side o' the barn. No doubt some o' them was sparkin' a bit.

Parker Newburgh an' his wife Heppie was settin' off by theyselves, faces all pinched and scrunched. They's hard-shell Baptists an' didn' much approve o' dancin' an' frolickin'. Made me wonder why they come at all. Mayhaps they's two boys—George an' Wayne—put 'em up to it. I spotted them two boys o'er with the other youth an' vowed to keep an eye on my belongin's. George an' Wayne was rounders fer shore—somethin' I could ne'er quite figger out. How could two plumb moral Baptists, who was theyselves beyond reproach, whelp two boys who was such dissolute cusses? Gels had best watch they's whereabouts, Buster'd best watch his likker, and I'd best lock the drawers on my medicine wagon with them two around.

I got Blancey settled in the corral an' commenced to walkin' toward the house. I glanced in the barn an' seed Cordy dancin' with Libby Garlick—the Widow Garlick. Her man had gone to the camp-town in the sky a yar or so afore, an' she was 'temptin' to run her place alone with her ten-year old boy, Rustin.

As I might a-figgered, Cordy was all lightfooted an' sprightly with Libby. They was dustin' up the place with shuffles an' swings. Cordy was a-makin' her dress tails pop. A streak o' jealousy run through me 'long with a feelin' o' deficiency an' scantiness. Cordy an' Libby shore looked to be havin' a grand ole time doin' what I couldn't do in a million yars.

I tried to shake out the mopes an' kept on pace to the house. Thar was Buster a-settin' in a rockin' chair on the porch smokin' that infernal pipe o' his. He was a-stompin' and a-clappin to Merle's music with a joy what warmed my green-eyed heart.

When I got to the porch, Buster's wife Lena stood to give me a li'l hug. "Mighty pleased you come," she said. "Set a spell with us."

Havin' no other options, I set myself in the open rocker. We didn' say much fer a time. Jes' sat thar listenin' to Merle who played on an' on 'thout a break. Finally, though, he guv his fangers an' elbows a rest. Folks spewed outen the barn to set up some games. Cordy come out too, Libby on his arm. They's tossin' they's heads back laughin' at somethin'. I felt lower'n a snake belly.

"Git you somethin' to drink, my dear?" Lena said, risin' from her rocker. "Got some soft cider an' some beer."

"Carn whiskey?" I asked.

"Oh, I s'pect Buster's got a jug or two squirreled away in thar somewhar."

"I'd be obliged fer a splash," I said.

"Me too," Buster said.

"Better watch mixin' laudanum an' carn whiskey," I said.

"Why? that laudanum you give me is right upliftin'. Tetch o' carn whiskey'd give it a li'l boost."

"That's my p'int, Buster. Don' need to be exacerbatin' the sitiation."

He smiled an' give me a li'l dismissive flick o' his hand. "I'll be *all raght*." He drawled out them words with a big ole grin.

"Shore you'll be *all raght* so long as Belle's hyar to pour syrup o' ipecac down yer goozle so's you kin purge."

"I'll be keerful. Promise." He hollered o'er his shoulder, "Jes' two fangers Lena. That's all Belle'll let me swaller."

I jes' shook my head, but I smiled a mite too.

Right then, Cordy come up with Libby still hangin' on him. Had to admit, she looked gargeous with her plumb black hair all crinkly an' spillin' round her face. Not a skin blemish in sight, an' I thought I spotted artificial red on her lips. Looked like a jaybird in pokeberry time. In them days, no woman o' decent repute wore lip colorin'. If'n I was right about my suspicions, it tole me a mite 'bout Libby. On top o' all 'at, she wore a flouncy red dress set with a new pair of leather high-top shoes. That no doubt set her right up as the queen o' revelry, so to speak.

"Afternoon, Belle," Cordy said. "Reckon you know Libby hyar."

She loosed her arm and smiled.

"I do," I said. I couldn't quite keep the frost from lacin' my words.

Cordy rubbed his hands together in oblivious delight. "Gonna be a fine day."

I took a swaller o' carn whiskey.

"Merle'll be crankin' it up ag'in afore long," Cordy said. "Gonna mosey on down fer some dancin' Belle?"

"Wouldn't count on it."

"Why? Music's right fine."

"Don' dance, Cordy. I tole you the same a few days back."

"Kin always be a first time."

"We'll see," I said, glancing at Libby who sported a ranklin' grin. I set to grindin' my molars. Needin' to vacate the premises, I stood an' fairly snatched Buster to his feet. I propelled him inter the cabin.

"Come on in hyar, Buster. Time fer a li'l check-up." I didn' really need to examine ole Buster. Jes' needed to get free o' Cordy and Libby standin' out thar. Jes' so's thangs was on the up an' up, I took Buster's pulse, peered inter his eyes. Got a bit o' a surprise when I took a gander in his left peeper. "You seein' clar, Buster?" I asked.

"Not up close. Gettin' on in yars, case you hain't noticed."

"I'm not meanin' that. I knowed you cain't see up close too good. Wonderin' 'bout seein' fer off."

"Maybe not too clar in the left un."

"'At's what I figgered. You got a bit o' pus in thar. Yer conjuctiva—that's the outer linin' o' yer eyeballs—is all red and kinder swole in that left eye. Prob'ly part an' parcel o' the white blood. Seen it a time or two afore. Don' reckon thar's much what kin be done. Sorrow 'bout it. We'll watch it. Now go on. Git on out thar an' enjoy yer party."

I stuck in the cabin fer a spell waitin' for Cordy an' Libby to mosey on. Couldn't wait too long though. After that long ride, I slipped outen the back door and picked up the path to the necessary. Fer reasons I cain't quite fathom, Buster built his necessary pert'neer fi'ty yards from the cabin.

As I'se walkin' down that long path I seed Cordy an' Libby off through the trees talkin' real close like. That done it. I resoluted to take my leave soon as I could 'thout appearin' ungrateful, make it a pop-call. Don' know what I'se thinkin' gettin' all lathered up 'bout havin' a good time with Cordy. He done found better game. No question 'bout it. No p'int in stayin' much longer. Felt a li'l tear sting but shook it off right quick. No use cryin' after the jug's busted.

I just come outen the necessary when I heard all kinds o' hootin' an' hollerin'. *Miss Belle! Miss Belle! Come quick! Need you right now!*

Couldn't fer the life o' me figger out what all the caterwaulin' was about. I tugged my skirt up so's to walk faster. 'Bout halfway back, Bradford Carver, one o' the youths what'd been sparkin' a bit, come runnin' toward me.

"Miss Belle, come quick! Rusty Garlick falled off the hay loft."

"Then we best be steppin' out," I said, an' we both lit out to the barn like a bat outen hades.

Rusty was a-lyin' on the barn floor howlin' like a moon-struck coyote. He's holdin' his left arm an' tryin' his best not to let them tears loose. I slipped down aside him an' put my hand on his back. "Rusty you look like the hindquarters o' bad luck. What happened?"

"Falled from up thar," he said, nodding to the rim of the hayloft.

"'At's a right poor idee, Rusty. Long way from up thar to down hyar. Where you hurtin?"

"My arm," was all he said.

I peered inter his eyes an' give his li'l body the oncet o'er. I agreed with Rusty's diagnosis. Arm's only thang banged up. "All right then, let's have a peek at yer arm." I said an' run my hand o'er the boy's forearm real light an' tender. He give a li'l wince.

"Sorrow, son," I said. "You brace yerse'f with this arm when you falled?" He nodded a bit. "Well, I reckon you got a fracture o' the ulna. Know what that is?" He shook his haid.

"Well, they's two bones in the lower part o' yer arm. Big un's the radius; little un's the ulna. I'm a-thinkin' yer got what we call a *greenstick fracture*. Ever heerd o' a greenstick fracture?"

Rusty shook his haid again and sniffed a mite. I kep' a-talkin. Doc J larned me if'n you keep talkin' it he'ps take the patient's mind off'n what hurts, leastways some. Seemed to be workin' in Rusty's case. "Ever snap a green branch?" I asked. Rusty nodded.

"Then you knowed it don' gen'rally bust all the way through, now do it? Top part cracks open but bottom part don'. You foller what I'se sayin?"

The boy nodded jes' as his ma—Libby the lover—come a-runnin' inter the barn makin' a big scene. She rushed up to Rusty an' falled on her knees. I held my hand out to block Libby.

"Don' be a-tetchin' him now," I said with plenty o' mettle in my words. "He'll be fine in a bit, but any jarrin' or bumpin' is gonna hurt like ole Billy Hades. So you best jes' set there quiet-like Libby."

She was taken aback an' stared at me all doe-eyed. I stared back 'til I'se certain she got my meanin'. I turned back to Rusty. "Yer gonna be fine Rusty. I'm fixin' to put that splintered ulna back inter place. Gonna hurt somethin' fierce fer a few seconds. Reckon yer man enough?"

He nodded but jes' a tiny bit. Afore he could think too long on it, I give a quick push on the bone protuberance an turned his palm toward the bulge. That set it back in position right nice. Rusty hollered like a stuck pig for three, four seconds afore takin' some li'l shudder breaths.

"Good," I said. "'At's all they is to it. Kin you feel the tips o' yer fangers?" He nodded again an' whispered a li'l *yup.*

"Kin you wiggle them fangers."

He done so.

"'At's good too. You keep a-wigglin' them fer a spell to keep the circylatin' goin. Now, you listen close Rusty. I'm a-gonna stabilize that bone, so's it'll heal up good as new. We-uns'll tie some sticks next to the arm—we call 'em splints. Fix up a sling fer yer arm too, so it don' go bouncin' 'round any more'n necessary. Gotta take it easy Rusty—no climbin', wrasslin', ropin', or nothin' else with that arm."

I turned to give Libby the eye ag'in. "Libby," I said. "You bes' keep a bead on that boy. Them splints'll be on a good month. Maybe more. Don' want that arm busted ag'in. Foller?"

Libby nodded and blinked with them irritatin' doe eyes o' hers.

I shook my haid an' hollered at Cordy to lop off some staves what lay o'er by the barn wall. "Cut 'em a coupla inches short o' his forearm length an' see if'n you can find somethin' to smooth 'em with. Don' need no splinters."

I repaired to my medicine wagon and brung out a roller bandage to bind the splints in place. Thirty minutes later, Rusty was up a-walkin' with his splinted arm in a sling. Look like he'd been chawed up an' spit out, that's fer sure, but he'd heal up good in a few weeks.

Havin' completed my treatment, I reckoned t'weren't enough room in that barn fer both Libby an' me. Time to head back home.

I thanked Buster an' Lena and took my leave. Oh, they was a-protestin,' but watchin' Cordy all moon-eyed o'er Libby set me on edge somethin' fierce. No need fer 'at. So I plastered a big smile on my face an' assuranced ever'body that everthin' was fine. Had to git home an' check on a newborn, I said. Bald-faced lie 'twas, but it seemed to work. Wasted no time in skedaddlin', an' two hours later, Blancey pulled me up to Doc J's house (still coudln't call it my own). I curried an' fed her afore makin' a beeline to the house and a dose o' carn whiskey, a big un.

————

Two days later, Cordy come by. I'se in the surgery doin' a highly del'cate procedure on li'l Marcus Showalter. Marcus had hisse'f a nasty infection o' his left middle ear. Eardrum was all swole up on account o' suppurative fluid built up ahind it. Most doctors was useless as a one-horned cow when it come to infections o' the ear. Doc J larned me good in ear medicine, so folks come from far away to get some relief from they's ear problems.

Far as I knowed, I'se the only one in 'ese parts who had one o' them concave mirrors what collected light an' 'lowed me to reflect a bright lantern beam inter the ear canal through a li'l cone-shaped tube what doctors call a speculum. With that light, I could stick a li'l skinny scalpel—sloshed with carn whiskey to kill the critters—right down that tube. I could nick the eardrum an' drain all that nasty pus. Then with a long pair o' forceps, I could stick a li'l rubber eyelet in that eardrum to keep it open fer further drainage.

I read 'bout them eyelets, called grommets, an' ordered four dozen from a famous Hungarian ear doctor, name o' Adam Politzer. Took most o' six months fer them grommets to get to the Ozarks. I even got a nice letter from Doctor Politzer hisse'f. Unfortunate, tain't no one in 'ese parts what could make heads nor tails outa them Hungarian words.

I'se gettin' fixed to nick the eardrum when Cordy come a-knockin'. Was a partic'larly inopportune time to be bangin' on the door. I'se chomped down on the handle o' my concave mirror what's held still by my clamped teeth so's my hands could be free. In one hand I'se holdin' the speculum. In t'other I had my skinny scalpel. Marcus was doin' kitty whimpers an' his ma was tryin' to keep him calm.

We-uns was busier'n a one-armed paperhanger, so I jes' let Cordy keep hammerin' on the door. Mighta thunk he'd a-knowed I'se busy and eased off a mite. Not so. Seems at times Cordy could be duller'n a widder-woman's axe. Finally, Marcus' ma hollered fer Cordy to desist with the knockin'.

After I finished with Marcus, I turned 'im o'er so's the ear could drain a bit more onter a clean towel. I set my surgical instruments aside an' let gravity take o'er. I wandered outta the surgery an' found Cordy settin' on the front parch o' the house. "What kin I do fer you?" I asked.

"I come by to see if everthin's all right."

"Everthin's fine, Cordy. Why ya askin'?"

"Seems you lit outta the hoedown quicker'n an eye blink. Don' rightly recall any farewells."

"Said my good-byes to yer ma an' pa. Seems you was perty busy."

"Busy?"

"With Libby Garlick. Didn' want to disturb you."

"Libby? We'se jes' dancin' some."

"You was doin' more'n dancing."

"I don' take yer meanin'."

"Seed the two o' you out in the trees, real close up."

"We'se jes' talkin' Belle."

"That what you call it? Talkin'?"

"That's all 'twas. No need to get all consternated o'er it."

"Not consternated 'tall."

Cordy give me a long look outa the corner o' his eye. "Why Belle Potts, I b'lieve you is a might green-eyed." He produced an infuriatin' grin.

"Don' flatter yerself, Cordy."

He jes' kep' a-grinnin'.

"Whaddya want, Cordy?" I said, makin' no effort to disguise my disdainment. "Got me a patient up to the surgery. Ain't got no time fer foolish jawin'."

"Belle, 'low me to 'splain. Me an' Libby is workin' on a transaction. I swear it to be the truth. She an' her boy cain't manage they's place no longer. Too much. Come spring, she's a-goin' to move on to Saint Louis where she got a brother. Wants to sell me her place or leastways have me manage it. That's what we was talkin' 'bout in them trees behind the cabin. Nothin' more."

"If you say so, Cordy. Seems you two was mighty cheery an' close fer business palaver. But makes no never-mind to me. Now I gotta git back."

I turned to leave.

"I ain't leavin' 'til we git the air clarified, Belle. 'Iss hyar is plumb ridic'lous."

"Suit yerself, but I reckon I'll be awhile."

I trundled back up to the surgery. Marcus was feelin' a good bit better. His earache was mostly gone, and he tole me he thought his hearin' had sharpened. I took 'nother gander at his eardrum, mostly to satisfy myself the li'l grommet was seated good. I coopered up Marcus' ear canal with a wad o' clean cotton. Sent him an' his ma a-packin'.

They hadn't no money to pay me so they brung some fresh milk what I put in the crick to keep cold. That's how a good many o' my patients compensated me in them hills. Presented whate'er they could. Truth be told, I et perty well with all the good food they brung my way. Mostly they give the best o' what they had to offer, and I surely 'preciated they's good will.

I took my own sweet time cleanin' up after Marcus' procedure. Fer all I keered, Cordy could jes' set thar on the porch an' make kitten britches fer tomcats. I hadn't got much to say to him anyway. Seems he wasted the trip, but I'd hear him out.

When finally I did rej'ine him on the parch, he's whittlin' away on a stick an' gittin' shavin's all o'er the parch flar. Set my mind to thinkin' 'bout Krieg hoppin' about on his crutch, sweepin', cleanin', an' tidyin' ever'thang up. Jes' thinkin' 'bout it ratcheted up my annoyance with Cordy a notch or two. I set down next to him. Follerin' sev'ral long seconds, I turned to him.

"Say whatcha got to say, Cordy."

He took a coupla strokes with his whittlin' knife. Then, he cleared his throat. "I'se right sorrow you come away with the wrong idee 'bout me an' Libby," he said. "Truth be tole, I was a-lookin' to dance a good bit with you but you was gone afore I knowed it."

"Cordy, I ain't blind. You was a-settin' up to Libby like a sick kitten to a jam rock. Don'cha try to say you wasn't. I'll admit it. Libby's a perty thang. Ole Belle hyar cain't compete. Ain't a-gonna try. It's why I pulled out."

"But that's what I'm sayin.' T'ain't no competition. Libby Garlick's a goner. Month or two she'll be plumb outen hyar. I'se dancin' with her jes' 'cause she was handy."

"*Handy?* S'pose that's one way to put it."

"Come on, Belle. Cut me a li'l slack hyar."

I stoppered up right then an' let what he said soak fer a minute or two. Reckon I was leanin' kinder hard on him. I didn't quite cotton to the notion that he's dancin' with Libby jes' 'cause she was *handy.* She was all gussied up fer shore an' flouncin' 'round like a peafowl with two tails.

S'pose I cain't rightly blame Cordy fer seizin' the opp'tunity, bein' he's a man an' all. Though I got to thinkin' 'bout his takin' the time to come by an' see me. Reckon he wouldn't a-done it if'n he'd no int'rest in me. Cogitatin' on it softened my heart a mite. I also had to allow I'se a bit too catty with Libby. If'n I'd admit it to myself, I was jealous. Jealous in two ways. She's so perty an' nice dressed I felt ugly an' plain. Then too, she got to Cordy afore I could.

As I sat thar thinkin' on it all, Cordy reached o'er an' took my hand in his. For some confounded reason, I let 'im. His hand skin was rough, calloused no doubt from his work. Still an' all, he held my hand gentle-like. Felt good. Felt mighty good. Didn' quite know how to take it. I looked up an' saw his eyes on mine, all soft an' pleadin'. I smiled. Couldn't he'p it. I knowed I'se starved fer 'tention. Seems I spent all my wakin' hours tendin' to the pains an' sorrows o' other folks. Had to keep up my concentratin' at all times an' had to show a stiff upper lip when it's heartbreakin' time. So when Cordy give me his fondness, my misdoubts 'bout his meanin' begun to founder. Tuckered as I was with it all, I cut my heart fences an' leaned inter Cordy. He cuddled me with his other arm. We jes' sat thar fer a long time, sayin' nothin'.

———

O'er the next few weeks, I made my way to the Mortons more'n oncet to check on ole Buster. Funny thang 'bout the white blood. Some folks suffer through a long debilitation, they's strength flowin' like molasses outen a cold jug. Others, why they jes' keep on a-goin' 'til all at oncet, they drop like a hailstone from heaven. 'Peared that's how Buster was proceedin'. 'Cept fer his eyeball, I couldn't hardly tell he's even sick, but I reckoned day would come when he's jes' curl up on the tickin' an' let 'er go.

Cordy an' me seed each other ever time I come by to see Buster. Then too, Cordy come gullin' 'round my place. We'd reached the bussin' stage after a coupla weeks but didn' go no further. I wouldn't cotton to any sprunchin'. To Cordy's credit, he didn't push his passion too hard, so we kep' things in proper confinement. Truth be tole, I didn' find Cordy's kissin' all that exhilaratin'. Mouth was hard an' bristled. Thought it orter be softer, but then h'ain't chalked up no comparatives.

I had to confess I wondered 'bout kissin' Krieg, sometimes even whilst I'se kissin' Cordy. I knowed it wasn't right thinkin', but jes' couldn' he'p it. Krieg was allus a gentle sort, an' he kep' his lip whiskers shaved good. I suspicioned that he'd be a fine man to kiss. 'Course as I thunk these thangs, I realized he'd no doubt be kissin' some other young gal what's all high-borned an' cultured. Even if'n an opp'tunity come by fer me to see Krieg ag'in, why'd he want to drag his wing with a peezaltree woman like me?

No, I'se beginnin' to think Cordy's 'bout as good as it'd ever git fer me. To be sure, he ain't asked to marry me or nuthin', but 'curred to me he's prob'ly thinkin' the same thang. Belle' 'bout as good as it'd ever git fer him now that Libby was 'bout to shuckle on down the road. Didn' rightly know what I'd do if'n he up an' p'inted to the altar. No doubt I'd have to ponder it some. Not too long I reckon or his ardor might cool. Problem was, I'se perty sure I didn't love the man.

I favor ponderin' the big idees, what's propounded in all them philosophy books in Doc J's liberry. When Krieg an' me'd be settin' an goin' o'er the thangs in them books durin' candle time, why I took to it like a lean tick to a fat kitten. Them words stuck in my brain too. He'ped me to see thangs in a diff'rent light. Folks come at the thorny thangs o' life in diversificated ways.

Readin' 'bout it an' listenin' to Krieg give me new perspectives. Kep' me from bein' so cock-sure 'bout everthang. Not so with Cordy. He's a good man, no doubtin', but when it comes to workin's o' the mind, Cordy bores with a small augur.

'Tain't that he's brain-numb. Not 'tall. He's jes' a simple feller what lives life as it comes to him. Don' have no drive to plow inter them spacious idees. To boot, he don' have the larnin' to do it. Course neither do I. that's why I needed Krieg to he'p me git a grip on what them philosophers was sayin'. If'n I'se honest with myself, I want to love a man fer his mind as well as ever'thang else. Cordy jes' don' seem to have quite 'nough nits in his haid fer me.

I'se cogitatin' on all these thangs one cold day late in September as I'se on my way to check on Buster. As Blancey pulled my wagon through the Morton gate, I intuited that somethin' was amiss. Most times, Buster, Lena, or Cordy'd hear me a-comin' an' step out to greet me. Help me get Blancey all sitiated an' such.

On this partic'lar day, though, 'twas diff'rent. Could jes' feel it in my bones. I slid down off'n the medicine wagon an' petted Blancey's nose. She's a-nickerin'. Mayhaps she figgered somethin' was off too. Strided up to the door an' give it a coupla hard knocks. After a spell— too long a spell—Cordy come to the door.

"Belle! Thank heavens you is hyar. Pa's in a real bad way." Cordy's brow was all furrowed and worryful.

"I'll git my bag," I said and high-stepped it to the wagon to fetch my black leather satchel what kep' them thangs I needed most often.

Cordy led me back to the bedroom where Buster lay on the bed, Lena by his side holdin' his hand. I scuttered to his bedside, sat next to Buster, an' laid my hand on his shoulder.

"Greetin's Buster," I said. "It's Belle hyar. Come by to see how you is farin'. 'Pears you is restin' good. I'se a-gonna have a little look. Don' you worry none now."

I opened my satchel an' pulled out my new Cammann binaural stethoscope. Peelin' back Buster's shirt, I put the chest piece atop his bony ribs. Heart was beatin' soft an' fast. Breath was a-comin' in irregular gasps through his mouth. Made his lips dry. I fetched a li'l tub o' lip salve what I made from hog's lard an' wax. Didn't smell too good but it'd relieve Buster's poor cracked lips.

I took each o' his hands in mine. They's mighty cool. Pulled back the sheet an' noticed Buster'd benastied his britches. I knowed he couldn't he'p it. I didn't say nothin' as I'se pullin' up his pant legs. Feet, ankles, an' calves was all mottled, speckled like a bluebird egg.

Buster was a-dyin'.

I stood an' beckoned Cordy an' Lena inter the keepin' room, shuttin' the bedroom door ahind us. I bade 'em to have a seat. Look on they's faces showed they knowed what I'se 'bout to say. I could feel my heart a-breakin' fer 'em.

"Lena, Cordy," I said keepin' my voice soft. "Buster's on the last leg o' his journey. I'se sorrow to say it, but I reckon he's only got a few hours left. He might not wake up but that don' mean he cain't hear us. So hard as it might be, we gots to set by his side, hold his hand, an' talk to him. Need to tell him we love him. Wouldn't hurt to give him permission to haid on out to meet the Lord whene'er he's ready. We'll all jine him afore long in the great bye-n-bye. Tell him so."

I let them words soak in fer a spell. I continued with my soft an' comfortin' voice. "He soiled hisself. That's narmal an' nothin' he kin help. So we need to git him inter some clean clothes. Keep him comfy. It's the main thang. Keep him comfy an' bathed in love. You'uns foller what I'se sayin'?"

Tears commenced to rollin' down Lena's cheeks. Cordy, hisself overcome, stood an' dashed outen the cabin. I knelt afore Lena an' pulled her ole gray haid inter the crook o' my neck.

"I knowed it's hard, Lena. He's a fine man, your Buster is. Gonna miss him somethin' fierce, that's fer shore. You go ahaid an' snub some. Tears is a gift from God, I allus say. They's a valve on the soul an' when God opens yer soul, tears come a-floodin' out releasin' some o' that pent-up sorrow. Makes room fer remembrancin' all them good times you-uns had together. It's a spiritual thang. I ain't much on spiritual thangs but I know tears kin be good."

As I'se sayin' these words, Lena commenced to quiet sobbin', wettin' my neck with her tears, shakin' in my arms. Could feel my own tears spill a mite. I rocked Lena 'til she finished her last sobs an' pulled back some.

"Thankee, Belle," she said.

I give her a clean hankercher what I kep' in the pocket o' my butternuts so's she could dry her eyes. "Come with me Lena. Let's git Buster cleaned up an' make him a bit more comfy."

When we finished our nursin', Lena asked if'n she could have some time alone with her man. That suited me, bein's as I needed to check on Cordy. Figgered I'd find him in the barn a-whittlin' away with his frog sticker. It's edzactly whar he was. Thar settin' on a board betweenst two logs, with whittle lashins an' lavins strewed on the floor.

I sidled up ahind him but said nary a word. I knowed some fellers preference to wear the willow quietly by they's self. Cordy'd be one o' them. So I jes' give his shoulders some gentle kneadin's, which I could tell he 'preciated a fair amount. He kep' on a-whittlin'. Seems like whittlin' a stick to no partic'lar end he'ped Cordy when he was out o' heart. He'ped him to sort thangs out an' swage his sorrows some.

Three hours later, Buster left we'uns to ourselves with one last shudder breath.

———

The buryin' took place two days hence in a stand o' big oaks jes' off'n the high pasture. Folks come from many miles around to pay they's last respec's to Buster Morton, surely one o' the finest men in these hyar Ozark hills. Leastways he's one o' the finest I ever knowed.

Brother Fryer led the service, an' it was 'bout as miserable as a frost-bit apple. He's a-jumpin' 'round, wavin' his Bible, an' hollerin' like a bug-eyed gollywompus. Made sure ever person thar knowed they was goin' to perdition lessen they 'cepted Jesus. Nothin' akimbo 'bout sayin' setch thangs, but I reckoned some o' his words shoulda been fer comfortin' and condolancin' to them what lost a loved one. All I could think 'bout was Krieger's warm voice sayin' them lovely words outen Doc J's li'l black prayer book. That woulda been a fur sight better.

I stood 'tween Lena an' Cordy durin' the buryin'. I draped one arm o'er Lena's shoulders an' t'other 'round Cordy's waist. I could feel 'em snubbin' a bit ever' now an' then. Put my heart inter a tight twist, an' I commenced a quiet whimper myself. Now that Buster was gone, Lena'd have to lean on Cordy to get the farm chores done.

Like I said, Cordy's a simple man, void o' deep thoughts, but he'd take good keer o' his ma. Sad to say, no more water fer Cordy. No more cricks an' rivers. Life run him aground. He'd been born, bred, an' buttered on the farm. Now he'd be a-workin' it fer the rest o' his days. I wondered, as I'se standin' thar, if mayhaps I'd be a-workin' it with him. I'd a hunch Cordy was gonna pop the question afore long. If'n he did, wasn't rightly sure what I'd answer. I did not want to abandon my healin' work to be a farm wife. On t'other hand, I'se runnin' outta options when it come to steppin' o'er the stick. I hankered to be a ma myself with two or three little ones a-runnin' 'round. Cordy seemed 'bout as good as ole Belle could do, an' I'd allow as to how I could do a whole lot worse.

After Brother Fryer finished his high an' mighty rant, folks lingered fer a spell while a few o' the men kivvered the pine casket with the rocky soil o' southern Missouri. I stayed with Lena an' Cordy through to candle-lightin' time. Didn' know what to say durin' most o' that time. Don' s'pose they's much to say, come to think on it. But they said they 'preciated my attendin' on them. Made 'em feel less alone, I reckon.

————

Two days after the buryin,' Cordy popped the question.

Ozark Glossary

plotches - same as *splotch,* now archaic
the necessary – outhouse
pop-call - short visit
jam rock - jam rocks are upright stones on fireplaces
gullin' 'round – courting
sprunchin' - petting, foreplay
drag his wing - court, woo
peezaltree - inferior, uncultured
hankercher – handkerchief
lavins - a great quantity
willow – mourn
swage - reduce, assuage

TWELVE

Bush

Late October, 1862

"I'm tetched to the core," I told Cordy. "But I'd favor some time to think on it."

Cordy must o' figgered I'd not answer immedjutly since he jes' looked at me with them big brown peepers o' his afore noddin' his understandin'. I give him a li'l peck on the cheek an' a thankee.

The next day, after granny-womanin' two new souls inter our Ozark hills, I sat down in candle-lightin' time an' pondered my sitiation with a li'l drop o' carn whiskey. I reckon I'd moved on from chewin' over Cordy's strong an' weak p'ints. I knowed who he was an' made peace with that. No sense in rehashin' it. Now I'se grapplin' with my callin'. As I tole Krieg, I felt a callin' to help thems what suffer, an' it give me no small 'mount o' satisfaction to see folks feelin' better when I give 'em what's been give to me.

On t'other side o' it, I got a powerful ache fer some li'l ones. I got some time to be sure. I'se only nigh onter thirty yar. But, save fer Cordy, I'd no prospec's 'tall. None afore, an' no guarantees goin' forward. Cordy couldn't 'bandon his farm. Mortons was one o' the first settlers in these hyar hills an' staked out a good spread. Cordy'd be expected to care fer his ma an' keep the place runnin' in good order. If'n I married him, seems I'd have to close the surgery an' take up as a farm wife. I didn' mind the hard work an' all, but the idee o' leavin' my house an' surgery cramped my soul somethin' fierce.

I took me another sip an' allowed as to how most hill gels didn't have to grapple with optionin' betweenst callin's like I'se havin' to. As I stood to mosey inter the bedroom, I'se leanin' toward assentin' to Cordy's perposal. I'd sleep on it fer a time an' see what the marnin' would brang. I sipped the last drop o' carn whiskey an' donned my nightshirt. Crawlin' inter the sack I reckoned I'd be needin' the extry quilt afore marnin'. Kitchen-settin' weather was a-comin' on to these Ozark hills, an' they's a chill in the air.

I falled inter sleep with Krieger Andrewes on my mind. A part o' me hated that weakness in me what brought Krieg inter my mind, but I'se too tard to fight it. Jes' couldn't conjur up no image o' Cordy fer some reason so Krieg kissed me goodnight in my weary 'magination.

––––––

Cain't rightly say edzackly when it happened. Lookin' back on it, I reckon it was 'bout two or three in the marnin' when the front door o' the house was busted open, an' five men come stormin' in. I'se in a deep sleep an' too bleary-eyed to figger what was a-happenin'. Afore I could snatch my gun, what I kep' propped by the bed, them five men surrounded me, pervadin' the whole room with stench an' menace. One held a musket barrel to my haid. In the dim light spillin' from a high-held lantern, I recognized two o' the men as Isaac an' Walter Jagger.

"Stay real still, Belle," Isaac said. "An' we won't hurtcha."

I'se skeered as a coon in a den o' wildcats, but I wasn't 'bout to show it to Isaac, Walter, an' them other three rowdies. "What in thunderation you doin' hyar, Isaac?" I said, risin' up in my bed. "Take 'at cussed gun away from my haid afore I snatch you bald."

Isaac studied me fer a coupla long seconds afore sportin' a half smile.

"Dare say she could too," Walter said, grinnin' a mite hisself.

"Could what?" Isaac asked, glancing o'er his shoulder.

"Snatch you bald. She's strong as a mama bear."

Isaac let out a li'l barkin' laugh afore lowerin' his gun a few inches.

"Better have a mighty good 'splanation, boys," I said, feelin' a bit o' grit comin' back. "What we gots hyar is trespassin' an' it don' go down well with me. You-uns might want to back away now an' close my broken door ahind you. I'se engaged an' fixin' to marry Cordell Morton an' he could whup all you-uns with one hand tied ahind his back. An' you knowed it Isaac Jagger." (Have to allow as to how sayin' I'se a-marryin' Cordy somehow set it a bit tighter in my mind an' made it more real, despite the extreme circystances I'se facin' at the moment.)

My mentionin' Cordy put 'em all inter fish-eatin' grins. They commenced to winkin' an' hootin' to one another.

"So the man-lady gots herself a beau," Isaac said amidst some chuckles what started my blood a-b'ilin'.

I th'owed the covers aside an' stood up. "Get out!" I hissed an' p'inted to the door. "All o' you-uns."

One o' the men, a fat, hairy, smelly thang, held his belly an' launched hisself inter a big ole guffaw. That did it. I smacked him a good one right in the kisser. Drawed a spot o' blood right quick, it did. He rocked back on his heels an' looked at me, betweenst winces, with eyes full o' surprise. That incensed him right good. He doubled his fists an' set hisself to retaliate. Them other men was enjoyin' ever'thin', but afore he could do nothin', Isaac put his hand on the fat man's chest to restrain him.

"Settle down, Groundhog," Isaac said. "Shouldn'ta laughed so loud. We ain't hyar to harm Belle. We need her. Now you go on out thar an' hitch up the medicine wagon. Belle, git yerself dressed fer some ridin'."

"Ain't goin' nowhere," I said, standin' my ground.

"Oh yes you is. Now git dressed, an' don' try to escape. We'll be watchin' the door an' the window."

"Nothin' doin'," I said. "Stayin' right hyar."

In short wink, Isaac's insouciance vanished. A snarl gripped his face. "You is goin' with us, Belle Potts," he said through gritted teeth. "Now git yerself dressed, or me an' my men will dress you. That what you want?"

I give my haid a li'l shake.

Without further adieu, them men left my bedroom, shut the door ahind 'em, an' waited fer me to slip inter my ridin' clothes what was hangin' on the wall peg. I reckoned I'd play along with 'em fer a spell, but keep alert fer an opp'tunity to escape. I dressed in my underclothes, butternut trousers, cotton shirt, an' tall boots. Tucked my hair under my wide brim an' put on my wool coat. Afore I left the bedroom, bein's as I'se all alone, I reckoned I orter leave some sort o' indycation o' what was afoot. I could leave a note but hadn't nothin' to write with. After a quick scurryin' 'round the room, I chanced on an ole belt what had a square buckle with sharp edges. I scratched *Jub got me* inter the plaster above my bed an' prayed them boys wouldn't spy the words. If'n I didn't return quick, why I'se shore someone would spot my message an' come to rescue me.

Soon as I walked inter the keepin' room, Isaac commenced to lashin' my hands ahind my back.

"No need to do that," I said. "I'll go along peaceful."

"Not takin' any chances," Isaac said. "Ever'one knowed you is strong enough to prize up creation and put a chunk under it."

After lashin' my hands, Isaac put a black sack o'er my haid.

"Yer runnin' up yer bill, Isaac. When Cordy gets a-hold o' you-uns, yer hide won't hold shucks in a tan-yard."

"He'll have to find us first, an' that will be pertineer impossible."

"Don' bet on it."

"We done jawin' now, Belle. Git a move on."

Isaac give me a li'l shove an' led me by my arm out to where Blancey an' the medicine wagon was a-waitin'. To my overwhelmin' disgust, Groundhog was fixin' to drive the wagon with me aside him. I could smell his owl-sour reek clean through the sack on my haid. I snapped my haid 'round an' said real soft an' slow, "Keep them hands o' yers to yerself." He give a li'l snicker, but I'se perty shore that snicker was laced with a tinge o' fear. Isaac must a-sensed Groundhog's leer 'cause he also warned him to leave me be.

———

And so, we-uns embarked inter the bush. I tried to keep my bearin's, but after several turns I couldn't orientate no more. We-uns traveled through the night. When the sun come up, it become clar our train was headin' east. No words passed betweenst Groundhog an' me.

Them other boys was quiet too, 'cept fer 'casional d'rections when we come to a fork in the trail. Ever now an' ag'in, one o' them would sashay up ahead to do some scoutin'. Bushwhackers had to be on the lookout fer Union soldiers what perty much controlled the southwest corner o' Missouri by this p'int in the fightin'.

'Bout noon, we come to a stop. Isaac noted that we was deep inter the bush, an' it would be safe to take off the sack. He reckoned rightly. I had no knowance as to where we was. He also took the lashin's off'n my hands so I could chew a couple o' strands o' deer jerky 'long with a few swallers o' water. After a spell, I convinced him to keep them lashin's off, promisin' not to try anythin' fancy. 'Twas a relief, too. The lashin's was cuttin inter my skin an' squeezin' off my circylation.

We-uns continued eastbound 'til the sun was low in the sky ahind us. The trail at several p'ints was so narrow them boys had to saw small trees down plumb close to the ground so's my wagon could pass. Groundhog kep' his meathooks to hisself but only 'cause I had my hands free an' Isaac kep' an eye on him. As the afternoon wore on, Groundhog sulled up good, which suited me jes' fine.

When dusk come upon us, we-uns crested a hill, an' I seed, through the heavy forest, a camp spread afore us. They's five tents, a corral with near a dozen harses, an' a scattering o' rough-hewed movables—chairs an' setch. 'Peared to be six or seven men an' two women roamin' 'bout the camp. Isaac p'inted to a narrow trail an' motioned fer us to foller him on down. Groundhog was so looby, he couldn't drive the wagon down that trail so I snatched the reins from him an' done it myself.

Oncet in the camp, I seed a cave cut inter the hill whence we jes' clumb down. 'Tweren't a deep cave, near as I could tell. Dark was a-comin' fast an' I couldn't see what's what inside that cave. I found out soon 'nough, howsome'er 'cause Isaac he'ped me down from the amb'lance an' steered me to the mouth o' the cave. One o' the women follered with a lantern.

Inside the cave, I seed ole Jubal Jagger laid up on the ground, sweatin' like a mule. His leg was elevated on a saddle, an' I could see it was tore up real bad. I turned to Isaac. "What happened to Jubal?"

"Run afoul of a Union patrol," Isaac said. "Jubal took a shot to the leg. Kin you have a look, Belle."

I nodded. "Bring the lantern o'er hyar," I said to the woman what was standin' nearby. Didn't take but a minute to see that Jubal's leg was all swole up, oozin', an' smellin' to high heaven. Gangrene. Bad. I stood up an' nodded fer Isaac to j'ine me outside. Seein' us emerge from the cave, Walter sidled up.

"His leg is a mess, boys," I said. "Cain't save it. Gotta come off jes' 'bove the knee. That's his only chance to survive."

"You sure?" Walter asked.

"Sure as sun rises in the marnin'. You gonna tell him or is I?"

Walter an' Isaac studied each other fer a few seconds.

"Don' b'lieve I kin tell him, Isaac," Walter said.

"Don' b'lieve I kin either," Isaac said. "You do it Belle."

"I'll do it, but first we got to thrash out a few thangs. You boys abduct me from my house, bind my hands, put a sack o'er my haid, an' haul me clear out hyar in the hide-out country. Takes a fair 'mount o' gumption to ask me to save Jubal, don'cha figger?"

Walter an' Isaac's eyes bored inter the ground. I let 'em stew fer at least a whole minute. I could see Isaac startin' to grind his jaw. He could git mean, as he showed back at the house. I didn't press the silence none fu'ther.

"Tell yer what," I said. "I'll do what I kin fer Jubal, 'cause it's what I'se called to do. *But*—an' that's pertineer the biggest *but* you-uns'll ever hear—I ain't figgerin' on stickin' round oncet I knowed Jubal is outen the woods. Foller what I'se sayin'?"

Isaac an' Walter nodded some.

"So you-uns will lead me back home when it's all o'er."

Isaac an' Walter nodded some more, kinder tentative like.

"I ain't gittin' a real good feelin' 'bout yer sincerity, boys. We have a deal or no?"

"I reckon that's fair 'nough Belle. If'n be up to me, it's a fair trade, healin' Jubal fer safe passage home, that is."

"If'n it ain't up to you boys, then who'd it be up to?"

"Reckon, Jubal'd be the one to decide," Walter said.

"He don' seem to be in too good a condition to be makin' decisions," I said. "He's plumb delirious with fever. So it follers that you-uns is now the bull geese."

Isaac an' Walter stared at the ground fer a spell more. Finally, Isaac give another li'l nod an' a raspy, "Okay Belle. Let's git on with it."

"All right, then," I said and commenced to shootin' out orders to git the long table near the cook pot, set it in the cave, an' round up as many lanterns an' torches as was in the camp. "I want two full jugs o' carn whiskey too."

The boys balked some that the notion o' surrenderin' they's whiskey, but when they seed me stare 'em down, they up an' complied right quick. I enjoined the Jagger brothers an' the others millin' 'round to bring me a clean sheet from my medicine wagon what to kivver the table with. Theys also told to figger out a way to suspend them lanterns above the table. Fortunately, a coupla o' them had 'nough in they's cerebrums to set up two poles, one at the haid an' t'other at the foot o' the table so's they could stretch a rope betweenst 'em.

Once them lanterns was hung, I shooed ever'one outen the cave save fer one o' the women, the young one who didn' look too fritter-minded, save fer the fact that she'd took up with these rullians. No time to do any biographin' though, so I got down to business.

"Roll up yer sleeves, sweet pea," I said. "Then pour some carn whiskey all o'er yer hands an' arms."

She looked at me with them perty brown peepers, wide-eyed some. I softened my voice a tetch. "I knowed it don' seem to make sense, pourin' whisky on yerself. Jes' trust me. I ain't got the time to 'splain right now." She nodded an' done what she was told.

Fer the next few minutes, I cut Jubal's pant leg off an' gathered the instruments I'd be needin'—knives, saws, artery forceps, tourniquets, needles, suture thread, an' the like. I also retrieved a small flask o' chloroform. Them ruffians whisked me away from my surgery so fast didn't have time to pack up my ether tray. So, it was chloroform fer ole Jubal. Once ever'thang was laid out an' ready, instruments soakin' in a pan o' whiskey, I jostled Jubal 'til he turned his bleary eyes in my direction.

"Jubal, don' know if you been a-graspin' the sitiation hyar. I'se 'fraid I gots to tender some bad news." He blinked a few times but 'peared to be follerin' me. "Yer leg's perty fouled up, Jubal. Sorrow to say, I cain't save it. Gots to take it off."

"Where?" he managed to wheeze out.

"Right 'bove the knee."

He cussed some. I let him shoot out a few choice words an' git it outen his system.

"I'se truly sorrow, Jubal. As it goes, Doc J. 'pressed 'pon me the obligation to treat ever'one—good an' bad—regardless o' what they done an' without no deemin' on my part. So, I'se a-gonna try an' save yer life. Yer leg's all cankered up an' doty. If'n I don' take it off, you'll die sure as a gun is iron."

A ripple o' sadness crossed ole Jubal's face, an' fer a split second, I had an inkle o' sympathy. That emotion slid away quick as it come. I motioned fer the young woman to bring me a clean cloth an' the flask o' chloroform. When I'd a-fashioned a cone outen the cloth, I poured some chloroform inter the fabric. "Lick yer flint, Jubal, 'cause hyar we go."

Oncet that cloth was placed o'er Jubal's mouth an' nose, he commenced to squirmin.' Even tried to rise up off'n the table. I tole the young woman to hold him tight to the table. Jubal was a strong man but too sick to overpower the young woman. His squirmin' soon abated, an' he muttered some afore slippin' unconscious. I took the cone away an' studied his respiratin' fer a half minute or so.

"'At should do it," I said. "'Preciate yer he'p sweet pea."

"My name is Pippa," she said, kinder stern-like. "My real name is Philippa Stetson but people call me Pippa."

"Okay, Pippa it is. You got any problems with blood?"

She shook her haid. "Seed plenty."

"I bet you have, ridin' with these paw-pawers. You go on o'er an' stand on t'other side o' the table. Put this hyar mask on. Do edzackly as I say."

Fer reasons I cain't quite pinpoint, I closed my eyes an' whispered a quick prayer to Jesus. One could argy that the world would be a whole lot better off rid o' Jubal, but I ain't got in in me to think that way. At that p'int Jubal was a patient, same as Krieg oncet was. Mayhaps deep down inside I'se skeered them brothers would rid the world o' me if'n I kilt Jubal. Mayhaps that wasn't it 'tall. Mayhaps a li'l bit o' Krieg was a-wanderin around in my mind. Whate'er, I took me a deep breath, poured carn whiskey on my hands, kivvered my nose an' mouth with a mask, an' sterilized the wound with carn whiskey. Then I snatched an ampytation knife from the tray.

"I'se fixin' to do what's called a circ'lar ampytation," I said, decidin' to norate my procedure. "First, we-uns put a tight tournequet high on the thigh, like so. Then we slice all the way down to the bone an' all the way 'round the leg, like this."

I done jes' as I said. When I'd made the incision, I p'inted to a cloth split half way up to form two tails. "Pippa, hand me that split cloth thar. We-uns is gonna retrac' all the tissue an' muscle by puttin' this slit down to the bone, crossin' the tails, an' pullin' up a tetch to expose the bone."

When I done it, I tole Pippa to hold the retractor. She complied in good order. I doused my capital saw with carn whiskey. "Hyar we go." Pippa watched the whole time, an' I had to admit a smidgen o' 'miration fer the gel. Didn' come anywhar near t' swoonin'.

I continued my noratin'. "Now, we'uns gonna smooth at bone down a bit with what they call a *rongeur*. Doc J called it a *gnawin' forceps*, what is a fair description, ask me."

Oncet I'd fixed the bone stump up good, I asked Pippa to remove the retractor so's I could snake out the main arteries and ligate them. 'Course, had to separate them nerves from the arteries so ole Jubal didn't suffer his remainin' days with neuralgia.

That bein' done, I loosed the tournequet an' brung them muscle flaps an' skin down o'er the bone. I sloshed the whole thang with some more carn whiskey and stitched it up. Some surgeons don' do no stitchin', but I thunk Jubal would heal some better if'n I stitched him up.

"Pippa," I said, when we-uns was all done, "You is one work-brickle gel, I have to say. I thankee fer yer able assistance. Now you keep an eye on this ole wampus-cat whilst I have a little parley with Isaac an' Walter. Make sure they keep they's end o' the bargain."

I found Isaac an' Walter settin' on a log a-waitin' fer me, lookin' all worried an' setch. They jes' kep' on a-settin' thar as I come upon 'em. Didn't rise up or nothin'. Don' s'pose they considered me a lady worth gettin' up fer.

"How's he doin' Belle?" Isaac asked.

"Surgery went all right," I said. "Time will tell. You-uns best hope I got all that nasty infection outen that leg stump, or we'll be treadin' high water ag'in."

"How soon you figger we'll know somethin'?"

"Should be outen the woods in a coupla days. Now, boys, we best be remindin' ourselves o' the 'rangement hyar. If ole Jubal rekivvers, as I reckon he will, you'uns best be fixin' to guide me fer enough so's I can find my way home. That yer remembrance o' the deal?"

"One day at a time, Belle. See how Jubal comes along. Then we kin talk," Isaac said rollin' a splinter round in his mouth. Couldn't rightly tell why he needed a toothpick seein's as he h'ain't got but two or three teeth left in his gob.

"Don' like the sound o' that," I said. "Seems like you is hedgin' on me."

"The *deal*, as you been referrin' to it, Belle, was mostly yer idee 'bout how thangs orter go down. Tole you Jubal'd be makin' the call."

"Oh no, yer don', Isaac Jagger. Oh no yer don'. You is a weaslin' outen the 'rangement. I tole you I'd fix up Jubal fer free passage back home. You 'greed. Now you is a-back-steppin' on me. Man's as good as his word, they say. You give me yer word—both you an' Walter. Ain't that right, Walter."

Walter stared at his shoes. Said nothin'.

I felt a niggle o' trepidation. What was these bushwhackers plannin' in my case? These boys was a-goin' back on they's word.

As I conjectured on it a bit, cain't say I'se too s'prised. Not a whit o' honor left in them Jagger boys. Oncet they's likely fair-minded an' all but the war's jibbled a number o' brains, bodies, an' souls. I concluded best fer me to let the matter set awhile. No use in rilin' Isaac an' Walter. Figgered I'd best let thangs stew a bit afore reprisin' the whole thang.

"We ain't finished with this hyar tête-à-tête," I said with a li'l sigh o' resignation. I felt a wave o' fatigue warsh through me. No sleep the previous night, a long ride, an' hard surgery had wore me out.

"I'se bone tired an' cain't hardly keep my eyes open. Figger Jubal will be out fer 'nother hour or so. Got a place I can take a load off?"

Isaac an' Walter looked at each other, an' it become clar they hadn't thought more'n 'bout two minutes ahaid o' theyselves. Finally, Isaac opined it might be all right if'n I took an extry Army cot (what I'se sure they stole) in the *li'l gel tent*, as they called it. Did't 'preciate they's condescendin' way o' puttin' thangs, but I 'cepted the offer.

When I pulled the tent flap back, I seed Pippa settin' on one o' the three cots arranged up parallel-like in the tent. She's lookin' down at her hands, mopey-like. Didn't look up when I come full inter the tent.

"What's troublin' you, honey," I said, soft-like.

She give her haid a li'l shake, as if'n she didn' favor talkin' 'bout it. I nodded an' headed fer the far bed, what was less rumpled. Figgered it'd be the one Isaac referred to. I'se plumb tuckered an' could use a bit o' sleep, so I pulled back a filthy wool blanket. 'Magine they's a perty big grimace on my face. No doubt they's more critters on that thar gray blanket than wool fibers. Stains o' unknown origin stared up at me an' give my gut a li'l turn.

Jes' as I was fixin' to crawl under them foul kivvers Pippa said in a real soft voice, "I'se sorrow."

I turned to face Pippa. "Don' take yer meanin'," I said.

"Sorrow you got cotched to come hyar."

"Have to say I agree. Walter an' Isaac promised if'n I he'p ole Jubal out, they'd let me go. Now, seems they's in a welshin' mood."

"Sounds 'bout right. They's bad men."

"So that leads me to the question as to why you is hyar."

"One of these men is my pa."

"Yer pa?"

She nodded with a look o' profound chagrin. "The one they call Groundhog."

"Yer greenin' me."

"No ma'm. He's my daddy," she said. Her face give away her chagrin at disclosin' this to me.

I found myself plumb perplexed. Couldn't 'magine Groundhog sirin' anythang as winsome as Pippa. She's right perty an' sharp as a hedgehog quill. Near as I could tell, she was virtuous to boot. How she come out so good with Groundhog as her pa give me a bit o' flummox. After a few seconds o' befuddlement, I regained my gentility.

"Feel like jawin' 'bout it," I asked

"Naw. Yer tired an' need some sleep. It'll wait."

I allowed as to how she was right. Not sure I coulda guv my full 'tention to her story. I nodded an' tole her we could talk later if'n she was still a mind to. With that, I slid under them kivvers tryin' hard not to let that mucky blanket touch my face. Have to find some clean warshin' water after I rested some. That was the last thought crossin' my mind afore sleep cotched a-holt o' me.

My peepers fluttered open two hours later. Pippa had left the tent. Took me a few minutes to shake the sleep outen me. Now that I'd 'complished what them durgens brung me hyar fer, I reckoned I needed to gin up a way o' gittin' away.

I'd take another poke at Isaac an' Walter in an attempt to prey on whate'er shreds o' decency they got left. Since I'se perty shore they's fixin' to break the promise they made, I'd have to figger out an escape. 'Course that would be pertineer impossible seein's as I had no clear idee where I was. Somewhar east o' home was 'bout all I could surmise. This hyar's perty dense hide-out country. I seed the last part o' the trail oncet the blindfold had been took off but I had no knowance o' it afore that. I'd have to free Blancey, slip away all stealthy like, an' then ride lickety split. Them boys would likely be in hot pursuit soon as they seed I was gone.

I'se cogitatin' on all o' this when Pippa come back inter the tent bearin' a steamin' bowl o' stew. Jes' the smell fired up my appytite.

"Yer awake," she said. "Figgered you'd be hungry. Have some o' this venison stew."

"Thankee," I said, settin' upright on the bed an' flingin' that sullied blanket aside. We said nary a word while I'se savorin' the stew what tasted a fer sight better'n I mighta foreseed. I left a big morsel o' venison 'til the last bite an' when I finished it, I handed the bowl back to Pippa an' repeated my gratitude for that much 'preciated repast.

"So, I'se compelled to ask ag'in why you be sallyin' 'round with them bushwhackers," I said. "Seems like you is a moral sort o' gel, not much given to wreakin' havoc in these parts."

She took a bit o' time to collect her thoughts. No s'prise thar. I reckoned she'd waded in some deep water in her short life. I kep' my gaze on her.

Oncet a body got past the grimy dress an' matted hair, they-uns would confirm my observation what she's a looker. Big brown eyes, what I noted afore, pearly white teeth all in place, and slender hands. Hands what had done a fair share o' work, but fetchin' jes' the same.

"Pa's a bad man," she said, breaking the silence. "I knowed that since I'se a shoot. I don' favor anythin' he an' them Jagger boys is doin'."

"Why do you stay?"

"Got no place to go." She looked up inter my eyes. "Ma an' me lived together 'til she died a yar back. Pa wasn't 'round much but he come back when she took to bed. When she slipped away, didn' know what else to do. Pa said I could ride with him. Said he'd keep me safe."

"He done that? Keep you safe?"

Pippa shrugged. "The Fed'rals don' know where we is camped. The Jaggers know these hills like the back o' they's hands. So they know how to hide good. When they go on a raid, they lose them Fed'rals ever' time. Even when they plugged Jubal, the boys was able to get away. We move ever' few weeks, so I feel safe. Have to say, howsome'er, if'n I had someplace to go, I would."

We lapsed inter silence ag'in, an' I stored all them thangs in my mind. Wondered if'n mayhaps Pippa an' I could conspire to slip outen hyar together. Didn't figger 'twas the right time to be talkin' 'bout that. Best see how thangs track fer a spell.

"How'd you git inter doctorin'," Pippa asked.

"Long story," I said, an' since nothin' else was snaggin' my time, I got down to tellin' her the whole long tale 'bout me an' Doc J. She hung on my ever' word, an' it 'curred to me that she might favor this kind o' work herself.

"I noted that you done good when we-uns was ampytatin' Jubal's leg. Not ever'one kin abide setch a thang. You ever of a mind to engage in healin' work yerself?"

She nodded. "Thought 'bout it some. I know they's what's called *nurses,* but I got no schoolin' an' no knowance as how one comes to be a nurse."

I seized a thought what come to mind. "Cain't make no promises, Pippa, but if'n I git outen hyar, I could use some he'p back home. Lot to do an' I could larn you how to do it—come to be a nurse that is."

She fixed me with eyes o' pure 'stonishment. "You really mean 'at?"

"I do. We-uns will ponder it some. Might jes' as well give you the first lesson in nursin' with Belle."

She sat up a tetch an' give me her full wide-eyed 'tention.

"Bein' clean is the most important thang," I said. "Meanin' ever' part o' you—hair, body, hands, fingers, an' clothes. All gots to be squeaky clean."

"Why?"

I proceeded to give her a li'l tutorin' on the animalcules. She asked a fair number o' insightful questions what confirmed to me that she had an astute mind. I took a deeper likin' to her.

Suppressin' a smile, she stood an' scooted outen the tent, my stew bowl in hand. Reckon that's 'bout the first time she had somethin' to smile 'bout fer a good long spell. Made me smile too, what confirmed fer me that even in dire straits, one kin 'casionally find a spot o' joy.

Thinkin' o' joy brung my mind 'round to Krieger Andrewes—

ag'in. Had a remembrance one night when we was conversin' about Aristotle who wrote about *eudaimon*. If'n I bethunk c'rectly, that word means "good spirit" an' comes from a life o' virtue what leads to happiness, leastways that's what Aristotle said.

Krieg helped me to unnerstand the diff'rence betweenst happiness an' joy. Happiness is from what's outside o' us, thangs what happen to us in life. Joy, he said, comes from that deep down inside feelin' o' peace an' 'ceptance. Comes from the Almighty tetchin' our souls, he said. We-uns kin be joyful but not happy an' vicey versy. He opined that Aristotle was really writin' 'bout joy.

I got in me a sense 'bout joy. I b'lieve I feel it ever'time one o' my folks starts farin' better an' gits well. Them li'l fragments o' joy don' seem to last fer a great long time, but I fer shore know the feelin' o' joy. Yup, jes' now, seein' the li'l smile on Pippa's face, give me a smidgen o' joy even in this turrible sitiation.

'Course not all o' my thinkin' was squandered on Krieg. Thunk a fair amount 'bout Cordy too. Afore long he'd note I was missin', an' I s'pose he'd come a-searchifyin' fer me. I growed sad at the thought that he'd have scadoodles o' trouble findin' me out hyar in the woods. I was surely hopin' he'd keep on a-lookin' 'til he located me. Maybe git with the Fed'rals an' come a-huntin'.

I'd perty much set my budget down on marryin' Cordy, but I wondered if'n I might pick it back up if'n he had no mind to find me. As I was ponderin' this matter, Isaac opened the tent flap an' informed me Jubal was awake an' moanin' up a storm. I give a big heave-ho an' follered him inter the cave.

Jubal was crimped up with pain, so I give him some morphine an' proceeded to my first inspection o' the surgical site. Preliminary indycations was favorable. I took his temp like I done with Krieg an' it was slightly up but not too bad. I'd keep an eye on it o'er the next day or two jes' to be sure it don' rise up on me fu'ther.

Though I hadn't much o' a mind to do so, I give Jubal some comfortin' words an' tole him I'd get one o' his men to fix up some crutches so's he could ham about in due time. The ole suggin ne'er give me a word o' thanks fer savin' his sorry life. Not that I done it fer praise an' thanksgivin', but still, seemed like he coulda showed a mite o' gratification.

I lingered with Jubal fer a spell 'til the morphine begun to take a-holt o' him. Then I sidled up to Isaac an' Walter who was lazin' 'bout the fire.

They give me a long look. "Time to go over our bargain, boys. Jubal's comin' along jes' fine so far. I'll wager it'll take a coupla days to certify he's outen the woods. If'n that comes to pass I want to know what plans you-uns got fer my return home."

'Tweren't no s'prise, but them grand-rascals jes' shrugged they's shoulders an' refused to answer my query. I could feel the steam a-risin' in me.

"You boys is actin' perty amnesiac, seems to me. I'll ask it ag'in. What's the plans fer me to be be set on the trail home?"

"Tole you afore, Belle," Isaac said. "'At's fer Jubal to decide."

"An' I tole you, Isaac Jagger, Jubal's not in a clar mind at the moment. 'Sides, I didn't bargainate with Jubal. 'Twas with you two."

They jes' stood thar an' said nothin'.

"You-uns is stirrin' up Gehenna with a long spoon," I said an' took my leave, madder'n a wet hen.

I went back inter the tent to ponder my sitiation some an' git my vexation under control. Not sure if'n I'd be safe after Jubal got on his hoof ag'in. Might jes' shoot me an' leave me to the buzzards. Course on t'other hand, way them boys was carryin' on, sure to be more injuries an' wounds. Mayhaps they's fixin' to holt me hyar to doctor 'em up.

Neither option was to my likin', so the idee of escapin' quickened in my mind oncet more. Didn' seem realistic to assume Cordy'd find me. As I'se ponderin' my sitiation, Pippa come back. I noted she had scrubbed up good, an' her hair was soft an' flowy like it'd been fresh warshed.

"You faired up right good," I said. "Where'd you warsh?"

"They's a spring crick over thar 'bout a hunnert paces," she said, p'intin' with one o' them perty fangers. "They's a canebrake what will give you some privacy. I'll spot fer you if'n you want to scrub up. Shoo away them boys, they come near."

I nodded.

"Hyar," Pippa said. "Some soap. It's kinder course, but it's all I got. If'n you want ter head on to the crick, I'll brang a fresh towel."

"'At's right kindly of you. B'lieve I will. Need to cool down some after jawin' with Isaac an' Walter. Need both cleanin' and coolin'."

"You'll be a-coolin' right good in this hyar cold air," she said.

I nodded ag'ain afore shruggin' it off. As I made my way in the direction Pippa was a-pointin' I seed the other woman in the camp carryin' some water up from the crick back to the camp.

"Who might you be?" I asked.

She set the water can down an' took a deep breath. "Name's Iris Monahan. I'se a cousin o' the Jagger men."

"How'd you come to ride with 'em?"

"Cussed Fed'rals kilt my man who was fightin' o'er near Newtonia coupla months ago."

"I'se sorrow."

Iris loosed a stream o' ambeer. "My Tom was ornery fer shore but I loved him all the same. When I got word o' his killin', I j'ined up with Jubal figgerin' to exact some revenge. Been successful too. Barreled inter three o' them Unionists."

I refrained from commentin' on Iris' jaded ambition. We parted ways, an' I found my way to the crick an' Pippa's canebrake. Looked 'round jes' to satisfy myself no one was a-gogglin' me. I doffed my shirt, butternuts, camysole, drawers, an' boots afore wadin' inter the crick nekkid as a plucked goose.

Ayee! that water was colder'n a pump handle in January. Took me a coon's age to dip myself inter a deep hole so's I'se up to my neck. I warshed quicker than a double streak o' greased lightning. Jes' as I'se fixin' to wade outen the crick, Pippa come by with a clean towel. She 'verted her eyes as she handed the towel to me, an' I 'preciated her respectin' my modesty, though I never did figger I'se the o'er-modest type.

Pippa kep' her back to me as I toweled.

"You is perty as a new-laid egg," she said.

'At stopped me tight. I ceased my dryin'. Couldn't b'lieve my ears. "Why thankee," I managed to say after an awkward spell passed by. "Cain't recall anyone callin' ole lanky Belle *perty*."

"But you is," she said. "You is strong, an' healthy, skin's all glowy an' satisfyin' to look at. Makes fer pertyfication, it does."

I couldn't he'p myself. I smiled an' give Pippa 'nother thankee. Come to mind, I needed to warsh my clothes too, but I'd had enough o' gelid water fer one day. I motioned fer Pippa to set a spell with me there on the crickside.

"You heerd anythin' 'bout what the plans is fer me?" I asked her.

"Cain't say as I have," she said.

"'Pears my options is next to none. I figger they's not plannin' to guide me home. No doubt, my espoused cain't find me, if'n he's even lookin'. But one thang's fer certain. I ain't berryin' in 'iss patch any longer'n I have to."

I locked my gaze on Pippa fer a long moment. "Kin I trust you, Pippa?"

She nodded. I kep' my gaze on her fer the better chunk of a minute. She was studyin' her knees the whole time. Finally, I let her in on what I'd been a-cogitatin' on whilst warshin' in the crick.

"I'm fixin' to light outen hyar soon as I'se satisfied ole Jubal's gonna make it."

She said nary a word.

"It'd favor me considerable if'n you would come along. Ridin' with the Jaggers is no place fer a gel like you what gots some real promise. 'Sides, two haids is better'n one out thar in them woods."

She kep' her silence, but I knowed she was assentin' to the idee in her mind.

"When we get free, you kin stay with me, an' I'll l'arn you how to nurse."

"But didn' you jes' say you was tyin' the knot with some feller?"

'At reminder slowed my ponderin' some. I still h'ain't got no resolution in my mind 'bout givin' up healin' to hep Cordy on the farm. I reckon my invytation to Pippa come close to solidifyin' in my mind that I'd keep on a-healin'. How Cordy an' me would work out the farmin' needed more study.

"Right," I said, hopin' by talkin' I'd make some sense to myself. "Cordy Morton has been a-settin' up on me. I h'ain't give him any affirmation yet but I all but made up my mind to marry him."

"I'd jes' be in the way."

I put my hand on her shoulder, gentle-like. "Naw. I'se got plenty o' room in the house fer the three o' us. Who knows, Cordy might stay on the farm some an' come to my house some. We h'ain't got it all chawed out yet. In any case, they's plenty o' room."

She give a few li'l nods afore turnin' to face me. "I'll go with you, Belle. Sure would like to he'p you in yer healin'."

'At pleased me an' I give her a good smile. "I'll be a-ponderin' how to slip outen hyar o'er the next day or so."

"I kin give it some reckonin' too."

I stood an' give Pippa my hand to haul her upright. We clumb up the crick bank an' back to the camp.

"I'll check on ole Jubal's stob ag'in," I said when we reached the cave. "Then I plan to ask one o' these cymlin-haids fer a splash o' carn whiskey. Seems I deserve a sip or two fer my services."

Ozark Glossary

kitchen-settin' weather - chilly period of early Fall
sulled - grow sullen, refusing to talk
rullians - course, unkempt person
deemin – judgment
all cankered up an' doty - rotten, decayed
paw-pawers - outlaws, fugitives. (Bushwhackers often lived on
paw-paws, a wild fruit.)
work-brickle - industrious, hard-working, anxious to work
wampus-cat - blood-thirsty animal in the wild
scadoodles - a large quantity or amount
my budget down - to make up one's mind, to decide
ole suggin - an inferior person
grand-rascals – cheater
barreled inter – shot
a-settin' up - expressed intention to marry
stob – stump
cymlin-haids - fool, dunce

THIRTEEN

Bush

November, 1862

A week slipped by. Ole Jubal done waded through his deepest water an' was makin' progress in hobblin' about with a set o' crutches. 'Course he's 'bout as pleased as a skunk in a churn to be perm'nently hipped up. He was meaner'n a cornered badger to ever'one 'round him so we-uns all give him a perty wide berth. I charged my mind a-plenty 'bout how we'd escape during them days. Pippa give me a clean set o' duckin's, allowin' me to warsh mine down in the crick.

One evenin' whilst them Jagger boys plowed inter' some likker they stole on a raid, I bade Pippa to j'ine me so's I could draw my idees on our escape.

"I noted a thang or two 'round hyar," I said. "That one durgin, name o' Corbett has took a fancy to yer."

Pippa nodded some, confirmin' that she knowed what I was sayin'.

"Also noted that he has a strong 'finity fer the carn whiskey. T'other night he's so drunk he had ter get a-holt o' the grass afore he could lean on the ground."

'At tickled Pippa an' she give off a short giggle. I smiled a mite myself.

"If you is of a mind, we kin couple them two knowances. One o' these nights, Corbett is gonna be on sentry duty. I was wonderin' if'n you might sidle up to him with a jug o' whiskey. Look at 'im all sweet-eyed and setch. Let 'im do some substantial pulls on the jug. Course you ain't a-gonna permit no funny bizness. You jes' keep him in the dark. Foller?"

She pondered my idee fer a few seconds afore noddin'.

"I kin do it," she said. "I reckon I kin git him to grab some long shut-eye."

"Be my thinkin'."

"Then what?"

"We'll un-hobble Blancey. She's a good mare what don' take to whinnyin' an' nickerin'. We-uns kin lead her outen hyar a fur piece 'til they cain't hear us no more. Then we mount up an' ride quicker'n buttered buckshot. Need some canteens o' clean water an' a gun."

"I kin git Corbett's gun oncet he's drunk hisself inter the ground."

"Sounds right good," I pernounced.

We set thar a spell mullin' o'er our strategem whilst I finished my laundry.

———

Thangs come to pass three nights later, when Corbett pulled sentry duty. Pippa an' me nodded to one 'nother in passin'. As the day wound down, I seed her slip a jug o' carn whiskey under her coat an' head off inter the woods. I done my part by selectin' a saddle what I could lay up on Blancey oncet we was benighted. Filled two jugs with fresh water from the creek an' secreted them away ahind some rocks near where the harses was hobbled. 'Twas the mercies o' the Almighty that we-uns had the run o' the camp. The men give us a fair bit o' freedom, within limits o' course.

That night Pippa an' me both et a good supper, knowin' it might be some time afore we could git back to the trough. Then we-uns waited fer dark to fall on the camp. To make thangs 'pear as if'n they's nothin' afoot, I checked on ole Jubal a time or two. Even he'ped him hobble outen the cave to set by the fire with them peckerwoods o' his.

Musta been feelin' a good bit better 'cause after a coupla snorts o' carn whiskey, he commenced to tellin' tales. To my great gratification, Corbett had a few belts hisself. That would make him a good sight more tractable in Pippa's hands. Pippa herself hung back in the shadows, jes' a-watchin' an' a-waitin.' This story-tellin' went on fer what seemed like well o'er an hour. Then, all o' a sudden-like, Jubal come to a full halt in what he was a-sayin'. He give Corbett a long odious look.

"Put that thar jug down, Corbett," he said. "'An git on up to the top o' the cave. Skin yer eyes fer Fed'rals."

Corbett staggered to his feet and stumbled up the rocks leadin' to the lookout atop the cave. Even in the wanin' light, seemed like his eyeballs was all bleary an' outa focus. I give a quick glance to Pippa an' noted her li'l smile. She seed Corbett's condition too. I'd be a-fibbin' if'n I said I wasn't narvish. My belly thronged with millipedes. I reckon Pippa was in 'bout the same fettle, but I had to hand it to her. Her visage betrayed nothin' 'bout how she felt.

Bein' as winter was upon us, the days was short. As night settled down on the camp an' the fire burned low, one-by-one Jubal's boys slunk off to theys' bedrolls and kivvered up ag'in' the cold. To my s'prise, Jubal wanted to talk some more with me, but my mind was too brimmed up with our plan to chew the fat. I humored him a bit with a "yes" hyar an' a "no" thar. Outen the corner o' my eye, I seed Pippa shuckle quietly inter the woods where she'd hid that jug o' carn whiskey.

So, it sets off.

I give Jubal another twenty minutes o' one-sided chatter afore announcin' I was fixin' to slip inter the tent fer some shut-eye. Howsome'er, jes' afore I stood, I asked Jubal if'n he was of a mind to send me home in the next day or so. Figgered if'n he assented, I'd call off the escape an' save Pippa from the loathsome task set afore her. Didn' take ole Jubal a second to confirm what I'd s'pected all along.

"Gonna head out to do some raidin' in the marnin' Belle. Who knows, might be needin' yer services ag'in."

Jubal's confirmatin' stiffened my resolve. *We'll be a-seein' 'bout that, Jubal,* I thunk to myself. *We'll be a-seein' 'bout that.*

When I got to the tent, Iris was snorin' like a ripsaw on rotten wood. I sat on the cot an' bided my time fer o'er an hour. When the moment seemed ripe, I slipped from the tent and skirted 'round the center o' the camp on my trek to where the harses was hobbled. When they sensed me easin' up to 'em, a few give off a whinny but nothin' outen the ordinary. I moved real slow as I retrieved a saddle and th'owed it gentle-like on Blancey. She allowed me to cinch it up good an' affix the bridle. I also picked up them jugs o' water an' slung 'em o'er her withers. She was patient as she could be, an' I whispered my thankees with a few strokes on her soft nose.

Oncet ag'in, I bided my time what to give Pippa a good stretch with Corbett. Worried me some to ponder what she had to suffer, but I had come to a place o' high confidence in her.

Whole camp was quiet as a graveyard an' a cold spell was a-movin' in. I shivered a mite an' sidled up to Blancey so as to warm myself. I give it thirty minutes afore slippin' the hobble off an' leadin' her step-by-step away from the other harses. To my great consolation, them other harses had settled down an' made nary a sound. In the dark, 'twas hard to spot the long pathway round to the top o' the cave, the one what I druv my wagon down when Groundhog lost his nerve. Thankfully, Blancey picked it out in due time, an' I jes' stepped along with her.

Jes' as we was climbin' the hill, one o' the men let out a stream o' choice cuss words. I stopped in my tracks an' felt my skin pucker inter goose flesh. I got a-holt of my breath. Seemed like a coon's age passed by afore I heard another o' them rullions spit out a few more cuss words right back at the first. I give a little exhalation, knowin' that they's an altercation a-brewin' what had nothin' to do with Pippa an' me.

I let a few more minutes slip by. I heerd Isaac rizz up to calm them boys down. When I'se confidant the ruckus was o'er an' they-uns was back in they's beds, I eased fu'ther up the trail. Me an' Pippa had agreed to meet by a big oak tree a couple of hunnert yards away from where high-hopin' Corbett was draggin' his wing 'round Pippa.

Oncet at the rendezvous, I leant inter the tree an' whispered a brief orisen to the Almighty. I come to prayin' a good sight more of late. Not surprisin', prayin' allus brung Krieger to mind an' I let him set thar a spell whilst I waited. 'Twas a comfortin' visage in the coal-black night.

I'se so occypied with my mental moonin's that I didn' hear Pippa slip up aside me. When she whispered my name, I like to jump plumb outen my skin. Seein' my scare, she put her arms 'round me an' held me close fer several seconds.

"You done it?" I asked.

"I done it. I jes' kep' pourin' whiskey down his throttle 'til his haid flopped on my laigs. Moved him off'n me easy like, picked up his gun and ammynition. Don' reckon he'll grasp onter what happened 'til we is long gone."

"I thankee Pippa," I said. "'Twas a nasty chore but God-willin' it'll aid our prospec's. No time to waste, let's cut mud."

―――

We mounted Blancey, knowin' she could see the trail a fer bit better at night than we-uns could. She set off at a good pace. Me an' Pippa had a sense the trail headed west, leastways fer some distance, but had no knowance if it kep' in that direction. I'se hopin' fer it to cross a bigger road what might be travelled more. As we moseyed on, we-uns kep' our talkin' low an' jes' a few words now an' then. Pippa was a-ridin' ahind and clutched onter me fer dear life.

Mostly me an' Pippa was lost in our own thoughts. Fer me, them thoughts ranged o'er a good many notions. I'se fer sure feelin' a mite o' relief at gittin' away so clean. Thunk to myself mayhaps the prayer I shot up hit its mark. 'Bout all I could do at the moment was to hope.

Krieger'd be assurin' me that prayer works an' our get-away come at the contrivance o' the Almighty. Wanted to b'lieve setch a notion, truly I did, but I'd have to confess to bein' a mite dubious. If'n Krieg was hyar, he'd be a-huntin' fer me sure as meat'll fry. I knowed it in my bones.

On t'other hand, I wasn't so sure Cordy'd be scoutin' in this hyar direction. Oh, oncet he'd found I'se missin', I reckon he'd go a-huntin' fer a short spell, but he don' have a ton o' pluck, Cordy don'. After a few perigrinations, he'd likely give up an' wait fer me to wander outen the woods.

I set to wonderin' should I marry Cordy, if'n we got clar o' these middle kits o' hades. Second thoughts was rizzen' in my haid. All of a sudden, I'se not at all persuaded I wanted to hitch myself to a man what got no sand in his craw. Course, if'n I seed him on the far side o' the trail come daylight, I reckon that would seal the deal. I'd marry him, I would. *Thar I go ag'in*, I said to myself. *Backin' an' forthin' on Cordy. One minute, I'se settled on matrimony; the next I'se fixin' to split the quill.*

"Whatcha ponderin'?" Pippa asked, her voice soft in the night.

"Oh, 'iss an' 'at."

"Thinkin' 'bout yer man?"

"Some, I reckon." I didn't allow as to the fact I'se thinkin' on two men. "How'd you figger?"

"I'd be thinkin' on my man if'n I had one."

"Ever had a beau?" I asked.

"I've had a few sparkin' me but none that was solid fellers."

"Hard to b'lieve, Pippa, you is a fence-corner peach, sure as a brook runs to river."

"Seems the hostilities has stymied courtin', leastways in my case. Never have found one that I'd favor spendin' my life with. Better to wait an' be sure than to be o'erhasty on it."

Pippa's bit o' sagacity right thar set me off inter 'nother round o' cogitatin'. Was I bein' o'erhasty with Cordy? Mayhaps. Then too, I reasoned, Pippa's a fair bit younger'n Belle. She gots a good many more fodder-pullin' days. She might think diff'rent, she gits to be my age. After a few more minutes o' backin' and forthin' all o'er, I shook my haid an' tried to focus on the serious sitiation ahaid.

"Gittin' tired, Pippa?" I asked.

"Yup, reckon I am."

"Come daybreak, we orter give it a rest. Slip off the trail an' find us a clarin' where we can bed down fer a few hours. Wish we had somthin' to gnaw on."

I felt one o' Pippa's hands slip off'n me. A few seconds later, she reached around with a good hunk o' jerky.

"Favor some?" she said.

"Where'd it come from?"

"I been a-squirrelin' it away fer the last two days."

"Well don' that take the cake! You are plumb full o' nits, Pippa Stenson. I thankee."

We-uns both give the jerky a good chaw an' swallered a few belts o' water.

———

A pale lemony sorta sun rizz in the east. Sky was clar and cold. Pippa an' me huddled tight atop Blancey to keep a-holt o' as much warmth as possible. We-uns let the sun mount up a bit afore dismountin' and scoutin' about fer a patch o' ground where we could rest a spell.

Turns out, Blancey was the one who found the spot. She led us to a patch thirty yards or so off'n the trail where some grass was still a-growin'. They's an ole fire pit in the middle, an' I surmised them Osages or Delawares once occypied the area. Even though the last ornery little leaves was a-fallin' like raindrops in April, leavin' the hardwoods nekkid, we was clean outta sight from the trail. Them Jagger boys would have to be lookin' right squar' in our d'rection to spot us an' even then it'd take more'n one look-see. We rolled out the saddle blanket an' lay down, spoonin' one 'nother fer warmth. Blancey grazed away.

"How far you figger we come?" Pippa asked, keepin' her voice to a whisper.

"Hard to tell. Been on the trail five hours or so. Could be fifteen mile but goin's slower in the dark. Maybe ten mile."

"They know we-uns is gone by now."

"No doubt, an' they'll be comin' after us like catamount chasin' coon. So we orter not sleep too long."

"Yup," Pippa said, stiflin' a long yawn.

Cain't rightly say how long we'uns slep', but I figger the better part o' two hours. We-uns awoke 'bout the same time, an' without sayin' hardly a word, got Blancey saddled an' regained the trail.

Weather was suddenly forebodin'. Clouds all gray an' poochy with rain, mayhaps e'en snow, had rolled in. True to form, Blancey soldiered on down that skimpy trail. We kep' our ears perked fer any noise ahind us what could mean them boys was closin' in. Didn' hear nary a rustle nor a clop. Fact is, them woods was eerie quiet as we-uns trotted along. Give me a tetch o' the jitters, it did. Oncet ag'in we kep' our conversatin' to the bare 'sentials. In my daydreamin' I seed Cordy comin' 'round the next bend. Sad to say, my hankerin' never come to reality.

A coupla hours musta gone by when me an' Pippa come to a cross trail. We-uns wasn't sure which way to go, so the twain o' us slipped off Blancey to cogitate some on it. Seemed like a good idee to have the last chaw o' jerky whilst ponderin' our sitiation. As I'se swallerin' the last bite, I snaked out a handkerchief what was still fresh from my earlier warshin' an' rubbed my teeth clean as I could. Mouth felt as filthier'n the bottom o' a joree-bird's nest.

When our skimpy repast was finished, we surmised a right turn on the cross trail'd be the best option. Settled on it, I he'ped Pippa inter the saddle since it'd come her turn to ride front. Jes' as I'se fixin' to heft myself up ahind her, I heerd a chillin' sound.

A hammer click on a musket.

No mistake 'bout it.

Someone had a bead on us.

I frizz.

Pippa frizz up too.

Them little neck hairs spiked.

"Marnin' ladies."

'Twas the horrifyin' voice o' Jubal Jagger.

He come 'round from ahind the trees on the cross trail, his musket butt restin' on that ampytated leg. A strange thought come a-coursin' through my mind. Figgered I must be one lolliper surgeon to have a patient ridin' a harse over hill an' dale within a fortnight after the cuttin'.

"You is temptin' fate, Jubal," I said. "Ridin' so soon after I sawed yer laig off."

He jes' sat thar on his harse chucklin'. "Come on out boys," he shouted. "Seems we out-duganed Belle."

"How'd you-uns git hyar so fast?" I asked as Walter, Isaac, an' Groundhog come inter view.

"Took a nigh-cut," Jubal said. "You an' Pippa come 'round the long way. Seems Corbett come to his senses earlier'n you mighta hoped. Reckon you-uns figgered if'n Pippa got feisty with him an' poured fox-head down his goozle, be hours afore he come to. Didn' quite turn out that way, it seems."

'Twasn't much replyin' I could make.

"What now?" I asked. "'Pears you is on the mend an' back to yer ole ireful self, Jubal. I best be gittin' on back home. Lotsa folk in need o' healin'. Pippa's comin' with me, case you was a-wonderin' why she rid with me."

"Reckon her pa hyar might have some say 'bout it."

"Naw, don' reckon he do. Pippa's a growed woman. She kin do her own settlin' on the matter."

I clumb up on Blancey.

Them rullians jes' sat in they's saddles eyeballin' us.

"Move aside now, gents, an' we-uns'll be on our way." I said this with a good deal more intrepidity than what I true felt inside.

"Ain't goin nowhere, Belle, 'cept with us back to camp," Jubal said. He shucked his nasty li'l grin and fixed his hairy lips in a snarl.

"We-uns had us an *enfoeff*, Jubal. My services fer freedom."

"Don' recall makin' any *en-* whate'er you is a-callin' it."

"*Enfoeff*. Means a bargain. You mightn'ta been in on it, but them brothers o' your'n did. Made us an enfoeff, we did. A bargain. Foller?"

Jubal's snarl intensified. Seems he ignored my notion plumb through. 'Thout sayin 'nother word, he motioned for the others to flank me an' Pippa. Didn' 'pear as if'n we-uns could outride 'em. Them boys had more shootin'-fixin's than me an' Pippa. Could easy barrel inter us whilst we-uns was lightin' out.

"Th'ow the pea-rifle down, Belle," Jubal said. "Walter, best snake them reins from Pippa an' lead them gels along. We-uns is headin' back to camp. Now!"

It took considerable less time to return by takin' the nigh-cut. When we arrived, Groundhog hauled his daughter off Blancy and prepared to mallyhack her. I jumped down an', lickety-whoop, I affixed Groundhog to a tall tree like a june-bug on a pin. He's so s'prised, he jes' stood thar with his eyes pooched outen his haid.

"You ain't layin' a fanger on her," I said.

He jes' nodded real slow like.

By then, Jubal'd had enough. "Fetter 'em," he said.

Pippa an' me was drug deep inter the cave what went further'n I knowed. To my chagrin an Pippa's, they's two ring-stakes hammered inter the wall with chains leadin' to wrist shackles. Seems Jubal an' his men was anticipatin' takin' some Fed'ral pris'ners, so they fabercated a cave dungeon. Them boys was afeard o' me, so they give me no trouble whilst affixin the shackles, but Corbett had the perverted pleasure o' puttin' them restraints on Pippa. She jes' stared straight ahaid an' uttered nary a sound durin' the whole insultin' episode. I'd a like to th'ow Corbett inter a den o' copperhaids an' stir 'em up good. No doubt Krieg would frown on that un-Christian sentiment, but I couldn't he'p my feelin's at the moment.

So thar we was, settin' alone on the cave floor, arms a-hangin' akimbo in them chains.

My high temper cooled a good bit now oncet Corbett and them others was gone.

"Sorrow, Pippa," I said. "Thought we had it licked out thar in the woods."

She nodded.

"Seems we best be compliant fer a spell. Mayhaps bye-an'-bye they'll let their guard down, an' we kin give it 'nother try."

She nodded ag'in.

Sev'ral silent minutes passed.

"Thankee, Belle," Pippa said, her words comin' low and soft.

"Fer what?"

"Fer intercedin' with Pa. He used to beat me when I'se a shoot, an' Ma wasn't 'bout to stop him. Jes' now it felt like it was happ'nin' all o'er ag'in."

"Hate to say it Pippa, but yer Pa has snakes in his haid an' has plumb lost his scruples."

"If'n he ever had 'em to begin with."

Jes' then, a niggle-thought come to my mind. Cain't rightly say from whence, but seemed under the circumstances we was facin' a prayer might be a fine idee.

"Would you favor me sayin' a li'l prayer," I asked Pippa.

She turned to me an' cocked her haid a mite. "Not much fer prayin'," she said "but don' seem like it'd hurt none."

Fer the first time in all my borned days, I said a prayer out loud in the presence o' someone else. Come to think on it, might well a-been the first prayer I said out loud ever. 'Twasn't a long prayer, an' I said it soft-like, not wantin' to draw 'tention an' not feelin' too secure in my petitionin'.

Thar bein' nothin' more to do, me an' Pippa lapsed inter silence.

———

Next marnin' dawned all mizzly an' damp. Jubal's barkin' orders like a Redcoat colonel, tryin' to get them boys a-movin'. 'Peared we was strikin' camp an' movin' on to who knows whar. An hour later, the wains was loaded, the harses saddled, an' Blancey all hitched to the medicine wagon. To my utter consternation, Groundhog's fixin' to drive my medicine wagon. And, insult added to injury, me an' Pippa was forced to walk behind with ropes tied round our wrists and affixed to rings on the back o' the wagon. Only good part was no sacks o'er our haids. Jubal musta figgered Pippa an' me had no knowance as to where we-uns was in the first place. He'd a-been acc'rate in that 'sumption.

Not knowin' where we-uns was located made it impossible to guage d'rection with any 'surance. To boot, the sky loomed so dark an' rumbly, I become misfooled as to where the sun was. By my best reckoning, we-uns 'peared to be headin' south, mayhaps a tetch back west. What give me this idee was them hills was risin' higher an' hollers was plowin' deeper. Mighta been coursin' towards Forsyth an' the Arkysaw line. Plenty o' wild country in that d'rection. Whate'er the case might be, Jubal's goin' deeper inter the bush. Settlers scarce as snake feathers outen hyar.

As early candle-light come upon us, we-uns rolled inter a clarin' what had an ole barn an' a single pen house burnt near to the ground. It'd been abandoned many yar afore, no doubt on account o' the fire.

"Early settler by the name o' Thurgood Turner built 'iss hyar spread," Jubal announced. "Nobody lives anywhars near. "Hole up fer a spell an' git some raidin' done. Make up fer the lost time lookin' fer Belle an' Pippa."

Walter forced me an' Pippa to set on the ground with admonitions to stay put. Come ten minutes later we-uns heerd a *chink, chink, chink.* I knowed 'mediately what was afoot. One o' them goober grabbers was drivin' ring-spikes inter a wall o' the barn. They's fixin' to shackle Pippa an' me in thar. My surmisin' come true as Walter marched us inter the barn. Roof was a-fallin' in on one side an' two o' them walls was mighty slantendicular. 'Twas pure luck the whole thang didn' come a-crashin' down when they's hammerin' the ring spikes inter the one good wall. So, there we was, settin' on dewy ground an' shackled like trade slaves.

———

Days an' weeks skimmed by. When we'uns was chained up, twice a day them boys would unhitch one arm so's we-uns could take a bait o' victuals. Ever few days, Jubal'd lead his men on raids. Oncet, I heered them suggins braggin' 'bout what they done to some womenfolk. Put me an' Pippa inter a state o' extreme vapors, but t'wasn't nothin' we could do 'bout it.

Seemed like them boys had a string o' good luck. Ever'time they come back to camp, they's unhurt. With no healin' to do, Pippa an' me jes' sat in the barn witherfyin'. I wondered if'n Jubal was re-cogitatin' they's need fer us. Couldn't rightly let us go, knowancin' we could fanger 'em if'n they's ever brought to justice fer the pandemonium an' bedlam they was fomentin' all o'er the land. I didn't squander 'is 'pinion with Pippa, but I hunched we was livin' on borryed time.

Ozark Glossary

o' duckin's - everyday clothes
benighted - to be overtaken by darkness
peckerwoods - poor Whites
split the quill – separate
solid fellers - a serious suitor with matrimonial intentions
a fence-corner peach - attractive country woman
lolliper - something or someone that is admirable
out-duganed - to outwit
fox-head - whisky, especially moonshine
enfeoff - bargain (often connoted a deal with the devil)
shootin'-fixin's - firearms and ammunition
mallyhack - beat severely
slantindicular - leaning, not vertical
extreme vapors - depression of spirits

FOURTEEN

Bush

Winter, 1862–1863

Jubal's raids slackened some in late November, and they pertineer ceased all together in December. We-uns hunkered in the Turner place an' simmered down on stayin' warm an' dry. Seems snow was mod'rate, comin' in short plunges, an' meltin' perty quick. Yet, still lef' ever'thang mucky, renderin' our camp like muddy spang. Kep' a golly-whopper fire a-burnin' 'round the clock, an' that come to be the gath-erin' spot fer most hours o' the day. S'prisin'ly, we et good. Jubal's boys was good shots, I'll give 'em that. Deer and turkeys was plentiful. As winter 'proached, them wassies give partic'lar 'tention to gatherin' stored taters, apples, beans, an' setch on they's raids. So, as I say, we et good, consid'rin' our circystances.

After a spell, Jubal loosed a mite on me an' Pippa. He freed us to roam about durin' the daytime 'cept our ankles was fettered together. At night, he run us back inter the barn an' chain us tight to the wall. Three links on each hand chain. 'Tweren't 'nough play to do nothin'. Couldn't bring our hands together an' couldn't twist 'round so's to work on them ring spikes. Lord knowed we was tryin', but to no avail.

Jubal tole us he figgered we wouldn't make a run fer it durin' the day, bein' as ever'body could keep an eyeball on us. Nighttime was a diff'rent story. Notin' that our sorry getaway attempt had took place in the wee hours, Jubal was squanderin' no chances. Good thang too inasmuch as me an' Pippa spent long hours whilst alone ponderin' some options. We had conceited up some poss'bilities too, but they's dependent 'pon Jubal an' his boys lettin' they's guard down an' forgettin' to chain us up. Should p'int out that they' allus careful to chain us when goin' on raids too. That'd be our best opp'tunity since ever'body in the whole camp, 'cludin' Iris j'ined in them atrocities. No one stayed back to watch us. However, to this p'int no openin' had come our way. We jes' bided our time.

Ag'in, to my brow-raisin' s'prise, Jubal's camp kep' reasonable healthy fer that time o' yar. Isaac come down with winter fever, an' Jubal tole me to tend to him. Had me some old man's beard in the medicine wagon, a lichen what grows mostly in them cone-bearin' trees. Doc J called it usnea, but most folks a-'ferred to it as old man's beard. I'd foraged it some time back an' made a tincture with carn whiskey. Found it to be partic'larly ameliorative when one's got sobby lungs.

So, soon's the winter fever come on Isaac, I give him a harse dose o' old man's beard. I ordered Jubal's boys build a cot lean-to fer Isaac what opened to the fire. Piled blankets onter him whilst he layed on the cot. Betweenst the fire an' blanket-warmth, I could burn the fever straight outen him.

Hydrated him consid'rable too 'bout which he complained right fiercely. "Gotta make water all the time!" ole Isaac would whimper.

"'At's good, I'd retort. An' quit yer fussin'." Took o'er a week fer Isaac to pull outen the fever. Weak as a cull-list kitten, but he minced on to full recov'ry.

Christmas come an' gone. Nary a whimper 'bout it round the camp. No s'rpise thar, bein' as them squirrel turners what prisonered me an' Pippa was 'bout as Christian as a pack o' hazel splitters. Jes' afore I falled asleep in my chains on Christmas night, I conjured in my haid what Krieg mighta been doin'. No doubt he's a-preachin' an' all joyful like 'mongst his people.

I'd perty much kep' the tears stoppered up good fer all the time Pippa an' me had been fettered, but on that partic'lar night, the dam ruptured good, an' them salty drops come in a torrent. I tried to hide ever'thang so as not to rile up Pippa lyin' by me, but 'tweren't no use.

Much as she could, she hitched herself inter a sittin' pose an' give me a long sad look.

"You okay Belle?"

I nodded but couldn't be certain she could see me, bein' as dark was a-comin' on.

"You is a mighty strong gel, Belle," she said, not waitin' fer no words from me. "Cain't 'magine how barb'rous this has to be fer you. Stole away from yer home in the middle o' the night an' kep' prisoner all these weeks by Jubal. Don' rightly know how you shut them tears in all this time. Seems fittin' to me you should have yerself a good ole fashioned snubbin'. Maybe flood a tetch o' that sadness outen you. Don' mind Pippa hyar. If'n I could reach you, I'd give you a good hug. 'Thout you, I'd a been in a sorrow state. No tellin' what them boys— even my own pa—mighta done to me. Even though you is they's captive, them boys is skeered o' you, Belle. Don' figger it's to they's best int'rest to cross you an' by 'sociation to cross me. We might be lashed up tight to this wall, but we is stitchin' together fair well an' you is the mucilage. I do thankee Belle."

I cried fer a minute or two more afore pullin' myself together an' sniffin' my dribbles away. "'Preciate yer words, Pippa," I said. "I ain't never been one fer Christmas, but me an' Doc J would have a nice meal, some rum puddin', an' give each other li'l gifts. I miss setch as that." I didn' allow as to how Krieg was mostly the cause o' my salivated 'motions.

We sat thar in silence fer a good spell on that Christmas night ruminatin' in our own thoughts. It was well past candle-lightin' time, an' Jubal's boys was quieted down out by the fire when Pippa give me some news what I h'ain't heerd afore. "Caught a few snatches o' what they's layin' out," she said. "They's fixin' on movin' ag'in, next week or so."

"Where to?" I asked.

"They's a little town called Colette Springs."

"Heerd o' it. Cain't say as to whar 'tis."

"Perty much a Fed'ral town seems. Jubal wants to rout them poor folks in Colette Springs an' take o'er the town fer a spell. Place is far inter the brush. Leastways that's what Jubal reckons. Figgers he can hole up thar fer a spell an' live more civilized like. Sleep in a proper house an' all. Jubal's tard o' campin' out an' wants to tuck some comfort 'round him."

"Wonder what that means fer we-uns."

"Hard to say," Pippa said. "I'd specylate they's fixin' to take us along. Don' see as how they'd be lettin' us go. Cain't 'magine they'd kill us, special since we doctored up ole Isaac good. Need to hold our taters an' look fer some gaps."

With that, we slipped inter sleep, huddled under some o' them nasty blankets what Jubal provided as a hedge ag'in' the cold. Me an' Pippa expected the Colette Springs raid to come to pass in short time, but day after day went on. Then weeks passed. Nothin'.

Ever' day a couple o' them mole crickets'd ride outen camp on reconnaissance forays. When they come back, they'd hole up with Jubal. Me an' Pippa never was tole what the happenstances was, but we figgered the delay meant they's Union patrols sashayin' about, an' Jubal wasn't takin' no chances. Men was gettin' antsy too, a-slaverin' fer some action. Ever'night they'd get inter the carn whiskey an' applejack. Musta drunk twenty gallon since we settled inter the Turner place. Ever' raid had as a prime objective the securin' o' more likker.

One night, near to the end o' January, Groundhog got a-sluggin' down what he thunk was some simon pure, water white applejack. Turned out 'twas a skunky batch what got him so drunk he's a-creenin' round crazier'n a boiled owl. Fell direck'ly inter the fire and sizzled hisself right good. Walter come a'runnin' to the barn, an' he unchained me an' Pippa, hollerin' fer us to tend to Groundhog. I'd jes' as soon leave him to blister up an' let the animalcules have they's way with him. Not too sure, but what Pippa wasn't o' the same mind. However, I let ole Hippocrates an' his oath have sway.

Didn' take an abundance o' insight to see that ole Groundhog was in a turrible state. He's all scorched up on his back an' right arm. Burnt the coat an' shirt right off'n his sorry hide.

Blisters was already formin' up. Not a good sign. Groundhog's openin' screams had subsided inter whimpers. Ag'in my baser nature, I give him some comfortable words whilst sendin' Pippa to the medicine wagon to fotch some necessary s'plies.

"I knowed that hurts bad, Groundhog," I said. "I got some opiates what'll ease the pain some. Heaven knows yer sorry soul deserves this. Whatcha git fer partakin' in that skunky hooch. Be that as it may,

Belle'll fix you up, ease the hurtin' some." When Pippa come back, I larned her how to make cold compresses an' to apply a plantain poultice. So happens, Iris Monahan had some honey an' after a coupla hours we-uns put a gentle smear on the burned parts. Kivvered it o'er with clean gauze.

"One o' you boys need to git a shirt fer Groundhog," I said. "Take it o'er to the crick, bust the ice, an' warsh it plumb good. Then bring it back hyar an' dry it by the fire. When it's dry, help him inter it. Don' tetch it no more'n you got to. Don' want the critters to git the upper hand."

Course they all looked at me like I'se some sort o' goomer-doctor, but they knowed Groundhog had a fair chance o' comin' out on the good side o' this calamity so long as Belle's in charge.

Jubal 'lowed me an' Pippa to stay up with Groundhog 'til the opiates took a-holt o' him. Then he marched us right back inter the barn an' chained us up.

"Yer welcome!" I shouted, loud 'nough fer all to hear. I muttered a string o' unsavories under my breath. Pippa nodded, an' we settled in fer some shut-eye.

Ever' few hours, we changed them dressin's on Groundhog an' kep' the wound as clean as possible under the filthy circystances what we was abidin' in. To ever'one's relief, no infection come upon Groundhog, and he set inter mendin'.

Pain come in spurts, but day-by-day, it cut back some. Scar tissue was a-formin' but wasn't nothin' we could do 'bout that. I didn' mention it to Groundhog, but I s'pected he'd have some restriction o' mobility in that right arm. Not only scar tissue but some diminution o' muscle seemed to be contributin' to his arm limits. Sorrow to say, but I'se certain he could still hold a rifle an' pull a trigger.

'Nother week passed by. Seems they's waitin' fer Groundhog's burn to heal up s'ficiently to ride. I liked to think Jubal didn' trust him to stay behind with us. Lord knows what he mighta done to me an' Pippa in spite o' his sorry state. He was burnt on the outside an' burnin' on the inside towards me, even though I doctored him up good. Man's evil an' ingratitude knowed no bounds.

Come the first or mayhaps the second o' Febuary, low an' menacin' clouds settled o'er the Turner place. To our surprise, they's a good deal o' activity in the camp. As we'uns was a-watchin' the goin's and comin's, Iris sashayed o'er to where we'uns set and proffered me an' Pippa a monstrous plate o' fatback, biscuits, an' bird-eye gravy.

"What's the 'casion?" I asked.

"Goin' on a raid," Iris said. "Don' figger on bein' back 'til lamp-lightin' time. So tuck it away."

When we finished our breakfast, we was back in them infernal chains. Less than an hour later, we-uns heerd the whole camp skeedaddle quicker'n a snake goin' through a holler log.

Jes' thinkin' on that turn o' phrase put me in mind o' Krieg as I ruminated 'pon his visage fer a time, half dreamin' he might come to find me an' be my knight in shinin' armor. Krieg an' me read some snatches o' Sir Walter Scott's *Ivanhoe*. Fer a short time, while ever'thin' was quiet as a graveyard, I set there an' fancied myself as Rowena with Krieg as my Ivanhoe. 'Twas a pleasant story in my mind.

After a spell, I shook my haid to scoot them idle thoughts away. Wouldn't be no knight in shinin' armor fer Belle. Fer certain, I didn' see Cordy in that role. He jes' wasn't a knight in shinin' armor. Have to confess, as the days an' weeks unfurled, my ardor had cooled a fair amount when it come to Cordy. Course I s'posed it all might change up when I seed him ag'in, if'n I ever seed him ag'in. The backin' an' forthin' on Cordy was never fur away in my mind. Seems at the moment, they's more backin' than forthin'. No sense in dwellin' too long on it. Better thangs to think about, so Pippa an' me engaged in some cogitatin' on what oppytunities fer escape might befall us in Colette Springs.

Hours rolled by. Me an' Pippa jes' set thar, all hobbled and fettered. Come candle-lightin' time, they's no sign o' the Jubal Jagger gang. We didn't worry none 'til what we reckoned was the wee hours o' the followin' marnin'.

"Where you figger them boys is?" Pippa asked when the light o' day come filterin' through the chinks.

"No idee, but they allus come back," I said, tryin' to sound courageful, but I'd be disingenuatin' if'n I didn' admit I was frettin' a good bit inside.

"Thirsty. Been kindly o' them to leave us a canteen."

"Had they knowed they' be so long, I'd like to b'lieve they would have."

"Wonder if'n somethin' happened? Remember, we heerd they's

Fed'rals patrollin' 'round hyar. Don' s'pose they cotched up with Jubal in Colette Spring, do you?"

"Hope not. Heinous as Jubal's been, them Fed'rals would shoot 'em all on sight as enemy combatants."

'At thought shuffled us inter a distressin' tailspin.

If that wasn't enough, the temp'ture had dropped a goodly amount. Pippa an' me curled tight as we could under them nasty blankets but 'twas comin' on cold as an Eskimo's hammer.

Plucky gel though she was, Pippa herself commenced to snubbin'.

"Honey, I'se sorrow," I said. "I'se shore they'll be back afore long. I tried to give her some more words to ease her frettin'.

Just then, a whiffle o' wind begun to blow. Could feel it comin' through the chinks an' skitterin' 'round the edges where the walls had fallen in. An' then, sudden-like, come the snow right on the heels o' them first puffs o' wind. To our risin' misfortune, they wasn't big, fluffy snowflakes neither but them hard, stingy li'l pelters what bored inter our skin.

We ducked our heads under the blanket best we could an' sunk down deep inter a fearful misery. Under that blanket, breathin' in the stench of sweat and dross, 'cumulated o'er decades in want o' a good warshin', I sensed the first tentacles o' deep dread. They coiled 'round my heart and wrung on it, like one o' them python snakes what I read 'bout long ago.

Snow coated my blanket, freezin' it an' intensificatin' the obscene horror and blackness inter which I had fallen. Me an' Pippa was set on a course what led to icin' o'er an' endin' our borned days frizz solid in Thurgood Turner's slantendicular, fallin' down barn.

————

Dark come upon me an' Pippa. Utter dark. Utter quiet. I woke up some, an' to my brow-raisin' s'prise, one o' my hands had slipped outen the shackle an' lay tucked up under the blanket. My fangers clutched a small tin. Couldn't fer the life o' me figger what had happened. I ruminated 'pon it some an' come to the conclusion that someone had unlocked one o' them iron wrist cuffs. Mighta been Iris comin' back to camp an' takin' a smidgin' o' pity. Cold as my hand was, that little tin was nice an' warm in my clutches.

After a spell, I managed to slide the lid off'n it, an' to my o'erwhelmin' delight, I could feel some locofocos nestled inside. My heart lept higher'n the hills o' Jubernaw. Locofocos! I could use 'em for light an' mayhaps cogitate a way o' loosin' Pippa an' me from them infernal chains. Havin' e'en one arm free give us a fightin' chance. Might e'en be able to reach them shackle keys what they hung high and outen reach.

I fotched a locofoco from the li'l tin an' scoured 'round with my hand 'til I found a rough rock. I struck the locofoco an' a flame burst from the tip.

Oh my, that was a delight. I give sev'ral long seconds jes' to starin' inter that dazzlin' flame. Seemed like all o' a sudden I'se warm as a new-baked 'tater. Made no sense to me, a li'l flame like that thawin' me out so thoroughly. 'Twasn't o' a mind to complain, mind you'uns. That's for shore. Jes' a bit mystifyin'.

I stole a glance o'er to Pippa. She's breathin' real heavy, so I'se confident full shut-eye had come 'pon her. I'd wake her in due time an' share the good fortune what had come pass. For now, though, I jes' wanted to waller in the warmth for a spell. Selfish, I knowed, but I'd fritter jes' one locofoco. Jes' one. The rest we'd use to 'luminate our escape, oncet we had a plan drawed up in our minds.

As I'se starin' at the flame, what had come 'bout halfway down the stick, I seed a figure, sorta shrouded like in the dim light ag'in' the far wall o' the barn. Skeered me half to death at first and I rizz up as fer as I could in my fetters. Feller was wearin' a white robe with a red sash 'round his middle. Didn' say nothin'. Jes' stood there lookin' at me. Edspression on his face piped a sense o' calm inter me.

I knowed in a quick tick he wasn't thar to do me an' Pippa no harm. "Who might you be?" I whispered.

He didn't answer me back but give me a teensy smile, jes' the barest o' smiles, but that smile rushed inter me the mos' joyful sense o' peace what I'd e'er knowed. Nothin' what'd e'er happened to me in all my borned days could tetch the deep down tranquility and concord permeatin' my soul.

Then, it come 'pon me like a bolt outen the blue. Standin' afore me was none other'n Jesus hisself, silent an' strong an' still. As I'se peerin' at him, all balmied inside, he stretched out one arm an' beckoned to me to foller him.

Jes' then, the locofoco flame guttered an' died.

Ozark Glossary

simmered down on - concentrate or focus upon
muddy spang - mixture of gravy and butter
wassies – wasps
conceited - imagine, contrive
winter fever – pneumonia
hazel splitters - wild hog, razorback
salivated - mangled, shattered
taters - be patient
some gaps – chances, opportunities
goomer-doctor - witch doctor
Jubernaw - Phrase of unknown origin, perhaps a malapropism
or a creation.

PART 3

KRIEGER ANDREWES

FIFTEEN

All Souls Parish, Saint Louis

Winter, 1862—1863

My work at All Souls increased through the fall and early winter of 1862 as Gridley piled more responsibility upon me. He now required me to preach three Sundays a month, leaving him but one sermon to prepare every thirty days. He added additional weekday services but refused to officiate at any of them. All funerals and weddings fell to me, except when someone specifically requested Gridley, which was never.

After several months of this grueling routine, I found myself drained of energy and despondent. It had come to affect my health as well. I suffered through a nasty bout of the grippe in November, and I never fully recovered. I found myself subject to wracking fits of coughing. It was so severe at times that I had to halt mid-sermon for several minutes before it subsided. Of course, the parishioners were concerned, and the two physicians attending All Souls prescribed a variety of concoctions, none of which had any ameliorative effect whatsoever. I yearned for the ministrations of Belle Potts.

I found Annie's reaction to my illness disturbing. She seemed at once annoyed and wary, irritated by my coughing and asthenia, fearful of contracting the disease herself. Thus, she kept her distance, interacting with me for brief snatches of time and only as necessary.

Understandably, this wounded my heart. I did not covet her sympathies, as such, but I began to worry if she could truly accede to that phrase during the Solemnization of Matrimony, which read, *Wilt thou love him, comfort him, honor, and keep him in sickness and in health.* Perhaps once married, her demeanor would change, but a trace of doubt had lodged in my mind.

In the matter of matrimony, Annie and I had established a date—the first Saturday after Easter, April 11, 1863. As the year of our Lord, 1862, drew to a close, plans for the wedding began in earnest. Of course the bishop would conduct the service with Dean Worthingham assisting. I had selected Marty Muldown as my witness, and he heartily agreed. It would mean traveling from his curacy in Kansas City, but he was more than willing to brave the dangers, and I felt humbled by his unbridled enthusiasm. My joy increased when Marty added that he had been granted a few days off following Christmas and would return to Saint Louis to visit his family. He promised to call upon me, and my spirits were buoyed at the thought.

The temperature plummeted on Monday, December 28, fixating a light dusting of snow that had freshened the grounds of All Souls the previous evening. The Christmas services had been completed, and I had at least this day for respite. I brewed some camp coffee on the potbellied stove of the Hermitage and savored the flavor before collapsing exhausted onto a rickety canebrake chair and throwing a quilt over my legs to ward off the chill in that drafty hut. Though I did not smoke, I cinched the smoking jacket I had inherited from my father and inhaled the lingering scent of Cavendish tobacco that had so permeated our house in south Saint Louis while Papa was still alive.

As I sat there, worrisome thoughts percolated to the surface of my mind. For a number of days, I had begun to wonder if parish ministry were indeed the right calling for me. I was so overwhelmed by the work that I found myself bereft of joy. The unremitting routine and oppressive administrative responsibilities ground me down.

I understood that divine supplication might be my only solace, and I did take my worries to God in prayer several times each day. Yet, I experienced no relief from the malaise that had lately engulfed me.

Anticipation of my marriage to Annie did little to lighten my mood. What I most dearly missed was the pastoral care of the sick and wounded in the company of the Sisters of Divine Compassion. When sitting at the bedside of one who suffered, I felt most fully alive, most fully myself. Of course, I had occasion to minister to the sick and dying in All Souls, but somehow it did not seem the same nor did it provide the sense of wholeness I experienced at Laclede Hospital. These thoughts evoked the memory of one dear occasion many months ago in the Ozark hills, not long before I took my leave from Belle.

I had offered to assist in the preparation of some stock medications from the varieties of plants she had foraged. We were busy in the shed making a tincture from a lichen she called old man's beard, which we immersed in corn whiskey. As we completed the task, several shouts could be heard outside the shed walls. Belle opened the door and there stood a man and his wife. He carried his toddling daughter who appeared asleep or unconscious. From the looks of wretched fear upon their faces, Belle and I immediately grasped the gravity of the situation.

"Charlie, Millie," Belle said. "Scoot on up to the surgery an' put yer li'l one on the table thar."

Once in the cave, I stood to the side as Belle began her examination of the little girl, asking questions of her parents with a comforting and confident air.

"Can you-uns recall what happened to her?"

"She falled outen the wagon yestiday," Charlie said. "Cracked her haid on a rock."

"Did she spew?" Belle asked.

"O my, yes," Millie said. "Sluiced outen her in a torrent. Shot plumb near acrost the room, oncet we got her home."

Belle nodded, gently drew the child to a seated position on the table, and asked her several questions, I presume to assess memory and recall, orientation, and concentration. Reaching into one of the mahogany drawers, Belle retrieved a small hammer, with which she tapped the little girl at several points on the arms and legs. She also struck a locofoco and brought it from beyond the girl's visual range in close to her eye and back again. She repeated this several times with both eyes.

When she finished her examination, Belle cuddled the small child in her long arms and turned to face the parents. "Seems she got concussed when her haid hit that rock. T'ain't much to do 'ceptin' to keep an eye on her. I reckon she'll be tard, like she is now, an' maybe carp some 'bout a haidache. Let her rest. That's the most important thing. Keep her bedtime reg'lar an' let her nap whene'er she's a mind to. Might be important to wake her up a few times during the night fer at least a week or so. See if'n she kin wiggle her fangers an' toes. Let me know if'n she cain't. I reckon she'll pull through in fine fettle, but it'll take some time, mayhaps a month or more."

Belle shot me a quick glance. "Pardon my manners," she said. "'Iss hyar is my friend Krieger Andrewes. He's studyin' to be a preacher."

I nodded to Millie and shook hands with Charlie.

"Krieg," Belle said softly. "Would you favor sayin' a quick prayer fer 'iss li'l one?"

I cannot describe how I flowered within at this unanticipated request. It took me several long seconds to recover my senses sufficiently to draw near to the child and place my hand on her shoulder, just above Belle's arm. I beckoned for the parents and Belle to gather with me. Instinctively, we held hands and bowed our heads. For the rest of my life I would count that prayer in a Missouri cave as one of the most intimate moments I have ever experienced.

Sitting there reveling in this memory amidst my shivvers, I heard a sharp knock on the Hermitage door. Without the energy to rise from my chair, I called out to my visitor. "Come in," and turned to see the grand shape of Marty Muldown framed in the doorway. He stomped his feet, removed his gloves and scarf, pulled me to my feet, and smothered me in a bear hug. He pushed me to arms length and inspected my visage.

"Krieger Andrewes," he said. "You look like you've been sorting wildcats. What gives, my friend?"

"Rough few weeks," I said and fell back into my chair. "Coffee on the stove and a cup there on the shelf."

Marty shucked his coat in a heap on the floor and poured himself a coffee. He retrieved the only other canebrake chair and tested it gingerly before settling his girth upon the wobbly seat.

"Good to see you, Marty. I've been looking forward to your visit."

"The sentiments are mutual," he said.

For the next several minutes, upon my prodding, he chronicled his work in Kansas City. To my great envy, his situation was far more accommodating than mine. The priest for whom he worked was a gentle and supportive mentor, one sensitive to Marty's neophytism.

As Marty's discourse wound down, the conversation inevitably turned to my situation, which I described with as much objectivity as possible, trying to keep whining and grumbling at bay. Brow furrowed, Marty listened intently. After several long seconds, he said, "I take it, you can't go to Gridley and beg for relief?"

"At best, it would fall on deaf ears," I said. "At worst, I would be subject to a violent tongue lashing. I fear the man is not in his full senses much of the time. His reactions are often explosive and unbefitting."

"But there is your marriage on the horizon. Surely that musters some delight."

When I did not respond, Marty's gaze intensified. "Is everything all right with Annie?" he asked, his words carried on a soft and supportive voice.

"I think so."

"That does not strike me as an overwhelming affirmation."

I nodded, perhaps admitting to myself for the first time that it was not. "I'm just tired and that no doubt suppresses my enthusiasm. I'm sure it will return if I can get some rest."

"I do hope so," Marty said, draining his cup and puckering from the bitter grounds that washed into his mouth. "But I have always known you to be a man of extraordinarily high energy. If anyone can carry Saint Gridley's water, it is you. Moreover, yours is a wonderful parish, aside from Gridley. One day I might favor serving it myself. But that is neither here nor there. I must say, to see you in this depressed state, gives me pause to wonder if there isn't something more, something other than the difficulties with your work."

Realizing I had no one else upon whom I might unburden myself, I inhaled deeply and gave off a long sigh.

"I'm not certain," I said, "if I am of suitable disposition for this work." Marty opened his mouth to protest, but I stilled him with a raise of my hand. "Hear me out. I shall admit that my thoughts are sullied by the illness. I grasp that our work is a calling, and I do not sense any diminution in my assurance that the Lord has a purpose for me in His ministry. Yet, I have wondered of late if this purpose is most fully expressed in the confines of a prosperous and comfortable cure. Perhaps there is another vineyard in which I should labor."

Marty continued to study me with furrowed brow. "Are you thinking of a professorship, of becoming a don?"

I shook my head. "Not at all."

"But you have that experience, at least in part, gained whilst teaching the ancient languages at Cranmer."

"True," I said. "But that is not where my heart rests."

"Then what?"

"I wonder if I might of better service as a chaplain. I feel as if I should be serving the poor, the sick, and the disenfranchised rather than tending to the needs of the affluent—though the good Lord knows they need kindly ministries as well."

"But where would be your chapel, Krieg. There are not many places in these States that seek the services of a private chaplain. Are you casting an eye to the military?"

"No, not the military as such, though I would be honored to tend to the spiritual needs of soldiers. I could not re-enter the field as an Army chaplain. My leg would not stand the stresses of battle. I fear there is no place for me...nat least no place where I might secure a living wage."

"Have you confided these concerns with your betrothed?"

"Therein lies my second worry."

"You have my ear."

"She is acting in a peculiar way of late, or at least so it seems to me."

Marty did not fill the pause ushered in by these words.

I continued. "She seems unmoved by my condition and the exacerbations caused by my circumstances. She is standoffish and even appears peevish at times."

"Perhaps you are misjudging her disposition."

"Perhaps, but I fear not."

"And how long...."

"Thinking back on the matter, it occurs to me that her attitude changed shortly after she accepted my proposal for marriage. It is as if that singular event jibed her sail, and she changed course. I can think of nothing I did to cause such a shift in mood."

"My counsel, good friend, is to divest yourself of these concerns with her directly. You have pledged yourselves to one another, and the banns of marriage will soon be published. It is better to seek resolution with her now rather than let matters fester, wouldn't you say?"

I nodded. "You offer wise counsel, but I do not know how best to broach the subject."

"Perhaps a spot of prayer on this will open the opportunity for you."

"Yes... well... who can argue with that?"

Marty remained in my company for another hour of reminiscing, pondering the course of the war, and pledging to remain faithful in correspondence for the weeks leading up to my wedding. When he left, I felt a measure of relief at having voiced the sources of my disquiet. Yet, the relief remained diluted by their uncertain resolution. I stoked the fire in the potbellied stove and crawled onto my cot hoping for the liberation that attends a long and uninterrupted nap.

It seems that when one prays for an opportunity, the Lord answers at the most inopportune time. I had just drifted into a pleasant dream state when a sharp knock sounded on the door of the Hermitage. It took the better part of a minute for me to reorient myself to my surroundings, the time of day, and the persistent knocks. When I finally did stumble to the door, I beheld Annie standing on the porch, shivering beneath her wrap.

"May I come in?" she asked, her voice laced with irritation at having to wait for me to assemble myself.

"Of course," I said and stood aside to let her enter.

"Why are you cooped up like an invalid?"

"I am trying to rest, hoping at last to shake this illness that has befallen me."

"I should say there is much to be accomplished and little time for naps," she said, settling on my canebrake chair with an air of urgent purpose. "Within the fortnight," she began. "We must busy ourselves with the invitations. I shall pen and address them, but I require your assistance with the invitation list. I have begun in earnest the gathering and manufacture of items for my trousseau. Daddy has supplied me with a beautiful trunk in which to place the items, though it will not be sufficient for the many items I *must* place therein. Already, I have had to commandeer one of the Effinghams' upstairs rooms to lodge the dresses, petticoats, shawls, and linens. And, did I tell you, Bobble's wife has agreed to take me into town to engage the services of a dress-maker? You know, white is the new color for wedding dresses, at least among those who can afford it. I am happy to assure you that Daddy will pay for a white dress. Now, dear me, I have the stress of finding suitable material. I shall spend an entire day at McClelland and Skruggs Dry Goods—you know, the one on Fourth Street—where I shall acquire several necessities. Perhaps they will have the white mate-rial suitable for the dress. And have you yet purchased my wedding ring? You might contact Mister George Collier Robbins. I understand he is a fine jeweler and skilled in engraving in gold. You *are* thinking gold, are you not?"

For long uninterrupted minutes, Annie prattled on about the details of the wedding, all of which furthered my despondency and drove me to nearly to the breaking point. When I could suffer it no longer, I raised my hand. "Stop! Please stop."

Annie halted in mid-sentence and looked at me, wide-eyed. "Whatever is the matter?" she asked.

"Annie, I know you are pouring your heart into this wedding, and for that I am very grateful, but I am bearing a heavy burden that I must confide."

The dilation of her eyelids increased. "What?"

"I am following the counsel of my friend Marty. He visited me earlier today and opined that I should share my concerns with you." Without waiting for her to accede to this conversational turn, I opened the dreaded topic. "For some time, I have been questioning whether parish ministry is for me." I then repeated much of what I had expressed to Marty, leaving open the unresolved consequences of a change in vocation and what it would mean for us as a married couple. When I finished, Annie simply continued to stare at me, her breathing arrested, and her mouth slightly ajar.

"Don't be silly," she said at last, on a long exhalation, and offered me the same patronizing smile she might employ with a misguided child. "You will soon be the next rector of All Souls. I overheard Uncle Thad disclose as much to Auntie the other evening. He had spoken to the bishop. Reverend Fitzsimmons's days are numbered here. The complaints from the parishioners have risen to a clamor, and some-thing must be done. In fact, the removal will be accomplished before our nuptials. You are the heir apparent. The bishop plans to ordain you to the priesthood *toute suite.* I meant to tell you this, but I had not yet the opportunity, consumed as I am with the wedding. And...." She clasped her hands in delight, staring dreamily at the dilapidated ceiling. "The house on the hill will be ours! The Fitzsimmons must move. Just think. That grand mansion will be ours. Oh, the receptions and entertainments we will host!" She returned her gaze to me, now with a stern frown. "So no more of this flannel about the unsuitability of parish ministry. I don't wish to hear of it again."

This declaration ushered in another thirty minutes of vocal perigrinations about the wedding. When finished, Annie stood and, with the barest of farewells, marched out the door of the Hermitage with nothing more than a tittering *ta ta.*

I closed my eyes. Rector of All Souls? I could not imagine a more crushing work. To be sure, I had been the *de facto* rector for some months, but the thought of this as a permanent assignment flooded me with an unremitting dread. By disposition and vigor, I could not have been more ill-suited for the work.

As evening drew near, I continued to stare at the flames in the potbellied stove. My mind churned with tormenting thoughts of my future—of a life with Annie Worthingham. *Annie, Annie! Is your love for me only to secure a place in high society? Do you not care for me as a man? For who I am deep within? For the genuine Krieger Andrewes? You show no concern beyond yourself, and that I cannot imagine is the proper attitude for a clergyman's wife.*

Pondering these matters plunged me into such despair that I came nearly to the breaking point.

After a long night of fitful sleep and more fitful prayer, I made the decision to journey into downtown Saint Louis and have a long conversation with my bishop. I determined that a preemptive disclosure on my part might stay his intention to ordain me prematurely to the priesthood and install me as Rector of All Souls. The following morning, I donned my clerical blouse and collar, hitched my horse to the church wain, and clopped my way to Saint Michael's, where our bishop served as rector along with his diocesan duties. When I arrived at the parish house, the bishop greeted me in his magenta cassock.

"Deacon Andrewes, what a fortuitous visit. I have been meaning to summon you for some important conversation. Do come in. May I have Alice brew you a cup of tea?"

"No thank you, your grace, I will be fine."

He waived me off. "No *your grace*. I've never cared for that appellation. It seems pompous and unsuitable for one called by grace of our Lord. It is *His* grace. Now please sit and tell me what is on your mind."

With stammering tongue, I disclosed my physical and emotional indisposition. He listened with his elbow upon his desk and a forefinger bisecting his lips. He said nothing. I then launched into my growing reservations about my suitability for parish ministry. As I proceeded, vertical furrows sprouted in the center of his brow. When at last I finished, I felt relieved to have it all off my chest but uneasy as to how the bishop might respond.

An exceedingly long pause ensued.

He exhaled and leaned back in his chair staring at the ceiling. "Well, I must say that is a most disheartening revelation. It has been my intent to make some changes at All Souls. Mister Fitzsimmons is to be removed. Complaints of his irascibility and failure to accept the full responsibilities of his office have reached me. At the same time, I have heard of your diligent work, brilliant preaching, and pastoral sensitivity. My plan is to ordain you to the priesthood within the month, force Gridley into retirement, and require he and Mrs. Fitzsimmons to move from the rectory to another house I have secured for them. Thence, I would install you as the rector. So you can imagine my consternation at hearing of your reticence for parish ministry. It is quite a fly in the ointment."

"Yes, sir, I do see that, but I fear I am not up to the task."

"Of course you are. You are already doing it."

Another lengthy and disturbing pause ensued.

"You realize I have the authority to direct the events I have just outlined," the bishop said. "You have taken a vow of obedience to me as your bishop, a vow before God."

I forced a dry swallow. "Yes, sir, I do know this."

"I have no one else to take charge of All Souls and no other vacant cure for you. So, I fear I have no choice."

"I see."

"However, you are a fine cleric and have served well under difficult circumstances. Your work at Cranmer Hall and your accepting the burden of working under Mister Fitzsimmons have not gone unnoticed in this office. I am not unmindful of your depleted circumstances, exacerbated I'm sure by your upcoming nuptials and all the preparations that attend thereto."

"Yes, sir, thank you."

"I would like to make a suggestion. Please take a brief time off. I'm thinking a fortnight, perhaps at the outside three weeks. Go to your mother's or wherever you desire. But remove yourself entirely from the premises. Entirely. Or the work will continue to hound you. I shall pen a directive to Gridley and a pastoral letter to be read to the congregation explaining that you are on furlough for two to three weeks. Take the time to recuperate physically and spiritually. When you return, I shall ordain you and have my difficult conversation with Gridley Fitzsimmons. What say you?"

"Mister Fitzsimmons will come unhinged."

"Of that I am quite aware, but I remain his spiritual authority and will remind him of the same. He will do as I say. But *you*, what think *you*?"

Realizing that this would likely be the best offer I would receive, I accepted with suitable gratitude.

"You should leave immediately. As soon as you can get your affairs in order. What will Miss Worthingham say?"

"She will be quite upset I fear, but when it is an order from the bishop, there will be little to which she can object."

"Very well. See to it my good man. Let us pray."

Following prayers for my recuperation, recovery, safe travels, and favorable reception by one and all, I made my way back to the Hermitage, my heart somewhat lighter but in no way fully unburdened. Now I faced the daunting task of breaking this news to Annie.

The occasion occurred that very evening when she stopped by to rattle away on the wedding. After fifteen minutes of enduring her minutia, I held up my hand.

"Annie, I beg of you, give me pause. I have something important to announce."

She widened her eyes and parted her mouth, as has become her expression when anything should halt her verbal barrage. I noted that her mien did not change when I had disclosed the direct order from my bishop. After perhaps ten eye blinks, unaccompanied by speech, she stood and put her hands on her hips, and effected a withering glare. In slow cadence and barely disguised vexation, she proceeded to excoriate me, concluding her invective with, "You put the bishop up to this. You do not have your heart in *our* future and I find it profoundly unsettling."

I shrugged and replayed my trump card. "I assure you this was the bishop's suggestion, and I have no choice but to obey. I've taken a vow."

"Where will you go?"

"I have no idea."

"Will it be away from here?"

"That is a condition of the bishop's directive."

"And away from me!"

"Just a fortnight."

Her pique rose to the boiling point. She slapped me across the face, burst into tears, and stormed out of the Hermitage.

For some strange reason, I found myself relieved. With these difficult conversations behind me, I turned my attentions to where I might go and when. It took little time to confirm the inkling I had developed. A fortnight—perhaps three weeks—would permit me time to travel to southwest Missouri and engage the curative powers of Belle Potts.

SIXTEEN

Southwest Missouri

January, 1863

The Federal government had a firm grip on the Southwest Branch of the Pacific Railroad, making the journey from St. Louis to Rolla quite safe. I boarded the train at 10:15 on January 5, 1863, and seven hours later after ten stops, I arrived in Rolla, the eastern terminus of the line. With each stop—Franklin, Saint Clair, Stanton— the pressures crowding my mind diffused. Sullivan, Bourbon, Cuba—I found myself breathing more easily, able to exchange large volumes of air without paroxysms of coughing—Rosati, Saint James, Dillon, Rolla.

When I finally stepped off the train and on to the platform in Rolla, I felt at last that I was on the mend. There lurked in the back of my mind that cloying trepidation of ministry and marriage, but with a two-, perhaps three-week buffer, I could keep it at bay and live rather refreshingly in the moment.

Of course, in my rationalizations for this westbound journey, I had yearned to seek Belle's medical advice and treatment. This pretext seemed to have faded along with my symptoms. Yet, I knew I would proceed to seek her out.

A nagging unease surfaced everytime I anticipated this pending reunion with Belle. I had no knowledge of her life in the eighteen months we had been separated. As with me, she may have found a life partner, could be happily married, perhaps even be a mother by now. I could not have expected her to live her life in the slim likelihood that I would one day return. And even if I did return, as indeed I now was, what would have been my motivation and what would I have desired? After all, I was betrothed and the wedding was nigh. I would have to present myself as a suffering man, in need of medical attention. This could be the only moral purpose, but its underlying reality seemed to ebb by the hour.

Most of the passengers on the train were military personnel reporting for duty down the line. Freight cars hauled ordinance, artillery, rifled muskets, medical supplies, and rations. Most of this materiel was destined for the military depot in Springfield. Following the Battle of Wilson's Creek, Union forces recaptured the town and began to fortify it. I learned all of this from one Major Marsden who sat opposite me on the leg from Sullivan to Rolla.

"Built four forts in and around Springfield," Major Marsden informed me. "All under the control of General Egbert Brown. Did you know he was the former mayor of Toledo?"

"I did not. I've been somewhat out of touch since being wounded at Wilson's Creek. I'm no longer in the service."

"You were at Wilson's Creek? A significant battle, I'm told.

"To be sure."

For the next several stops, I replayed the battle for the young Major and he, in turn, gave me something of a picture of the situation in southwest Missouri and the Union *Army of the Frontier.*

"I'm bound for Springfield and south from there," I said as we neared Rolla. "Can I expect safe travel?"

He shrugged. "It gets more dangerous once you leave Rolla. Of course, Bushwhackers abound. That's the real danger."

My stomach knotted. "Is Jagger still wreaking havoc?"

"He's the worst. There are other smaller, less threatening groups, but Jagger's the nastiest of the bunch. In point of fact, I have new orders to report to Springfield where I am to recruit a small detachment for the sole purpose of locating and neutralizing guerrilla raiders. My first mission will be to find Jagger."

I nodded and a new disquiet entered my mind.

I booked a room in the new Grant House Hotel, arriving in time for the simple supper of scrapple, potatoes, and honeyed coffee served in the dining room. A fellow traveler, Abraham Waugh, sat opposite me. I learned he planned to travel west as far as Lebanon where his daughter lived. We agreed to ride together for the next two days, and I found myself relieved to be in the company of another on this more perilous portion of the journey. It would take me four days to reach Springfield and points south, which meant I would have to travel the last two legs alone, but I resolved to worry about this when the time came to part with Abraham.

Early the following morning, I used the money given to me by the bishop to buy a horse at Thompson's Livery along with a serviceable saddle and tacking. The off-white mare had been appropriately named Buttercream, and I found her to have a delightfully gentle gait. Abraham and I took our leave of Rolla in mid-morning and arrived in Waynesville where we spent the first night. Out bright and early the next day, our trip proceeded without incident until we reached Lebanon. Very light traffic greeted us during these first two days of travel. We occasionally met a Union patrol, and this provided additional security and peace of mind. Abraham's daughter graciously agreed to put me up for the second night. When I left the following morning, I extended my heartfelt thanks for her hospitality, bade Abraham farewell, and clucked Buttercream down the Old Wire Road with a prayer for safety on my lips.

To my great relief, the third day proved uneventful, and I arrived in Marshfield by early evening. I found suitable lodging and a meal in a boarding house near the Old Wire Road. As my head hit the pillow, I resolved to be up early the following morning with hopes of making the final leg to Springfield safely and in good time. At the crack of dawn, Buttercream and I were off at a good pace. The moderate weather continued and a pale sun shone through the wispy clouds above. I chewed some stringy venison jerky and munched a tart apple, a cold and unsatisfying breakfast.

Shortly after noon, I approached a sharp left-hand turn in the road and, as I rounded it, six secessionist soldiers burst from the tree line and surrounded me, muskets at the ready.

I reined in Buttercream and waited, my heart in my throat.

I said nothing.

Nor did they.

The leader, a sergeant, studied me with hooded eyes, unwavering, even as his horse sidled.

"Who might you be?" the sergeant said.

"I'm Deacon Andrewes on my way to the west for medical attention."

"You look fit to me."

I mustered a brief cough. "Lungs are inflamed, I fear."

He continued to stare at me for several long seconds.

"Are you armed?" the sergeant asked.

"No sir."

He nodded, first to me and then to his pickets. "This way."

Twenty minutes later, I was escorted into a massive encampment of Confederate soldiers near a village called Sand Creek. The sergeant led me at gunpoint to a command tent and ushered me into the presence of Brigadier General John S. Marmaduke. A tall man with a handlebar mustache and thinning hair stood to greet me, offering me his hand. "So you are a clergyman?" he said.

I found myself somewhat flummoxed that a Confederate General with three stars on his collar would rise to greet me.

"Yes, sir. A deacon in the Episcopal Church," I said.

"I see. I'm a Methodist myself, though not particularly active at the moment. Tell me what brings you here."

"I'm not physically well, and I know of a... a physician in the countryside near Ozark whose medical expertise I seek."

"I see. Are you a *Union* man?"

My heart returned to my throat, and I telegraphed a quick mental prayer to the Lord. "Yes, sir. I have to say I am."

"Have you seen duty as a soldier?"

"Yes, sir. Wounded at the battle they call Wilson's Creek. Lost a bone in my leg."

General Marmaduke nodded and studied me in silence for several long seconds before rapping his field desk with his knuckles. "Just retired from a hard-fought battle in Springfield. I would have taken it too if Colonel Proctor had joined me in time. No other prudent course but to pull back." He sighed. "Tell you what Deacon Andrewes, I will let you be on your way on one condition."

"Yes sir."

"I had to leave some of my wounded in Springfield. I would ask that you approach General Brown, the commanding officer there, to be certain my men receive medical care and if you would give them the Lord's succor, I would be forever grateful. Oh, and one more thing. A number of my brave men gave their lives yesterday. I would pray that General Brown might prepare a soldier's sepulture for the Confederate dead."

"I would be honored to carry this message," I said.

"Then be on your way," General Marmaduke said.

"Yes, sir. Thank you sir. I shall see to your men."

Three sighs of relief, ten quick steps to Buttercream, one spur of her flanks, and I was rid of that Confederate camp. I made a beeline for Springfield and arrived in the late afternoon. A dreadful scene greeted me. Smoke still wafted in the air from the burning of a number of houses. An eerie silence enveloped the town, broken now and then by a moan or shout. The fallen and wounded were borne on carts to what I presumed were makeshift morgues in the first instance and hospitals in the second. Citizens remained fearful, knowing that Confederate Colonel Proctor had arrived in the vicinity to the east and would unite with Marmaduke. Union cavalry members remained near their horses and at the ready to advance should there be renewal of the attack.

"Where might I find General Brown?" I asked one soldier passing by.

"He's likely at the hospital," the soldier said. "He was wounded in the arm."

The hospital was but a short ride away, and I found General Brown in a private room, sitting up in his bed and in obvious pain, the color drained from his face. A bandage shrouded his right upper arm. I introduced myself and presented General Marmaduke's petitions for medical attention of the wounded, proper burial of the dead, and spiritual aid for his Confederate soldiers. Wincing, General Brown nodded. "Wounded Rebs in a house, Mrs. Mary Campbell's house on Roanoke Street. More are in a Mrs. Owen's house in the south part of town.

Doctor Caleb Whitney and several other surgeons, including Reb surgeons, are attending to them as time permits. I've already ordered burial of the dead in a proper manner. I'm sure Post Chaplain Fred Wines could use your help."

Wishing the general a full and speedy recovery with promises of intercessory prayer on his behalf, I took my leave of the hospital and found my way to the Mary Campbell house. I did not get an exact count, but I estimated some thirty wounded Confederate soldiers suffered in various degrees of agony throughout the house. The kitchen had been converted to a makeshift surgery. A surgeon performed amputations on a long table. This sight brought into bold relief my own experience of many months before and the divine grace that not only spared my life but my limb as well.

One surgeon glanced in my direction and, seeing me standing in the doorway of the kitchen in clerical attire, inquired of my business.

"General Brown sent me here and asked if I might lend my ministrations to the wounded and dying."

The surgeon nodded. "There is a young man from Arkansas in the keeping room yonder. He isn't going to make it, but he's conscious and has been asking for a chaplain. Be good of you to see to him."

"Yes, sir," I said and made my way to the adjacent room where I found the young man lying *in extremis* on a couch, covered by a woolen, tan Army blanket. I knelt beside his bed and touched his shoulder, prompting his closed eyelids to flutter.

"I'm Deacon Andrewes," I said. "I understand you've been asking for a chaplain."

He nodded slowly.

"What's your name, son?"

"Marshall... Marshall Clark."

"And where are you from?"

"Pocahontas, Arkansas."

"Are you in pain?"

"Not much. Cain't feel much below the waist. Nothin' in fact."

"Where were you hit?"

"Took two rounds, one in the back and one through my belly."

We lapsed into silence for several long seconds.

"Not gonna make it, am I?" he asked, fixing his eyes upon mine.

"Your wounds are grave," I said.

He nodded and closed his eyes.

"Are you a man of faith?" I asked.

He nodded again. "Pray for me, will you Deacon? Death is crawling up my body. It'll hit my heart and my haid afore long. Like to have a prayer while I can still hear it."

"Of course," I said and prayed silently to the Lord for the right words. Grasping Marshall's hand, I began my prayer, "Almighty God, merciful Lord, look upon this your servant, lying in weakness. May it please you to pardon all his sins. Comfort him with the promise of life everlasting. Receive him into your loving arms and, we pray, give him refreshment, gladness, wholeness, and joy in your Kingdom with all of the saints who have gone before. May his soul and the soul of all of the faithful departed rest in peace."

I whispered two *amens* and opened my eyes. Marshall's remained closed. His slight smile betrayed a peaceful end. I pulled the blanket over his head.

———

Despite my mission to see Belle, I knew I had to remain in Springfield for an indeterminate span of time. The need for Christian ministration overwhelmed Post Chaplain Fred Wines, and no one was serving the Confederate wounded, a responsibility I assumed for myself. For the next thirty-six hours, I visited and prayed with those wounded that had been billeted in the homes of Mrs. Campbell and Mrs. Owens. Finally overcome by exhaustion and hunger, I accepted a tin bowl of chicken soup and coffee from Mrs. Owens before lying on the floor among the wounded to catch a brief rest. I slept for several hours during which, unbeknownst to me, someone covered me with a blanket.

Upon awakening, I resumed my labors. Those Confederate prisoners and the ambulatory wounded were loaded in wagons and trundled off to prison under guard, presumably to the military prisons in Saint Louis. Sixty-three Confederate soldiers were too injured to be moved. I continued to minister to them. While in prayer with one poor lad who had lost both arms, Post Chaplain Wines approached me from behind. When I finished my prayer, he tapped me on the shoulder. I turned and beheld a weary man.

214 JOHN HUTCHINSON

"We'll be burying the Rebel dead in an hour. Can you assist?" he asked.

"Of course. Where?"

"South of town a ways in a vacant field. Follow Jefferson Street. You'll find us."

"Very well," I said.

Chaplain Wines took his leave, and I returned to my ministrations with the young Confederate amputee.

Despite my fatigue, I felt a new vigor and purpose in ministering to the wounded. It was what I would call a joyful exhaustion, and it imprinted more indelibly upon my mind that this work resonated deeply within my soul. I had no idea how to actualize it in my future clerical life, but I had come to realize in a deep and radical way that I was at heart a chaplain, not a parish priest.

Yet, Marty had been correct in his observation that short of the military, which was out of the question, I had no outlets for such ministry. And, there was the matter of Annie, All Souls, the rectory, and the wedding, all of which pointed me in the direction of my life journey for years to come. The weight of it all depressed me as Buttercream, and I clopped down Jefferson Street to the site of the Confederate burial.

When I arrived, I saw three to four dozen bodies, shrouded, and stacked on wagons near a shallow pit. I dismounted and strode to where Chaplain Wines and a sergeant were engaged in conversation.

"Deacon Andrewes," Chaplain Wines said. "Thank you for coming. This is Sergeant Dolman, who is in charge of this detail."

Dolman and I shook hands.

"Is this the grave?" I asked.

"It is," Chaplain Wines said.

"For all of those on the wagons?"

"Yes."

"It's too shallow, I fear. And must it be a mass grave? Can there not be individual graves with appropriate markers?"

"Don't have time fer that," Sergeant Dolman said. "'Sides, they're Rebs. Lucky to have this much, ask me."

"I promised General Marmaduke when I met him that I would assure a proper burial for his dead. General Brown agreed. This is far from a proper burial."

"I got my orders," Sergeant Dolman said. "Don't much care what Marmaduke wants and General Brown gave the command, so he must assume this is acceptable. Let's get on with it."

I took a step forward, my ire rising. "But do you not understand? One good rainstorm and these bodies will float to the surface."

Dolman jutted his face to inches from mine. "Deacon, them men is traitors. The enemy. All due respect, you have no authority here."

"God loves these men as much as he loves you Sergeant. They are therefore worthy of an honorable interment. I protest your actions in the strongest words."

"Protest away," Dolman said and turned to the six Union men flanking the wagons. "Load 'em in."

The men on duty wasted no time in lowering the shrouded bodies into the grave. When the last corpse had been deposited, they shoveled the reserved dirt and sod until a mound of earth spread before us. Chaplain Wines asked me to read a suitable Scripture passage, which he followed with a rather ill-formed commendation and committal. That was it. Sergeant Dolman, his men, Chaplain Wines, and the empty wagon beat a hasty retreat back to the city center. I remained by the gravesite, chagrined by the whole slipshod affair, my mood matching a day that had turned cold and cloudy. A light breeze rattled the few lonely and resilient oak leaves that clung to their branches in defiance of the seasonal demand that they flutter to the ground and rot into new soil.

The burial would be my last service to the Federal Army of the Frontier. The following morning, Buttercream and I took our leave after more than three days of ministry among the Confederate wounded. By noon, I had reached the village of Ozark where we passed by the charred remains of a Union fort that General Marmaduke had torched in his drive toward Springfield. Two grizzled gentlemen—one with hands on hips, the other with arms folded—surveyed the wreckage, no doubt wondering what would happen to their little town now that the Union detachment had fled north to join the Battle of Springfield. I waved and they reciprocated before returning to their study of the blackened fort.

Turning to the east, I picked up the road that would lead me to Belle's place. Strands of excitement and anxiety twisted within me as I rounded a curve and spied her house in the distance. Drawing near, I sensed something amiss. The front door stood akimbo in the door-frame. I dismounted and walked slowly up the steps. The door had been torn off the hinges and simply propped up in the entryway, leaving an opening through which the wind whistled carrying leaves and light debris into the keeping room. I lifted the door aside and made my way into the room. *Nothing colder than an empty building in winter*, I thought to myself.

"Belle?" I called. "Belle, are you here?"

Nothing.

I made my way through the house and found no sign of her. The bed in Belle's room remained unmade and her rifle leaned against the wall. Unusual. She always made the bed each morning and removed her rifle to the two pegs on the keeping room wall. That she had not done so did not bode well in my mind. I inspected the rest of the house, retrieved the surgery key from the kitchen drawer where it was kept, and made my way up the hill to the cave. When I entered the surgery, I found everything in good order. However, three swipes of my finger revealed a thin layer of dust on the surgical table, armoire, and instrument table. No procedures had been performed in the surgery for several weeks, it would seem. I made a last foray to the herb shed and, as I feared, it gave evidence of a long span of disuse.

Since Belle was so well known in the region, I reasoned that someone in Ozark might know of her whereabouts, so I made a quick return to the town center where I found the court house that housed the Christian County sheriff's office. The sheriff, one William Friend, sat behind his desk reading a newspaper when I crossed the threshold. He looked up and nodded.

"Yes, sir," he said. "Can I help you?"

"I'm a friend, a former patient actually, of Belle Potts. I've just returned from her place, and it seems she's not been there for quite some time.

Sheriff Friend folded his paper and laid it aside on his desk.

"We don't know where she is," he said. "Back before Christmas, she just disappeared."

"Her horse and medicine wagon are gone too," I noted.

"Yes. We think she may have been dragooned for medical purposes."

"Did you mount a search party?"

The sheriff nodded. "Three of them. We covered at least twenty five miles in all directions, but there is a lot of wilderness out in these Ozark hills."

"Who could have taken her?"

He turned his palms up and shrugged. "Possibly one of the Bushwhacker gangs. They are masters at hiding."

"Have you given up?"

"I don't really know what more we can do. The war is on, and it is dangerous to scout around the area. Ozark is staunchly Union and has voted as such. These Confederate sympathizers have no compunction when it comes to violating and killing loyal citizens. We can only hope that one day she will show up. Lord knows we miss her and her services."

"I can't accept that outcome," I said, taken aback by the sheriff's off-handed attitude. "I will take up the search myself."

Sheriff Friend shrugged again. "Up to you, but I don't know how one man can succeed where dozens have failed."

"Nevertheless, I shall try. One must not underestimate the aid of the Almighty in such ventures."

"I'm sure the Almighty has already been consulted many times on this case."

"That may be," I said, "but she is a very special woman and deserves unremitting effort to find her. Remember the proverb, *The slothful man roasteth not that which he took in hunting: but the substance of a diligent man is precious.*"

He rose from his desk and put his hands on his hips. "I do not appreciate your throwing the Good Book at me, sir. Are you implying we have been slothful?"

"I'm not implying it, sir. I am stating it as a fact."

"We have lives to live," he said. "We have neither the time nor the manpower to stage an ongoing search. You should know that. We gave it a good effort."

"Not good enough," I said.

"I think our time here has ended," he said, circling around his desk. "I believe you should move on. Search for her if you must, but do not bother me with it further."

"I shall leave. Before I do, have you any advice as to where I might begin? Any clues that you have uncovered?"

"Not a clue to be found. There is a farmer named Cordell Burton who has asked Belle to marry him. You might visit him and see if he knows anything more."

This announcement of Belle's betrothal brought me up short. I simply stared at the desk for several long seconds before recovering some measure of my wits. The Sheriff cocked his head. He seemed to sense the jarring of my soul, and his demeanor softened. "Don't know that she accepted his proposal," he said. "Still, that's the best place to begin."

He gave me directions to Cordell Burton's farm, clapped me on the back, and wished me good luck. "If you discover anything and if we citizens can help, let us know." I thanked him and took my leave.

Once back on Buttercream, a worm of shame wiggled within me. To be sure, it was out of character for me to behave in such an insolent way. Sheriff Friend most assuredly did not deserve my hurling a proverb at him. His position was quite appropriate and necessary. They had sent out three search parties without success. At some point, futile search operations involving volunteers must come to an end. I resolved to extend my apologies to the Sheriff the next time I saw him.

As the day was growing short, I returned to Belle's house reckoning that she would not mind my taking up residence there and using it as a base for my search. Upon arrival, I spent an hour by the lamplight repairing the front door and reseating it upon its hinges.

That night, I crawled into Belle's bed, the very bed of my convalescence. I rolled about in it trying to pick up her scent, her residue, her essence. I prayed I might find some sign or pointer that could lead me to her. Of course, in the back of my mind I knew that my discovery of her could be devastatingly grim. I could not allow myself to dwell on that possibility. So, as I lay under the blanket that had once warmed her, I prayed fervently for divine guidance and a joyful outcome. I had already spent more than a week of my furlough, but I resolved to pursue this mission until I reached its resolution. The wedding and my return to service of All Souls would simply have to wait. I sensed clearly I was under the hand of God.

SEVENTEEN

Springfield

January, 1863

A brutal frost ushered in the morning. I rose from the bed, shrouded myself in Belle's blanket, and repaired to the cooking room in desperate need of food. Rummaging through the cupboards, I found some dried meat of unknown origin. Thanks to the chill in the house and a careful curing, the meat had not become rancid, and after a confirmatory sniff, I ate several strands hoping it would sustain me through my visit to the Cordell Burton farm. I found some of Belle's tooth powder and gave my dentition a good and long overdue polishing. After feeding Buttercream a pail of oats from a bin in the barn, and following the parting directions from Sheriff Friend, I set a course to the encounter with Belle's beau.

While in Saint Louis—out of sight, though not out of mind—I hoped I had come to accept the reality that Belle would move on with her life. However, roaming about her house and land, in dreadful fear for her, I could now barely abide the notion that she had come under another man's sway. Of course, it was utterly irrational but a green glow of jealousy enveloped me that morning. I prayed I would be civil to Cordell Burton. After all, it would be unseemly for a man of the cloth to succumb to envy. Unseemly in the extreme.

An eerie stillness greeted me as I passed through the gate to the Burton farm. No signs of life could be seen—no livestock, no horses, no farm cats, not even the trill of a songbird. I dismounted, stepped up the porch, and knocked on the door. An elderly woman in a long gray housedress and white bonnet greeted me, an ancient double-barrel flintlock shotgun in hand.

"Who might you be?" she asked.

I pinched the brim of my hat. "Sorry for the intrusion, ma'am. I'm Deacon Andrewes, and I've come in search of one Mister Cordell Burton."

"What would you be wantin' with him?"

"I'm a friend of Belle Potts and lately discovered she is missing. Sheriff Friend over in Ozark thought Mister Burton might know her whereabouts."

The elderly woman relaxed and set her shotgun aside. "Sorry to greet you with a fowlin' piece. Cain't be too careful these days what with them Bushwhackers roamin' the countryside. Come on in. My son Cordy's mendin' fence but due back soon for dinner. You say you're lookin' for Belle?"

"Yes ma'am. A number of months ago, I was mortally wounded on the battlefield near Wilson Creek. Belle rescued me and saved not only my life but my leg. I was in the vicinity and thought I'd pay her a visit. I've come to find out she disappeared a number of weeks ago."

Lena Burton's sorrowful nod confirmed what I had expected. She and her son had no idea of Belle's whereabouts. "Strangest thang," she said. "Cordy's been out three times scourin' the countryside for her, but to no avail. You know...." Lena fixed me with her gaze willing me to understand what she was about to say. "Cordy's fixin' to tie the knot with Belle. If and when she turns up, that is."

"Yes," I said. "I had heard as much. She is a fine woman and will make a wonderful wife."

"She's a blessin'. That's for sure. I'm o'er the moon that Cordy had the gumption to ask for her hand."

I could not resist asking, fearing the answer: "Did she accept his proposal of marriage?"

Lena shrugged. "Cordy said she wanted to ponder on it a spell. They's a good bit to consider what with her healin' work and this farm. Cordy's plannin' to stay an' run some cattle. She'd be a big he'p out hyar. But, afore she could give an answer, she vanished. Cordy's perty sure she'll accept though, an' I reckon she will too. Cordy's a good man, an' I knowed she wants some li'l ones. So does Cordy, for that matter. Jes' wish we'uns could find her."

"Has he stopped searching?"

"For now. He's waitin' 'til somethin' breaks. Some news. Figgers they's no p'int in traipsin' aimlessly 'round these hills."

Were I betrothed to Belle, I could not imagine abandoning the search for her. I would have made it the sole purpose in my life to *traipse* around these hills. I had little expertise in such things, but I could not simply sit around idly, and I certainly had no incentive to return to Saint Louis knowing that Belle was lost, imprisoned, or perhaps even dead. No, I would recover the crude maps of Missouri and Arkansas from where I had placed them during my cleaning and cataloguing of Doc J's library. With them spread before me, somehow I would develop a plan to search the area, no doubt retracing the steps of those who had served on the three search parties. Perhaps I could uncover something they missed. Perhaps some of the homesteaders and farmers in the area would have spotted her and have news to share.

Just then, Cordell stomped his feet on the porch and blew through the door obviously concerned for his mother, having seen Buttercream tied to the porch rail. When he saw us sitting peacefully before the fire, he relaxed and doffed his hat. I beheld a giant man, brawny and handsome, with a shock of wheat-colored hair and large brown eyes.

"Cordy, this is Deacon Andrewes," Lena said. "Come lookin' for Belle. Thought you might know of her wharabouts."

Cordy stepped forward and offered me his hand as I rose from the chair. "Cordell Burton," he said and shook his head. "I've no idee where she might be. Been gone nigh on two months. Searched high an' low but cain't find no sign o' her."

"What do you think might have happened?"

Cordy shrugged. "Her medicine wagon an' harse is gone, too. No tellin' what happened. Somethin' mighta spooked her, but Belle ain't one to spook easy. Cain't 'magine her up an' runnin' 'thout tellin' no one. Some specylation she's snatched for healin'. Or mayhaps she lit

out on her own accord to he'p someone. Still, don' make no sense she'd
be gone so long. Might be a pris'ner. Her repytation is knowed far 'n'
wide. Could be them Rebs abducted her an' took her south to he'p
patch up they's wounded in some hospital safe ahind the Confed'rate
front."

"Makes sense," I said.

"We'uns is hopin' she'll jes' show up one o' these days, fit as a
fiddle."

"We can hope and pray," I said.

Lena invited me to remain for dinner, an offer I readily accepted,
not having eaten well for several days. When I returned to Belle's place,
the day was nearly gone. I lit a lantern and, as I had planned, retrieved
the maps. They had only rough approximations of the regional roads,
and I feared they were seriously out of date. Of course, none of the
trails and *nigh-cuts* were shown.

I was intrigued by Cordy's suggestion that Belle may have been
kidnapped by Confederate soldiers and spirited south where her
services could be put to good use in a hospital setting. Though it
would be very risky, I decided to take a southerly route on the morrow,
toward the Arkansas line. My previous good fortune with General
Marmaduke gave me some hope that, as a clergyman, I would be
deemed low risk and not worthy of detention. Perhaps my ministrations among the Confederate wounded in Springfield would become
another credential in my favor.

As dark settled upon the Ozark hills, I slipped into Belle's bed
and passed a fitful night. The morning dawned with sunlight
streaming through the bedroom window. I sat up on the bed and
noted again Belle's rifle leaning against the wall. I picked it up,
hefted it, and considered whether or not to take it with me for
protection. After several minutes of internal debate, I decided against
it. I would place myself in the hands of the Almighty. With a self-
confirming nod, I stood the rifle against the wall where Belle had
placed it and, as I did so, I beheld some scratches in the wall,
suddenly visible in the bright sunlight. I could not quite decipher
them, but I knew they were recent. During my convalescence, I had
come to know every square inch of that room. If the scratches had
been there during those days, I would have known it. I stepped
quickly into the front room and swiped the chimney for ash residue.

When I rubbed ashes over the scratches, the pit of my stomach dropped.

JUB GOT ME

A flush of terror spread through every particle of my being. Not Confederate soldiers, but ruthless and pitiless Bushwhackers.

Jubal Jagger.

I knew from my own encounter with the man that he bore a cold-blooded cruelty. I reckoned that one of his men must have been wounded, and he seized Belle to save the man's life or limb. Weeks had passed since she scratched these letters. What would have become of her? Jubal would have no qualms about killing her once her services had been rendered. Of this I was certain.

My mission had taken an abrupt turn. I needed to find Jubal Jagger. No easy task. I pondered where to begin and remembered my recent conversation with Major Marsden on the train west. I recalled his orders to locate and neutralize Jubal Jagger.

Marsden would be my first contact. I dressed quickly, saddled Buttercream, and made a beeline for Springfield, where I hoped to find Marsden. Luck favored me. Upon arrival in Springfield, I located the so-called Fort #4 on South Street and chanced upon Major Marsden sitting on a stone fence, smoking his pipe, and joshing with several Union soldiers. He recognized me immediately upon my approach.

"Deacon," he said, rising to shake my hand. "Good to see you again. What brings you to these precincts? I assume you are feeling better. You seem in the pink."

"Indeed I am," I said. "My health has returned, praise be to God. I am here to determine if you have discovered the whereabouts of Jubal Jagger."

Marsden spread a wide smile, turned to the nearby soldiers. "Gentleman, Deacon Andrewes here wishes to know if we have any notion as to where Jagger might be."

Oddly, the soldiers smiled as well, nodding, and one even burst out laughing. I could not fathom their good humor.

Marsden returned his smiling gaze to me. "I'm not at all sure why you want to find Jagger," he said. "But you certainly have come to the right place."

"How is that?" I asked.

"Follow me."

The Major led me some fifty paces up South Street to a low slung house, partially charred from the fires ordered by General Brown. Pushing the door open, he led me into a front room. There laid out in a neat row were the corpses of the one-legged Jubal Jagger and seven of his men. "There's the old civvy cat himself," Marsden said with a proud placement of his hand in the in the unbuttoned flap of his uniform blouse. "Caught up with him two days ago as he was preparing a raid on a little settlement called Colette Springs. A good old gun battle ensued. We shot them all without one of our men taking a hit. A splendid day it was!"

My heart surged into my throat. "Was there a woman with them?"

"Yes. One."

"But she isn't here. She's still alive?"

"Last I knew but I doubt she will survive her wounds."

"Where is she?"

"With the other Confederate wounded from the battle a week ago. Mrs. Campbell's house."

"Thank you sir," I said beating a hasty retreat, my heart and mind blown about in a hurricane of dread. The thought of Belle lying mortally wounded in a makeshift Confederate hospital, one in which I had lately ministered, filled me with terror. I could only hope I would arrive before she succumbed.

I burst through Mary Campbell's front door and grabbed the lapel of the first ambulatory person I saw. "The woman," I said. "The one they just brought in. Where is she?"

The man simply pointed up the stairs.

I sprinted up the stairs and dashed from room to room in search of a woman with long blonde hair.

"Where is she?" I asked of no one in particular. "The woman they just brought in."

"Lyin' in the front room bed," one of the wounded said.

"No, I just looked there."

"Only woman here," the man said. "Leastways only one I know of."

I shot back into the front room. Indeed, there was a woman lying there, but it was not Belle. I knelt beside the bed and shook her shoulder to awaken her. She was unresponsive, save for a soft groan.

"Ma'am, were you with Jubal Jagger? I must know."

Still no response.

I shook her harder.

"Wake up," I said. "Please, wake up."

Her eyes fluttered.

I repeated my inquiry, to which she gave a small nod.

"Were you with Jagger?"

Another small nod.

"Was there a blonde woman, tall, a doctor of sorts with you?"

She turned to me. "Belle," was all she said.

"Where is Belle?"

"Daid, I reckon bein' chained up all this time."

The woman slipped away again.

"Where? Where is she chained?"

I shook her again. Roughly. Frantically.

"Where!"

Her eyes fluttered once again and she whispered, "Thur Turner."

With that, she gave one last gasp and breathed her last.

Her death jarred me into my senses once again, and I lowered my head in shame. My urgency had robbed me of the chance to pray with her. "Does anyone know this woman's name?" I asked.

I heard a woman's voice behind me. "That's Iris Monahan, Jubal's cousin."

I turned to see a slender nurse with a soiled apron.

I nodded. "I shall pray for her."

I voiced a brief prayer for the repose of her soul before rising.

"She whispered 'Thur Turner' just before she died. Nurse, do you have any idea what that means?"

"None," she said. "Clearly it is someone's name, but I have no idea who it is."

"Very well. Thank you."

I raced back to Fort #4 where Major Marsden had resumed his perch on the stone wall.

"Thur Turner. Does that name mean anything to you?" I asked.

He shook his head. "Wo, 2hy do you ask?"

"Iris Monahan just died. She whispered this name to me before passing. I had asked her of the whereabouts of one Belle Potts, a friend of mine who has been abducted by Jagger. That's when she said 'Thur Turner.'"

Marsden shook his head again. He called to the other soldiers milling about the area. "Any of you know of a Thur Turner?"

None did.

"Most of us are not from around here," Marsden said. "We wouldn't know the locals. You might inquire in the saloons and boarding houses. Ask people on the streets. Somebody probably knows of a Thur Turner."

I followed his advice and for the next several hours questioned as many people as I could on the streets and in business establishments. Not one person recognized the name, and I grew fearful that Iris Monahan had given me the wrong name or a false one. Still it was all I had, and in desperation I pressed on. My anxiety soared to galactic levels when I stopped long enough to consider Belle's circumstances. Iris had said she was chained. Chained where? I glanced at the dark and foreboding sky. A front had moved in and the first shots of an icy sleet pelted my face. Was she sheltered? Did she have food and water? Had Iris been correct, was Belle *daid* by now? And who, by the mercies of heaven, was Thur Turner?

As I scurried to and fro about Springfield, I shot darts of prayer to the Almighty begging him for a break. The storm and short winter days brought early darkness to Springfield. Exhausted, I finally took shelter in a boisterous saloon whose regular patrons had not been deterred by the weather. Indeed, they may have been emboldened by it, gathering to ponder and prognosticate. I plowed through the crowd to the bar and asked the barkeep for a metal cup.

"Gentlemen!" I said, banging the cup on the bar. "Gentlemen!" The clamor subsided. "I am trying to find a man named Thur Turner. Has anyone heard of this person?"

In unison, the clientele shook their collective heads.

I nodded in despair. "Thank you," I said and returned the cup to the barkeep.

Defeated, I raised the collar of my coat and prepared to face the mounting storm. As I neared the door, an old man, toothless and nearly bald, grasped my arm with his claw-like hand.

"Come down close, sonny," he said, his voice a wheezy reed. "So's I kin hear you."

I complied.

"Now who is you lookin' for? I couldn't quite heer you."

"Thur. Thur Turner."

He raised his eyebrows. "For 'nother cup o' ale, I might be of help." A broad grin revealed his eroded gums.

"Do you know who Thur Turner is?"

"Could be. How 'bout that ale?"

I nodded. "Sure. I'll buy you a cup of ale."

When I gave him his liquid fee, he downed it in one gulp and wiped his flaccid mouth with the back of his sleeve.

"About Thur Turner," I said.

"It's Thurgood. Thurgood Turner. He's a recluse what lived out in hide-out country. Leastways he used to. Heered his place burned down an' he took off."

"Where did he go?"

The old man shrugged. "No idee."

"Do you know where his place is? The one that burned down?"

"Like I said, out in hide-out country."

"Can you be more specific?"

"Don' b'lieve I kin. I never knowed for shore whar 'twas. Thurgood's been gone ten, twelve yar now."

I everted my lips in the frustrated realization that I would extract no more information from the old man. I stood once again to leave.

"Pardon me," came a voice from behind. I turned to see a Union soldier approach me from a rowdy pack of fellow men-at-arms. "I couldn't help but overhear. I know someone who might be able to help."

"Please, sir. Tell me."

"There is a man named Injun Jim—I don't know his real name—but he has served as a scout for the United States every now and then. He knows these Ozark hills and hollows. If anyone can find where this Thurgood Turner once lived, it would be Injun Jim."

"Where do I find this Injun Jim?"

"He has a small farm east of here about five miles. Took him a white wife. Has a son I believe. He can track a light-footed mouse on a bed of rocks. Don't know if he'll help but might be worth checking."

"Thank you, my good man," I said. "Thank you very much."

"Can't miss his place. Head out east on Walnut Street. Five miles out, you'll see a big boulder on the right, marking the lane leadin' down to Injun Jim's place."

The soldier extended his hand. "Good hunting," he said and slipped back into the crowd.

EIGHTEEN

Search

February, 1863

G iven the brutal storm and late hour, I had no choice but to take lodging in Springfield and wait until the next morning, the dawning of the first day of February. When I arose, the proprietress of the inn prepared two eggs and several slices of salted ham for my breakfast. As I wolfed down my food, I considered the possibility of rounding up Cordell Burton to accompany me but decided it would consume too much time. If we found Belle alive, Cordell would be notified immediately, and he could assume his proper role as her betrothed.

The thought of their pending marriage brought to mind my own. I had been gone for ten days and thus far had no longing desire to be in Annie's arms, no pining for her. While a bolt of discomfort—perhaps guilt—shot through me, I dismissed it immediately, mindful of the important task I faced.

To sustain me on the journey east, my gracious innkeeper packed two cold chicken breasts that had been fried the previous day. "It's faired up some," she said as she handed me the food. "Make for faster ridin'. Leastways for a spell."

To my relief, it had *faired up some*. The sleet storm had abated but spread the ground with a sheet of frozen ice. Buttercream picked her way along the road at an agonizingly slow pace, but I appreciated her prudence. I hoped the temperature would soon rise sufficiently to melt the ice. It took most of the morning to reach Injun Jim's place. I spotted the big boulder from nearly a mile away and spurred Buttercream into a gallop, relieved that the sun had melted most of the ground ice.

When I rounded the boulder, I could see a dog-trot cabin several hundred yards to the south. I reined in, dismounted, and spotted a boy perhaps ten or eleven years old sitting on a porch rocker, whittling.

"What are you carving?" I asked.

Without a word, he showed me a perfect facsimile of a fox, precise in every detail save for the bushy tail, which required his finishing touches.

"That is an excellent carving," I said. "Where did you learn to do this?"

He shrugged. "It just comes in my head, and I make it real."

"Well, I say that is a rare talent. I wonder if you can help me. I'm looking for one they call Injun Jim."

Before he could answer, one of the cabin doors opened, and an attractive woman with silvery-blonde hair stepped on to the porch, pistol at the ready.

"Who might you be?" she asked.

"Beg your pardon, ma'am. Permit me to introduce myself. I am Deacon Krieger Andrewes, and I am looking for a man they call Injun Jim."

"He's my man," she said. "He doesn't favor that name."

"My apologies. It's the only name I've been given."

"His name is James Darrow. He is of Scottish and Cherokee descent. What do you want with him?"

I quickly outlined my purpose and the need for his services to locate Belle Potts.

She studied me for several long seconds. "Charlie, go fetch your pa."

The boy jumped from the rocker and ran around the side of the cabin, presumably to the barn from which I detected the sound of hammer on anvil.

"Jim will be along shortly," the woman said. "I'm Harriet Darrow. Come in and rest for a spell."

I followed her into the cabin and took a seat in a caneback chair before the chimney. Moments later, a tall, leather-skinned man with russet hair pushed through the door followed by Charley. His leather apron matched his complexion. I stood to greet him. Cautiously, he accepted my proffered hand. Harriet slid to his side, put a hand on his shoulder. "It's all right, Jim. Please sit, you will want to hear what he has to say."

Jim nodded and lowered his lanky frame into a chair. He peered at me with dark, inscrutable eyes. I repeated the purpose of my visit, my offer, and the desperate hope he would know where Thurgood Turner once lived. I added, "I have a small amount of money with which to pay you." My cash reserves were nearly gone, but I would give all that remained to Jim if he agreed to assist me.

Save for the crackling of cedar logs in the chimney, silence descended upon the room as Jim considered my offer.

He took a deep breath and glanced at his wife and son standing together arm-in-arm. "Belle Potts," he began in a low measured voice. "Brought the boy into this world. Saved his life and the woman's. Boy was satchel first, an' Belle turned him. Yes, I will help you. No pay."

"But do you know where Thurgood Turner's place is."

He nodded. "Southeast. Rising and falling country. Not much left of Thurgood's cabin. Burned down," he said, confirming what I had earlier been told.

"How far."

"Maybe fifty miles. Best get a start."

"Can't make it fifty miles today," I said.

"No. Best get a start. Camp tonight and reach Thurgood's tomorrow."

He nodded to Harriet, who leapt into action preparing food for the journey.

Without a word, Jim slipped from the cabin, motioning the boy to follow.

"Can I assist?" I said before he latched the door.

He shook his head, leaving me on the caneback chair to wait and worry. Belle had been chained for a long spell in severe weather, presumably with neither food nor water. I had a grinding fear we would be too late, if we found her at all.

As the minutes ticked on, a low thrumming murmur of doubt began to bubble. This doubt had always simmered below the surface of my consciousness, but I had heretofore been successful in keeping it from a roiling boil. What did Iris Monahan mean when she said "Thur Turner"? Did it truly point to where Belle had been imprisoned? Or did she intend something else? Were we on a wild goose chase? Were we so misdirected that any hope of saving Belle would soon be absorbed into the future like a cup of water poured into the ocean?

———

An hour later, Jim reentered the cabin clad in a long fur coat fashioned of beaver pelts. He tossed me a similar wrap, along with a pair of fur mittens and a fur hat with earflaps. "Gettin' cold," he said. "Best git a move on."

Harriet gave her husband a quick hug and kiss on the cheek. Jim nodded, squeezed the back of his son's neck, and turned to leave.

"I shall pray for you," Harriet said.

I nodded in Harriet's direction. "Thank you," I said, donned the fur garments, and followed my guide out of the cabin.

Jim had outfitted a packhorse with cookware, the foodstuffs his wife had prepared, a lantern, and other necessary materials. Before mounting his horse, he examined Buttercream. "Good horse," he said. "Let's ride. Hard."

We set off at a brisk trot in a southerly direction, Jim leading. Passing through Ozark, we veered south by southeast along an unmarked trail into the wilderness. Around two o'clock in the afternoon, another sleet storm erupted, pelting us with icy buckshot. Fog rolled in, and visibility dropped to but a few hundred feet. Our progress slowed as the horses lowered their heads and pressed on. The storm brought early darkness, and Jim called a halt near a small stream.

"Flows into the Garrison Branch," he said, pointing to the creek, as if the location had meaning to me.

With skill and dispatch, Jim laid a canvas sheet on the ground to serve as a floor and pitched a small tent. At his direction, I led the horses to the stream for a long overdue drink and fed them oats from one of the saddlebags.

In short order, Jim had the lantern lit and a fire started with dead-fall kindling. He added wood. The flames grew, sparking and cracking. Smoke dispersed into the clouds aloft. I watched my guide as he slowly poured milk from a canteen into a cast-iron skillet, added flour, and formed a thick sauce to which he added sliced potatoes and chips of fatback. Despite the wretched conditions in which we found ourselves, the meal was nourishing and satisfying. Two cups of campfire coffee punctuated our supper, a welcome hedge against the plummeting temperatures.

We slipped into the tent and hunkered under several blankets and our fur coats. In the lantern light, I saw Jim withdraw a small leather-bound volume, which he placed upon his chest, and began to read.

"Scriptures?" I asked.

He nodded. "You seem surprised."

"No. Not at all. Comforted, actually."

I confessed to a modicum of wonder that this taciturn Scot-Cherokee was a man of faith. At once, I was convicted of my own recent neglect of the Bible and vowed to put right this lapse in my discipline, ever more necessary under the menacing circumstances we were facing.

On the morrow, however. I was too tired and too disquieted to take much solace from the written Word. I knew this to be a sad admission indeed, particularly for a man of the cloth, but in that instant, huddled for warmth and in the soft glow of the lamp, I finally let go and drifted into much needed sleep. A prayer for protection lay unspoken upon my lips.

I awoke not long after daybreak to the smell of roasted potatoes and onions cooking over the open flame. Jim had obviously arisen at least a half hour earlier and set about preparing breakfast. We wolfed down the food and, while I scoured the skillet in the creek, he made short work of breaking camp. The snow and sleet had succumbed to the new day, but ominous clouds continued to roil overhead and a frigid wind lashed the surrounding forest.

"How far?" I asked once we were back on the trail.

"Ten miles. Mayhaps a bit more."

"Can we make it by noon?"

"I reckon, barring problems ahead."

I left unasked the question as to *what* problems might lie beyond the next bend in the trail.

———

As anticipated, within minutes of high noon, we halted near the boundary of a five-acre clearing. Through the trees, we spotted the scorched remains of a cabin, confirming that we had at last arrived at Thurgood Turner's secluded patch of ground. Several military-issue tents had been pitched within a few yards of the burnt-out cabin, no doubt the stolen remains of Jubal Jagger's encampment. Two inches of snow covered rough-hewn camp tables, folding chairs, a sizeable stack of cordwood, a cold fire pit, and *Belle's medicine wagon*!

Jim dismounted, handed me his reins, and drew a revolver from his hip holster. He motioned for me to stay back. Crouching, with quiet speed, he covered the ground between the tree line and the tallest fragment of the cabin wall. Rubbing Buttercream's neck to soothe my own fears, I watched as Jim peered around the corner of the wall, pistol pointed skyward. No movement or sound could be detected save for wind high in the surrounding pines and oaks. With his pistol now in firing position, Jim slipped into Jubal's camp and sequentially opened all of the tent flaps. Satisfied that all was clear—and shaking his head to signal no sight of Belle—he beckoned me forward. My stomach flipped like a hot johnnycake as I clucked Buttercream forward, the other two horses in tow.

"No sign of her?" I asked, trying to remain composed. My emotions betrayed me as the question spilled out in frantic haste.

Jim shook his head.

"Barn," he said. "Stay here."

With the same crouching stealth, he dashed to the barn and pressed himself to the wall, just to the right of the open door. He shot a quick glance within and pulled back. Several seconds later, he repeated the glimpse before slowly rounding the door and entering the barn.

I waited.

He did not emerge.

Unable to contain my trepidation, I inhaled deeply, closed my eyes for a tiny shot of prayer, and ran to the barn.

As I blinked to clear away momentary snow blindness, I saw Jim rising from a mounded blanket.

He shook his head.

"She's gone," was all he said.

I let out a low moan.

"Another one," he said, stepping over the first and kneeling by the second blanketed body.

I joined him and as he pulled the blanket away.

I blinked.

There I beheld the pale-blue face and flaxen hair of Belle Potts.

Jim placed two fingers on the side of her neck.

I closed my eyes. "Is she...?"

Breathless seconds ticked by.

"Alive," he said. "Found a pulse."

"Oh thank heavens!" I wheezed through clenched teeth.

Jim drew a hatchet from his belt and hacked the chains from the barn wall. Jim snatched the shackle keys from high on the wall and unfettered Belle's wrists and ankles.

"To the tent," he said.

I scooped the unconscious Belle into my arms and raced across the snow-laden yard *quicker'n a snake goin' through a holler log.* A sense of irony filled my mind as I recalled her carrying me off the battlefield many months before. I laid her on what I presumed was Jubal's cot since it was wider than the typical military issue. For a fleeting second I wondered where Jubal had managed to steal this enhanced piece of camp furniture.

"Crawl in next to her," Jim said. "Cover up and let your body heat warm her. Rub her, but not vigorously. Gently and firmly."

Without hesitation, I complied, deferring to Jim's superior skills in coping with extreme weather conditions. Her hands were frostbitten into curled stumps of ice, and I wrapped them in my own. I let my warm breath stream over her neck and face, praying that she would survive. Jim added two more blankets and slipped from the tent.

Through the flap, fluttering intermittently in the wind, I could hear him laying a fire with wood that had been stacked near the rock-rimmed pit. Some minutes later, the crackle of pitch and scent of smoke eased my angst a trifle, and I began a slow massage of Belle's arms and legs, careful not to violate her in any way by my warming strokes.

I whispered to her unhearing ears. "You're safe now. Jubal's dead. We've got you Belle. Safe and sound. You rest. Awaken when you're ready. Take in all of my warmth."

And so it went for an hour or more.

She gave no response.

Her breathing remained regular.

Grasping any strand of hope, I delighted to see some flush of pink return to her face, and I redoubled my gentle stroking and closed my eyes in prayer.

My supplications were interrupted as Jim pulled back the tent flap.

"The fire is roaring now. Let's get her by the fire."

I slipped from beneath our shared blanket. Jim and I grabbed the ends of the cot and bore Belle to the fireside.

"The other woman," he said. "Died of exposure. I put her in the back of the medicine wagon. We should try to waken Belle. I've got sugar water warming by the fire. She should drink."

We let another hour pass, turning Belle's cot every ten minutes or so to provide uniform warming.

"It's time," Jim said.

Together we lifted Belle to a sitting position. She lolled like a rag doll, limp and unresponsive.

While I held her upright, Jim knelt before her and slapped her face, sharply.

She gave no response.

"Wake up, Miss Belle," he said several times and slapped her again.

Still no response.

I jostled her, calling her name.

Nothing.

Jim jumped to his feet and sprinted to Belle's medicine wagon. With reckless abandon, he tore open drawers, rifled their contents, stared at bottles and vials, until finally he uncorked and sniffed one, wrinkled his brow, held it in the air and raced back to the fire pit.

"Sal ammoniac," he said. "Smelling salts."

He held the bottle under Belle's nose.

We waited.

Seconds later, she squeezed her eyelids, wrinkled her nose, and shook her head.

"She's coming to!" I shouted.

Jim withdrew the bottle.

Her eyelids fluttered.

Then opened.

I squeezed her shoulders.

Slowly, she turned to face me, her eyes unfocused, her mind uncomprehending.

She turned away.

Jim issued another whiff of the smelling salts.

She turned back again, her brow furrowed in confusion.

After an eternity of seconds, she whispered, "Krieg?"

"Yes, Belle. It's Krieg! I'm here."

She lowered her head, gazing at the blanket around her legs. She shook her head in slow motion.

Then she looked up at me again.

"Krieg. Is it really you?"

"It is! That mule-headed Private Andrewes. Your greatest surgical success. Remember me? I'm right next to you."

She slumped against my chest. "First Jesus," she mumbled. "Then Krieg. I must be in heaven."

"No, dear Belle. You are still with us. Right here on Mother Earth."

With effort, she trained her gaze on Jim.

"Injun Jim?"

With a rare smile, he said, "If you say so."

Suddenly, she gasped and shot to rigid attention. "Pippa! Where is Pippa?"

I shook my head. "I'm sorry, Belle. She didn't make it."

A low inhuman moan sounded from deep within Belle. "No! No! No! Not my Pippa. She's strong. She made it. No. I know Pippa's hyar. Where is she?"

Neither Jim nor I said a word.

"Where! Where is Pippa?"

"Too much," I said, softly. "Too much. She could not hold up against the weather."

Belle let out a piercing scream that shattered the forest calm and nearly curdled my own blood. She struggled to rise, but I held her to me. She fought for several long moments before succumbing to exhaustion and slumping once again into a rag-doll sprawl.

"She needs to drink this sweet water," Jim said.

I nodded. "Let's give her a spate of time. The shock of the other young woman's loss has affected her deeply. She is somewhat delusional. Seeing Jesus? A spectre. A phantasm brought on by her condition. Let's give her some time."

Jim agreed and, as I sat on the cot holding Belle, he outlined his plan. "We'll stay the night here. Try to get some food down her. Keep her warm and as calm as possible. In the morning, we'll head home. You and she can ride in the wagon, your mount and the packhorse behind. I'll lead you. We cannot make it all the way back with the wagon, but I know a widower named Carsten. He has a place south of Ozark. He will take us in tomorrow night. The following morning, I'll take my leave. Belle will know the way to her place."

"I can't thank you enough."

"You will. Or I should say, she will. We are not immortal nor are we immune to sickness and adversity. We will call again and again on Belle as the years roll on. It'll all come out fair in the end," he said, smiling. "It's the way the world should be. The way the Great Spirit intended."

Ozark Glossary

a dog-trot cabin - cabin with two rooms separated by a breeze-
way, common in the southeastern US in the nineteenth
century
satchel first - breech birth

PART 4

BELLE POTTS

NINETEEN

Belle's Place

February, 1863

I 'se still perty doddly the next marnin' an' grievin' heavy fer Pippa. That gel had some genuine promise what got cut short too early on. Since I got no knowance o' her kinfolk, I drawed an idee to bury her next to Doc J. Krieg 'greed to funeralize her, say some prayers usin' his book words, an' readin' from the Bible some. When we'd clumb up on the medicine wagon, I asked Krieg to drive. I needed jes' to lean inter him and soak up the comfort what oozed outen ever' pore o' his body. I'se all warm 'n' gluey inside settin' aside him. Don' rightly know what I'd expected to come o' it all. Tried not to think too much on it. Jes' wanted to gorge on his bein' with me.

That feelin' didn' last o' course. 'Round noon, Krieg said 'twas time to talk squirrel. I knowed it was a-comin'. I cain't 'member edzactly how our conversation played out, but what follers is a fair 'proxima-tion. Unless I disremember, Krieg got ever'thin' goin'.

"I hear you and Cordell Burton are going to be married," he said, starin' straight ahaid.

I took my haid off'n his shoulder 'n' looked up. "Who tole you that?"

"Well, Sheriff Friend, for starters."

"Sheriff Friend? How'd you come 'pon that ole chicken hawk?"

"I sought him out when I realized you were missing. He told me to check with Cordell, that the two of you were engaged. Then Cordell himself confirmed it."

"You talked to Cordy too?"

"I did."

"He say why he didn' come a-lookin' fer me?"

"He did search for you. He was a member of three search parties. None of them could find a trace of you."

"And so he give up?"

"I think he felt there was nothing more he could do."

"Searched three times, you say?"

"That's what he said."

"Three times for Cordy—turned up nothin'. One time for Krieg—turned up Belle. That tells me a good deal more'n Carter has oats." I snuggled Krieg some. "Naw," I said sorter soft like. "I ain't steppin' o'er the broomstick with Cordy. He mighta reckoned so, but he's misfoolin' hisself. I never did give my consentin' to his proposal."

We let the matter drop fer a spell. Blancey jes' trotted 'long ahind Jim.

Krieg stirred it up ag'in. *Roiled* it, might be a more acc'rate way o' puttin' it. "I have to tell you, Belle," he said. "I myself am engaged to be married."

Them words was a hard punch to a soft belly. I stopped breathin'. In one short second, Krieg plumb salivated my heart. When a stitch o' my senses come back, I sat up an' loosed Krieg's arm what I'd got a-holt of. Though he was my Ivanhoe, right then didn' feel right hangin' on him like an ole apron. He did'n' say nothin' more. Jes' let thangs bogue around in my haid. When I got a bit more o' a grip an' pondered it some, thangs was makin' no sense. If'n Krieg was fixin' to tie the knot, why was he a-quill-wheelin' round these hyar parts? If'n he wasn't comin' to see Belle, he'd a-had no knowance I was gone. I'se right certain he didn' wander all the way down hyar jes' to tell me he was bespoke to some city gel.

Me 'an' Krieg 'peared to be corked up fer words an' save for the sound o' iron hooves on hard ground, t'ain't a sound to be heerd as we driv down the road. I s'pose ten minute, maybe more, reeled off afore I gathered the gumption, to pose a query.

"Krieg, I'se mighty beholdin' to you fer rescuin' me. Truly. But why'd you sashay down hyar in the first place?"

Krieg copped a big breath. "I was sick. I had a terrible case of the grippe and couldn't seem to shake it. On top of that, I was worn out by the unremitting workload that had been placed upon me. My bishop directed me to rest for a couple of weeks. I determined you would be able to help me with my illness. As I traveled here to meet you, I began to recover so I decided, as long as I had made the trip, I should at least stop by and pay my respects. You know the rest."

I nodded. "Sometimes, sickness in the haid an' heart kin keep a body from healin'. Seems you come to be well oncet all that strain slipped away." Emboldened some, I kep' a-goin'. "When you'uns fixin' to get spliced?"

"Ten weeks from now."

"Ah," I said. "So, you'll be a-movin' on from hyar perty quick."

"Yes, if I may, I'll spend the night with you and begin my trek back to Saint Louis tomorrow. I was given two weeks of leave, three if necessary. I've been gone around ten days already. It's time to head out."

A wave o' lonesome sadness warshed o'er me. Thought o' Krieg ridin' away a second time set-up a sorrow-pain in my soul. The tomorrys I'se now facin' loomed cheerless an' forelorn. I'd fixed in my mind not to plight my troth with Cordy an' Krieg jes' sawed off any hopes what mighta sprung up o'er the last few hours with him. Felt some li'l tear stings but managed to sniff 'em away.

"I fixed your door," Krieg said, changin' our course o' talkin'. "I was able to tidy up the house as well, but the surgery needs a good cleaning."

"I reckoned it would," I said. "Don' worry none 'bout it. I kin clean it up good in due time."

I harbored a hunnert questions 'bout Krieg an' what he'd been up to since we last seed each other but couldn't bring myself to pose 'em. An', truth be told, I truly did not want to hear a thang 'bout his wooin', so I kep' a-holt o' my tongue. Silence kivvered us ag'in. That is, 'til we come near to Ozark, an' Jim bade us farewell in knowin' I could git us the rest o' the way to the confines o' Doc J's white clapboard house.

———

We come upon the place 'round noon. Krieg strode up the parch steps, selected the pick-axe an' shovel what he'd a-pegged upon on the logs eighteen months ago, an' 'thout a word, trod back ahind the house whar Doc J was buried. Fer the next three hours, he clawed through the frozen an' rocky ground 'til he had a grave dug fer Pippa. Whilst he was a-spadin' up the dirt, I thunk it an opportune time to crawl inter a hot bath. I'se mighty flowsy after all them days in the bush. Clothes was all dotty 'n' soiled. I fired up the wood stove an' heated me some water what I poured inter a big tin tub in the back room. Mis'rable as I was, the warshin' did restorate my spirits some.

'Spite the outside chill, Krieg come in after diggin' Pippa's grave soaked from his laborin'.

"Favor a bath?" I asked.

He nodded.

I heated some more buckets o' water an' left him to his scrubbin' mindful o' the time he had a cool bath on a hot day down to the spring. That remembrance sent me down the road o' desolation oncet more. Havin' him 'round the place jes' churned up one remembrance after 'nother.

After a spell, come to realize, since they's a foregone conclusion what he'd be outen my life ferever, best thang'd be fer him to move on so's I could squench him from my haid. Have to be honest with myself, that li'l chore might be pure imposs'ble. Deep down, I had to 'cept the fact that Krieger Andrewes'd be part o' my mullin' fer the rest o' my borned days. Shakin' my haid o' them thoughts, I walked slow-like to the back o' the house an' took a gander at the hole Krieg dug fer Pippa. Poor li'l thang. She'd be put to ground in a sheet, since they's no box to be had. Leastways it'd be a proper burial fer an improper dyin'. Didn't come close to balancin' out, but it give me some comfort.

Whilst I'se standin' thar grievin' some, Krieg slipped up ahind me. He's all proper dressed in a black suit an' strange neckpiece what I'd ne'er seed afore. Must be his deacon garb, I reckoned. I s'pose 'twas some wearables what he'd left ahind when he come a-searchin' fer me. I snatched a glance at his face an' seed 'twas all shaved smooth. His coal-black hair was still a might curly-wet. Jes' lookin' at him upsurged my heart rate some. Breathin' fast as a field mouse too, if'n I was truthful 'bout it. I noted the tiny book with them lovely words tucked under his arm.

"Are you ready?" he asked.

I nodded.

He handed me his book and fetched Pippa's body from the wagon. When he come by the graveside, he laid her down.

"Do you want to have a last look?" he asked.

I give my haid a wee shake. "Let's put her to rest," I said, an' try as I might, I couldn't keep the tears from streamin' down my cheeks. I'se weepin' fer both Pippa 'n' me both of us daid in diff'rent ways.

Krieg noted my snubbin', stood an' tried to take me in his arms. I stiffened. *No...no...no*, I said to myself. Cain't let him comfort me. Gotta resist. Only thang to do. Meltin' inter him would put me off my rocker an' I might ne'er get clumb back on. I sensated what he's puzzled by my dissuadin', but he didn' push it none.

Kneelin' back down, Krieg lowered Pippa inter the grave an' retrieved the book I was a-holdin' fer him. Then, in that coarse, honey-soft, mesmerizin' voice o' his, he commenced to recite them beautiful book words.

He h'ain't spoke more'n a few words when I heerd, "I know that my redeemer liveth, and that he shall stand at the latter day upon the earth; and though this body be destroyed, yet shall I see God: whom I shall see for myself and mine eyes behold, and not as a stranger."

When them words tetched my eardrums, the strangest thang come upon me. Quicker'n a brim can slip a net, I'se back in Thurgood Turley's dry-wilt barn where I seed Jesus fer the first time. Thar in that hammer cold poke, I met the Lord in the light of a locofoco. Now, standin' aside Pippa's grave, a new brighter, more refulgent light dawned upon me. In that instant, sure as I live an' breathe, I knowed in the deepest way o' knowin', one day ag'in I'se a-goin' to meet my Lord *and not as a stranger.* My soul felt queerish warm an' reposeful.

Truth be told, I've no remembrance o' the buryin' from that p'int on. I'se plumb lost in the deep believin' that whatsoe'er might transpire in the days ahaid, I'se safe in the lovin' arms o' Jesus. Bestirred as I was 'bout Krieg leavin' me in lonelihood, on that chilly Feb'rary afternoon, a serene deepwater peace flowed through Belle Potts, a peace the likes o' which I h'ain't ne'er felt afore.

I sensed his hand 'pon my shoulder.

"Are you all right, Belle?"

'At snapped me outen my reverie. I nodded. Didn't know quite what to say so I jes' smiled an' nodded. He seemed to have a feelin' 'bout what mighta happened to me, so 'thout a word, he took my upper arm an' guided me back inter the house. He lowered me inter the short settee what stood afore the chimney, stoked the fire some, an' come set aside me. I'se in a kind o' dreamy trance an' stared blank-like inter the fire as it crackled an' sparked. I yearned to hang onter the peace 'an tranquility what suffused me fer as long as poss'ble. Krieg jes' sat thar quiet as a play-dead possum. A tiny part o' my mind 'preciated his reassurin' silence an' his willin'ess to let me be fer a spell.

Couldn't be able to say how long we'uns set thar afore the fire, but I reckon it was a good long bout 'cause when I finally blinked back inter the moment, we'uns was in late evenin'. I turned to Krieg an' put my hand on his leg, not in an over-rimmin' way, mind you-uns, but in tender gratitude. "Thankee," I said. "Fer ever'thin'." Then I snapped to. "Hungry?"

"A little," he said and put his hand o'er mine.

I couln't let his hand linger thar, much as I favored it, so I quick-slipped my hand back and stood. "We'uns got no victuals. I'll be back quicker'n a snake goin' through a holler log." We both laughed, thereby relievin' the quietude an' settin' thangs back on a safer shelf.

I th'owed my coat on, grabbed a basket, fished out some specie from a jar in my bedroom, jumped bareback on Blancy, and galloped to Garland and Norma Larimore's place a mile down the road. I asked if'n I could buy some eggs, milk, butter, an' meat. They's so happy to see me, wouldn't hear o' takin' a cent. Laid on me a dozen fresh eggs, a half-pound o' fresh butter, a jar o' milk, an' a hunk o' salt pork. I give 'em my gratitude with assurances I'd be by when I could spend more time, and festinated home.

One hour later, Krieg an' me set down to a fine meal o' biscuits and red-eye gravy. Our supper palaverin' mostly circled 'round my time with Jubal Jagger an' his rullians. I tole him 'bout the kidnappin', the ampytation o' Jubal's leg, the raids, Pippa's an' my futile 'tempt to 'scape, the chainin', an' other aspects o' livin' when we was bushed up.

Follerin' supper, we repaired oncet ag'in to the settee where I favored a coupla fingers o' carn whiskey an' Krieg sipped tea from a li'l china cup. He couldn't get his digit through the handle so he sorta pinched it with his thumb and forefanger. Fer some reason, it tickled my fancy an' set me inter gales o' laughter.

"What is so amusing?" he asked, starin' at me o'er the rim o' the cup.

"Seems what we got hyar is a perfec' metaphor for we'uns," I said. (Krieg larned me that word *metaphor* when we was readin' some poems by an English feller name o' John Donne.) "Ole hill-granny Belle is quaffin' carn whiskey from a cannin' jar, an' high-borned Krieg is sippin' English tea in a dainty china cup all saucered up."

Without warnin', Krieg set his teacup down, took my glass o' carn whiskey right outen my hand, put his hand around my shoulder, an' with a strength I couln't resist, pulled me right inter his embrace. He tipped my chin up an' bestowed 'pon my mouth the sweetest, softest, most luscious kiss I could possible 'magine. An' he kep' it up a goodly spell. Suffice it to say, my 'nitial s'prise flied away, an' I plumb thawed inter a puddle. Somewhar in the back o' my haid, I gripped the fact that none o' what was happenin' could be deemed proper, but I couldn' he'p myself. I participated in the kissin' jes' as much as Krieg. Save fer that feelin' by Pippa's grave, I'd never been assailed by any sensation so unbidden but so welcome.

When we finally did come up to cotch our wind, Krieg looked me long inter the eyes. "I love you Belle Potts. Love you with all of my heart."

I pulled back an' studied him some, comin' at las' to my senses, and frowned in the natural befuddlement a gel orter feel at such a moment. "Whar'd all this come from?" I asked. "You ought not be bussin' when you is fixin' to stand on the flar with someone else."

"Well," he said lookin' down to the flar as if I'd jes' triggered him to do so. "Over the past number of days, I've come to some new clarity about my life."

I cotched a-holt o' my breath, waitin' to see which way this cat's a-gonna jump.

"I'm not going *to stand on the flar* with Annie Worthingham," he continued. "Down here in the clear air of the Ozark hills, I now realize that she and I do not share the same values nor the same purposes in life. And, while at one point I thought I loved her, it's no use pretending any longer. I do not. I have one love in this life and that is you my dear Belle. You and only you. It has been that way since the day you found me on that field of battle."

"But...."

He hoisted his hand. "Let me finish. While you were gone to get food, I spent my time in intense conversation with the Lord. He and I have agreed that parish ministry is not where I am called to serve. I have an uncommon security in this decision. I will not continue my work at All Souls Church. My service is with the sick and dying. I am a chaplain at heart, not a parish priest."

"But...."

He raised his hand oncet more. "I will leave tomorrow as I planned in order to set my affairs in order, but if you will have me, I will return to ask formally if you would be willing to *stand on the flar* with me."

I stared at Krieg fer a poke o' stretched out seconds, misbelievin' his words. Finally, I brung to mind the need to breathe. "Mind sayin' it oncet more, Krieg? Not quite certain I heerd you clar."

"I want to come back to the hill country and marry you."

I swear I couldn't he'p myself. My hands shot up to my mouth, I reckon to kivver the silly grin what had split my face. They's not thar fer long—my hands on my mouth that is—'cause I stretched 'em out an' flung myself at Krieg, tumblin' him o'er on the settee, sulterin' him with kisses, 'til he whooped fer mercy.

"Sure as I live and breathe, I'll marry you Krieger Andrewes! Sure as I live and breathe." Then, tears burst from my eyes, tears waggin' scadoodles o' joy.

That night, me an' Krieg maintained our propriety. I curled under my own kivvers happier'n a butcher's dog. I finally drifted inter sleep, warmed by a day wherein I come to know Jesus an', to boot, set forth a future with the only man I'd ever love.

Ozark Glossary

doddly - shaky, unsteady
funeralize - to hold a funeral or memorial service
more'n Carter has oats - a large amount
bogue - move aimlessly about
a-quill-wheelin' - to cover or patrol a large area
bespoke – betrothed
flowsy - dirty, unkempt
squench - to extinguish, obliterate, subdue
brim - small fish
dry-wilt –
in late evenin' - *Evening* in the Ozarks means afternoon
over-rimmin - sexual or suggestive
flar - be married
sulterin - to smother
waggin - to carry
house plunder - household items—furniture, carpets, bedding,
kitchen utensils, etc.

TWENTY

Belle's Place

May, 1865

I reckon it's time to reel in 'iss stemwinder, snag the loose ends, and tie some knots. It's been more'n two yar since Krieg kissed me good-bye an' promised to return soon's he could squar thangs away back in Saint Louis. The bloody madness o' the war betweenst the States had ended in April, 1865, an' fer the mos' part, life got on more narmal-like in the hills.

They's still some secessionist lunatics what tried to set up a li'l skirmish hyar an' thar, but we'uns rizzed up some vigilante folk called Bald Knobbers. Name come from the grassy summits o' the hills mostly down 'round the Arkysaw line. Them Bald Knobbers done a fair job o' keepin' the maraudin' gangs from gittin' the upper hand. At times they's not much better'n the Bushwhackers, but leastways they favored the pro-Union folk an' give some pertection fer which we'uns was all thankful. Gumment was nigh unter useless when it come to any sort o' restitution. Folks what had seed they's prop'ty razed by Jubal's ilk mostly jes' rebuilt on they's own. The Fed'ral fort in Ozark what was burnt down by Gen'ral Marmaduke ne'er was rebuilt. T'wasn't no p'int to doin' it after the war ended.

Now, back to Feb'rary 5, 1863, the day Krieg lef' fer Saint Louis. I gathered my gumption an' rode Blancey out to the Morton farm. I found Cordy millin' 'round in the barn. I set him down on a sawharse, an', as gentle as I could, I give him my declination to his proposal o' marriage. To my momentary chagrin, he kinder shrugged the whole thang off as if'n it didn' amount to a sneeze in a tornado.

"Figgered as much," he said. "Bein's as you ain't said nothin' since I made the offer." I decided ag'in' remindin' the mullet-haid that I'd been a tetch preoccypied an' outta pocket o'er the previous number o' weeks an' hadn' really come 'pon the oppytunity to answer him one way or t'other. Come to think on it, when I initial sashayed inter that barn an' he seed me fer the first time in a coon's age, alive an' well, he didn't seem all that overjoyed to know I'se up on the hoof.

So, I give a big sigh an' took my leave, poppin' in to pay my regards to Lena afore hightailin' it. As I rid back to Doc J's an' clared my mind a mite, I felt a dose o' gratytude what it had come off so easy. Turns out Krieg had much whiter water to shoot through. I best 'splain what I mean.

Krieg took a good deal longer to put his affairs in order than I reckoned it would. I'se worried sick somethin' had happened to my man. I'se hopin' fer a letter or a telegram insomuch as they'd been a telegraph line runnin' from Saint Louis to Springfield three yar or more by then. Nothin'.

In the back o' my mind, I apprehended he might git cold feet. After all, leavin' all what made him who he was—his citified raisin', all that edycation an' book larnin', his preachin', an' keerin' fer souls was 'bout to be th'owed to the wind when he come to be with Belle hyar in the hills and hollers, home fer mostly rustic folk. Could hardly blame him if he come to recogitatin' the whole thang.

As I'se waitin' in setch disquiet, my healin' work took off like a hungry hummin'bird, an' I'se only able to worry in li'l snippets betweenst patients. I took to prayin' a good deal more an' diskivvered my talkin' with the Lord was a boon an' balm to my worryin' mind. Read the Bible a good deal in candle-lightin' time. Even memorized one bit from Song of Solomon:

The voice of my beloved! Behold, he cometh leaping upon the mountains, skipping upon the hills. My beloved is like a roe or a young hart: behold he standeth behind our wall, he looketh forth at the windows, shewing himself through the lattice. My beloved spake, and said unto me, rise up my love, my fair one, and come away.

Ever night afore shut-eye I'd say them words to the walls o' my bedroom an' dreamed o' my Krieg "leapin' 'pon the mountains, skippin' 'pon the hills," and callin' to me, "Rise up my love, my fair one, and come away."

When he finally did come leapin' back inter my life late in after-dinner time one May day, he was ridin' a wagon pullin' 'nother wagon full o' house plunder. Soon as I seed him, I run so fast if'n I'd a feather in my hand, coulda called it flyin'. I jumped inter his arms, curlin' my legs 'round him an' lockin' my ankles tight as bark on a tree. I inhaled his musk an' give out li'l whimpers o' bliss. We kep' a-holt one 'nother fer a pocket full o' minutes. Reluctantwise, I 'ventually pulled away. Took most of an hour to git him unloaded afore we could set a spell an' ketch up. '

Twas a warm day so we 'stablished ourselves in the big ole rockers on the parch. I took the first bite o' the apple an' norated what I'd a-been up to fer nigh unter the three months Krieg 'n' me was apart. Then, we flipped the coin an' he set in motion what come to be his long tale o' difficulty.

O' course the hardest task what lay afore Krieg was informin' Annie Worthingham the nuptials was off. Way he tole it, she plumb lost all her wagon wheels an' took to him with fists a-flailin', whuppin on him fer all the money, marbles, an' chalk in the whole world. He jes' stood thar an' let her whale on him. That ended it.

She starmed outen his life, an' he says he h'ain't seed her since. He allowed as to how he felt right poorly fer havin' to rend the relationship, an' I confess to some guilt nigglin' 'round in me as well, but in the end, I knowed 'twasn't my choice. Krieg's the one what made that bed an', much as I loved the man, I reckoned they's nothin' much I could do but give an ear an' some sympathizin'. It all made fer my everlastin' benefit, to be sure, but neither of us could shuck the baleful thoughts 'bout poor Annie what curled 'round us as he sat thar rockin' an' re-paintin' the scene.

After a poke o' long seconds, Krieg turned his recitation to church matters. Seems thangs went right awful with the bishop also. He charged Krieg with "conduct unbecoming of a clergyman" for disobeyin' him an' breakin' the engagement, which made no sense 'tall. How can honesty, vacatin' a loveless union afore it's too late, an' bein' true to one's own self be *unbecomin'*?

Oh, an' the bishop said Krieg *abandoned his cure*, meanin' he 'elected not to continue at All Souls. Ag'in I'se puzzled at the reasonin'. Why was it 'bandonment when Krieg had heerd what he heered from Jesus hisself: His work wasn't to be in a church as such but in succorin' the sick an' dyin'? Seems to me a bishop orter pay 'tention to a word what come from the Lord. To my way o' thinkin', payin' no heed to the Almighty is a perilous trail to foller.

Come to pass, the bishop summar'ly defrocked Krieg, took away his preachin' papers, and *reduced him to the lay order*. Still h'ain't quite figgered why bein' in the *lay order* is a reduction, but then they's a lot what don' take root in my haid when it come to 'clesiastical matters, to use Krieg's word. An' ask me, the punishment was a mighty big box fer whate'er li'l crime Krieg mighta c'mitted.

They's a few other transpirations to report. Jes' afore leavin' Saint Louis to come back to Belle, Krieg got word his friend Marty Muldown had been called to be the bull goose at All Souls an' su'prise, su'prise, he'd been seen in the comp'ny o' one Annie Worthingham. Seems she's favored to git her fancy house on the hill afterall. Don' know if'n it give Krieg any comfort to heer o' this, but I hoped so. He prob'ly tasted a tetch o' bittersweet swirlin' 'round in his craw, but he never brung the subject up ag'in, so I cain't say fer shore.

But 't'ain't all. Turns out they's a reason Krieg took so long to come home to the hills. His mama died all of a sudden from apoplexy. Happened while Krieg was with her settin' an' talkin' in they's home. She slipped away in his arms.

As he's tellin' 'bout it, I seed some li'l tears slide down them precious cheeks o' his. I slipped from my rocker an' kneeled by his side, pullin' his haid down inter the crook o' my neck an' holdin' it tight thar. I'd ne'er seen him snub afore, an' it ripped my own heart inter tatters. When he finally cotched a-holt o' his feelin's, he pulled me inter his lap.

"I had to put her affairs into order," he said, squeezin' me some whilst we rocked. "I sold the house and retrieved a small inheritance. I also sold most of the furniture. The items we unloaded I wished to keep because I could envision them in this house."

I nodded, not carin' one whit 'bout the money or the house plunder. Jes' o'er the moon to be sittin' on his lap backin' an' forthin' in the rocker on one wonderful May afternoon.

———

Krieg an' me stepped o'er the broomstick three days later. He 'ranged it all earlier when he come through Springfield. Found a Methodist preacher what 'greed to marry us down in a grassy field by the spring. Me an' Krieg plaited an arbor with branches an' wildflowers. The Methodist preacher, Kreig, an' me stood under the arbor for the cer'-mony itself.

People come from far 'n' wide to see ole Belle git spliced to a city feller. All them folks I'd a-healed in one way or 'nother an' them's I'd a-grannie-womaned showed up. Krieg an' me was tickled to see Jim an' Harriet Darrow come by 'long with they's boy Charlie. The boy give us a small wooden fox what he'd carved as a weddin' present. To this day it sits in a special place on our chimney mantle.

'Mong the last to arrive was Cordy an' Lena Morton. An' guess what? Hangin' on Cordy's arm, all flits an' smiles, was none other than the Widder Garlick. It brung a wee grin to my face. That perty much said it all.

We'uns used the inheritance and house sale money to build a small hospital not far from the surgery cave. Krieg hired some carpenters and masons to put it up. Made it outen stone what we retrieved from farmers' fields. They's quite happy to part with them rocks you'uns kin be shore. Called it the Joachim Jeremiah Johnson Hospital, but right quick it come to be known as The J. It had a dozen beds cordoned off fer privacy, indoor terlets, a small cook room, an' a medicine room.

Right 'bove the door we affixed a perty wooden cross what Krieg had crafted so's we'uns could let ever'one know the Lord was allus the source o' healin'. We merely he'ped Him out some. Krieg was happier'n a pig in mud to minister in The J. Oh, an' did I mention that Methodist minister what married us turned out to be a bishop in that partic'lar brand o' salvation? He heered Krieg's story in the 'Piscopal Church, give it a big *pishaw*, an' restored Krieg's preachin' papers, thus bestowin' 'pon him a measure o' redemption. He's now what they call a Methodist elder.

———

An' one more thang: We-uns, my Krieg an' me, gots us a li'l one.
    A gel, name o' Pippa Andrewes.
    She gots a li'l chug in her chin.

———

The End

OZARK GLOSSARY

Chapter One
ginger ooze – decoction
narvish-like - worried, uncertain
called to straw - gone into labor
granny-woman – midwife

Chapter Two
heired - inherited
josie - long undergarment
civvy cat - small spotted skunk
victuals - a meal
stopper - small quantity
greenin' - teasing
chubs - sweethearts, lovers
jibble - cut to pieces
aggerpervoked - to provoke
poke – bag
cooper - treat an open-head injury
snubbin - weep, sob, snivel
half-hammin - skip, hop, and jump
chimney – fireplace

Chapter Three

looby - clumsy, awkward
ming-mang - mixture of butter and molasses
furrin - as in *foreign* but connotes anyone or anything from
outside of the Ozark region
a sack 'o pum-grannies - small gourd-like fruit of uncertain
attribution
gales - gleeful, cheerful
chug - dip, fissure
simples - refers to a dull-witted person, one whose skull ought
to be bored to vent the dullness
a-fawnchin – disturbance
edzacktly - accurately, precisely
kill-devil stout - strong, high proof
jes' a shoot - nearly mature
gee-wholliker - marvel, wonder

Chapter Four
benight - overtake with darkness
gap - opportunity
miration - wonderment, from *admiration*
git triggered up – dressed
cook-room – kitchen
citireen - old-timer, long-time resident
clabberin – cloudy
crimpy – cold
gammoner - one who talks incessantly but is unreliable
soozified - uncouth and conceited

Chapter Five
take the studs – grow stubborn
durgen - uncouth, unsophisticated hill person
come a-wingin' - to court or woo
a nigh cut - a back road, generally private
chaunk – to chew

Chapter Six
Papists – Catholics
Puseyites - followers of Edward Pusey, a leader in the Oxford

movement
middlers - second-year seminarians

Chapter Nine
locofocos - early term for matches

Chapter Ten
all lanky an' little with it – slender
wingin - courting, dating
jakey – countrified
jillikins – backwoods
puffy white cells – leukemia
snaky - long and winding
gaily - in good health, lively spirits
mannersome – polite, kind
ambeer - tobacco juice
croaker - physician, doctor
got a tick in yer naval - native of the Ozark hill country
noodlin' - catching fish, particularly catfish, with bare hands
git-flipper - guitar player
blinkied – soured
swallered a watermelon seed - became pregnant
o'er-rim – promiscuous
franzyin' – immoral

Chapter Eleven
plotches - same as *splotch,* now archaic
the necessary – outhouse
pop-call - short visit
jam rock - jam rocks are upright stones on fireplaces
gullin' 'round – courting
sprunchin' - petting, foreplay
drag his wing - court, woo
peezaltree - inferior, uncultured
hankercher – handkerchief
lavins - a great quantity
willow – mourn
swage - reduce, assuage

Chapter Twelve
kitchen-settin' weather - chilly period of early Fall
sulled - grow sullen, refusing to talk
rullians - course, unkempt person
deemin – judgment
all cankered up an' doty - rotten, decayed
paw-pawers - outlaws, fugitives. (Bushwhackers often lived on
paw-paws, a wild fruit.)
work-brickle - industrious, hard-working, anxious to work
wampus-cat - blood-thirsty animal in the wild
scadoodles - a large quantity or amount
my budget down - to make up one's mind, to decide
ole suggin - an inferior person
grand-rascals – cheater
barreled inter – shot
a-settin' up - expressed intention to marry
stob – stump
cymlin-haids - fool, dunce

Chapter Thirteen
kitchen-settin' weather - chilly period of early Fall
sulled - grow sullen, refusing to talk
rullians - course, unkempt person
deemin – judgment
all cankered up an' doty - rotten, decayed
paw-pawers - outlaws, fugitives. (Bushwhackers often lived on
paw-paws, a wild fruit.)
work-brickle - industrious, hard-working, anxious to work
wampus-cat - blood-thirsty animal in the wild
scadoodles - a large quantity or amount
my budget down - to make up one's mind, to decide
ole suggin - an inferior person
grand-rascals – cheater
barreled inter – shot
a-settin' up - expressed intention to marry
stob – stump
cymlin-haids - fool, dunce

Chapter Fourteen
simmered down on - concentrate or focus upon
muddy spang - mixture of gravy and butter
wassies – wasps
conceited - imagine, contrive
winter fever – pneumonia
hazel splitters - wild hog, razorback
salivated - mangled, shattered
taters - be patient
some gaps – chances, opportunities
goomer-doctor - witch doctor
Jubernaw - Phrase of unknown origin, perhaps a malapropism
or a creation.

Chapter Eighteen
a dog-trot cabin - cabin with two rooms separated by a breeze-
way, common in the southeastern US in the nineteenth
century
satchel first - breech birth

Chapter Nineteen
doddly - shaky, unsteady
funeralize - to hold a funeral or memorial service
more'n Carter has oats - a large amount
bogue - move aimlessly about
a-quill-wheelin' - to cover or patrol a large area
bespoke – betrothed
flowsy - dirty, unkempt
squench - to extinguish, obliterate, subdue
brim - small fish
dry-wilt –
in late evenin' - *Evening* in the Ozarks means afternoon
over-rimmin - sexual or suggestive
flar - be married
sulterin - to smother
waggin - to carry
house plunder - household items—furniture, carpets, bedding,
kitchen utensils, etc.

AUTHOR'S NOTE

In order to bring Belle Potts's character into bold relief, her nineteenth Century Ozark dialect has been exaggerated, but not by much. Virtually all of the vocabulary words, sayings, and comparatives are genuine. I am indebted to Vance Randolph, an early-to-mid-twentieth century folklorist and ethnographer who studied the dialect and customs of the Ozark region, which covers northwest Arkansas, southwest Missouri, northeastern Oklahoma, and the extreme southeastern corner of Kansas. He lived among, interviewed, recorded, and observed native Ozarkers for nearly sixty years. Arguably, his book, *Down in the Holler*[1], which he co-authored with George Wilson, remains the preeminent volume on the dialect of the region. A substantial majority of the footnoted definitions in *Whiskey Woman* have been drawn from *Down in the Holler*.

Though it is beyond the scope of this Author's Note to present a historical treatise on the origins of the Ozark dialect, suffice it to say that much of the linguistic heritage derives from early modern English, particularly the variations brought to America by the Scotch-Irish. Some have incorrectly assumed that those who immigrated to the United States settling in Appalachia and later in the Ozarks were sufficiently isolated to preserve historic dialects and vocabulary from the British Isles. While there may have been some remnant constructions from the old country, the dialects in these mountain regions evolved and changed, as did dialects in most other regions of the country.

Moreover, local residents often made up words to suit a particular situation and they became part of an area's lexicon. Thus, it is safe to say that the Ozark dialect, as presented in *Whiskey Woman*, is unique and elaborated.

It is very important to emphasize that this dialect does not represent ignorance, limited education, nor social regression. The dialect has its own distinctive vocabulary, syntax, and pronunciation patterns. It is a rich, colorful, and vivid dialect. In rendering the speech of the hills, I had an interesting challenge. As a trained phonetician, it would have been possible for me to craft Belle's grammatical structures and pronunciation with far greater orthographic accuracy. However, it would have made the dialogue extremely laborious to read. I had to strike a balance between accuracy and intelligibility. As a result, many standard English phrase and spelling conventions have been retained. Sadly, with the expansion of mass communication, much of the Ozark dialect and many of the lively sayings and non-standard pronunciations are disappearing. However, one can still hear them, especially in the rural areas among native residents. My wife's ancestors settled early in the Ozarks and at family gatherings I have heard such words as *we-uns* (first person plural), *you-uns* (second person plural), *heired* (to inherit), *snub* (to weep or cry), *stob* (jagged stump), *hyar* (here), *thar* (there), *gaumed* (cluttered), *fair-up* (to clear as in weather clearing), and many more.

With respect to the historical context, the events relating to the Battle of Wilson's Creek and the Battle of Springfield are accurately portrayed. There were women in the region who, in the wake of the battle, entered the area and provided help with the wounded. Both Union and Confederate field surgeons provided medical care to the soldiers from both sides. Generals, Lyon, Sigel, Marmaduke, Brown and Price are historical characters, as are Post Chaplain Wines and Christian County Sheriff Friend. All other characters are products of my own imagination and bear no resemblance to people living or dead. Jubal Jagger is fictitious but his activities truthfully reflect the guerrilla raids fomented by Bushwhackers during the Civil War.

Cranmer Hall Seminary, All Souls Parish, and the divines associated with the Episcopal Church in Missouri are also all fictitious. However, the ecclesiastical structure, quoted prayers from the *Book of Common Prayer* (1789), and clergy offices are accurate in what was then known as the Protestant Episcopal Church in the United States of America. In addition, the curriculum, pedagogical technique, and daily routine of Cranmer Hall are realistic. Biblical quotations are taken from the King James Version, which would have been in widespread, if not exclusive use in the Church during the 19th Century.

Conventional medical practices and natural healing remedies mentioned in this work are consistent with the care of sick and wounded patients during the Civil War era. Doctor John Snow is a historical figure and did publish a paper entitled, *On the Mode of Communication of Cholera* in 1849. He was an early proponent of germ theory, which did not become a prevailing explanation for the transmission of disease until late in the 19th Century. In 1847, Doctor Snow also published a paper *On the Inhalation of Ether* and designed the *inhaler* described in Chapter One of *Whiskey Woman*. Snow preferred the use of ether to the more potent chloroform, once the dosage and temperature could be properly regulated. As Michael Ramsay has noted, "John Snow's accomplishments in medicine, anesthesia, and epidemiology constituted an achievement that changed the face of medical practice."[2] Doctor Adam Politzer, mentioned in reference to middle ear surgery, was also an important innovator in otology. He developed a prototype tympanostomy tube (middle ear tube) out of hard rubber. However, it should be noted that it had limited success because of high rates of infection. Presumably, Belle reduced that risk with her considerable attention to sterilization.

No work of fiction, especially historical fiction, is written in isolation and that certainly has not been the case with *Whiskey Woman*. I am deeply indebted to the following individuals for helping me to bring this work to fruition: Dr. Katrina Bogdon, a licensed naturopathic physician of Our Healing Roots in Springfield, Missouri; nurse educator Paula Linden, MSN, RN; and fellow novelist Laura Kingston (*The Gardener's Gift*). As one might imagine, the most incisive critique and the most lavish encouragement came from my wife Jean Ann. We read the text over aloud to one another more than once in long evening sessions. For that time together, I am deeply grateful.

NOTES

Author's Note

1. Randolph, Vance & George P. Wilson, *Down in the Holler: A Gallery of Ozark Folk Speech*, (Norman: University of Oklahoma Press, 1953).
2. Ramsay M. A. (2006). John Snow, MD: anaesthetist to the Queen of England and pioneer epidemiologist. *Proceedings (Baylor University. Medical Center)*,*19*(1), 24–28. doi:10.1080/08998280.2006.11928120

Made in the USA
Las Vegas, NV
19 August 2023

76316470R00154